THE WORLD CHRONICLES BOOK ONE

IN THE SHADOW OF BABYLON

*"I have given them thy word;
and the world hath hated them,
because they are not of the world,
even as I am not of the world.
I pray not that thou shouldest take them out of the world,
but that thou shouldest keep them from the evil.
They are not of the world,
even as I am not of the world."*

John 17:14-16

JOHN JOHNSON

Copyright © 2021 William Johnson

This is a work of fiction.
Names, characters, businesses, places, events, locales, and incidents are either the products of the author's imagination or used in a fictitious manner. Any resemblance to actual persons, living or dead, or actual events is purely coincidental.

All rights reserved. No portion of this book may be reproduced, scanned, or distributed in any printed or electronic form without permission. Please do not participate in or encourage piracy of copyrighted materials in violation of the author's rights.

Purchase only authorized editions.

Paperback ISBN: 978-1-945169-55-7
eBook ISBN: 978-1-945169-56-4

Orison Publishers, Inc.
PO Box 188
Grantham, PA 17027
717-731-1405
www.OrisonPublishers.com
Publish your book now, marsha@orisonpublishers.com

Printed in the United States of America

Other books by John Johnson
The Byzantine Chronicles series
    The Blade – ISBN 978-1945169-29-8
    The Brothers of the Blade – ISBN 978-1945169-40-3
    Sons of Light – ISBN 978-1945169-45-8

"So he carried me away in the [Holy Spirit] into the wilderness:
and I saw a woman sit upon a scarlet coloured beast,
full of names of blasphemy,
having seven heads and ten horns.
And the woman was arrayed in purple and scarlet colour,
and decked with gold and precious stones and pearls,
having a golden cup in her hand full of abominations and
filthiness of her fornication:
And upon her forehead was a name written,
MYSTERY, BABYLON THE GREAT,
THE MOTHER OF HARLOTS AND
ABOMINATIONS OF THE EARTH."

Revelation 17:3–5

CHAPTER 1

The patrol walked through the fields in a wedge formation; eleven men in the wedge, with five scouts ranging ahead in a wide arc. Behind the wedge, like the shaft of an arrow, the lieutenant, the commo man, and the three men of the air/vehicle defense team followed. They had been on patrol many days, their numbers dwindling from sniper fire and hovering ordnance, pressure mines, trip wires. The three females of their patrol were dead as well as the novices to long-range patrols. The fields were spacious, flat, fertile, fields of Eastern Europe.

They walked east, parallel to a highway a half mile to their right. The highway was straight, raised above the fields on an earthen bed. The highway was littered with antipersonnel mines the size of a man's hand. The mines were clearly visible on the black road surface; a surface ripped, peeled, torn by obsolete tracked vehicles – long ago superseded by the airfoil and spidery walker. Perhaps the mined road was intended to channel soldiers into a kill zone; perhaps the patrol was already in that zone.

A river was to their left, a quarter of a mile away. The young infantryman named John could not see the water, only the levee green with lush grasses occasionally splotched with the rotting carcasses of milk cows. The trees by the river offered shade. The trees were without movement. Nothing on the earth seemed to move but the patrol. He listened to the fabric of uniforms rasping as weary legs pushed through the thick hay. The men were forced to lift their feet high or be tripped in the densely growing blades. John was gaunt, had no energy—they had been on patrol a very long time.

Summer—ninety degrees easily and humid, cumulus clouds in a glaring blue sky—in the year 2240. Two thousand two hundred and forty years since Christ walked the earth. The thought of Christ lifted John's veil of depression and weariness. He looked over the wedge of sullen men. They would like to be hugging the flanks of the road and not upon the open fields. In the open, covey and flock bombs could descend upon them in seconds—before they could blink twice—and rip their bodies apart. Then, a soldier would lie screaming, with his bowels upon his chest, staring at the sky, praying for death.

He was different than the others—he had no fear of the openness of the fields or of death. His Lord could hide him anywhere. God made the earth, knew every fold and recess. God knew every man's appointed time to die. If it were God's will, he, lowly John Johnson, could stand before his enemy's eyes and not be seen. He laughed to himself; those around him would think him crazed if they knew his thoughts. He knew the Spirit heard and laughed with him in celebration of his incomprehensible faith. His thoughts were always heard by God—they were prayers, yearnings, seekings, conversations. The Creator, the Living God, watched over him.

This war he fought within was a political war, a constrained war, and no doubt the loser would receive some guarantee or compensation. He was on loan from a United States government that he neither loved nor felt allegiance to. In Europe there was the dream of a new and glorious day, the rising of a new empire like that of ancient Rome. An empire of peace, stability, prosperity, a united Europe, geographically whole, politically united, an economic power second to none, affecting the course of the world.

He knew the dream was a lie. The idealism begotten of intellectuals and politicians and glorified by a news-starved media was a sham. The citizenry was given the historical precedent of the Roman Empire to energize their actions. Those seeking wealth, status feigned belief so as to foster a new consensus in the power struggle that was evolving. This war was fought for power, wealth—the same motivations of the first war ever fought. He thought liberty, freedom, patriotism would never again be motivations for war.

There was nothing in this war for Christ. John sensed he had consciously sinned by allowing himself to be selected for military service. Perhaps, before the amendment of 2100, he could have believed in the Empire dream, felt a loyalty and duty to his country. The amendment made him a lawbreaker if he spoke of his Lord. He knew that at one time, his government had honored God, had given Christ an environment in which to work freely. Once, his government had honored truth, the truth that is not of mankind, but which men can know. He wished he could go back to that time; then he could have fought with his whole being.

What did he owe his government or the world? Government provided law and order. Law and order were good, but did this justify the wrong that had been done to his Lord? Was it right to honor this government? He waited for God to give him the answers. Only the Lord Himself could break the oath John had given, the obligation undertaken. If he broke his oath, there would always be self-doubt, the haunting belief that perhaps John Johnson just couldn't take the combat soldier's life. Enough thought. No escape from combat was granted or possible—except death, wounds, or the end of one's enlistment.

Jesus! Jesus! Would he see heaven today? Life wearied him. He glanced over the wedge; each man was fifteen meters apart, almost perfectly spaced. His throat com was on as ordered. Speaking was forbidden, except in an emergency. Somewhere an enemy soldier was hunched over a sound-detection unit, waiting for the formed patterns of speech to arise from the chaos of nature's sounds. The yellow line would jump, the computer screen would flash a recognition signal and the text of the words spoken, then calculations and a fix. The enemy would press a button, and the birds of death—the covey or flock bombs—would come. It was rare that a few words would reveal a location but not impossible. Some sound technicians could pick out the patterned sounds of human feet moving upon the ground. Bonuses were given when hunches brought success.

The sweat ran in rivulets down his skin. His uniform was one piece and airtight. The air circulators always failed to cool. He looked into the sky; the fluffy, towering clouds had not moved. His throat com clicked twice. He fell to the ground instantly, face up, feet toward the expected enemy. He pulled down his hooded face mask and zipped it to the collar of his uniform. He waited. His chamele suit, the name an abbreviation of chameleon, gradually began to imitate the color and pattern of the high grass above him.

A shadow passed across him. Big it was and dense, seeming to carry icy coldness under its wings – along with the darkness of death. An observation drone, probably heat-seeking and visual. If all masks were zippered, there would be no register of body heat. One unzipped mask, and the body heat would radiate from the face and around the collar like the flame from a cigarette lighter.

The replacement, Jones, had had trouble with his zipper in practice runs. Nerves. John knew the others were now lying on their backs, silently cursing not only Jones's past incompetence but also raging against his weak and worthless flesh. It seemed strange to John they were so desperate to preserve their self-willed, hate-filled lives. He chuckled to himself; their lives were all they had. At the age of twenty-two, John had already come to realize there wasn't anything worth holding unto in life—except the Lord. God's will be done.

The throat com clicked twice. The patrol rose warily from the tall grass. The masks were unzipped, peeled back. John straightened the chamele cover on his laser rifle, moved the sling that supported the weight of the rifle from his neck to his shoulder. The constant friction of the sling had created a burning chafed swath upon his neck. The pouring sweat soaked into the swath. His sweat mingled with the fibers of his undergarments, creating a repugnant odor that dissipated as he unzipped his collar.

The walk continued. No one uttered a sound. John watched the lieutenant; positions were rotated at his hand signal. The lieutenant was the timekeeper; each rifle squad member was to receive equal time on the vulnerable point and scouting positions. The lieutenant was a Churcher, the leader of the "civilized men." They believed in the Empire dream, the World Church, the perfectibility of humanity. The lieutenant's kind were mannered, educated above the norm; their families had money; they climbed the ladder of success.

To these men, the Empire dream was arbitrary—any dream would have sufficed as long as it gave standards. Standards were the rules of the game;

standards decided winners and losers, those who would have and those who would have little. All officers were Churchers. Those who wished to be officers, or wished to play the game, clung to the lieutenant. John exhaled in disgust as he thought of the Churchers. He knew what these men became when their paths to achievement and dominance were blocked: hateful, spiteful, arrogant. Beliefs, manners, breeding were tools to separate themselves from the less educated or spiritual—tools quickly discarded when no longer serving their purposes. They loved their Church, their god of self-delusion, human spirituality.

John knew he was next on the point, the scouting position immediately ahead of the center of the wedge, one half hour away at seventeen hundred hours. Ahead loomed a paved roadway intersecting the highway they paralleled. They would be upon the road in less than ten minutes. Sergeant Towels, who was on point, slowed. "Pointers" always advanced alone across a road. The road held danger—cover for an enemy patrol in ambush, a sniper, an electronic trip wire, or mines. Towels was a coward. Towels wouldn't cross the road. The porcine-faced, violent-tempered, cowardly Towels was of the group of men bound by their atheism.

These men believed nothing, found no need to give life reason, logic, purpose. Right was what kept them alive and happy; wrong was what ended their lives and took their happiness away. Life just was, and abstract thoughts such as justice or purpose were tools invented by crafty men to take power from the credulous masses. Sergeant Towels looked at his watch and smiled. True to himself, he signaled the new pointer, Johnson, to the position. He would cut his time on point short a half hour. The lieutenant would do nothing. The lieutenant knew who had the power in the platoon. The lieutenant raised his hand, legitimizing Towels's early departure from point.

John smiled sardonically as he moved forward. He knew that if he had left the point early, he would have been punished. The unfairness did not haunt his conscience; he expected unfairness. Rank had its privileges. The scouts, knowing the next order, removed themselves to the flanks. The platoon sank into the field, the chamele blending; they would provide suppressive fire.

John studied the earthen bed topped by the roadway. He intended to walk up the slope, as he didn't have the power to run. Gaining the point position, he looked quickly back at the platoon gazing at him. He wore a smile of irony. These men cared nothing for him. To them he was the Baptist, a name of scorn and amusement. He was an outsider, an oddball tolerated only because he did his work well. He held their lives in his hands now. Why was he in this war? Was it faith or sight in which he walked? The Lord had a purpose.

He turned away from the now invisible platoon, studied the high slope of weeds and shrubs. He crouched as he walked, instinctual fear and physical exhaustion pulling him down. His muscles quivered. The body seemed so eager to fall into death. Suddenly, energy and strength came to him. He grunted a satisfied and thankful chuckle. The Lord was giving life to his body.

He hit the edge of the drainage ditch before the embankment at a sprint, his eyes searching for movement or shape. He leaped the ditch, his legs jarring into his hips as he landed on the slope. He scrambled upward. His pack swayed and shuddered upon his back, digging into his flesh. He zigzagged up the slope, bounding through the brush, low in profile, erratic in movement.

Upon the road he threw disrupters to his left and right. He felt the nakedness of the roadway stretching to distant dark trees. He felt the heat of the macadam and smelled the tar where tracks had churned. The disrupters rolled—they simulated natural glitches in electronic fields—to mask his passing. Roads were favored for the placement of electronic surveillance-beam devices.

His mind paused from the mad flow of uncertainty, speed, to a moment of lucidity; he saw a blown, jumbled bridge rising from the flatness of the roadway far to his left. He leaped from the roadway, down the embankment, into tall grass. He felt coolness pressing against his boots and calves; mud, water enveloped his legs. He grunted from the force of landing. He saw buildings ahead, a farmstead blocked from the patrol's view by the road embankment.

He rushed toward the buildings, knowing he must not give an enemy time to react. The house, barns, garages were made of preformed plastic panels. Expansive shade trees, overgrown flower beds surrounded the buildings, as did a wide and level area of uncut lawn. The stench of dead cattle entered his sinuses. He was within a depression—a foot-wide channel of water bordered by rushes. He sensed the enemy watching. Water and rushes were erupting ahead of him as silent laser fire moved toward him.

***

Henry Johnson rose early, even though he had been up past midnight the night before. The day held a newness, an anticipation—as if God were going to bestow a gift. Henry believed the knowledge of this gift had already been implanted within his mind and slowly would be unwrapped. He stood at the second-story window and looked out over the vast fields of the ag lands. The sun was just peeking over the long, forested ridge of a mountain. Sunlight streamed into the room, flooding it with golden light.

He gave thanks to God for the warmth of his home—a glistening dew spoke of a morning chill. He gave thanks that he had a home and not some city apartment for the elderly. All the old-timers were crammed into apartments. He thought of his grandson, John, in Europe. He prayed that the boy—a man, really—might be delivered safely home. Henry had been in a war—the Philippines Insurrection—as a military intelligence officer. That was as crooked a war as this European Empire business. Politics.

Every minute of his military experience had been agony to his soul. Daily he prayed that John would be brought safely home. Henry derived great comfort in the assurance that John had eternal life. They would meet again, whether in this world or the next. Henry took his robe from the back of a chair, felt the immediate warmth upon his body as he enrobed. He slipped into his bedroom shoes and shuffled downstairs.

He thought he could remember a time when his body and mind were alert from the first waking moment. Now, waking seemed to be a gradual process. Perhaps the remembrance was just a lie; he didn't know. He was tall, lean, tanned. He gardened and cut and split firewood in season. He still had muscle tone—he lifted weights—and had an impressive chest and arms for a man eighty-two years old. He walked every day. His hair was white, but the Lord had kept him well. There was work to do for the Lord—always work to do; that is why he lived.

His book, *A History of God and Civilization*, had been developing in surprising ways. Using an historical perspective, he protected himself from the

In the Shadow of Babylon

Church's label of heresy or *Enslaver*. After all, he was only stating what Christians had once believed. At every opportunity, he destroyed the new beliefs and strengthened the old truths. His narratives held a cutting incisiveness that couldn't have come from a feeble mind like his. The writing had passed beyond his intelligence and capabilities into the realm of the Holy Spirit's wisdom.

He had traced the vine of Christianity from its origins in the Middle East 2,200 years ago and chronicled its growth and spread, even as the root had been pulled. Now the last bloom, the United States, was withered and brown. The vine was dead, the stem rotten where it had first risen from the earth. Weeds rose above the decaying remnant. Humanity's desire for the world, its pride in life, had subverted all that was good.

The subversion had come rapidly in the last four hundred years and was easily witnessed through the history of the United States. God was removed from all aspects of government affairs—from the Senate chaplain to "In God We Trust" on coins. Moral law was separated from civil and criminal law and abolished. Abortion, sexual perversion, polygamy became rampant, creating a weakness, as yet hidden, in the vitality of society.

The lack of moral law would not create the coming catastrophe—the Tribulation, God's wrath upon mankind. Moral law had never created morality; it only defined the human condition. A righteous theocracy could not have changed the hearts of men. It was very close, the end of this world. Or was it that he was an old man, and his own end was the shadow across his mind?

The course of events had made such good sense. The merging of Protestantism with Catholicism was hailed as the beginning of a new age, and the World Church was born. Greater power meant greater good could be done. Mankind was served; but strangely, unnoticed by anyone, Christ was not. Why should a coin say, "In God We Trust" when no one trusted in God? Why shouldn't there be abortion when no one valued life? Why shouldn't unwanted life come into being if the state would become mother and father? Why shouldn't there be sexual perversion as long as that perversion was not forced upon anyone? Why did people with certain beliefs have the right to tell others how to live? It all made sense, even the amendment of 2100 that labeled the old beliefs antisocial, antihuman rights, against the interests of mankind, and forbidden to be spoken.

Anger coursed through Henry. It all made sense, except that humanity's logic was not God's truth. Pride and lust, using the intellect, imitating logic could not attain God's wisdom.

No one knew Christ as Savior. What was there to be saved from? No one knew the working of the Holy Spirit within their hearts. Now the Holy Spirit only restrained mankind from being given over to man. The world was better than at any time in history: there was almost no war, no starvation; there was an abundance of material comforts. People were healthier, stronger, more intelligent. People were spiritual, believing in honor, truth, duty. These spiritual, healthy, happy people were dead to God. Without truth, their souls lived a lie.

Yes, the end was very near.

The house smelled of musty paper, old books; Henry loved the smell of antiquity. The aroma of his breakfast—eggs, coffee, oatmeal, toast, selected the night before and cooked automatically—caused his mouth to water. He felt an embarrassment at his body's instinctual desire for food but not the pleasure of taste or the energy that would be provided. He had been thinking about someone…John. He needed John, needed young legs, an agile mind, for he had found a personal mystery within this history of God and man.

John's great-grandfather, a pastor, one of the last visible true believers, had left an odd note. Henry had seen his father's note many years ago and thought nothing of it. Two weeks past, he had discovered the note again while searching his father's private papers. His father had played a semiprominent role in church history and would be included in his book. This time when he read it, the note seized his mind; the note was disturbing, puzzling, fantastic in its implications. He needed to share the contents of this note—more a clue—with someone he could trust.

***

John's breathing was labored. He dove into the channel of the ditch beneath him; began a low crawl that became a slithery glide. Water and mud were in his face. Hidden in the rushes was the stone foundation of an old spring house. He gathered himself up behind the protective stone wall, clicked his throat com three times: enemy ahead. The patrol would flank left or right. Flanking to the left, the troops could receive fire from the river levee; flanking right, they could receive fire from a wooded area. Lord, his heart was beating loudly.

From the corner of the stone foundation, he peered at the buildings. The house, which resembled a dormitory, had two stories, a narrow porch. The plexiglass windows were shattered, curtains hung listlessly. He was certain from the angle of fire that the enemy was in the farmhouse. No movement came from the buildings. John ran toward the front door of the farmhouse. He aimed his rifle at doors and windows but did not depress the trigger. He pulled a grenade from his web belt. The perfectly spherical grenade was heavy, potent in his hand. He wished to toss the grenade, then another, into two of the downstairs windows. But the flashes of light, muffled roars, debris blowing out the windows would register on sound-detection units; the flying debris would be seen by drones or enemy scouts. He dropped the grenade into a cargo pocket.

Intuition said the enemy had already retreated. He burst into the house, saw furniture cast wildly about. The stuffed sofas and chairs were dirty and stained; glass, lamps, pictures were on the floor. He searched the downstairs rooms, then ran up the stairs, straining to hear sounds over his own footsteps and hard breathing. The bedrooms were empty.

As he ran down the steps he sensed the farmworkers might still be in the building. Clothes in the rooms, beds recently slept in, an absence of dust on furniture were proof of recent habitation. The workers would be hiding in the cellar. The enemy would not hide in a cellar—no escape. The stench of rotting cow flesh pulled at his guts as he ran to the barn. He saw a tractor, a freshly dug pit, bags of lime, carcasses—the remainder of the dairy herd not yet buried.

He moved quickly through the barn, searching, reflexes heightened. Behind the barn was freshly ground earth; tracks had pivoted—three or four vehicles? He wasn't certain. Far out in the fields, racing for a distant tree line, was a man. The man wore a gray-green camouflage uniform, carried a rifle. John brought his laser rifle to his shoulder, sighted on body mass. The barrel jumped with each heartbeat. He ran to a fence post, steadied his barrel upon the post. The sight pasted a fluorescent dot upon the torso of the man, belt high. John pressed the trigger. A gray puff of smoke came from the man's torso. The man was gone—down in the grass. One scout, mechanized infantry, dead. The silence of the kill always astonished him. The "silence of violence," the soldiers called the laser blast.

farmhouse cellar. Furtive hand signals among the men spoke of women. Till Animal angrily cut short the signaling.

Female farmworkers had evidently been found. There were no allies or noncombatants to these men he fought beside; people were valued for what could be taken from them. The lieutenant gave the hand signal indicating high-ranked men. The gathering knew they were being watched, and the women would be protected by the judge advocate's office. John followed the platoon into the building, thanking God that no harm would come to the women. He scraped the mud from his boots on the edge of the porch. He shook his head, the cleaning an ingrained response to his former life as a farmworker. Others in his platoon gave no thought to this building as a home and delighted in their disrespect.

The lieutenant was a figurehead, his orders broken when circumstances warranted, but severe penalties safeguarded the well-being of women and civilians, and high-ranking men were eager to use power in their defense. The lieutenant retained some semblance of leadership among the Churchers by appearing to be the collector and judge of opinion, facts. The true power lay in the coalition of atheists and pagans. Simply by their numbers, through acts of passiveness, disobedience, sabotage they could make the lives of the ruling authorities miserable and ineffective. Unable to physically intimidate or threaten, the lieutenant skillfully used his rank to coerce, frighten, and deny off-duty privileges.

The lieutenant sat at the kitchen table; three women and an old man were gathered in a corner to his left. It had been so long since John had seen women or living people dressed in civilian clothes that they seemed almost alien. By their eyes, he understood that he was the alien, from a world they could not imagine.

His body stank of sweat and sodden fabric. His eyes were wide upon that place beyond weariness. His gear was rugged, worn, dirty. He carried the laser rifle—the death stick. Soldiers were an obscenity within the home; their sweat, mud, rifles, bulky forms, rough faces filled the room. He was like a beast, a horse from the field, standing within the home.

The women were beautiful, one tall, lithe; one short, ample; one petite, vulnerable. The lieutenant smirked as if he had acquired the rights to the women. He had the superior rank and breeding; he was entitled to their favors. John was pulled aside as the men filed down into the basement. He stood by the lieutenant, who had his battery-operated writing pad upon the table. He wrote: "Good work, John. Lots of hustle. Hear you wasted one." He smiled as he looked up at John. He continued. "You'll have your pick of the special service women when we get back, I assure you."

Each battalion had its escort women or men—government employees, who were used as rewards, incentives for good or outstanding service or conduct. The lieutenant watched John's eyes narrow into a sneer.

"Your rank will be coming soon."

John's sneer became an amused gaze.

The lieutenant disliked John. John always made him feel like a fool. Yet it was John who was the fool, the oddball, a religious fanatic, an ascetic, an introverted loner. The lieutenant's printed words were enlarged, and the hand movements producing the words emphatic in reaction to the overtures not accepted. "One hour. Eat. Refill your water bag, shave, clean your weapon. We'll sleep in the wilds tonight. Dismissed."

John thought he saw the lieutenant immerse himself in an anger. He hated the wilds, hated combat, the feeling of dirtiness, sweat, sleeping on the earth. He had an intense hatred for the natural world—the world outside of man's making. Old John didn't seem to mind, never complained, mostly smiled at the inconveniences, hardships. The lieutenant despised and envied John.

John nodded in affirmation – in a combat zone saluting was forbidden. Only the Baptist gave the nod – yet it always seemed an insult.

Save for one guard in the kitchen, the platoon had collected in the cellar. John descended the steps. Here they would escape the heat of the day, sound-detection units, and heat-seeking drones. A spring issued from a rusty pipe in the side of a stone foundation wall. No one greeted John as he came down the steps, crossed the floor to the pipe. Each man sat up against the smooth stone walls, absorbing the stones' coolness. Body odor and heat filled the cellar as the men opened their airtight uniforms to wash and cool themselves. A cloaking disrupter had been turned on. The windows had been covered with heat-deflecting blankets. The men were weary, yet relatively relaxed in the safety of the cellar.

John was filling his water bag. Sergeant Towels was speaking in a whisper to his group of men. "The old man says three tracks were here. One carrying electronic gear and drones. One a covey launcher; the other, mech infantry. They sent out drones all last night. That one today was probably theirs."

The voice held an irritation, the words had been spit upon the listeners as if Towels welcomed a dispute.

With the water bag filled, John sat against the wall, looked over the groups of men; the Churchers, the atheists, the pagans, and by black-skinned Sergeant Scott were the pagans of color. Scott and his men worshiped an African god of maleness, blood sacrifice, cult sex, voodoo. This god had come out of South America, a malleable god, branching, bending, and grafting hundreds of primitive beliefs and gods onto its stem. Scott was Black in a world where a true black skin was rare. He had great size and strength, preferred intimidation to reason. His genitals were his god; sex, his worship.

Each group was divided by racial, cultural, philosophical criteria, sometimes overlapping. Each group had its dominant personality: the lieutenant, Sergeant Towels, Animal, Sergeant Scott. Personality? Personalities did not exist—personalities demanded character, and character was nonexistent. In the absence of character were pleasures and loathings, likes and dislikes, each one formed by the hundreds of variations in experience, inborn lusts, and upbringing that is the fate of men. They had been selected for recon work by intelligence, inborn traits, mental reflexes, past work records. Physical discomfort, fatigue had no effect on their equanimity, nor did covey bombs hovering around them. In an odd way, they were specialized for their craft.

John thought upon the twenty-one soldiers who had once been a platoon of forty. He had carried their burdens—their packs and weapons. He had taken their sentry duty, their scouting assignments, their point positions. He had always given and never taken. He knew their evil and depravity. The Lord had given him calm, an even temper; his mind retained a purity. He had spoken the Word, not with condemnation, but with love, and had been scorned. These men despised him. He sensed something had gone out of the world—a decency, a kindness. Perhaps only in his imagination had these existed. His duty was done; whatever debt he owed his government had been paid. He was weary and broken in spirit.

Animal had found a Federation newspaper in an upstairs room and was reading, in whispers, selected pieces to his men. His keen-witted comments elicited laughter and admiration from his small band. John began to sink into sleep, then was jolted awake. Animal's followers were laughing with a hysteria born of utter fatigue. Animal's voice projected a grave seriousness, his every word embellished with emotion.

"'The Old Order has been reconvened; the New Empire established. We have order, peace, freedom—from hunger, joblessness, want. Freedom to achieve man's desires are our world's destiny. A new patriotism is needed, a loyalty to the Federation, and through this loyalty, a loyalty to mankind. With God as our partner, truly there will be heaven on earth.'"

"On and on he speaks of a new patriotism! What is the old patriotism? What do we get from this new order?" Animal's voice seethed with hatred. "The mighty words of this pompous ass are written in our blood! It's all shit!" He looked deeply into the eyes of his men. He held their gazes, impressed upon them his sincerity. "There is only the blood that will take us to Valhalla. Someday this Federation will understand where its power comes from"—his voice became an angry whisper, cloaked from the hearing of Scott's men—"from white men's blood, and then we'll seize what is ours! Odin watches."

The lieutenant was halfway down the steps, his hand rapidly crossing his neck, signaling the men to be silent. Almost simultaneously, the disrupter status light glowed red. All conversation ceased. Many men inhaled deeply; some closed their eyes. John closed his eyes and smiled faintly. Was this moment the end? What enemy ordnance would send him to heaven? Eyes opened and watched the red light. Deep, measured breaths, the rise and fall of chests. Some eyes looked inward, and some eyes studied the cellar and the men within. Survival plans were being formulated.

John decided not to run for the steps, as men would jam that narrow escape route. The narrow cellar windows would not allow escape. Rodriquez, a mixed-blood Churcher, was the nearest man to John. He was mentally dull and morally vacant, yet beyond the distrust and paranoia common to every man in the platoon, he had a desire to be liked and sometimes spoke with John. John thought of grabbing Rodriquez and shielding himself with the wide man's body if a blast occurred. No, he would shield Rodriquez.

The red light turned yellow, then green. Body postures, facial expressions, breathing patterns changed. Tension was gone, relief and happiness dominated. The lieutenant went up the stairs. Scott stared hard at Animal; the hatred in the eyes threatened death. He spoke. "Die for what? Blood? Odin?" He contained his contempt but hoped for a rejoinder from Animal to trigger his rage.

A Churcher chimed in. "I'll die for mankind. There is a world wanting what those words represent."

"No." Animal's voice was rigid. "Those words are to make men slaves to an idea instead of masters over their own sweat, blood."

The Churcher felt the irresistible power of Animal's zeal and had no desire for discussion to turn to argument. "Well, you've got the opportunity to take some of the wealth if you play by the rules."

Animal's eyes softened in merriment, his voice projected laughter. "No." The voice became soft, coaxing, patient. "They made the rules to exclude my kind. Ask the Baptist; he'll tell you it's a lie. He's one of you, and he knows it is a lie."

The Churcher's voice hardened. "He's not one of us. His god is an Enslaver. To him, humanity is evil. The Baptist is full of mysticism, holy spirits, doomed flesh, a thousand and one laws. The true God has taken us past that." The words were angry, but the Baptist had no power; diplomacy was not needed.

Animal's eyes gleamed. He enjoyed pitting the Baptist against the Churchers on the slightest pretext. John smiled, knowing he was being used. The label of *Enslaver* would have been a serious charge anywhere but on the front. The sect had been banned by the amendment of 2100; punishment was life in prison. He had never stated he was an Enslaver and had never uttered a denial. On the front, no one cared about a man's political or religious views as long as he did his job and kept his beliefs to himself. John spoke.

"If this Federation were for the glory of Christ or even if Christ was tolerated, then there might be merit in the new order."

The Churcher winced when he heard the name *Christ*.

"The Church is part of the Empire dream, a large part of the impetus." Talking to the Baptist was like conversing with a brick wall.

"You speak of the Church...I speak of Christ. Who in the Church knows Christ as Savior?" John turned to Animal. "You talk about blood, so you should understand this: if one of your men fell on a grenade that would have killed all of you, his blood would then have shielded you from death."

"Yes." Animal drew the affirmation out warily even as his eyes narrowed.

"So why don't you believe in the Christ, whose sacrifice shields you from sin and death?"

The conversation irritated Sergeant Towels. "You all talk shit. Gods shmods. When you're dead, you are dead. When you live, you live. Attach any meaning you like to your actions or attach none; there wouldn't be any difference."

John said nothing. Animal smiled slyly at Towels. The Churcher had given up. John had seen a flicker of doubt on Animal's face, just a momentary confusion before the hardness returned. John pulled out his dinner, stripped the protective seal from the flat, wide container. As the container was exposed to the air, it began to heat. He set the meal down on the cellar floor to cool and wiped his rifle. Waves of sleep passed through his mind; his head began to nod. After his meal he would shave...

CHAPTER 2

Under the high, interlocking tree branches lived a perpetual gloom now made deeper by dusk. John stared into the forest of well-kept trees, the trunks straight and branchless for at least twenty feet. He was on point again—they said no one was better in the forest than he. He did not protest; he wanted to be away from them.

He was certain he had heard metal on metal, a dull clank sounding from somewhere in the forest. He slipped out of his pack. The perspiration that had collected along his waist and back seemed to freeze on his skin. He had no fear of his own side dropping ordnance on the sounds and he and his patrol becoming collateral damage. The Federation forces were actively engaged in combat operations far to the north; this river "front" held no interest. It was uncontested—a place of patrols and surveillance, nothing more.

He would sit a moment, or into eternity—what was time to him? He signaled to the patrol behind him; they melted into the forest floor. The sound came again, echoing coldly from the trees. He smelled the river beyond the forest. No doubt electronic trip beams had been placed somewhere ahead on the forester's rugged trail. The sudden coughing and whir of engines echoed for a moment through the forest, then silence.

Tree branches crunched; saplings slapped against solid hulls. Three squat, black forms lumbered through the trees toward the river.

The tracks were in amphibious mode—long air pipes rose from engines and exhaust, paddles projected from the tracks. A mechanic must have dropped a wrench while installing a pipe, and that is why the patrol hadn't blundered into a confrontation. Bags of shock-deadening chemicals clung to the hulls. Like his uniform, the three tracks were of a chameleon material. These must be the tracks the old man had described to Towels, John thought. The enemy had great confidence in its sound-scrambling capabilities against counter fire, and as no fire was raining down upon them, it was justified. Or perhaps the enemy thought this zone truly held no interest to the Federation.

Tracked vehicles, antiques, of a design over two hundred years old. Rarely seen even as construction vehicles in the trackless vastness of Africa, Asia, Australia. These machines worked, were inexpensive and simple to operate and repair, and there was plenty of fossil fuel to burn. What the vehicles carried—the weapon system—was state of the art and frighteningly deadly.

John studied the covey launcher—the "nest," in military slang. The covey was more responsive than artillery or mortar fire, as the ordnance hovered over the battlefield. A target could be engaged independently of a human spotter. Depending on the model, lightweight discs or winged bombs would rise from the nest, five to twenty at a time. The discs or wings were made of plastic explosives reinforced with fiberglass and metal shrapnel. Lift was accomplished by heat and sunlight, propulsion, by microwave, electric motor, or chemical combustion.

The covey could hover in the air or lie on the ground to conserve fuel, patiently waiting for a target and avoiding fire. Some models were designed to destroy vehicles, but the covey was most effective on infantry on open ground. When hover time was nearly exhausted, the covey was dropped on likely target sites—behind a hill or ridge, along a creek—or on readings of unusual sound or heat.

The covey could be put on target by sight, television cameras, drones, or heat- or sound-seeking devices. When the covey was in a heat-seeking mode, one soldier shooting could bring the covey down upon himself. The covey never concentrated upon a source but maintained a formation. If a platoon or company was widely dispersed, a flanker shooting could save a part of that platoon or company. A dummy heat source had yet to be issued to the troops in the field.

John had experienced coveys in flight a hundred times, by his rough calculations. The weapon's incredible speed, the target's helplessness, and the whirring, shadowlike death imprinted deeply within the mind. Coveys screened by ridges, forests, buildings, moving at blurring speeds, skimming over men by feet and inches, and dropping on patrols, companies behind, beside, took breath from lungs, heartbeats from existence. The speed, relative silence, unpredictability terrorized soldiers. A soldier feared being the designated shooter—the man obligated to bring death upon himself in order to save his comrades.

Darkness was fully upon the earth. John pulled down his night-vision goggles, and with a few clicks of his throat com, brought the platoon forward. They moved in and out of reality as they walked, floating in the depths of fatigue. One moment the mind would have a calm, a lucidity; the next moment nerves would race in fright and unreality. On the breadth of the river, a buoy light shone as if peacetime commerce still rode the glassy water. They felt safe from coveys in the dense woods. Sound units or heat-seeking sources, if able to penetrate the trees, might mistake them for herds of deer or boar.

The woods ended. They walked through extensive fields, pastures of river grass. Fog came; the river air was cold, numbing. They bedded for the night on the river levee. In the damp high grass, spread apart, masks zipped to collars, they slept. John thought they should have separated into groups, half the number on the far side of the levee, but this was not done.

John awoke to the sun intensely hot upon his face, magnified by the clear plastic vision window of his mask. A peculiar stillness surrounded him. He sensed fear. He slowly raised his head over the tall grass. Hovering over the patrol was a covey, five birds, carrying enough destructive power to annihilate the platoon. The birds would fall in a star-shaped pattern, spreading their concussive power and fiberglass splinters over a maximum area.

Was an enemy soldier watching—joystick in his hand—unable to discern the nature of the objects in the grass? Had someone slept with his face mask off, allowing the covey to home to the source of the heat? Or had a drone passed in the early morning, marking their location? The immediate question was: Why hadn't the covey dropped?

He had no fear, only an anxiety for rational thought. If the covey were being controlled by sight, the enemy would have landed the birds, knowing this act was so unnerving as to cause someone to bolt, thus identifying the target. A drone-directed covey would have dropped immediately, not hovered. Sleeping soldiers make no sounds, so a sound unit had not pinpointed their location. This covey must be heat-seeking and had found a source of heat. Perhaps the heat source was so low as to cause hesitation, confusion. John did know that a cutoff of that heat would cause the covey to drop.

John rested upon his elbows, searched the grass, saw other heads staring. To his left was Rodriquez, the designated shooter. Rodriquez stared at the hovering death, listening to the faint whisper of air upon the wings, listening to the soft static of solar cells converting heat to lift. The small electric motors made a whizzing sound, like flies. The eyes of Rodriquez expressed shock, uncontrollable fear. The face was contorted, the body shook. The patrol watched and waited.

John scrutinized the heads barely discernible above the grass. He saw a collar and face mask partially separated—Jones, the new replacement. Jones was sobbing but still maintained some control of the utter terror that had seized him. Jones and Rodriquez would be executed if they survived the landing of the covey. Rodriquez would die if he did fire and would die if he didn't fire. The covey was the preferable death.

Rodriquez was afraid to die. This thought seemed strange to John. He had no anger toward Rodriquez, just a sadness. Who was the secondary designated shooter? Towels, it appeared—beating John by a few feet at most. John raised his rifle. He knew Towels would never shoot, never admit that a few feet made him the designated shooter. The movement of John's rifle jolted Rodriquez, and instinctually he raised his rifle. He did not fire. Twice Rodriquez aimed, and twice he took his eyes from the rifle sight.

John turned his eyes from Rodriquez and took aim. There might have been a 50 percent chance of survival for him had Rodriquez fired; now there was none. John aimed at the bird on the far right of the covey; he was on the left flank. This shot might save lives. He sensed the humor that their lives weren't worth saving. Yet who knew the inner heart but God? Was there one among them who would know Christ?

He fired. The hit bird spiraled toward John with a speed seemingly motivated by vengeance. The four remaining birds fell, then all five exploded into air bursts for increased killing efficiency. The heads had vanished as each man rolled onto his stomach, willing himself into the grass, the earth. The explosions were muffled, weak; the birds careened to the earth in broken sections. John jumped up, ran for the crest of the levee, threw himself over the top. Other bodies were tumbling over. They heard muffled explosions as pieces of the covey exploded upon the ground. The patrol peered over the levee. A circle of grass had been mown down. A faint smoke hung over the circle like a ground fog but having the tangy odor of high explosives.

The platoon knew the birds had been defective.

John heard a violent striking sound coming from behind him, the sound of a fist upon a skull. He turned quickly. The platoon had already gathered around Jones and Rodriquez, who had been cast together. The Churchers and the lieutenant were on the fringe of the gathering. Rodriquez had been knocked to the ground by the blow; he was shaking in terror. Animal had zippered up Jones's face mask. Animal cuffed his head, and Jones stumbled to the ground. Sergeant Scott and John moved toward the gathering.

Animal moved quickly to the bulletproof cigarette-sized container on the lieutenant's torso. Within were the injectors that administered a death dose to any soldier who was incapable of continuing the mission, whether for physical or mental reasons. All knew they could not stand in the open for long. The lieutenant opened the container with a small, attached key. In one deft moment, Animal had injected Jones in the thigh. John, remaining close to Rodriquez, was scribbling on a small tablet. Rodriquez was a Churcher; perhaps the lieutenant could do something for him, thought the Baptist. Jones was an atheist; he'd had no one to come to his aid. Animal looked around at the gathering. John held up his note, flashing it at the face of Animal and the gathered men. TIME IS SHORT.

Jones had crumpled to the ground dead. Fear was in Animal's eyes. He frantically gave the disperse sign, moving his arms from his elbows with speed. The entire platoon moved back up the levee. John pulled Rodriquez up the embankment. Suddenly the patrol reversed direction. Rodriquez froze as he saw the others running out onto the vast, flat grassland stretching to the unseen river. John let him go. The sound of falling ordnance split the sky. The earth shook, sod rained down, a vast column of blackness came over the embankment as John turned and moved toward the blackness, over the levee's crest. He fled down the embankment, headed in the direction the patrol had come from.

The blackness lifted quickly. From the corners of his vision, John saw missiles streaking toward earth, saw the explosions, the columns of smoke. The green flatland of grasses, dark-green copses, mature forest, levees, and raised roads; the columns of smoke; and the vast cumulous-clouded sky held a wild beauty. He sank into the lowland along the levee's base. He turned south, following the levee. He saw coveys filling the sky, moving quickly, dropping just as quickly.

It was by coincidence that the enemy had taken its preemptive strike along the front just as the platoon had gathered. Hundreds of Federation patrols, perhaps thousands of soldiers, had been stealthily moving east to the river. The heavy ordnance always came first, then the antipersonnel coveys. John found a drainage culvert in the side of the levee and tucked himself outside and against a concrete wall, hidden by brush. His job was to wait. This mission had a preordained wait time of an hour and a half, then he was to find his platoon.

In an hour and a half, he rose. The sky was dense with clouds, rain squalls raked distant fields, the wind blew, and the temperature had dropped. He crawled to the top of the levee at a place where he could peer across the green flatness and search for his patrol. The plan had been to meet a quarter of a mile south if the enemy and terrain allowed. The vastness had been swept by rain squalls. He saw a slice of water—the river—and a jumble of concrete rising—the city, far in the distance. The field grasses, heavy with moisture, laid when walked or crawled upon. He saw individual trails leading out and then turning south. He saw a burned swath where the trails had converged. These men were dead, not realizing the drone cameras could see the trails. The drone master had waited till the trails converged—more carnage with less ordnance. The clever men in the platoon would have remained at the levee base or hugged the base as they crawled south, as flattened grasses at the crease of levee and plain could not be discerned due to the optical distortion cause by the steep levee. Animal and his group were likely alive.

John turned and backtracked to his culvert hiding place, then followed the base of the levee a quarter of a mile south before dropping over the embankment. He would then travel up the levee to the point where his platoon had last been.

He had no sooner dropped down the embankment when he saw a blasted culvert. Someone had hidden in the culvert—a rookie mistake like standing before a window in a lit room on a dark night. Drone jockeys had passed the concrete for days or weeks, and any form silhouetted on the concrete backdrop, and blocking the opening would have been blasted. He found two left boots.

He saw them peering at him. Deep underneath the watery weeds, a hundred yards from where he had departed their company. John clicked his throat com once. Imbedded in the brief sound was his individual code. He would be known if the lieutenant's commo equipment and computer had survived.

A click was returned. John could not see Rodriquez. Likely he was atomized by ordnance, but just as likely he'd gotten an injector in the thigh for his failure to shoot. Once men began to kill, the killing seemed hard to stop. It was like a drug invading the mind. Had Rodriquez followed him, he'd still be alive. Rodriquez had had that herding-instinct mentality.

John remained where he was; no need to join the group. Slowly he pivoted his body toward the vast plain and unseen river. Jones and Rodriquez had almost completed a mission. In a day, maybe two, it would be over: the river reached, the assault would begin. They were exempt from the assault; they were recon, nothing more. Brutal were the times, the death injectors, and men who liked to kill—the enemy or their own. Well, they would all answer on their judgment day, reap their reward or punishment. Darkness would be upon the land soon.

***

The patrol came upon the river and its objective, a ferry landing of antiquity—a tourist attraction. The men were buoyant from their success, carried

In the Shadow of Babylon

a weary joy in their hearts. For sixty miles they had followed a preplanned, unalterable route through disputed territory. One of hundreds of patrols revealing paths of least resistance to the generals at headquarters. Now the lanes were marked, and the offensive could begin. The patrol's work was done; the stress, fear, anxiety cast away.

The patrol was left naked and exposed at its objective. The river shoreline was devoid of cover except for a rubbled ticket building and a thick band of rushes. The broad gray river seemed to reflect, expand, elongate a man's form for all the world to see. The city on the far shore, looming thousands of feet above them like a vast mountain range, harbored the enemy. They could imagine the enemy in the tallest buildings where the wind always blew, cold, bundled, peering through high-powered ocular devices at the land across the river. Even so, the elation could not be suppressed; an impudence came from success. They had survived the worst; what could hurt them now? Rest, peace, were their due. All they had to do was sit and wait.

They didn't know how long they would have to wait. This was their destination, said the lieutenant; there were no orders but to wait. If this meant eating the last of their rations and starving, they would do so. If this meant receiving artillery fire till no one was left alive, they would do so. Not from patriotism or duty, but because they made a light blink on a three-dimensional map, and if that blinking light moved from an assigned position, they would be hunted down and killed. Killed as deserters, rogue soldiers, hanged by their necks at some heavily traveled place for all to see.

The patrol spread along the length of the river, away from the rubble of the ticket building. The building made a good rocket or artillery coordinate for the enemy. They dug in and hit water at two feet; bricks, planking, sheet metal were put into the holes to keep feet dry. The clear skies of the morning were now as gray as the water. The summer heat had vanished with the previous storms, replaced by an unseasonable coolness. The sky and the river moved, and the men were giddy with fatigue.

Behind the patrol stretched a large parking area, empty save for one derelict civilian airfoil; beyond that, empty marshy grasslands. In the water before the patrol, two dirty white ferries lay half submerged. The sightseeing decks and the pilot houses protruded from the water. The metal was flecked by shrapnel, pocked by rocket fire, burned by laser. Rust was already spreading from the wounds. Sea gulls lined the railings, their gray-white excrement running down the sides like drips from a can of paint.

Across the river, along the waterfront of wrecked docks, cranes, roadways, storage tanks, and warehouses, lay sunken ships; plastic-hulled barges, hydroplaners, solar clippers—their wide expanses of rigid sail tilted and jumbled in geometric patterns, ocean vessels, river work ships. All the boats had burned and twisted superstructures. Above the waterfront rose the skyscrapers of the city.

A stillness lay over the city, an absence of movement that stunned the eye. A silence came from the stillness that was eerie. The buildings touched the clouds like high mountains of stone. The buildings formed canyons and solidly blocked the horizon. In their vastness, they reached across the expanse of water and lay upon the men. They heard the wind—torn by the steel and concrete and shrieking through the interlocking pedestrian ways that tied the buildings together. The wind's sound made them empty inside, lonely, vulnerable, and afraid.

The enemy was surely in the city. Every building fortified, every street covered by grazing fire, every underground chamber crammed with ammunition and supplies. The men thanked whatever god they worshiped that it was not their duty to go into the city. No doubt the enemy had its shock troops within the city. Men of phenomenal size and strength, the result of genetic engineering, synthetic hormones. Men who, with stimulants, could fight without sleep, live on nothing but pills for weeks. Men whose gigantic bodies could carry the most advanced equipment, special optics, hearing devices, armor, flight packs, and laser weapons with twice the power of conventional arms.

All of the men had seen shock troopers while in basic training, each side had such men. Companies of lesser soldiers vacated the roads when shock troopers passed. They knew these men to be keen minded, pragmatic, even intellectual, and absent of social or moral scruples. Enemy or friend, they were the same. Many had soaring egos, seeing the awe and fear they inspired in others, knowing the power within them, they sometimes imagined themselves as gods. Because of their value to society and the expense of their creation and training, their asocial behavior was overlooked. No normal soldier wished to meet a shock trooper in battle.

In the Shadow of Babylon

The patrol hunkered in the rushes and gave thanks the city was not theirs to enter, gave thanks that the mission was done, gave thanks that all they needed to do was wait.

***

Henry sat down at his desk and immediately propped his feet up on the only empty corner. Lying on the desk was the message his father had written seventy-five years earlier. He had read the message twice since the rediscovery a week past. After each reading and a few moments of thought, he would busy himself with housecleaning or outdoor chores. He allowed the deeper levels of his mind to work on the message while that part of the mind tied to the body was occupied. The longer the words lay upon his mind, the more disturbing and fantastic they became. Henry picked up the message and read again:

I have seen the followers of the cherub and have read their book and know of their ways. The time is near for the birth of his son. See with your eyes and hear with your ears. The stone which the builders rejected, the same is become the head of the corner; this is the Lord's doing, and it is marvelous in our eyes?

The date on the message was two days prior to his father's death. The signature on the paper was that of his father. An address on the outside fold of the paper was that of a small but influential seminary where his father had taught. The note had been written on indestructible paper and had been placed in a fire/water-proof pouch, which in turn had been placed in a cloth bag. The bag was found in a trunk loaded with his father's papers. He remembered his mother telling him the trunk had been the private domain of his father. Therefore, his father had placed the message in the trunk.

"The cherub" was easily traced to Ezekiel 28: 14–19. This fallen cherub, a type of angel, could only refer to Satan. The cherub's son, or Satan's son, could only be the "Beast" of the book of Revelation, the Antichrist who was coming to establish his rule upon the earth. His father had hidden the message from laymen's eyes by calling Satan a cherub. Laymen thought of cherubim as pudgy, childlike angels, though the cherubim were spiritual beings in immediate contact with God, living in His presence, and not of human form. One cherub had rebelled—and taken a new name: Satan.

His father had challenged those who knew the Bible with the phrase, "See with your eyes, hear with your ears." This phrase was borrowed from Christ's words in Matthew 13:15, who in turn had quoted Isaiah. The phrase was an exhortation to hear with the heart and a method to hide meaning from the dead of heart.

What was fantastic was that his father—a sane, godly man, who walked in the Spirit—should write that he knew the date of the birth of the Beast. If you knew the birth date of the Beast, then you knew, within a few years, the time of the end of the world. Christ, the man, when He walked the earth, did not know the exact time of the end. Why would such a close approximation of the end be given to an obscure pastor?

Perhaps the answer was in the fact that his father had looked upon their book, evidently a Satanic bible. This information was disturbing, fantastic, and to Henry, highly believable.

"The stone which the builders rejected, the same is become the head of the corner; this is the Lord's doing, and it is marvelous in our eyes?"

The Lord's words were spoken in Matthew 21:42, and he was quoting Psalm 118:22, 23. This passage had to be a clue. But a clue to what? A clue to the location of the same information his father had looked upon? Did this clue reveal the hiding place of the Satanic bible, the time of the birth of the Beast?

If all these assumptions were true, how had these documents escaped discovery by others? Satanic forces would kill to hide or repossess this knowledge. A few people remained in this corrupt world who would die to make the truth known.

***

The offensive came with an unexpected suddenness that dazed the men of the patrol. They had expected the city to be bypassed or flanked, certainly not attacked in the limited amount of daylight remaining. It was as if they had been the last pawn moved; all had waited upon them. Hundreds of rockets hissed over the patrol, skimming the ground. Far up the river and far below, the rockets swarmed out of the west like bees returning to a hive.

In the Shadow of Babylon

The rockets seemed alive—thinking creatures—neatly moving around and over obstacles, lining up approaches. Rockets flew into windows and doors, entered subway passages, slammed into air-conditioning and heating ducts. Antimissile fire streamed out of the city like water from hoses, bursting some missiles in midair.

The gray concrete city shook with concussions that reverberated from the canyon-like walls. The patrol felt the thunderclaps as sharp pain in their ears, as quivering viscera, as shaking hearts. They watched the brilliant flashes, saw glassy auras of superheated air, fragments of buildings cast into space. Thin trails of smoke drifted up from the city. The earth trembled into infinity, it seemed. Aircraft came just as the sun was setting behind the city. Explosions and concussions became constant as the aircraft made their passes, dropped their ordnance. Aircraft exploded and burned, streaking across the sky like meteors. The waterfront burned; flames leaped high. The water danced, agitated by fragmentation bombs. The fragments caught the last of the setting sun, shone as silver slivers as they flew. Then, the aircraft were gone from above the city. Bombers, flying low, bypassing the city, streaked over the river, moving east to targets deep within the enemy's lines. Secondary explosions rocked the city, slammed into the hearts of men, stole their breath away.

The air became cool, damp as the patrol watched in awe. They had a sense of safety in their insignificance to the grand event. They were on the sidelines, unnoticed spectators. They watched the flights of air platforms hovering over the city, entering canyons, landing upon buildings. Like clouds issuing lightning, the platforms streaked laser fire. Explosions were heard far to their rear, distant rumblings coming through the ground. Flashes of light were seen against the western horizon like heat lightning—only of longer duration. The enemy was fighting back, attacking staging areas.

The trembling behind them, the scene before them renewed hidden fears. They zippered their masks, closed their uniforms, went to internal breathing. They lay in their shallow holes, the wet coldness entered them. The sun was gone, mist came from the river lowlands. Fires were scattered about the city. In the tallest buildings, the flames were enraged by the wind and burned with ferocious intensity that could be heard on the river shore. Air platforms still hovered between buildings, casting light beams and bullets, explosive rounds. The ripping sound of high-speed rounds tore the air. Perhaps the ferry landing would be seeded with mines or be made into a chemical dead zone to block the advancing forces. Perhaps the enemy would contest the ferry landing, sending in shock troops to establish a point of resistance.

A whirring, humming noise filled the senses of the patrol. The men instinctively ducked; the sound was at a crescendo within the blinking of an eye. Hundreds of airfoils skimmed over the shallow holes. John felt the rush of air, smelled the super-revved motors, heated to maximum tolerance. He flinched. Had he been sitting upright, he would have been decapitated. The speed of the craft were beyond a man's reaction time, making him feel slow, stupid, vulnerable.

The craft outran defensive fire. John saw the backs of shock troopers in the rapidly disappearing craft. They were lined up in neat rows, jerking stiffly with any erratic movement of the foil. The river water, lifted into a fine spray, twirled behind the craft.

Laser and rocket fire came out of the city, bouncing off the water and over their heads. Their attention was diverted from the attack by the sound of a damaged airfoil to their rear. The craft wavered, a rotor had been hit; still, speed was maintained. As the craft passed over the parking area of the landing, its nose dipped, and its speed caused the air to deflect the nose into the pavement. Sparks flew up, the craft skidded, its nose shuddering. The shock troops gripped the safety bars with straining hands and arms. The airfoil flipped and twisted—for a second, the furiously turning rotors were exposed. The troopers spilled out, skidding and tumbling across the cement. Arms and legs were flung out from the bodies as centrifugal force humbled the strength of the big men. Bodies rolled, skittered along the ground. A man fell into the rotors; body parts flew out. The rotor blades made the sickening sound of grinding as they whacked into flesh. Shattered flesh, blood, bone were scattered across the cement and into the patrol.

The airfoil tumbled end over end through the patrol's position, into the water. Shock troopers lay at the rear of the trenches, bunched against a drainage ditch from the parking area. They lay like leaves blown against a fence. A transported demolition charge exploded as some of the patrol raised their heads; flesh splattered into their bodies, sticking to their uniforms. Not all the shock troopers were dead, some moved groggily, others began raising themselves. Their armor had protected them.

"Shoot the bastards! Shoot them!" Towels's crazed voice came over the throat com. Animal and Scott had their lasers aimed.

"No! No! They're our men!" The lieutenant's voice cut into the static. He stood, hands waving; he was incensed.

John had his rifle raised. The huge men, dizzy, weakened, wounded, were attempting to rise to their feet. In confusion they might fire upon the patrol, or simply from anger and rage.

Animal yelled into every helmet and to the lieutenant, "You can't trust them!" The desire to live and the ingrained fear of disobeying a direct order from an officer fluxed through his determination.

Someone fired as the lieutenant turned his head toward the troopers. Others fired upon the same target, a trooper who had risen to his feet. He was knocked back to the cement.

The lasers sought out his face and his weapon arm.

"Damn it! No!" The lieutenant rushed toward Towels. A shock trooper, who had risen to his knees, fired. The lieutenant was blown apart. The patrol's fire turned upon that trooper. His head hit the ground; he remained in a kneeling position till his laser blew apart.

The men of the patrol blasted the groggy, disoriented forms, laughing as they did so. Tension and sanity were destroyed as each trooper disintegrated. The men laughed as blasted flesh clung to them.

Sergeant Towels bellowed out a challenge, his vocal cords tightened, his voice raised to a woman's pitch. "I'm in charge now! When I say you fire, you damned well will fire!" His face had flushed dark red; his eyes were unfocused and wild. The patrol laughed insanely at Towels's outburst. Towels began to laugh from the headiness of his new power. Scott did not laugh.

"I've got higher rank." Scott's voice was uncharacteristically weak.

"You dumb nigger. You was just staring at them troopers! They kill 'cause they like to kill. You've got no combat sense. I'm boss!"

The laughter stopped; a tense silence held each man. Scott fingered his trigger. His men were outnumbered. The lieutenant's men would not aid him. The men knew what Towels had said of Scott was true. Scott chose to bide his time. Towels would die by his hand; it was just a matter of time.

The tension broke when the canisters dropped. The canisters dropped quietly, did not roll or bounce, and quietly exploded yellowish-gray gas. John's eyes scanned the perimeter even as he began checking zippers and seals. He saw five canisters neatly covering their position. Men ducked into their holes, securing masks, feverishly feeling their uniforms. If they had not been zipped up, all would be dead. John checked his suit and mask a second time. All secure. He jiggled his wraparound water pack—more than half full. That was good.

The gas was stubborn, lingered for hours, bonding almost like a solid so that light winds could not disperse it. The gas had completely surrounded him. Visibility was one to two feet. The time of terror had begun. One small tear in the suit, someplace you couldn't see or your hands, feel: the gas would touch your nostrils, and there would be terror. Then, there was the fear of the antidote and the injectors every man carried for chemical biological warfare. Were the injectors defective or damaged? Was the antidote potent? Had the enemy used a new gas that made the antidote obsolete? Would you be so flustered as to inject the wrong antidote, or mix the biological and chemical needles? Even if everything went right, you had to find the leak, patch it within an hour, or death would come.

He had been through such attacks before. At first you are afraid to move, thinking movement might cause a rip. Then you dumbly trust the suit and worry of other things. Is the enemy advancing through the fog? Men stare with such intensity that they see their aberrations and fire. Sometimes the wrong men are killed. Sometimes men simply run away from the fog, never to be seen again.

He had advanced beyond those fears and worries. There were simply the hours of waiting that needed to be filled. Where did the canisters come from, who had targeted the position, and why? Had the patrol been seen or were the canisters dropped on the coordinates of the ferry landing as a precaution or a prelude to an offensive move? He believed the enemy didn't know the patrol was at the landing. Had the enemy known, antipersonnel rounds would have been dropped. Gas was used to mask an operation or create the illusion of movement. Perhaps his patrol or the storm troopers had been spotted, and the enemy had no antipersonnel rounds remaining.

John shook his head sadly. How lucky Jones and Rodriquez were already dead; they would have been in torment in this gas attack. It was better to think of home, the memories of the past. Now even these had faded, become so worn and threadbare they gave no covering peace. All was gone; only Christ remained. Christ each moment of the day. No future, no past, only Christ now. Resentment came to him. Like the children of Israel, he was tired of manna, tired of the Christ he fed upon each moment. Bitterness was creeping into his heart. Strange how the heart could one moment glory in Christ and the next feel as if it had never known Him. He must think of other things. They said this was the only conflict anywhere in the world. When it was resolved, the world would know peace for the first time. What did he care of the course of the world? A world populated by the same type of men who were in his platoon.

The earth was still rumbling. From the city, he heard the thunderclaps, could see white-yellow flashes through the chemical fog. A stillness surrounded him. He heard no movement of equipment or bodies, no coughs from those around him. A wind stirred; he watched the chemicals suspended before his eyes bend with the wind.

In time, the chemical fog broke apart and was pushed upriver by a breeze. The small monitoring device on his chest read *safe*. One of the sergeants should be out, planting the more complex and sensitive detection units issued to platoon-sized forces. His lungs were tired of pulling air from within the suit. Towels had evidently decided to sit tight. The only reason that came to mind was laziness. John slowly lifted his mask, though technically he was disobeying orders. After a few short breaths he breathed deeply, sighed in relief.

The dead shock troopers lay scattered about, the exposed flesh had turned black from the chemical fog. The wrecked airfoil had floated down the river half submerged and caught on some invisible underwater obstruction. No stars were seen; the clouds were a solid gray. The city glowed dully where fires smoldered. The walls of the buildings retained heat from heat bombs and had a dull luminescence. The fires on the upper floors of the skyscrapers burned brightly, and the yellow light reflected on the clouds. The wind caught and fanned the flames. The towers, walkways were shredded, torn; some upper stories looked like rubbly mountain peaks. Many walkways hung, swaying wildly in the winds.

The city's great depth and height, the wreckage, imparted a primeval beauty and power to the scene. John looked upon volcanic mountains rising into birth rather than a civilization subsiding. The sounds of explosions were intermittent. Most of the explosions were muffled, coming from within buildings or from the subterranean city. Flames reflected from the water, flickered upon the patrol's position.

By looking closely, John could see soldiers, tiny figures, or see the results of their laser fire, grenades bursting, rockets streaking. Air-platform gunships still hovered or darted through canyons. The red crosses on the hospital craft were visible. He saw a missile launcher transported, dangling under an air platform, to the top of a building.

The firing to the rear had increased. Flashes of light, rumblings, revealed an engagement upriver. Perhaps the assault on the city had only been a feint and the true thrust was to the north. The shaking earth seemed determined to release the suppressed fear within.

He ate hurriedly, then secured his mask. Why hadn't a detection unit been planted? Why hadn't orders been given to unmask? He could smell his own stink now that the mask was secure. His scalp itched from infrequent washing and the irritation of unevaporated sweat trapped by his helmet. His underclothes were twisting, sticking, binding, and he could not straighten them. His socks had rolled down close to his heels. Though he had just eaten, his stomach churned in hunger. His web belt pulled at his waist. All this discomfort could make a man edgy, distracted, angry. He had no anger, only an indifference.

A dry sleep taste was in his mouth. Mist came from the river. The blackness of the river increased as the flames from the waterfront receded. Sleep took hold of his mind. His head began to nod. From the black river came a flock of ducks. The ducks drifted so peacefully in the mist. The river was a good environment for the ducks—broad, safe, with weedy areas along the shore for food and nesting. The river smelled very much like ducks. The ducks circled the ferries, came into the shallow water.

In the Shadow of Babylon

Since a child, he had liked ducks. The ducks rose up and became deer. Deer from the outskirts of the city, from the neglected land along the wharves and storage areas, seeking a quiet place away from war. The deer walked quietly on the shore, browsing and watching, alert for danger. It was so peaceful—like his grandfather's country home—the deer grazing in the yard. He wondered if the deer would eat from his hand as they had done at his grandfather's home. They were big deer; they became bears in his mind.

God! Lord! Christ! His eyes widened; his body tensed. Enemy storm troopers walking toward the patrol's position. The enemy's chamele uniforms as gray-black as the river water, the mist and the night. They moved slowly in a long sweeping line, so stealthily, so confident in their prowess.

John's grenades were neatly laid on a ledge in his foxhole. He pulled the pins of all three grenades without visible movement. The enemy trooper before him turned his head in a wide scan. When the head was turned away, John threw the grenades. As he threw, he heard astonished cursing over his throat com—the patrol was aware of its desperate situation. The grenades exploded before the trooper even as the line charged the patrol's position. In the flash of light from the grenades' blast, he saw the trooper fall to his knees as if only stunned. John knew his only hope was to find sanctuary—past the sweeping enemy line, in the river.

Laser eruptions burst through the reeds into the wet ground. Over the throat com came the anguished cries of his platoon. The advancing troopers had not closed the hole left by their grenaded comrade. John dashed toward the man, hoping to run by him before he regained his senses. Just as John was cutting around the kneeling trooper, the trooper looked up, his laser arm aimed at John. With no time to fire, John deftly blocked the aimed laser with his own weapon. The trooper grabbed at John with his free arm, pulled John into his armor-encased body. John could smell the man's sweat, the heat welling from the great muscles. John frantically ripped his knife from the sheaf on his web gear even as he ducked a blow from the trooper's laser arm. John continued his motion, slipped behind the man, now struggling to his feet. John jumped upon his back, attempting to pull the helmeted head backward. The knife desperately sought the jugular through clothing and armor. John pried the knife, seeking some entrance.

The trooper was in a frenzy—he twisted, fell to the ground, intending to crush his assailant between his body and the ground. The knife blade struck flesh. John jiggled the blade. An anguished roar promising vengeance came from the trooper even as his throat filled with blood.

John ran into the rushes of a small, narrow, weed bank within the river's channel, heard the thrashing of the trooper in his death throes. He tensed for the laser shot into his back. The water pressed against him; his suit gave him buoyancy. The coldness of the water could not match the heat of exertion or the numbness of fear. He ran, then swam with his hands, pushing himself into deeper water until only his head was visible. The mist lay about him. The current carried him downriver past the sunken ferries, the wrecked airfoil, to a jetty that provided deep water for the crossing.

As he drifted, the shore lit up with explosions—a rocket attack. He knew it was common practice for an advancing enemy to overrun a position by stealth, then follow up with a missile strike to destroy the wounded, those in hiding or in ambush. He wondered if any of the patrol would escape. It flashed through his mind that the enemy had wanted to advance through the chemical fog but that the confusions of war ruined their timing. He smiled at their ill fortune or incompetence.

He came ashore and hid, in thin cover, till the hours near dawn. The morning mists helped to hide him. He was not wet, but the water's chill had penetrated him. He circled the ferry landing, coming in behind the ruins of the ticket building. Fresh chunks of concrete lay strewn about, evidently damage from the missile attack. He saw movement in the ruins and distinguished the forms of men. He realized with a start that Towels, Animal, Scott, and seven men had survived. He saw none of Scott's men and none of the Churchers.

He surmised that during the chemical attack, Towels and Animal had moved their men to the wetlands. They had anticipated an attack. This is why Towels had not placed a detection unit out after the chemical barrage—he and his men had been gone by then. The absence of the men explained the unusual quiet. Only the Churchers, Scott's men, and he were in position when the enemy shock troopers attacked.

Scott may have seen the pullout, as his foxhole was nearby, and followed, or pulled out later when the troopers attacked. Scott would have led his men to safety had he had sufficient warning. Scott and his men, the Churchers, and John were a welcome sacrifice. John could feel the presence of Animal behind the plot; Towels didn't have the cunning.

John spoke his name into the throat com, then entered the ruins with a thankful smile on his face. He spoke not a word; his eyes showed no emotion or surprise to the survivors. Towels's and Animal's eyes widened in disbelief. Then Animal's eyes narrowed and held the light of laughter. The Baptist seemed to live a charmed life. Perhaps his Christ had power.

Animal spoke. "Played dead, they passed over us, we left before the rocketing."

John noticed Scott glaring at them from his position at the end of the ruins, nearest the river. A rage clung to Scott. John knew his theory of betrayal was correct.

"Where's my position, Sergeant?" John looked at Towels.

"Over there." The position pointed out was across a wide opening from Scott's position. Towels didn't want the two of them to talk but wanted them in proximity.

John turned to leave.

Animal spoke. "Got all your equipment?"

"Yes." John had picked up his laser when he returned to his foxhole.

"Let me see your knife."

John handed the knife to Animal. Animal examined the blade. He saw no traces of blood, but there were fresh nicks and scrapes in the bluing.

"Okay." Animal returned the knife. He noticed the cheek flaps on the Baptist's helmet were damp—the material held moisture, unlike most of the uniform and equipment. John sheaved the knife and walked away. He knew Animal was retracing the events of the night.

When the Baptist was out of hearing, Animal said, "He's the only one who could have killed that trooper. He must have moved into the river to escape. The water washed the blood from the knife but soaked his helmet flaps. The damage to the blade came from the trooper's armor."

Towels spoke. "He's goddamned clever and lucky." The voice was traced with envy.

Animal added, "But he's no danger to us. He'll keep his mouth shut. He doesn't want any part of our games." Animal laughed.

Towels cut into the laughter angrily. "He's goddamned dangerous. He just hasn't had his chance."

CHAPTER 3

The first ground units of the offensive began appearing soon after the Baptist had settled into his position. The advancing units were disheveled, worn, but nowhere near exhaustion. Their pace was exceeding all projections. Enemy scouting units, sniper complexes, firebases were being annihilated. Cockiness and success gleamed in the soldiers' eyes. The advancing units ignored the patrol even as they established temporary defensive positions along the river. Soon the river was lined with airfoils.

The city had been quiet, with only sporadic explosions through the course of the morning. Now aircraft strafed the city in preparation for the final assault. A lone enemy fighter strafed the riverbank lined with airfoils. The patrol watched the airfoils become shredded scrap metal. They saw the fighter explode in a yellow ball of flame, just a small dot in the sky, far on the horizon.

The troops were in a jovial mood as they commented on the strafing and the downing of the aircraft. It was good to have unlimited speech, to be free of the threat of covey bombs. They watched the damaged airfoils being replaced from the underbellies of huge cargo air platforms. The river's edge was a mass of movement, of engineering and infantry units, machines, weapons systems. The patrol knew its job was done. They had survived. Rest, good food, showers, sexual companions, alcohol, mind relaxants, passes awaited them. Forty soldiers had become eleven, but death was forgotten and life—good, easy life—beckoned them. Every man's thoughts were on the future.

In the afternoon, their captain, a man seldom seen, came to them. He appeared when it was necessary to order, punish, or reward. He was a harsh man among harsh men—career officers. Whatever personality he possessed was hidden from them. He always spoke to them with condescension, choosing simple, vulgar words. He had Scott gather up the patrol.

Scott's shoulders squared, his posture became erect with the responsibility, with the affirmation that he was the ranking man. Towels watched the strutting Scott evilly, wondering if Scott was stupid enough to mention the incident of the past night. The captain stood on a concrete column that had fallen intact. He was in normal fatigues, no chamele suit, no body armor. John assumed the advance had been a walk in the park. It seemed this podium had been made for him. He removed his helmet.

He was a man in his middle thirties, lean, with a "cruits" haircut. His thickly muscled neck engulfed the sides of his skull. His countenance was severe. He was a man who liked destruction, liked manipulating people, liked the climb up the career ladder. He knew every aspect of the soldier's trade, from small-group tactics to clothing maintenance. Not simply the book knowledge but the knowledge that came from doing. Even sergeants respected him for his knowledge. He looked over the gathered men and after a long silence spoke.

"You did well. You reached your objective without leaving your ordered route. Your patrol's lane was the main avenue of the advance."

The patrol's lane being the main avenue of advance was a matter of chance, yet the inflection was that it had been their skill. John became suspicious—praise was rarely given when deserved.

The captain continued. "You even stood up to the enemy's best, their shock troops, and survived the friendly fire incident that killed them."

John looked at the faces of the gathered men; they were hanging on his words like adoring children on a mother's apron. Their tension had dissipated when their guilt was overlooked and excused as friendly fire. John had no admiration for the captain. He knew the men were dreaming of the rewards that might be bestowed upon them through this man's power; unlimited access to the company whores or a week-long pass to one of the cosmopolitan cities. Towels's eyes were bright with cheer.

The patrol was in its own small world; the activities of war swirled around them. They didn't hear the noise of airfoils, boats, tracks, walkers, ammunition carriers, antiaircraft batteries; the shouts of men communicating above the noise of engines. The captain stood before them like a god. His entourage of messenger, driver, commo man were at his feet. He continued speaking.

"You did well and will be rewarded. But the enemy is far from beaten. His resistance is stiffening like the prick on a junkyard dog." The men revealed ludicrous grins. "Because of this resistance, I was ordered to collect my company and move forward into the city."

The grin on each man's face slowly emptied into a blankness. A stunned silence hung on the gathering. Animal was the first to react.

"Sir, does that mean we're goin' too?" Animal's tone was humble, subservient.

"You're part of the company, aren't you?" The captain's voice was mocking and steely.

The brightness left Towels's face and eyes. Scott's countenance was twisted into a murderous rage, every facial muscle tensed. Animal's head shook numbly as he looked inward at the conflict taking place for possession of his sanity. Animal spoke contritely.

"Sir, we were forty men; now we're eleven. Can't we sit this one out?"

"I have orders. You're soldiers. There is no exception. I'll see what I can do to compensate you after this is over."

"None of us will be left to compensate when this is over. Moppin' up in the city is certain death!" Animal struggled to maintain respect in his voice. Infantry troops have a dread of urban warfare. Every window, door, manhole, roof, vehicle, rubbled structure could hide a sniper. Even if you were aware of every danger—sniper, ambush, booby trap—in any one place, by taking three steps you come upon a thousand new places where death might lurk.

"You exaggerate...and I don't need to explain myself. I have my orders. You will—I repeat, You *will*—obey!" The voice was brutal and uncompromising. The captain's body tensed with physical intimidation, as if he might leap from the podium.

The once adoring children became peevish, resentful. They had no understanding of this war. If their work did not bring them reward, then why did they fight? Now the small compensations they had earned were taken away at a whim or postponed, if not for eternity. What were eleven men in the scheme of things? They had done their job. They hadn't undergone privations, fear, hardship for a cause but for what others consider their due: sleep, food, warmth, sex, life free of anxiety. They feared their captain, knowing his severity and his absolute power over them. Their helplessness made them more desperate and resentful.

Scott spoke. "Beggin' your pardon, sir. Isn't—"

"Sergeant, shut your mouth! You will do as I say or face the penalty."

Scott's eyes looked inward in disbelief. The patrol knew the penalty the captain referred to was immediate death. Rebellion in the ranks had been common till draconian measures had been implemented, such as the death penalty at the commander's discretion.

The captain stared hard at the men; a contempt gleamed in his eyes. He had been more lenient than he had intended to be—hinting of compensation. Motivating men was a matter of reward or punishment. He couldn't appeal to patriotism, manhood, or a higher cause; they no more believed in these things than he did. Iron, brutal discipline could never be relaxed. Such were the soldiers he led, such were the people of his nation and the world.

Animal raised his rifle muzzle from the ground to waist level. Towels's rifle moved. Scott shifted his rifle to face Towels. Towels was hated as much as this ass of a captain. The captain's men tensed; one fumbled slowly for his pistol. The captain glared, confident in his rank and his physical power.

Animal spoke harshly. "We damn well deserve better than we're gittin'!"

The captain's posture of intimidation goaded Animal's manhood.

The captain spoke. "You were going to get better than you deserved until you raised that rifle. Put it down and you will walk away with your life."

Animal's eyes had never left the captain's eyes; baleful stare was locked to baleful stare. They were daring each other. The bonds of restraint snapped in Animal.

"If I walk away now, it's just to die later, in the city, with no pleasure between. You shithead. You don't frighten me. Not your goddamned rank or your attitude. You're a fucking man just like us!"

The gathering tensed; each man tightened his hold upon his weapon. In a rage, the captain jumped off his concrete podium and grabbed Animal by the neck, even as he knocked Animal's weapon to the ground with one savage kick. Animal seemed momentarily stunned by the captain's actions. When had an officer ever touched an enlisted man?

The captain's moves had been quick, brutal, but he had underestimated Animal's ego, his hatred, and his combat reflexes. With the slightest movement, Animal had jerked a hidden, spring-loaded wrist knife into the captain's taut stomach muscles. Animal's hand went into the hot stomach as he sought the aortic artery and spinal column. He twisted the knife into hard bone, even as he smiled into the captain's face. Animal studied the captain's eyes and gloated at the dying man's confusion and pain. The captain hunched over; Animal supported his victim as if he meant to help him. The crowd suddenly realized what had happened. Men scrambled; lasers were firing. John found cover behind a foundation wall.

John withheld his fire. Scott had known joy when Animal pushed the knife deep. Scott admired Animal for his manhood even as he hated him for his race. The mutiny was a convenient excuse for killing Towels. The captain's commo man had rolled over a pile of debris even as he was calling for help. Towels knew the situation was out of hand. If they had quietly led the captain into the weeds and killed him, they might have had a chance of escaping punishment.

Animal realized the captain, the captain's men, and Scott must die for him to live. He knew the odds were against him. He could not be taken prisoner. His men willingly fought beside him; they were bonded by blood; they were not afraid of death. Towels understood his chances of survival were slim. He had raised his weapon in the direction of the captain and on such slight and ambiguous movements, soldiers had been put to death. Still, he had to back the winner, the power.

Towels turned his weapon on Animal and his men even as Scott's laser sought Towels.

John remained hidden; he would wait and would fire only to preserve his life. Within minutes he saw clean solid green uniforms moving around the perimeter of the laser fight. They were security police, ruthless psychopaths who enjoyed killing and torture. They were upon him; they said nothing; he offered no resistance. Still, they kicked his weapon away from where he had dropped it, stripped him of his knife, rifle-butted him to the ground. He sensed the firefight had ended.

He was prodded viciously to his feet and moved to the lifeless forms of the captain and his men. Only the captain's commo man had survived. All the bodies were being collected. Towels was dying; red foam frothed his lips, he breathed convulsively. John looked upon his dying exertions without remorse. Scott was dead. Animal and one of his followers lived; all the others were dead. Three men were needed to drag Scott to the collection of corpses.

The commo man looked at the three living men. He was shaking, his eyes were glassy. He had never been in a shootout, rarely saw any action. His body was coursing with fear and hatred for those who had made him fear, uncovered his weakness. The commo man spoke as he hyperventilated. "You're all gonna die for this."

A security guard viciously raised his rifle butt toward the commo man's face; the commo man ceased talking. The prisoners were segregated.

John assumed they were waiting for an officer, and when one arrived they would all be shot or hanged. The commo man was so shaken that he would swear everyone had been part of the mutiny. The commo man's eyes had held desperation, a forlornness, a sorrow when he had glanced at the body of his captain. The captain had been a father figure, a protector from the discomforts, the brutalities of army life. The commo man wanted revenge, blind revenge.

The security patrol wanted to kill; killing gave them pleasure. Investigation or reasonable doubt were not part of their vocabulary. John knew that if he were to escape death, the commo man would have to make an assertive, unequivocal statement in defense of his innocence. John knew that statement would never come.

Animal sat on a block of cement, a guard beside him. The second prisoner was out of John's sight. Some of the security patrol had to be new; it was against procedure and common sense for prisoners to be able to see each other. John gave thanks that blindfolds hadn't been used. Animal felt the gaze and slyly tilted his eyes upon John in a quick glance. Animal smiled wryly as he looked back to the earth. He sensed something in the Baptist greater than the circumstances. Was the Baptist's god truly *God*?

John saw the spark of bravado in Animal. They both knew they were doomed. Animal's posture—the slumped shoulders, the passive hang of arms and hands, was an act. Animal was formulating an escape plan, waiting for the proper time. John could see this in Animal, for he knew him. The guard looked upon a man in remorse, resigned to his fate. For a brief moment, a gleam entered Animal's eyes—a gleam of respect for John.

Was escape a possibility? Not just momentary escape that would buy a few minutes or hours, but time enough to feel life free from fear? He was on a foreign continent, deep within a war zone. His uniform, all uniforms, were marked electronically for easy tracking. Security patrols roamed the front lines and behind the lines. How could he purchase a ticket home without money, with an identity number stamped upon his flesh that would tell the authorities he was a deserter?

Perhaps the commo man or some witness to the mutiny would stand up and say, "This man is innocent." He snorted sarcastically at the thought. No one bothered to volunteer the truth unless there was something tangible in it for them. Cynicism didn't produce this realization, only the reality of the times. Besides, that man, had he existed, would have already stepped forward. Everyone knew how quickly punishment was administered on the front.

John watched the ants at his feet, working between a crack in the concrete, heaving up the soil. He didn't feel his body; he lived within his eyes. He was weary. Did he truly wish to escape death? Heaven was so near. Why should he live? The obstacles in life were insurmountable. Death would come quickly. He hoped they would not hang his corpse beside a roadway. The thought of his empty flesh on display angered him.

Peace came to him. It would be good to leave this foolishness. A laser to the heart, a broken neck, a quick death. He wasn't bitter at the thought of death, neither elated nor depressed. He had lived the best he could—God knew. In a sudden but gentle lucidity, the presence of the Holy Spirit was upon and within him. With the absence of his own will, he would clearly know the will of God. The Lord would decide life or death.

Animal sprang. The guard had turned his head slightly to watch a construction walker topple as it entered a boat. The guard was absorbed in the accident. Animal had been waiting patiently. He twisted the guard's neck, wrested the laser from the dying grip, and ran. Another guard saw the escape and shouted.

John's guard took four steps in the direction of the fleeing prisoner, attempting to paint a bead. Without thought, John crawled to the pile of confiscated weapons, grabbed his knife. He slunk away through the rubble like a snake, entered the high rushes in a blur. He saw a wide-shouldered security guard—a woman, by the projection of her chest. She seemed to be looking at him but not seeing him. He ignored her, moved downriver, making no effort to hide or hurry. He wouldn't have been disappointed had they found him.

He came upon a six-legged walker facing the river. One of the foot pads had caught in a tangle of rusty cable. The cable had probably come from a dredging operation years in the past. Men were working to free the pad. He joined them, putting his weight against the stubby leg. His added weight caused the pad to slip from the cable. No one spoke to him or seemed to think his presence odd. No one thanked him. They were engineers, by their insignia.

They jumped onto the empty bed of the walker, he joined them. He assumed they had been laying all-terrain road along the shore, as the road ended near their walker – which had a mounted derrick. He thought they were heading back to a distribution center for more roadway. They were sullen, tired. They looked upon him and knew he didn't belong but hadn't the curiosity to ask why he was among them. He smiled inwardly at their deadness and relaxed ever so slightly. He resolved not to put any effort into this escape but to simply follow the opportunities the Lord would bring his way. He knew the Spirit was guiding him. He had been too weary, the prize of Heaven too real for him to have escaped on his own. Was he going home? The thought was ridiculous. But then, what was impossible for the Lord?

The walker followed the river, then entered the bustle of a staging area. Here, air platforms were being harnessed to loads; walkers were crawling about with their caterpillar-like gait; huge, tired marsh vehicles squatted under immense loads, tires bulging. Great mounds of pontoons, bridging, roadway, fuel cells, food pods, were swarming with laborers, eaten into by machines. The walker came to a stop before a regimental command post; the engineers silently jumped out, walked toward one of the huge inflatable tents near the headquarters tent. None of the engineers looked back at John.

He stood by the bed of the walker and scanned the mass of activity around him. His eyes could not focus; he was vulnerable, nervous. His mind was blank as to what he would say if someone challenged him as to his unit or purpose.

He was paralyzed with indecision.

"Hey, soldier!"

John searched the moving crowds and vehicles, his eyes glazed. An officer stood by a jeep parked in front of the regimental headquarters. John then pointed to himself questioningly.

"Me?"

"Yes, you. Come here."

The officer stared and seemed to smile at John's discomfort. Walking toward the keen-eyed officer, who was in his midthirties, John saw the chaplain's collar. Women would call him handsome because of the large eyes and strong jaw. His clothes were clean, showed no signs of hard wear. John noticed boxes, a rolled-up tent, and acoustical equipment on the far side of the jeep. The chaplain's eyes were piercing; John could not hold the gaze. The chaplain seemed to have a perpetual smile.

"I'm not taking you from anything?"

"No, Chaplain." John understood he was to load the jeep.

A chaplain's duties on the front had become monotonous to Father Desmit. The setting up of the tent, the altar, the sound system; the packing and unpacking of the jeep were wearying and degrading to his abilities. They had promised him an aide a month ago, and still he had no one. He liked a soldier who didn't need a direct order, could read between the lines. This soldier was conscientious, treating the boxes gently, arranging the heaviest gear toward the center and bottom of the jeep.

The worn uniform, the smell, the thin frame, languid movements, pale skin, the wide staring eyes told Chaplain Desmit a combat soldier was before him. Combat soldiers wore no patches of rank or unit. Probably a recon man. Such men intrigued Desmit—men who had killed, men who had seen others killed, men who knew the fright of combat, were a breed apart. This young man named Johnson, according to the faded name tag, was in trouble.

Desmit knew the moment he had seen him standing forlornly behind the walker. No gear, no weapon, no purpose, fear and confusion in the eyes. Deserter? Without a doubt. But why? Answering that question, perhaps helping this Johnson, or turning him in, would give life taste, add excitement to the dull routine, and provide sermon material.

John completed loading the jeep. Desmit extended his hand.

"Father Desmit, now at your service."

John grasped the hand; the grip was strong.

"I could use a driver. Just to my next service, fifteen minutes down the road. I'll make it right with your commander." John looked deeply into Desmit's eyes. John knew Desmit suspected something.

"All right, Father. Let's go."

Desmit seemed to like the title *Father*—the eyes had brightened. Desmit's perpetual smile broadened. Fifteen minutes, enough time to learn Johnson's story. If Johnson had redeeming value, he would use his influence upon a number of generals who owed him favors. He needed a driver/helper, a companion, even a soul to enlighten. If Johnson was incorrigible…well, then the authorities could deal with him. Desmit's goodness and righteousness spread a warmth throughout his body.

John moved into the driver's position, turned the ignition, felt the rotors giving lift. Desmit seemed relieved to be in the passenger's seat.

"What are you called?"

"John—a name as common as dirt."

"Who's your commanding officer?"

"Captain Van Ord." John supposed this was a lie since Van Ord was dead.

Desmit noted John's tone of voice. Self-deprecating—a lack of self-worth?

"What's it like in combat?"

"Weariness, loneliness, perpetual fright."

"Killed men?"

"Yes."

"Why are you running away?" Desmit's tone was nonjudgmental.

"My staying serves no purpose."

Johnson hadn't blinked an eye as he answered—no denial or uneasiness—as if he knew the question was coming. Yes, Johnson could read between the lines. For a moment, the intelligence frightened Desmit. He could be sitting beside a clever murderer, a compulsive killer or thief. Desmit found peace in his collar—the Church was feared even by murderers. The Church had power no sane man willingly tested. This Johnson was sane, he was certain.

"You're wrong. I can think of many reasons to stay—positive and negative." Desmit sought John's eyes for encouragement to continue.

"Go on, Father."

"The negatives are: If you run, you will be hanged as a deserter. If you escape, you will live in perpetual fear. Your ID number can't be used to buy or sell. You will not be given work and thus will have no food. You will have no place to call home, no clothes, nothing. You will be forced to live by theft and deception, and eventually the police will catch you. Your ID is imprinted upon your skin, man! You're marked for life.

"Now the positive side. You might be promoted—rank equals more status, more money—if you stay. You could become an officer! You might be moved into a support role, a behind-the-lines job, a clean job, one that will translate easily to the civilian job market. You will be out of danger," Desmit said.

"With all this personal satisfaction comes a deeper joy: fighting for the Federation, the New Order. History and mankind will record you as one of those who brought prosperity and order to the world.

"There is plenty of purpose. You have just got to choose to do right, then develop the will to see your plan through. The Church can help you do this."

John smiled thoughtfully. Why was Desmit concerned? He spoke. "I thank you for your concern. I took the officer's test when I was in basic training and passed easily. I was interviewed by a panel of captains, men of the Church. They believed in a god who gave man passion, ego, self-will, and who gloried in man's achievements. Then it came out that my God abhorred man's passion, ego, self-will, and gloried in the achievement of human submission and weakness so that His will could be done. That was the end of becoming an officer."

Desmit heard no bitterness but perhaps a trace of wistfulness.

"They told you that was the reason for your rejection?"

"Yes, they wondered how an officer could have such a god and achieve victory on the battlefield. They may have even believed me to be an Enslaver."

Desmit tensed visibly, instinctually; he did not understand why. He thought back to his seminary course on Church history and antagonistic doctrines. He remembered that the Enslavers had had a brief but powerful reign beginning with the Reformation and ending in the Scientific Period. Their reign was called Protestantism, the theology of a few dissidents that was given power by nationalism, a rising middle class, and the discovery of new worlds.

The power of reason had eventually reasserted itself, and at the turn of the second millennium, most Protestant denominations had merged back into the true church, the World Church. Those who didn't join the Church espoused Church doctrine. With this new power, the Church had wedded the state, and heaven on earth had truly begun.

The Enslavers were radicals who broke from their own Protestant faith before and during the merging with the true Church. If it had not been for the amendment of 2100, they still might be organized. He remembered the history, but for the life of him, he couldn't remember the Enslavers' doctrine in any great detail. He knew they were pessimistic, doomsayers, mistrustful of their own motivations and those of others. They saw the world as evil. The intellectualism and rational thought that could have lifted their burden was denied by their own beliefs.

In the quiet that had followed the last words spoken, John silently recited the amendment of 2100:

It is the right of citizens to be free of harassment, persecution, and discrimination from religious, moral, and ethical beliefs that are in excess of or deny or impugn civil law. All such religious organizations, creeds, movements, and persons that express said beliefs are lawfully restrained from the promotion of such beliefs.

Desmit broke the silence. "You're not an Enslaver, are you?"

John wondered on the consequences of his answer. Some men might laugh, amused by a law that outlawed a doctrine they knew nothing about. Some men might turn him over to the nearest authorities. He could not deny his Lord.

"I believe in Christ as the Savior, Redeemer of a fallen race."

They were passing through batteries of self-propelled missile launchers scattered through the fields and open forests. The batteries were forming up columns; the heavy engines revving, whirring into a high-pitched whine; the drivers' faces showing their keenness to move.

To remain in one place too long was to invite death.

Desmit's eyes gleamed merrily at John's response: he had not denied he was an Enslaver. Desmit studied John's face. Studying faces was a habit he had acquired that gave him the appearance of thoughtfulness and concern. He wished he had a firm grasp on the doctrine of the Enslavers instead of remembered bits of hearsay and negative comments. *Enslaver* was a word much like *Satan*, a nebulous, undefined something that was alluded to and wide in application, but never really explained. The popular conception was that if you were against a good time, you were an Enslaver.

This Johnson seemed a good person—intelligent, with something to offer society. He had wanted to make something of himself and had a setback. Was this setback a catalyst to his archaic beliefs? Had anyone taken the time to bring him to the truth—to the Church? He was worth the time and would be given a chance if all he had done was desert his unit.

"Is desertion your only crime?"

"I deserted because I was to be executed for a crime I didn't commit—a mutiny that led to murder, and I happened to be there."

"Did you take part?"

"No."

Desmit believed John Johnson.

John wondered at this Desmit and his kindness. Priests were supposed to be humanitarians. Was that his motivation? Did he wish to live up to the priestly ideal and bind another to his goodness—feel the warmth that would be returned to him for caring? Or did he wish to be the righteous one in a just cause? Nobility certainly stroked the ego. Did he want to lead a man up out of the mire, be the teacher, mentor? Or was he a good man who loved justice, truth, and nothing else? Who could know a man's heart except God? Could there ever be purity of motive for a man who hadn't given himself to Christ?

John wondered if a time would come when the beliefs he professed would make Desmit so uncomfortable as to reject him, turn him over to the authorities. He felt confident of Desmit's silence and protection for the moment. How long could he make that protection last without compromising his faith or being sidetracked from his escape? Even with Desmit's aid, he would not give himself up to the authorities. The covenant had been broken between him and the state.

"Pull in here. The last mass of the day."

John entered a wide field enclosed by inflatable tents. Desmit jumped out before the jeep had come to a full stop. Desmit suddenly stopped in full stride and turned to John. He studied John's face. A calm came through Desmit's voice. "We're not done talking. I want to hear more. I'd appreciate you setting up over by the headquarters tent."

John had noticed signage announcing the end of the combat zone. John saluted. "Yes, sir."

Desmit laughed, strode away purposely.

***

The service had begun. John sat on the back bench. The pews consisted of three sections of twenty benches, each taken from the mess hall. All the benches were filled. The soldiers were well groomed, clean, their uniforms and equipment new, their faces fat and shaved.

He was aware that these soldiers kept their distance from him. He was gaunt, unshaven, his eyes wide, his movements of a trancelike quality. A strange pensiveness came over him as he realized the day was Sunday. The field rations he had found in Desmit's jeep and had eaten induced a sleepiness. He thought he was forgetting something, something important.

His mind was hollow, he could not remember.

Music. A feeling of warmth, comradeship, understanding clung to the seated soldiers. Symbols, crosses, incense, statues of saints, candles surrounded them. Desmit wore a robe. The congregation sang. By the time of Desmit's sermon, John was nodding into sleep. His homesickness ached within his heart. His uniform seemed a prisoner's garb.

Desmit talked about the importance of knowledge, the perfectibility of humanity, the freedom that comes as knowledge increases and laws decrease. He stressed the importance of the war, of protecting the values of the Church, of God's assistance to men who seek Him. John heard the mixture of foolishness and truth and fell asleep.

Desmit found his driver lying on the grass, sleeping in a fetal position. They packed quickly, Desmit working more quickly than John. They drove away from the tents, away from the front.

"Did you catch any of my sermon?"

"Parts."

"How did it compare with your beliefs?"

Desmit wished to close the gap between the Church and John. The Church needed men like John, and John would benefit from the Church. How strange could his beliefs be? Every religion, denomination, sect that had submitted to the power of the Church had found a room in the Father's mansion.

"I know Christ is the Savior—the Redeemer of a fallen race. How can mankind be saved by God when they refuse to believe they are sinners? Your Church believes men are inherently good and so can strive, through their will, to a more perfect state of being. I say man is inherently evil; he has fallen, the law proves this. He can't be made perfect through his corrupted will. A man must die in Christ to live an acceptable life."

Desmit listened carefully to John's words, smiled. He needed to be sharp to win this battle. This wasn't an average frontline soldier. John, who had tensed with his outpouring of words, was now chuckling, so relaxed he seemed to melt into the seat. This philosophical talk was good, the repetitious pastoral duties had been dulling his mind. Johnson was a blessing. God would give this man into his hands.

"Is your problem, then, between law and man's striving for perfection?"

"Yes, that is a good bit of it." John decided not to contest the word *problem*.

"A vestige of sin still remains in the world. I admit this. As our knowledge increases, our tendency to sin will decrease. That is how we reach a higher plane, become more perfect."

The words began to flow. Desmit's mind felt relaxed, confident. God was speaking through him. He continued. "Once the Jewish people thought more than one wife was acceptable. Then they were told it was not, and now it is acceptable again. Christians thought homosexuality was evil till it was revealed that it was only cult homosexuality and the abuse of the young that was evil. Christians once thought they were God's children till it was revealed through scripture that all were God's children. Christians once thought they should be separate from the world till the scripture revealed they are part of the world. On and on it goes. As we fully interpret the Bible and discover new knowledge, we live closer to what God intended. The old thoughts, laws, become obsolete and are repealed."

"Well said, Father, and I could answer each one of your examples and prove it false, but that would be tedious."

Desmit was surprised by the intellectual arrogance of Johnson.

Johnson spoke again. "Did Christ come into the world to do away with the law or to bind us even more tightly to His perfect standards? The law is to tell us we are sinners, to activate our consciences and root out our egos, our self-will. Sin resides in every child born—sin isn't a social concept. How can sin be done away with simply by calling wrong right, evil good? Sin can be suppressed, rerouted, hidden, denied, or ignored, but it lives within us. Knowing it is there doesn't give you the power to reject it. To me, this talk of perfection is just a scheme to call what has been wrong since the fall of Adam—man's heart—right."

Finally, a pause. Johnson liked to hear himself talk. His supposed intelligence was irritating. How many theological works had he read? How many years did he spend in a seminary? Yet kindness would win in the end.

"John, what kind of a god wouldn't want us to be free, perfect like himself?"

"Yes, through Christ, with His new life coursing through our bodies dead to sin. Can the naturally born man have motivations other than evil? Freedom comes from a new birth in Christ, not from denying the law and our sinful hearts."

John's voice was flat, unemotional. Desmit seemed at peace when he spoke.

"To live free and enjoy life—that is the motivation behind the Church's beliefs."

"What part of man is living free? The evil or the good? What does *enjoying life* mean? Doing what you want or what God wants? Is your enjoyment serving God or your own self?"

Desmit understood the problem now—the idea of a dual nature warring in humanity. The idea of a god who wanted the opposite of what you wanted. Ah, Enslavers bound people to the law; his seminary course came back to him. Christ, to them, became a parasitic being or an alter ego who lived within them instead of a guide to wisdom, a helper, who allowed man to be all that he wished. Such a system of beliefs could make anyone unhappy. No wonder an amendment had been added to the Constitution, though it seemed unnecessary. Who would want such beliefs but those with intense self-hatred?

"Tell me, Father. If God told you that you were inherently sinful and your thoughts and actions were not within His wisdom and love, were not animated by His Spirit within you, would you give up everything that you are to have that wisdom, love, and Spirit?"

"Everything? No, He'd never ask for everything; that makes no sense. Why does He need to energize me, animate me, when I was born with life in me? Look at what I have accomplished. I've sinned and will sin, but I was made in God's image. I leave the sin behind, learn, grow, become better."

"And the world knew Him not."

"What?"

"You were made in the image of God. When Adam sinned, mankind appropriated God's image for himself. We've stolen what is rightfully God's."

"Or were we given those things?"

"Adam was given the Garden."

"A Babylonian folktale."

"Christ died for my sins; that's why I am free. He lives within me, and that is why I remain free."

Desmit smirked. John Johnson was the least free man he had ever met—miserable, having nothing, going nowhere. But why kick a man when he's down? Desmit kept those thoughts hidden and spoke of others.

"You talk mysticism. He lives inside of you! The personality—Christ? Does He talk to you?"

Desmit had attempted to keep cynicism from his voice and had failed. John spoke quietly even as Desmit unknowingly moved away from John.

"I have my own personality. The Holy Spirit is in me."

"Tell me; how does He talk to you?"

Desmit wondered if Johnson had mental problems. John was sentient of the underlying fear.

"From somewhere beyond the human soul, He speaks within, and then I discern. I don't hear audibly. I discern from within. Then a will comes with discernment, a power, and you know it is genuine, not of you."

John smiled at Desmit, who had lost his perpetual smile.

Fear and loathing twisted Desmit's lips. This god even thought for a man! Why is something "genuine" when it is not of you? Foolishness!

John spoke. "You ought to discern."

"I think it is impossible to discuss this subject with you, as your beliefs are not based on logic but mysticism. I haven't had any experience near yours, nor have I ever heard of such experiences."

"Do you want to have such experiences?"

"What must I do?" Desmit threw up his hands. He would humor Johnson; the talk was absurd.

"Believe you are a sinner," John said. "Then, want God more than anything else in this world, including yourself. God will do the rest."

"That's unacceptable." Johnson had such self-loathing that he escaped himself by this alter ego, Christ.

"Why?"

The road had jammed with traffic, mostly damaged weapon systems moving to repair areas. A tank carrier was before them, loaded with hunks of metal once tanks.

"John, I say this with love in my heart. You are not a happy man. You've looked on the dark side too long, and it has warped your perception of reality."

The traffic was inching through a crossroads. The corpses of ten men hung from a crossbeam of metal piping supported between two trees. The necks had stretched grotesquely, the nearly naked bodies were mutilated and streaked with a single line of yellow paint. The only clothing, underpants, were stained with feces and urine.

"There, Father, is the work of your perfect men, your perfect society. I don't mean the hanging—brutal as it is, perhaps that was justice. No sign to explain the reason. The public display, the mutilation, those come from hearts that are sick, perverse, evil."

"Yes, of course, those things happen, especially when men are put under stress. Think of all the men who wouldn't have mutilated the bodies. Look, a better world is coming, and the Church is a part of that movement. Let's bring light to your mind and then find you a place within this coming world."

"I don't want to help build the new Tower of Babel."

Another ancient folktale. Best not to debate it. "You're against peace and prosperity?"

"When society doesn't allow Christ Jesus to be preached. It is better if there is war and poverty, and the true Christ is allowed to work in men's hearts."

"That's seditious. You'd rather see the world in ruin because your idea of god isn't allowed to be mentioned?"

"Without Christ in your life, peace and prosperity satisfy nothing but the self, not God. You can do great works, and your soul can be dead to God. Peace and prosperity come from the benevolence of God. They are not signs of his presence within a society."

Yes, it was true. He would rather see the world in ruin. Desmit would never understand that thought. To Desmit, life continued for the enjoyment of men. For God, life continued so that men might be saved. God would bring the world to its knees someday, for the world had rejected his Son. Noah saw the wrath of God upon the world, as did Sodom and Gomorrah, and the people of Israel.

Desmit heard the uncompromising stubbornness. Why couldn't the "self" be satisfied with peace and prosperity and anything else it so desired? How had the "self" become the enemy of John? Why was God against the very creation He had made? A good psychiatrist might have the answers for John. He still had something to offer society. How many times in a day could such strange beliefs cause aberrant behavior? Probably none. It was just philosophy, talk.

"I'd like to help you, John. I can see that justice is done in your case. I know important people. You are innocent, and truth will prevail—if enough pressure is brought to bear on the right people."

"It's over, Father. I played by your rules, fought for peace, prosperity, the Federation, and would have died for this government that doesn't allow me the freedom to worship my God or tell others of Him. I can no longer be a part of a system that denies me my reason for life—my God."

Desmit said nothing. He had described what life would be like if John chose to run. John was choosing to run. Perhaps there would be a change of heart in the time remaining. He would allow Johnson to walk away and only then would he alert the proper authorities. No doubt they were monitoring Johnson's location now. His uniform was electronically marked as were all uniforms, a fact John seemed to have forgotten. A man sympathetic to his flight would have reminded him.

"How far to your home base, Father?"

Christ warned His disciples to call no one Father but God. The warning seemed appropriate. Desmit would turn him in.

"Another fifteen minutes."

The voice seemed curt.

"How long do you stay at the front?" John asked.

"Thirty days, then I go back for two weeks. Two weeks of travel, sightseeing. Europe is incredible, prosperous—*rich* is a better word." Desmit's mood had changed from resentment to excitement, a lust for life. "Here there is a rich history, a respect for the past. I'll be glad when this Federation is fully established. I want to remain in Europe. It's incredible how the heads of government have controlled the destructiveness of this war, how little the economy has been affected, or people's lives disrupted."

People's lives disrupted. John thought back to a small town the patrol had passed through. All the inhabitants had died upon the road as they had attempted to flee. The bodies had been in different states of putrefaction. The bodies on the road, where the sun's heat cooked the macadam, were dried, shriveled, mummified. Within the shade of cars, the bodies were wormy, slippery, oozy, wet. It was the memory of the bodies of women and children that hurt him.

"This week I'm flying back to my home diocese to put in a request for a transfer."

Desmit seemed cheerful again. John vowed to keep him in that state till they parted.

"Where's home?"

"Los Angeles."

"Miss it?"

"No, I was raised by the state—all orphanages look the same. Besides, Europe has what I need: wealth, antiquity, intellectual ferment, and people who enjoy life and aren't afraid to be different."

"Was it difficult to get a flight? I heard they cut back travel to save fuel for the war effort."

"Hey, I'm a priest. I'm important. They bumped a guy off a flight to give me a seat. People know the importance of the Church."

From the corner of his eye, Desmit saw John wince. He would have to turn Johnson in. He would make one last appeal to reason and then it would be to the authorities. Johnson was intelligent, and so his intransigence was a danger to himself and the Church. This Enslaver philosophy was more pernicious then he had first realized.

Potholes and ruts increased. The traffic had loosened when the tank carrier turned off a mile back, then it thickened again behind a convoy. The convoy consisted of crowded troop carriers filled with infantry as ragged and worn as John. Traffic stopped. The jeep came to rest on a slight rise on the tree-lined road. John scanned the empty wheat fields to his left and right. To the right, within the wheat fields, was a defoliated forest. A warm wind and heat came from the fields. John's body was numb from fatigue. The fields filled his senses. The summer heat was coming back after the cold front of storms. Life smelled good, and the air reminded him of other times, in his past, when he had been free. He was free for the moment; hope was still alive. He savored the moment. The warmth was pulsing him into sleep.

The peace was gone! He sensed what was coming before his mind formed the thought. Instinctually, he leapt from the jeep and ran full speed into the fields of yellow wheat. He yelled a warning to Desmit without a turn of his head. No time to wait, or repeat a warning, or even to jerk Desmit along. Life and death were only a matter of seconds.

Desmit was numb with wonderment, fumbling with his briefcase, when the bombs struck. John heard the explosions behind him. Would his eardrums burst? The ringing was intense. Concussions jolted his body. Could a man be shaken apart? When would the burning shrapnel shred his body to a tattered pile of gore? The bombs were the largest he had experienced. He heard the ordnance rumble up the road, past him, into the distance. He dove upon the ground.

The sound seemed to roll on forever. He rose when the sound was past him. He wasn't dead, felt no wounds upon his body. The ordnance had stitched the road like a sewing machine needle, straight, without a skip. Such accuracy was seen as a blessing by the infantryman who could run to that zone of invisible shelter. Soldiers feared the stray, the rogue bomb. To stationary targets, the satellite-controlled bombing was devastating.

John turned to the road as the first moans came to his ears. Shrieks and screams cut the still air. He smelled burning plastic, metal, cloth, flesh. He shuddered as he remembered the soldiers packed into the troop carriers. Only one other man was in the field; he was at least a hundred yards away. As they looked at each other, John could feel the man's relief as his body shrank in a sigh and filled with thankfulness.

John ran loosely, staggering to the jeep, his strength and equilibrium gone. Desmit was dead. John sighed painfully. He had relaxed in Desmit's presence, felt a measure of safety. Now he was stripped bare of that benevolence. An aching loneliness overcame him. He had an anger toward God till he remembered that God had brought him Desmit. God knew the future, and so John trusted.

CHAPTER 4

Desmit had no visible mark upon his body, and John was inclined to believe the concussive power of the bombing had ended life. As John propped Desmit upright in the seat, he felt a wetness on his hand. Searching, John found a small cut at the base of the skull—a shell fragment had been driven into the flesh. Only a fingertip drop of blood oozed from the wound, half of which was a clear liquid.

John sat down on the punctured hood of the shell-splintered jeep and then jumped away as the hot metal seared his nerves. He sat on the earth; even that was hot. He was tired. He rubbed his hands in the dirt, pulling the dirt into a pile. He remembered the peace of his childhood; then, he'd had no worries. He could have heaped the pile of dirt upon his head in anguish.

An explosion of anxiety and fear burst upon his mind. He had not rid himself of his uniform and the location chip within. At this moment, the security patrols could be bearing down upon him. He thought of sitting and waiting for them. The odds were that some time could elapse before he was tracked and found. Hundreds of thousands of soldiers were in a small area, all sending in signals. Perhaps the order had never been given to track him, or it was backlogged in some overworked private's computer. He rose stiffly and grabbed Desmit's briefcase, picked up Desmit in a firefighter's carry, and moved across the wheat fields into the defoliated woods.

He would become Desmit, and Desmit would be the body of John Johnson. He hadn't thought out the ramifications of this switch except that it might buy time. He moved too quickly and found himself winded and rubber legged. He needed privacy to make the switch and to think in peace. He slowed his pace. Already traffic had resumed around the wreckage, as ambulance crews worked, and an emergency center was organized. He moved deeper into the barren woods; the trees began to show leaves. He came to a stream. He looked around and saw no one; the road was out of sight. The security forces could be moving through the woods at this moment.

He stripped, chuckled sadly. He would die clean. He stepped into the small stream of cold water and with a packet of cleaning powder from his hygiene kit and washed. His plastic razor was sharp. Using his small mirror, he shaved his cheeks and neck, leaving the outline of a beard. The beard would add a few years to his age. He stripped Desmit as far as his undergarments and then methodically dressed him in the battle uniform of a recon scout. Desmit had been heavier, though of equal height.

John discarded his own undergarments. The material held a naturally bad odor, and the constant flow of perspiration had not helped. Desmit had narrower and slightly smaller feet but the shoes had to be worn; chamele combat boots on a priest would bring undo attention. John loosened the shoes as far as possible and wore Desmit's dress socks. John placed the chaplain's collar in his shirt pocket—he had seen priests without their collars and assumed the absence would not draw attention. He exchanged dog tags. He took Desmit's ID card. He also kept his own ID card. John pulled out his knife.

"I'm sorry about this."

He stabbed Desmit in the right lung. If the security patrols found the body, they would surmise that after being wounded in the bombing, the deserter had sought shelter in the woods. He thought a moment then placed a small cut in the uniform by the neck to match the small sliver of an opening on the neck from the shrapnel. He paused and rethought the body again. He hoped the epidermal ID number, unseen, stamped on wrist and forehead, was not checked by infrared scanners. Thankfully, the ID number was for buying and selling only and contained no location chip. This epidermal ID number was also printed on the ID card. There would be no reason to check a scanner. That would be extra work to men not interested in work. The security men would search for an ID card first. Not finding this, they would check the dog tag. Why should they check further? A body switch would be far from their thinking, and even if it did enter their minds, they might, from laziness, find it more convenient to close the case.

He was not satisfied with his assumptions. He pulled the left arm out of the airtight uniform and sliced across the wrist number. Only the coroner would take the body out of uniform hours or days in the future. To cut the wrist with his knife through the uniform would arouse the curiosity of an investigator. Once the arm was back in uniform, he raked the knife across the forehead as if shrapnel had struck. He sliced off edges from the clean cut. He had hopefully taken the invisible number with the skin.

He thought of placing the body in the stream, hoping that water acting on the ID ink would leave the numbers unreadable or the scanners inoperable. Or was it better to leave the body to decompose in the heat? He decided heat would destroy more thoroughly, and cool water would only preserve the skin. He dragged the body to exposed sedimentary layers at the base of the hill by the stream. He turned the body facedown so there was facial contact with the soil. The heat would be greater on the rock, and the soil would hold bacteria.

John fastened his sheaf and knife on his belt, at the small of his back. The priestly jacket hid it well. The briefcase remained unopened. He had tarried long enough by the body. He moved downstream for five minutes then went back to the road. He had passed beyond the bombed portion of the road. Looking back, he saw that the destroyed vehicles had already been pushed to the side. A few ambulances lingered. Traffic moved again.

Away from the dust and the noise of the road, he sat and opened the briefcase. He found Desmit's personal computer full of sermons, letters from friends, notes on the personal problems of his charges, orders to Desmit's billet—with the address given. John found codes for entrance into the billet, a gym locker key, an airline ticket to Los Angeles, bank account numbers. The ticket didn't assure him of access to the States. The IDs of all passengers were checked against their infrared numbers. His identity number wouldn't match Desmit's identity card number. The obstacles seemed insurmountable. He would continue. Perhaps God would provide an answer.

***

John opened the door, stepped into the dark room, and listened beyond patience. He turned on the light, desperately hoping not to find a roommate asleep. Desmit's room was empty; John sighed. Two beds were in the room, one was a bare mattress. A locker, a chair, a desk, a refrigerator completed the furnishings. A pair of woman's red panties hung on the back of the chair. A Desmit trophy from a brothel? John sat heavily in the chair and thought back over his journey.

He had encountered fewer difficulties than expected. He had stood by the road less than a minute before being given a ride—by a soldier needing intercession with the commander over a minor offense. The checkpoint leading out of the war zone had stymied him for an hour as he thought of schemes and subterfuge. Finally, it dawned on him that he could crawl underneath the guard house window by approaching via a screening building. He then caught a shuttle bus, showed the driver the address, sat, and slept till awakened by the driver.

The billets were old, a long stone building with an antique slate roof. The building had an historic marker that placed construction in the early nineteen hundreds. The guard on duty was involved in a lovers' spat with his boyfriend. He glanced at the raised ID card and allowed entry.

John rose from the chair, carefully examined the contents of Desmit's locker, chose appropriate civilian clothes. He showered thoroughly, allowed the hot water to penetrate his muscles, then changed into civilian clothes. He was unsure whether Desmit's clerical clothes had a tracking device embedded. Not taking chances, he taped the clothes into a bundle and carried it to the service center near his billet, where he placed it under the trailer of a semitruck with Italian plates.

Back in Desmit's room, he found a paper ticket to Los Angeles in the desk, along with a paper bank statement - both inside a small ledger book. The flight was in two days from a civilian airport in Paris. He found a keypad to a car and registration documents. He found the same documents in the personal computer. Looking out the window, he scanned the parking lot; one of the vehicles must be Desmit's. The refrigerator was empty except for some electrolyte sports drinks. Desmit had some field rations stored in a box beside the desk. John ate and drank.

John lay back on the bed. The problem now was changing his epidermal ID numbers to match Desmit's identity card. He knew a method existed, called masking, that printed new numbers over the original numbers. Such a procedure was illegal and punishable by death. Somewhere in the city of Paris were men who would perform the procedure—for the right price. He would pay from Desmit's account—money was certainly no object. He chuckled. Desmit had a sizable account. Chaplains were well paid or Desmit was moonlighting. How could he make contact with a masker? This was the next hurdle.

He had to push on. Only when he was in the States would he be able to relax. He must move fast. It was imperative. Someone could be pursuing. He attempted to lash his body into movement. His will was dead, or perhaps his body from lack of sleep. He didn't know what to believe. He trusted the Lord, turned out the light, and slept.

***

The two inspectors stood over the body. Dusk was closing quickly. The body lay facedown on the embankment within the wooded area of foliated trees. A small rill or stream gurgled nearby. The water slipped over rocks; minnows darted in the pool of water formed. The younger of the two inspectors spoke in the warm gloom of night. "It seems as if our deserter/murderer has escaped punishment."

"Perhaps," said the older man. Tree frogs were busily trilling, filling the darkness with an eerie quality.

The younger man bent down, felt around the corpse's neck till the dog tag chain was in his hands, then yanked. The older man shone a small flashlight on the neck. The entire body rose up with the yank before the chain broke.

"More and more quality goes into these chains." The younger man laughed at his observation. He read aloud, "John Johnson. That's our man. Let's get out of here and back to base. I don't like this frontline business."

The younger man touched the older inspector on the shoulder breezily, as if turning him to the vehicle. The older man resisted the movement and stood, looking at the corpse. He had been working with Hanson only two weeks, and the relationship had already become an irritation.

The kid was competent, knew all the latest techniques of investigation, and was meticulous in his computer work. He could learn to live with the rapid talk, the slang speech of Hanson's generation. But he couldn't live with the arrogance, the dominating personality, and the cute techniques of establishing that supposed superiority.

Some people—most people—you had to put in their place. He was especially tired of being called "old man," and didn't like Hanson's assumption that he, Hanson, was now lead man. Well, one year to retirement, one year of the kid, then it would be over.

Hanson called from the field, "Are you coming, Old Man?"

Borelli didn't answer, though he heard. They didn't often handle desertion cases or even frontline murders—the security patrols investigated and administered punishment on the front lines. But this man, John Johnson, who allegedly killed a captain, had entered the secondary zone. This zone came under the Inspector Advocate jurisdiction, a civilian branch of government that oversaw military affairs. Few criminals entered the secondary zone because of the competence of the security patrols. This meant that this John Johnson had been lucky and/or clever, of what proportion of each, Borelli didn't know. Why hadn't the uniform been tracked in a timely manner? What glitch in the system was responsible for that oversight? Then, there was the call from a general, a good friend of the deceased captain, who had impressed upon them his desire for John Johnson's head. The call was unnecessary—every case received the same thoroughness.

Hanson was beside Borelli. Hanson was blond-haired, in his middle twenties. He looked like an all-American kid, one who belonged on a beach somewhere, playing volleyball. Yes, this accurately described his attitude and youth. Another side of the kid seemed to say he belonged in a giant corporation, playing interpersonal politics, caring for no one, moving ever upward.

Hanson was of a thin build, aggressive and probing in intellect, arrogant in demeanor. Hanson was boundless in energy; quick motions characterized him. Borelli had seen Hanson stripped for the shower. He was taut, toned, but not muscled. Physically, you thought of Hanson as a long-distance runner, capable of handling prolonged pain, having an unconquerable will.

"What's the problem?" Hanson sighed in mild disgust.

"There isn't any." Borelli didn't move, though he felt Hanson's impatience and anger attempting to move him.

"Look, the dog tag matches the name on the uniform. We've been following Johnson's beep on the screen since the general gave us his uniform code."

"How many hours elapsed from this man's escape until we picked up his trail?" asked Borelli.

"Eight hours." Hanson became irritated, not understanding Borelli's line of reasoning. "He was a played-out recon man with sixty days of combat behind him. His mind was gone. He kept the uniform on, and before he could find new clothes, an airstrike got him. These frontline troops aren't experienced criminals. It's obvious we've got our man."

"It seems that way. But don't belittle the cleverness of the common man when his life is on the line. He will surprise you. There is an instinct to live that is incredible in its power."

Hanson sighed resignedly. He wanted a hot shower, a hot meal, Borelli knew these things. Borelli knew driving at night in unfamiliar territory, in a war zone, was not a favored activity. All these things he had impressed upon Borelli in the past. He looked at old man Borelli, hair in his ears, wrinkled skin, all the elasticity gone. To his credit, he kept the weight off. Though he was of a stocky build, he kept his stomach flat with sit-ups. Hanson knew he wouldn't be in the field at that age. Borelli must be a loser, not to be sitting in some plush office before a console.

"Okay," Hanson said. "What's wrong?"

"Nothing is wrong. I just like to think. I come to a body, and I like to think. Maybe it's reverence or respect. There is something fascinating in it. This guy once lived. He had dreams, hopes, desires that made him live, motivated him. To fulfill these desires, these dreams, he thought certain thoughts, planned, applied himself to remaining alive.

"Now, I can stand here and know these things to a degree—by studying him—the way he is dressed, where he went to die, how he died. I have a feeling of omniscience. I feel like I am in the eyes of God staring down at this scene. I was here for his death, too. I can see the last moments of his life. I can't interfere, but I can watch. You know what I mean?"

"Yeah, I know what you mean." Sometimes Borelli could weave a spell, say something profound.

"This is fascinating to me, standing here imagining. From curiosity, I want to know more. Turn this Johnson over for me, please."

"I'll get contaminated." The uniform would hold trace elements of biochemical agents, defoliants, and human decomposition.

"Get contaminated." Borelli's voice had a curtness.

Hanson, with one hand, rolled the body over. Borelli's eyes went immediately to the slashing wound on the forehead and showed alarm. In an instant Borelli knew the body before him was not John Johnson. He had read the observation data of Johnson in his file and had seen a detailed picture of his face. Hair color, cheekbones, jaw more or less correct. The ears and the nose did not match. The face was plump -recon men were devoid of fat. The science data: facial recog, finger prints, DNA were not needed. He would use id number only to establish identity. Borelli spoke. "Take my knife and cut out the skin to the boundaries to the forehead ID number. We'll try to rejoin the slashed portion and run a scanner." He held out a small pocketknife.

"Let's just take the wrist number," said Hanson.

"There is no wrist number."

"All of them have wrist numbers." Hanson spoke angrily, knowing that Borelli knew.

"Just cut the forehead. It's a waste of time to take off the uniform for a nonexistent wrist number."

Hanson cut the skin in a neat rectangle around where the invisible number lay. "Why argue with senility?" showed in his body posture and facial expression. He marveled at the blade's sharpness but said nothing. Borelli noticed Hanson had no squeamishness as he cut. He seemed to enjoy the task. The strip hung over the blade like a piece of uncooked bacon as Hanson stood.

"Now put some body glue on the underside and try to rejoin the slash." Body glue was a staple in first-aid kits on the front lines.

Borelli bent down by the body, examined the lung wound. In a panic, the man had run from the bombing into the woods. It wasn't the smart thing to do, as help would come by the road. But panic did strange things to a person's mind. The trees were shelter, the bombing might begin again; these were the thoughts, perhaps. There had been no blood trail. He came to a small rip in the collar, body fluid had stained the fabric, mostly clear fluid. He stuck his finger in the slit and felt a wound at the base of the skull. He retrieved his tweezers from his small forensic tool kit and probed the wound, going in deep. He pulled a piece of shrapnel from the wound. Here was the cause of death. The wound in the lung had every appearance of a knife wound—he had seen many. He had known instantly the slash wound on the forehead had been from a knife.

Hanson came to Borelli, shaking his head, holding a scanner and the rectangle of flesh.

"The numbers are incomplete." His mind was irritated, and his voice held the tone.

"Now you can check the wrist number, if it exists, in hopes we can get a few partial numbers, and placing them together, get a list of names as to who this could be."

"Why…" Hanson did not continue his thought: Why wouldn't there be a wrist number? Instead, he bent to the body and began pulling the stiff arm from the sleeve. "I'll be damned." Hanson spoke under his breath. The wrist had been slashed. Borelli had known the wrist would be slashed. Borelli stood, stretched his back; his knees ached as well. The night summer air smelled green and rich. Next summer he would be retired, sitting on a deck, sipping iced tea, looking at the starry heavens over a retirement community in somewhere, USA.

He shone his light on the ground and began an ever-widening circle around the body. He found the place where the corpse had been dropped from the shoulders of John Johnson. He saw a dull glint of metal. Stooped down, dug it out with his larger pocketknife, as he realized Hanson still had his smaller blade. He smiled, bemused by his luck. He held an old Roman coin bearing the head of an emperor; he could not read the name. He heard Hanson tapping away on his computer– entering the partial numbers.

"Let's go." He began walking across the field, back to the road where their vehicle was parked, back where the convoy had been bombed. Likely, John Johnson had been riding with the now-deceased man. By instinct or luck, Johnson had survived. He saw where the destroyed vehicles had been collected and walked over. Among them were only three personal vehicles: a general's airfoil, a plastic-tired civilian sedan, and, by the plates, a chaplain's all-terrain multidrive.

Hanson had caught up. Borelli spoke. "How long is the list?"

"Seven hundred and fifty."

"Is there a chaplain on the list?"

"A Father Lucas Desmit."

"Does that plate number match?" Borelli pointed to the chaplain's plated vehicle in the scrap park.

Hanson typed in his computer. "That's the one." He walked a few more steps and spoke again. "You're on your game, Old Man. John Johnson is alive, and he killed Desmit."

Borelli stiffened, his shoulders lost their slump and were pulled back, his chin was raised. He went from introspective to aggressive; time to play the game of life. "Cut the 'old man' stuff—permanently. And from now on, be more concerned with your work than a hot meal and getting out of the field." Borelli held out his hand as he stared into Hanson's eyes. "The knife."

Hanson slipped the pocketknife into Borelli's hand. He was hoping Borelli had forgotten it. "I wasn't thinking of a hot meal or getting out of the field."

Borelli stared down the lying Hanson. He knew men and how they thought; they weren't much above animals, really. Borelli began walking back to their vehicle.

"And you are wrong again. Johnson didn't murder Desmit. Desmit was killed by shrapnel—instantly." Borelli held up the thin sliver of metal before Hanson's eyes. "From the back of his neck." He paused. Should he continue? "You missed the lung wound caused by a knife, the forehead slash caused by a knife, the fat on the face and the overall body weight." He really ought to stop. "Was there a blood trail leading to the corpse? Johnson carried the body of Desmit to the woods and plunged a knife into the lung to give the appearance of a wounded man fleeing. Johnson then traded uniforms, took Desmit's ID card, slashed the forehead and the wrist."

They were at their vehicle. "Get on the compuphone. Get Desmit's electronic code for his uniform—if any; Johnson might keep Desmit's clothing for a while. Find Desmit's billet. Johnson might know the location. In any case, till we have an electronic marker, that is where we are going. You might want to call the MPs and inform them of our destination." Request a facial recog of Desmit – just to dot the "i."

Hanson began to turn toward the vehicle's passenger door. Borelli put his hand on Hanson's arm and held him in place, then spoke.

"I want the in-depth records of Desmit and Johnson. Contact the security patrol that collared Johnson. I want to know for certain whether Johnson killed that officer, and if so, why. Don't settle for opinion. Demand the facts and probe for information they don't volunteer."

Borelli tightened his grip on Hanson's arm. "And Hanson." Borelli waited for an acknowledgment.

"Yes, boss?"

"You have the habit of touching me. Never touch me again."

Hanson stared blankly as if Borelli were odd and then turned toward the vehicle. When Borelli was to his back, a smirk came to the face of Hanson. He had counted on Borelli being a pro—Borelli's record had said as much. The situation was perfect. Borelli believed him to be an arrogant, on-the-rise rookie. Hanson laughed to himself; that was all true. All was well. Except, why was Borelli interested in the initial crime? What did it matter if Johnson were guilty or innocent?

***

It was early evening in the red-light district. He saw a prostitute standing on a corner. The freshness of her posture and clothes told him she had just come to the corner. She wore the red lapel button issued by the Federation to show she was disease free and working. He pulled up directly beside her.

She was seventeen or eighteen. She had green eyes that held an iridescence and close-cropped brown hair dyed blond. Her ears were small, her cheekbones prominent. Her face had a certain breadth but not a flatness. The jaw was square and feminine, the teeth even and white. The lips hinted at fullness. He had not studied a woman's features in many months. His gaze would have been rude to anyone not a prostitute. He couldn't help his stare; she fascinated him. He saw the pain in her eyes, and his soul hurt for her.

She did not make eye contact at first but allowed his eyes to wander over her. When she thought he had had enough, she looked directly into his eyes. Before she met his gaze, she had sighed in disgust—or impatience or submission. He couldn't tell which. She wasn't anxious to work, and she didn't enjoy enticing men. She preferred to be icy, aloof—her only means of holding onto a semblance of dignity.

She had already outgrown the world and was weary of life. She had seen a man murdered. She had seen a coworker beaten senseless. She had seen countless drug overdoses and incoherent rampages. She had had so many men enter her that her soul was numb. She felt nothing now but a momentary shiver of revulsion, then it was just her body there, nothing else.

She still had a youth's hope and dreams, as if some answer existed to life, and some thought or person would show her the way to some other world. She thought there was another world better than the one she was in—this was her hope. She still harbored romantic thoughts even as all men treated her as an object, even those who had given her respect. She fought the romantic thoughts with a cynicism; hope was battered by the cynicism. Unbounded hope could hurt worse than none at all.

He was parked and staring. He annoyed her. He was just another face, nothing special. She walked the few steps to the window. He noticed her legs—long, straight, well formed. She was thin in the waist, ample in the chest. A solidity, a health were apparent in her build. Her clothes were fashionable, tasteful, modest, not like a low-class prostitute baring the legal limit. His body was dead; he couldn't lust and did not complain of the absence. He was wise enough to know that many men had lusted after her. She was beautiful. Had the Lord chosen her to be his Rahab or should he look for another?

"Do you want something?"

Her voice was ice. Her words froze him into indecision. He needed a woman with a heart. Was it her coldness that assured him she had the heart he needed? She was young; did she know the underworld? Could she make the contacts?

"I...uh...I'm new to Paris and need a guide. Have you ever done that?"

"Been a guide?"

Her intonation was that he was an ass. Her English was spoken with an American accent.

At least he wasn't a tough guy with a smooth act. No anger flashed upon his face. She chose to reward him with kindness.

"Yes, I've done that. But down the street at the visitors' center are less expensive guides for hire."

She didn't want anything to do with him. He looked dead on his feet, mentally slow. Who knew what drugs he did? Thin! Not a handsome face. Bills had to be paid, she had to eat. But he looked easy, maybe all he wanted was a guide.

"No, it is you I want for a guide—not sex."

She entered the car even though they had not agreed upon a price. She always established a price first. She was good at judging people; appearances said he was the type who hit. Faces lied. He did not have the spirit of a brutal man. He was no danger. He pulled into the stream of traffic.

She stared at him. He felt the eyes upon him.

She was toying with him, wanting to see what would flush from his mind under the pressure of her gaze. She moved closer, her eyes wide, until she was only inches from his face. She hoped he would think her crazy and let her go. At a stoplight he returned the stare. His eyes held no lust or mental instability. A warmth emanated from his body that relaxed her. She resisted. Whatever he was thinking frightened her. His eyes broke contact first.

"What are you looking for?" He smiled and laughed, perplexed and confused.

"For the man...for the man." She spoke slowly, thoughtfully, sadly.

"The man in me, the man of your dreams, the man of the flesh?"

The light turned, he accelerated.

"I have no dreams." Her voice was bitter, defensive. "Man of the flesh?" She mocked him as she spoke. She had never heard the phrase before but sensed its meaning. "You're all men of the flesh." She stared into his eyes. "But you don't want sex, remember. The man in you is lonely, empty, cringing; you're dead to life." These were the most bitter words she could have spoken; she hated him because he was so much like her.

He suddenly pulled into a parking space just vacated. She tensed, grabbed the door handle. He calmly turned his body to face her and looked her in the eyes. Her face fascinated him; the greenness of her eyes was startling. His mind was absorbed in his own plight, and he asked the Lord to allow him to step outside of himself and see her. He sensed the Spirit resting upon her.

She let go of the door handle when she realized he held no anger. She averted her eyes. "Stop that." She was annoyed, angry.

"What?"

"Feeling pity for me."

"It was just concern."

She turned away from him and slumped into her seat heavily, morosely. She'd better keep her distance from him. Concern. A lie, a tool to manipulate her emotion. She spoke.

"What do you really want?"

"Your name."

She grimaced at his avoidance to her question. So now he was going to run through the let's-get-to-know-you routine.

"Diana."

"My name's John."

She laughed. "Yeah, that fits. The everyday John."

He hadn't answered her question, but he would be her work for the day. She would be that woman or collection of women of the past who had created his dream, his fantasy. He was an innocent romantic. Hold his hand, cling to him, show affection every moment. Encourage his every word, mirror his own thoughts, allow him into a mind he would think was hers.

Delusion. They would be young lovers, innocent, true. He would become so involved in his dream and her mirroring of it that he would never touch her. Occasionally, to make him hurt, to reassert her power, to make him want her more, she would become icy, moody. The formula was simple; she had done it a hundred times before. Something within her heart told her to be wary.

He knew he was a fool. She was beautiful—what did beauty have to do with having a heart? He was weary, losing concern, patience; he would tell her everything. That wasn't the plan. The plan was to establish a friendship, take her to dinner, a park, a museum, to wherever and whatever interested her. When he had won her trust, he would ask for her help. Did he have the time to establish a friendship? Was anyone in pursuit? To her, such friendship would be a lie, a tool to get what he needed: her trust. He sighed. "Listen carefully."

He stopped till he saw she was waiting expectantly for the next word. A bemused smile was on her face, one that said, "Tell me the big lie now; I'm waiting."

"I'm a deserter from the front. I was going to be shot for a crime I didn't commit. I'm impersonating a priest who had befriended me and was killed in a bombing attack. I've got his ID card, access to his bank account, a ticket to the States. All I lack is his number on my body. I need a masker. I thought you might know one."

She laughed at him; not merely a few chuckles, but with unrestrained hilarity that fed on its own unruliness. He listened to the laughter. He hurt. He would never see home. What a fool he was. Then the hurt was gone. He began to laugh through his anguish, laugh with her at his predicament, his absurd request. His laughter slowly died in wrenching pain. He had no tears to shed but wished to God he did. She glanced at him, felt his hurt, the longing of his soul. He was a broken man, a man in despair.

She realized his story had been the truth. His despair entered her. If caught, he would be killed—pushed around and beaten, no doubt, before he tasted death. That was the way of the world. To be so far from home, to have no one, to be empty, weak, helpless: she knew these feelings, and she had compassion for him.

She swore to herself she would never let him know he had touched her soul. What foolishness! He didn't want sex. He didn't want to abuse her. He wanted her to flirt with death—aiding and abetting a criminal, counterfeiting.

In the Shadow of Babylon

"You have a deal." He changed subjects. "Why is your English with an American accent?"

"Get the car moving. I want to get this over with as soon as possible."

He obeyed her brusque command.

She sensed his disbelief in receiving her help. "Our English teacher in the state school was an American. She was one of the few people I respected. So maybe you're getting a free ride on my respect for her."

He heard but only half believed. Traffic was thick, even at this early hour, and his reflexes were gone—lost to a sleep-deprived mind. Diana relaxed; her body sank back into the seat. A strange peace came over her. She wasn't afraid of the fate that awaited her if she were caught. Maybe she did trust him, because something in him was like Miss Ames, her teacher; something more than being an American.

She had been twelve when Miss Ames had come into her life. If anyone had asked her what she wanted to be, she would have said a nurse. She didn't think people should hurt, and nurses helped hurting people. So simple. This teacher, Miss Ames, made her feel loved. Miss Ames had been a nurse before becoming a teacher, and Miss Ames would tell stories of the hospital.

To be twelve and have no one, no mother or father, no brothers or sisters, only cold, impersonal staff and teachers—except for Miss Ames. Miss Ames took her shopping, though it wasn't her job. Miss Ames invited her, and select others, to her house for dinner. Miss Ames took them to church. Miss Ames laughed with her and cried with her for a year. Then Miss Ames was gone, and nobody knew why. Little Diana was alone again, and life hurt even more. Poor Diana. Diana cringed at her own self-mocking. They said Miss Ames went back to the United States, but nobody knew for sure. God, she hated to think back. She hated her emotions, her past.

"Can't you drive any faster?"

That was all death or life imprisonment, according to the Federation. She smiled evilly. She would like to throw her life to the winds of fate.

She wanted to hurt that system that had hurt her. She wanted to tell the whole damned world how much she hated it. She didn't just want to hate the world, she wanted to make it cringe, make it moan in anguish, and she wanted to exalt over its pain. She wanted to taunt it and spit upon it. This stranger was giving her a chance. She kept her smile. Was he real? Was he an undercover inspector of vice testing her ethics?

"Why should I believe you?"

He spoke slowly, resignedly. "I guess there isn't any reason…the world's full of liars. God knows I'm telling the truth."

He rummaged his tired mind for some defense, some proof, and found none.

God knows, he said. She wanted to curse God, and she could not. If she cursed the idea of a God, then there was no hope anywhere. She studied him. He was dead on his feet, as though he had come from the front. His thinness validated his story. Inspectors got their three meals a day. An inspector wouldn't have concocted such a farfetched story; an inspector would have had a perfect reason for her to believe.

"I believe you." She spoke with no kindness or sympathy.

She watched his face closely as she spoke to him. His startled expression convinced her again that he was telling the truth.

"Are you being followed?"

"Not that I know of."

"I want whatever is left over in the bank account when the masking is paid for." She wanted him to believe she was after the money.

He hadn't expected her to trust him. The trust was so easily given that he was wary. Wariness took mental diligence, and he had none left. He couldn't understand her motivation—money, was that it?

CHAPTER 5

The orderly led them down the hallway. He had known Desmit and shared freely with Borelli. Borelli stopped halfway down the hallway from Desmit's room, turned to the orderly, spoke in a whisper. "See if you can locate his car." The orderly nodded as he left. Borelli and Hanson soft shoed to the door. Hanson unlocked the door, his pistol drawn. Hanson led, with Borelli close behind, not knowing what they would find. They had never received Desmit's electronic marker from authorities and had no idea where Johnson was. Hanson spoke, but it was unnecessary.

"He's been here."

Blankets were disturbed on the bed; field ration containers were in the otherwise empty trash can. Hanson was happy—they were out of the field—canned or dehydrated food, unwashed bodies, mud, chamele uniforms were behind them. He knew they would never return. Borelli would begin to feel pressure for the unseemly protraction of this case. Hanson spoke.

"I'm almost rooting for this guy—as long as he doesn't leave the Continent and I have to leave my family."

Borelli smiled; Hanson had a wife and child on the Continent. It seemed God made a wife for every man no matter what kind of fool he was. Borelli knew what Hanson knew—the longer Johnson remained free, the more incompetent Chief Inspector Borelli appeared. This was the true reason Hanson wanted Johnson to roam free. Borelli spoke.

"Only a year ago, you wouldn't have been permitted to leave the Continent in pursuit; another department took over."

"Do you think we could be leaving?"

"It is a possibility this guy could do it."

Borelli spoke as if he had no responsibility in the case, felt no pressure to make a quick apprehension. Hanson grimaced as he looked over the unmade bed. Borelli thought the grimace had been directed toward him. Borelli wondered why Hanson hadn't contacted the military police. The MPs may have caught Johnson entering or leaving Desmit's room. On the other hand, MPs were amateurs. They might have botched the job and alerted Johnson. Why hadn't Hanson mentioned the absence of the MPs? Borelli decided not to bring up the subject—what would be gained? Hanson could easily lie—"I called them, but they didn't show." There was the possibility Johnson had rested at the billet and was gone before the MPs could have been called.

Hanson became edgy when Borelli didn't question him on the MPs. Hanson spoke.

"If we hadn't been caught in that bombing. If the MPs hadn't fouled up, we would have our man."

"They fouled up." Borelli said it as a statement of fact with only the tinge of an accusing question.

"Yes, and I will find out who." Hanson flashed with anger.

Borelli let the subject drop; the anger seemed a sham. He thought aloud. "Eight hours plus six. Fourteen hours."

Borelli began searching the locker and the desk. Johnson had been free eight hours before they had picked up his trail. It took another hour to locate Johnson's uniform on Desmit's body. Five more hours had passed in the bombing and the travel to the billet. Borelli didn't mention the fact that Hanson had gotten them lost. Being lost had placed them, by fate, in an area that was bombed. Their vehicle had suffered minor damage, and repairs had eaten into their time.

"Fourteen hours behind?"

Strangely, Borelli felt no need to blame Hanson for becoming lost.

"No, fourteen hours that Johnson has been free. He could be right down the hall at this very moment or in Paris or Madrid." It struck Borelli that Hanson appeared not to be thinking of timelines and was pushing all responsibility onto the "old man." The fourteen hours quoted was too generous, as Johnson didn't technically leave the combat zone till Desmit was killed in the bombing. Borelli knew the attack had happened an hour and a half after Johnson fled the murder scene of his captain.

Hanson said nothing. Borelli turned to the orderly who had just burst into the room.

"Desmit's car is missing?" stated Borelli.

"Yes, sir." The orderly spoke crisply.

"Bob." Borelli had decided to call Hanson by his first name, hoping to take some of the antagonism from their relationship.

"Yes?" Hanson hid his contempt for Borelli's effort to calm their rivalry.

"Place the missing car on Federation police records. Monitor Desmit's bank account. Call Federation Travel Security and give them Desmit's and Johnson's identity numbers." Borelli turned to the orderly. "You mentioned earlier that Desmit was going on leave. Do you know where?"

"Los Angeles."

"Do you happen to know what city the flight was from?"

The orderly brightened. "Yes, Paris. He was debating whether to drive to the airport or take a train."

Borelli didn't return the cheer. He felt sorry for Johnson—his freedom was almost over.

"Thanks. You may leave us now. Close the door, please."

The orderly left with a quizzical arch to his eyebrows. Borelli eased into the desk chair, studied Hanson's eyes. Hanson—hunched on the bed, shoulders forward, body leaning, eyes staring—seemed like a bird of prey ready to strike. "Bob, how long will it take for Federation Travel Security to act on our request for a blockage?"

"Maybe an hour or two. Codes have to be verified, the information sent to every port and terminal. The information must be disseminated to every security guard."

"Let's review and organize our thinking," Borelli said. "One. In one to two hours, air and water travel will be closed to John Johnson and Lucas Desmit. Our fugitive will either be caught by security personnel or escape capture. If it is the latter, he will remain at large on the Continent until he bumps into the law, probably for a petty misdemeanor.

"Two. John Johnson has already found a masker, used Desmit's bank account, and is, or will be within the next two hours, on a flight to Los Angeles. To counter this possibility, give his info to United States Travel Security. We don't want him to slip into the US.

"In the meantime, we will stay put and sleep. We can't be certain he's headed for Paris."

Hanson shrugged his shoulders and walked out, without comment, to send the necessary information. Borelli studied the unused bed and pillow upon the bare mattress. Good enough—no crumbs, no stains, clean smell.

He checked the time, 1:00 a.m. He sat on the mattress—firm—and lay back as he closed his eyes.

***

Borelli awoke to the insistent sound of Hanson's voice and a rough hand on his shoulder pushing him into the mattress. Instinctively, before answering Hanson, Borelli checked his watch, 6:00 a.m. "Where's the fire?"

"Somewhere over the Atlantic."

"Johnson?" Borelli bolted upright in shock that just as suddenly turned to a satisfied amusement.

Hanson clenched his teeth and spoke. "Johnson was already on a flight to the United States when the hold was placed."

Borelli shook his head in amazement and respect. Hanson saw the look and took offense.

"You like this kid too much."

"I like his speed and cleverness. Besides, I read the account of his supposed crime. He didn't kill that captain. The security patrol that caught Johnson didn't want to investigate; just wanted to expedite the matter. They had one frightened and revenge-minded witness. What could he have seen dodging laser fire? Johnson had a spotless record prior to this charge."

"We don't have to take the outlaw's side, just catch him." Said an irritated Hanson, who then added. "Are we flying from Paris to the States to pick him up?"

"When he's caught. His flight will touch down somewhere within fifteen minutes. I hope he doesn't hurt anyone." Hanson noted that Borelli sounded like a concerned father. Borelli believed Johnson could beat the initial charges. A legitimate murder or assault charge would certainly hurt his cause.

"With what?" Hanson said sarcastically.

"He's still got his knife, as far as I know. A damned belt can kill." His voice rose in irritation. Borelli had an eye for detail. Johnson had stabbed Desmit in the lung with a knife and now that he thought of it, there had been no knife on the body of Desmit. A knife in personal baggage would have been picked up by security as illegal but not when transported in luggage. Or the knife could have been thrown into the woods by the body.

"He's a combat soldier; he'll kill if he has to," Hanson said knowingly.

"Not if he can help it." Borelli spoke defensively, then continued. "Los Angeles still the destination?"

"No, Harrisburg."

"Where's that?"

"Pennsylvania—the capital. He used the money for the Los Angeles flight to buy two tickets and changed the destination to Harrisburg."

"Two?" Borelli laughed. Who was this second person? He pulled himself into a sitting position in bed, his back against the wall. Hanson was edgy and attempting to hide it. Why would Hanson be edgy? Everything was going his way—the chief inspector was bungling the case. So he would need to make a transatlantic flight; roundtrip, a day of flying time. Maybe Johnson would stay in the United States for his trial and incarceration. Maybe they wouldn't make the flight at all.

An unease seized Borelli even as his stomach rumbled. Hunger, maybe that was the cause. No, it wasn't hunger that produced the unease; this was coming from a deeper level. It was like his premonition of his father's death three days before it occurred. As if something, someone was poking him in the mind, trying to get his attention. Rule number one, take care of the physical first: eat. "Let's get to a restaurant. You pick it; just make it close."

If only the MPs had been at the billet. If only he and Hanson hadn't become lost and caught up in a bombing raid. The timing had been fouled up and that had cost them their man. He should have placed the hold on travel as soon as they identified Desmit's body. But then it seemed improbable if not fantastic that Johnson could escape the Continent. Something wasn't right. The uneasiness borrowed deeply into Borelli's patient confidence.

Borelli reviewed the oddities of the case. Johnson escapes the military security at approximately nine thirty to ten in the morning. They should have been tracking him immediately through the device in his uniform. He should have been caught within the hour. By protocol, if he had not been caught in two hours, the Inspector Department should have been notified as part of fugitive protocol and as to a possible overlap in jurisdiction. But it was not until six thirty that evening that he and Hanson were notified. Not until seven thirty did they find Johnson's uniform on Desmit's body. That was screw-up one.

Screw-up two or possible screw-up: the military police never made it to Desmit's billet when they should have been there close to seven thirty. Johnson was likely already gone.

Screw-up three: because of getting lost and a bombing raid, it took five hours to make what was, at most, a two-hour trip from Desmit's body to his billet.

Two of the three screw-ups were Hanson's. Even the first, the lag between picking up Johnson's uniform tracker and his escape, may very well have been Hanson's. If he verified that Hanson had purposely given Johnson time to escape by misreporting when the tracker was picked up...then what?

Borelli had theories.

One. Hanson wanted John Johnson to escape because of some unknown connection between the two. No proof supporting the theory. The possibility seemed absurd.

Two. Hanson wanted John Johnson to escape for personal gain. The longer Johnson was at large, the more incompetent the chief inspector appeared. At some point, Hanson would contact higher authorities and complain of the incompetence, ask to take over. This was absurd as well, as it could be proven that Hanson made the mistakes.

Only theory one still had validity. But this theory had no credibility if Johnson were to be caught, as it appeared he would be. No payoff, no purpose, no reason. Borelli wondered if indeed his mind operated in paranoia. Maybe he needed to retire sooner. Maybe it was all in his imagination. Maybe Johnson had luck on his side. Johnson couldn't escape the stateside authorities unless Hanson had pulled some kind of trick. The only way to be certain was to call Travel Security and ask when the hold had been placed—but not while Hanson was present. He could challenge Hanson's story now. He turned his phone within his jacket to recording mode.

"Bob. You did contact the States about Johnson?"

"Yes, sir. They're waiting for him."

"Did you send both Desmit's and Johnson's ID numbers to the States?"

"I sent Desmit's—that's the ID and number he would use. He entered the plane as Desmit! He couldn't use his own name entering the States."

Borelli listened carefully to Hanson's intonation for any sign of duplicity. The emotion seemed genuine. Borelli spoke calmly.

"The authorities in the States are looking for the name *Desmit* and *his number*. What if by some fluke or cleverness, John Johnson's ID is used. The stateside people don't pick up on the fact Johnson isn't on the flight manifesto. There are possibilities for evasion."

"Slim possibilities! Johnson thinks he's home free using the name of Desmit. There is no reason to risk everything by suddenly changing names."

Borelli studied Hanson's face. Consternation was dominant. Hanson began frantically punching numbers on his compuphone. Was the consternation from the fact that Hanson had blown it? Both names should have been registered with the stateside authorities. Or was the consternation due to the fact that Johnson's last possible avenue of escape had been closed? This last hypothesis assumed that Hanson believed Johnson was clever enough to use his own name. Or had Hanson given any names to the stateside authorities? Or was there collusion between Hanson and someone in the States? Was he just playing along with this last possibility of evasion to hide the truth: that no names had been sent?

***

John walked down the corridor connecting the supersonic to the terminal. He was nervous to the point of uncontrollable shaking. He had slept fitfully on the flight. Instead of waking refreshed, he awoke confused and frightened. He had something to lose now. Before he had no chance of success. He had simply followed the Spirit's leading. Now he was in the United States, almost home, almost to food, rest, peace. More than ever, he must be keen minded, collected, focused. The emotion, the mental strain must be hidden.

He glanced behind; she was still following. He didn't understand why she had come. He had appreciated her company on the flight, but now she seemed a burden. His own problems were overwhelming; how could he care for her? She had done nothing illegal in coming to the States if she reported to the Department of Immigration within twenty-four hours. If questioned, she could feign ignorance of his flight from the law. Still, it was better that she kept her distance.

His mind raced to the obstacle of the checkout gate. Had the authorities been alerted, warned of a passenger named Desmit? If the authorities knew of Desmit, then Desmit should have been caught at the Paris airport, unless he was running ahead of the police. Or were the authorities searching for John Johnson? Or had some clever inspector put it all together so that Desmit and Johnson were both being sought?

He knew they were behind him, pursuing; the Spirit of God or angels told him. Were his angels and his intuition the unfounded fears of an anxious, desperate man? Were they gaining upon him, or were "they" simply the hallucinations of extreme stress?

It seemed perfectly logical to use Desmit's ID—Desmit had cleared Paris. The police obviously hadn't made the connection between himself and Desmit. They should have - right? The body should have been found within hours by the security police tracking the uniform of Johnson. Hadn't anyone noticed the difference between John Johnson and Lucas Desmit? Desmit was older by ten years and weighed twenty pounds more. Facial differences should have provoked questions. The partially destroyed identity numbers on the body did not match the uniform.

But then, there was a war. The tracking device may have been defective. Days could pass before the body was recovered. The body could have been hit by stray ordnance and destroyed or disfigured by a chemical attack. The men who found the body could have been tired, apathetic, unconscientious, or lazy—wanting an easy end to their manhunt. It made sense to use Desmit's ID.

Diana watched her John. He was nervous to the point of distraction. If he didn't find his poise, he would never be allowed to pass through the exit gate unchallenged. He had slept with tossings, turnings, mumblings, moans, gasps for air. Life on the front must have been tough. Well, life in the red-light district was tough too. She found it easy to look upon his distress without being affected. That is how you survived in her world. She really didn't want him to be caught; he gave her some sense of security and purpose.

All had gone well until now -even the actual masking had only taken minutes. She'd found a masker through a friend who had a client who knew a man. The client owed a favor, and the friend owed her a favor. The masker had been a top-rate pro, making big money by the appearance of his clothes and the organization he had around him. She really felt as if she were hurting the system through John. Hate and revenge slipped away at some point, and she had a thought—a dream—to go to the States. Go to the country of Miss Ames.

Maybe Americans were more kind, more caring, more decent; maybe this country had something she needed. She knew her thoughts were a lie—everyone was the same the world over: civil, selfish, and cruel. She wanted to believe, believe in goodness, even though it was a lie. She could go to the land that had produced a Miss Ames and start over, a new life. She would become a nurse, never touch a man—not even to talk to one socially. She would simply never return to her Paris apartment, never be seen on the streets again.

The authorities would know where she was; Immigration had rules. She would really be leaving herself, walking away from herself, her few friends and customers.

She had been ready to crush the dream until she entered the Paris airport. People were going places, moving, free, and she wanted to be one of them. They could only be what they said they were. Who knew where they came from or their past lives? They were coming from one place and going to another, and those places defined them. But between, they were free. She wanted to be free, to be only what she dreamed she was, a nurse. All she had to do was buy a ticket. Her John bought her that ticket without even a question. For the first time in years, she had smiled a smile of happiness.

She looked again for John at the luggage belt. She had none; he had checked one small briefcase he could easily have carried with him. She realized with a start that she was staring directly at him. She hadn't noticed him; she was looking for a nervous, distracted man. He was so calm, relaxed, natural that he melted into the crowd. He was good when the situation was tight. Everybody had an act.

Lord, the terminal was so large, crowded, so brightly lit. Calm had come to him when he had placed the situation into the Lord's hands. The Lord hadn't brought him all this distance to abandon him suddenly to his own self-efforts. The Lord wanted him to succeed, and he would. He attached himself to the shortest exit line. She was directly behind. He could not decide which ID to use. Maybe it didn't matter—both names being known or unknown. Logic said Desmit.

As he stood, he watched the personnel at the exit gates. Down the line, new personnel had come on duty—the next shift—except at the last three gates. These workers appeared tired, bored; a monotony clung to their movements. One worker John's own age seemed exasperated. His eyes constantly darted to the large clock hanging from the ceiling. This man stopped checking the passenger manifesto and then turned off the screen completely. This saved him a few extra seconds per passenger, as the computer did not have to match IDs with the passenger list.

In a moment, John decided to change his ID back to Johnson. Paranoia? Cleverness? A dulled mind? Intuition? John stepped out of line quickly and casually; Diana followed. John whispered, "I'm erasing my number and entering the far line."

Diana unconsciously gasped. The masker had given John an airtight, foil-wrapped gauze pad that could erase the new number, exposing the old. Once the new number was wiped clean, it would not return. Why was he undoing what had worked?

She noticed the screen that had been turned off. What if the new man came and turned on the screen before John passed through? John Johnson would be caught. Even if the screen were not activated, the authorities could be searching for John Johnson. Desmit had worked. Why change now? She clenched her jaw and smiled. What was it to her if he was caught?

John moved around a column by the wall, and in the quiet recess, wiped his forehead. The stinging brought tears to his eyes. She watched for a moment then hooked onto the line to save him a place. He emerged seconds later, moved in front of her.

The gate worker had become sullen on his lengthening shift, even as his replacement walked up beside him. John was before the scanning computer. The sullen man was about to leave.

Johnson's ID went into the computer, a light flashed green. Diana noticed the new man looking at the blank screen of the flight manifesto. He began to reach for the on switch.

Diana wilted to the floor. The new attendant rushed to her side. The sullen man did not notice the irritated forehead of John. Both gate workers had their eyes on Diana, who insisted her blouse be loosened. The firm breasts were momentarily exposed. The men were leering. The computer scanned John's forehead, and a second time the computer flashed green. John passed through the gate. He could hear the men calming Diana, flattering her, hoping for a bedmate that night.

She watched him walk out of the terminal into the darkness. She wondered if he would wait for her, or if she was now considered a piece of trash to be discarded. She wondered if security had already cuffed him. She buttoned up her blouse, refused medical aid, thanked the men, and was gone. She ran out through the doors, into the cold air, searching the crowded streets for a group of men, a commotion. He stood by the side of the exit, staring at her, smiling. This was the first time she had seen him smile. She caught his eyes and felt his joy.

He hugged her, thanked her over and over. She had never been hugged, never, never felt human warmth that wasn't attached to sexual lust. Something else was in the embrace—a power, a message. He needed her. She spoke.

"I wonder if Desmit would have passed through without incident?"

"An interesting question that we will never know the answer to." He looked over the streets. "The United States of America! Praise God that He has brought me home! Cold weather, but my heart is warm. He laughed pensively then added, "Are you frightened?"

"Why should I be?" She didn't want his concern. "You're the one who should be frightened," she taunted. Why did she want to make him hurt?

"I am frightened." His tone was sober, heavy.

She felt a tinge of remorse for her sharpness. He was facing death if caught. How long did he have to live? He would be caught eventually, probably soon. Her coldness was lost on him—he was too good to be enticed or repelled by her hardness of emotion. She hadn't wanted to be cruel. Perhaps she couldn't control her ugliness any longer, turn it on and off at will. How was she any different than the world she despised?

He took her gently by the arm; they crossed the street, searching for an all-night restaurant. She could see her breath; the cold entered her clothing. They had outrun the sunshine of Paris. Early morning darkness pressed against the city's lights. Were summer mornings always so cold here? She was curious and somewhat fearful of being in a strange country. The people crowding the streets were aliens. She saw, felt, heard, smelled the differences. Fashions, street signs, architecture, vehicles, even the way people walked were different. Subtle differences but enough to make her feel alone, bereft of confidence.

She willingly took his arm. Why did he return kindness for her evil? Why did he use the word *we*? The word made her uncomfortable. She wasn't planning to remain long with him. She would buy him a meal; she owed him that much. She didn't owe him a damned thing. She knew he needed her, her thoughts, opinions, support; she had no confidence that she could help. Why should she help?

The crowded streets forced her close to him. He was different. He didn't want her sexually. He was honest, treated her with concern and respect. He was an oddity, and strange sometimes when he talked; he was beginning to intrigue her. Maybe the appeal was that he was an outlaw—the world was against him. They entered a restaurant; the heat, the smell of food, coffee made him sigh. They sat in a booth in a far corner.

She spoke. "The meal is on me. I've got plenty of money and will have more as soon as I transfer my account."

"Thanks."

"How much do you have?"

"Thirty dollars—more than enough to get me to my grandfather's. I have money in a bank account, but that is probably frozen or being watched."

Thirty dollars was the limit placed on money card cash; anything above that amount was handled by ID number and the electronic banking system. She studied his face, his eyes, saw nothing but sadness, then spoke in a low whisper.

"Fill in the blanks about this crime you were supposed to have committed."

He talked, she listened and believed him. She saw into his heart, just glimpses, and knew he was good, yet she did not understand him. He finished his story.

"Why are you so strange?" Her voice held no animosity.

He smiled softly. "In what way?"

"You are kind—even gentle—and you were a soldier? You do not love life or people, and yet you respect life and are forgiving of people. The world irritates you, and yet you have peace. You have nothing and are going nowhere, and still you have purpose. You always ask how I am doing, if I want this or that. You act as if I could say something important—like I'm worth listening to. *Mon bébé*, you just don't fit into this world!"

She shook her head in anger and affection as she closed the gap between them. His innocence angered her; his kindness was endearing. She looked into his eyes. She knew her perfume was now in his senses. She waited for the eyes to melt in desire. She saw the tug in his heart. He eased back in his chair; the spell was broken. He could be tempted. They pressed their orders on the menu. He began to talk.

"I don't fit, Diana. Before I was outside the law, I was outside this world. I'm despised by people; my platoon shunned me."

"Why?"

"Because they sense I don't belong—just like you sense it. I know who God is, and He lives within me. Most of what people call *good*, I call *evil*. Even if we agree, we agree from a totally different line of reasoning. I'm what the Church calls an Enslaver. Did you ever hear of my kind?"

"No," she answered calmly. Her heart was pounding in fear.

"That tells me how dead the world is to God."

"How do you mean?"

"We're so few, we aren't known."

An anger came into her. Why was she talking to this John? Why did she want to help him? He wants to talk about God—of all things under the sun, God! She wanted to hate God. Look at the life He had given her. Or had she given it to herself? Make the John happy, talk to him.

"What do you enslave that angers the Church?"

"They say we enslave the natural man, the man or woman you are born, whom they claim is good, made, and ruled by God."

In the Shadow of Babylon

"And you say…" She held out her arm, fingers tight, hand opened, palm extended, as if presenting a guest to her talk show audience. Her voice impersonated a man, a talk show host, no doubt. The humor was lost on him—he had not watched the electrascreen in years.

"Every person born on this earth is born in rebellion to the God who made them," John said. "It is infinitely more agreeable to live for ourselves and from ourselves than for or through God. To leave this rebellious state, you must be born again, a second time, through Christ, God's son."

"What's the conflict? Why should anyone care that you feel you should be born again? You don't force people to believe like you, do you?"

"No."

"Then what is the problem?"

"The problem is, to know you are in rebellion you need to see yourself as God sees you—as a sinner. He uses the law to convince you of your rebellion. No one wants to hear the law; no one wants to know they are wrong. Living apart from God has its pleasures."

"I see the philosophical difference, but what does it have to do with life? The government has laws; the Church has laws. How are yours different?"

"The government has laws to keep order between people. The punishment keeps order, not the law itself. The Church has laws that are designed to create a powerful organization and to address the human condition—poverty, injustice, social issues. But the Church has become silent on the laws that identify the heart's rebellion. The laws that identify us as sinners. In the Church's eyes and in the eyes of government, these laws restrict social freedom."

"Ah, there's the rub. Now I see friction."

She had taken on another persona, one unfamiliar to him. He smiled despite himself. She continued. "Some for instances."

"Well, for instance, God says one man and one woman marry for life and are sexually true to each other. The rest is wrong—same-sex marriages, child lovers, plural marriages—all of it is wrong. Even to lust in your heart. You can imagine the hostility generated by expressing such a thought," John said.

"I know you would anger a lot of people. You think these people should change?" Diana asked.

"Yes, and not just them. Everyone needs to change—and they could, with God's help. Only Christ has the power to conquer the natural man, reverse our tendency to do what isn't right."

Strangely, she understood his line of logic. He would say these people needed to be born again through Christ. He saw himself bound to Christ, and the Church saw him as bound to laws that opposed social freedom. This talk had brought the spark of life to his being and so held her interest to a point. She had been trained to listen and had heard more aggravating and less interesting talk from her johns.

"Getting back to why you are strange…" Diana laughed. John continued to shovel food into his mouth—he had no recollection of the waitress bringing their orders. Diana continued.

"At some point in time, you recognized yourself as being in rebellion to God through His laws. The natural man that you were born was somehow left behind, as you were born a second time through Christ, God's son. Now your value system is different than the world's, and they hate you for it. Sharp, huh? I should get some kind of award."

He shook his head in annoyance at her tone even as he smiled at her keenness. Her tone had held a sarcasm she really didn't feel. He was sincere; he truly believed his words. Being sincere didn't make his words true. She had known priests who had been sincere and wrong. His talk of sex troubled her. What was a prostitute considered in God's scheme of things?

She was tired of this religious talk. One last thought, and she would let it die.

"Why don't you keep quiet about your laws and just live the way you think you're supposed to?"

"People notice the difference, and it irritates them," John said. "Deep down, in their hearts, they know I am living the truth, that God exists, and

He lives within me."

His last statement was difficult to understand. Perhaps he had developed a persecution complex in his evident loneliness. In his defense, people were cruel, selfish, and no one liked to be told they were wrong, either through word or example. But he was saying that people instinctively knew. Change the subject, Diana.

"This is Harrisburg, the capital of Pennsylvania?" she asked.

"Yes—two million or so inhabitants. Once a dead city till the western droughts came. Then eastern farmland became as precious as gold. I worked on the ag farms."

"Tell me about it." Diana motioned the waitress for a refill of coffee.

"At the age of sixteen, I went to the agrifarm to work. You have a two-year obligation to the state, which can be filled in a variety of fields. I chose ag because I didn't have to travel far and because I like open spaces, nature. Like I said, ag's big business on the East Coast since the drought. Homes, towns, old highways were torn down, cities were doubled into high rises and expanded underground to make way for the ag machines."

His eyelids were beginning to droop. The weariness eroded his characteristic reticence, unleashed his memory; thoughts flowed.

"The work was rotten at first—inside all day in the barns. Nothing but lines of cows. Feeding troughs, treadmills, showers, automatic milkers, artificial light. The smell of cows. You were a slave to the cows."

"Any women there?"

She wondered if this john was a virgin. He wasn't married, and to him, sex outside of marriage was a sin.

"Lots of women—wild parties in the dorms. They all became pregnant, gave their babies to the state, and collected their money."

"Did you sleep with any? Any little Johnnies in the state schools?"

He winced as she knew he would. Hurting him had brought no enjoyment.

"I wasn't always in Christ. But no, there aren't any little Johnnies."

He sometimes wondered if the past was worth remembering. Satan always seemed to take a piece of your heart when you remembered. He continued.

"I did my job poorly, purposely, and was moved to the fields for planting, harvesting work. This was supposedly worse work, a step down—lonesome, no women, out in the elements. Only one job was lower: working in the expansion crews, cutting timber, brush, tearing down homes, leveling hills, filling in depressions.

"I loved my new job—open spaces, greenness, the smell of the soil. Wild animals were in the fields—possums, raccoons, fox, coyotes, deer, rabbits. I worked alone, rode a huge machine. The size and power of the machine was good underneath you. On the night shift, with the high-power beams reaching out, the animals darted across your path. I loved being alone. I loved watching the green mountain ridges. I liked spying work crews half a mile away and thinking of all that freedom between us. On the street, ten feet of space seems like freedom."

She preferred this talk over the religious discussion; his story was interesting.

"What are the machines like?"

"Longer than five personal vehicles laid end on end and about half as wide."

"Personal vehicles?"

"Army talk: regular cars. Back to the machines. A heat jet came first, burning the stubble from the last harvest; then fertilizers were sprayed, then seeds planted—each seed encased in the necessary minerals, nutrients for the type of soil. The eggs of helpful insects came next, timed to appear with the new crop. The seeds were watered. I sat about fifteen feet off the ground as all this happened below me.

"My grandfather lived only a few miles away. Every weekend, that's where I went. He's in his eighties but has the strength and health of a forty-year-old.

In the Shadow of Babylon

He lives in a wooden house. Can you imagine? The house has received lots of attention from the media, one of the few of its kind still standing, an old farmhouse. Over four hundred years old. It's been treated with plastic preservatives. The state won't tear it down because of the historical value. When my grandfather dies, the state will take control.

"He's an historian, written many books. He's working on one now called *A History of God and Civilization*. He's a walking history book. He remembers the beginnings of the Afro-Asian droughts, the Sino-Indian wars, the earthquake of 2170. His house is filled with paper books, discs, even the first model of the electrascreen."

"I would read the weekends away. When I'd tire of reading, I'd take a walk in the woods, through the fields. I began reading the Bible on one of those weekends. I started with the Old Testament and thought it one of the worst books I had ever read. I only continued reading because I liked history. Then I read about Christ, and a war began in my heart."

She didn't want more talk of religion.

"What about your family?"

"I love them, I suppose. My mother and father, I mean. I am not as close to them as I am to my grandfather. Growing up, I rarely saw them. They always seemed to be working or enjoying each other's company. My older brother and I were left out. I was an object named *son*. My brother is ten years older; he's more like an uncle. He's a college professor—a geologist. He knows where the deserted places are. I'll have him pick one. I'll hide out, eat locusts and wild honey, and wait for the end."

"Of the war?" she asked. Why would he eat locusts and wild honey?

"Of my life."

"Long wait."

"I have no choice. Unless my name is cleared."

"So, then you joined the army."

"Yes. Biggest mistake of my life." He didn't need any more depressing thoughts. "Tell me about yourself."

"There's nothing to tell. I was raised by the state—Mother's protection failed, and she decided to make money by not having an abortion. I received a decent education in the state schools. Lived in dorms. Most people were cold, impersonal. I had no close friends. We were required to attend church, and the ritual was appealing. Some of what I heard seemed to make sense. At sixteen, I was pregnant, but I didn't want my child to live the life I was leading, so she was aborted. I didn't want their money."

She swallowed with difficulty, confusion and pain swept across her face.

"At the end of our schooling, at eighteen, they had speakers come in and give career choices. One speaker was a priest. He talked about serving mankind; making people feel less alone; giving them warmth, comfort; sharing their problems; helping them to like themselves. He sounded so honest and sincere. He gave a list of professions. Prostitute was one, though it was called by another name. It required less schooling than the others, so I went, learned how to care, handle all situations. Then I was registered. And here I am."

He did not ask about her mother. He knew the type—active, absorbed in their own lives, visiting their offspring once or twice a year. The visits would be crowded with sweet and loving words, gifts, and then Mother or Father would be gone.

"After the first time, I knew it had all been a lie. They wanted a dream, not me. They wanted to hurt me with their love. I've been working just enough to feed and clothe myself and save some money, so I could start over. I helped you hoping in a small way to hurt the system, and to earn enough money to make the move to another job. Then a voice deep inside said, 'Go, start over, in a new place.' The only decent person I ever met was an American—my English teacher in school. I mentioned her before. I thought fate was behind our meeting. I found myself in an airport with an American and took a chance."

He saw the working of the Holy Spirit upon her life. She called it fate. He smiled.

"Visit my grandfather with me. If you want to start your new life here, he could help. This city is as good as any other. You have nothing to do today."

She shrugged her shoulders, repressed a smile and hope. "Why not?"

She picked up the check, paid the cashier, and was out the door while he was still rising from his seat. Why was he being so damned kind?

He burst out onto the street. She was waiting. He saw an emptiness, an aching in her eyes. Another emotion was present, which he couldn't identify. She spoke immediately, wishing to thwart his probing thoughts.

"Seems cold for late summer."

"It is four in the morning, but you're right. The western droughts—caused by volcanic ash—affected the weather, as did sun abnormalities. It once was warm this time of year."

A commuter trolley pulled up to the corner where they stood. John smiled. "This is the one."

They boarded; half the seats were filled. She sat by the window.

"What's your God's law concerning a prostitute?"

"Prostitution is a sin. God loves you, Diana, even while you are a sinner."

"If I get out of prostitution, then I'm okay in His eyes?"

"No, you are already okay in His eyes. The law wasn't given so you would change your behavior, your line of work—though that will happen. The law was given so that you would recognize you are living apart from Him. If it were possible to obey all of His laws, you would still be a sinner because He would not be living within you. The issue is mastery, control of your life—freely given because of your love for Him."

"Love?"

Her contempt for the emotion burned in her voice. She didn't love herself, her life, or the world. How could she love God? She shuddered, cringed as a revulsion passed through her from the memory of her past—so many men had entered her. What were the choices with this God—to live like John? Where had God's love gotten him?

"I couldn't live like you. Are you a product of this love?"

Her eyes were beginning to moisten. This God of his was a lie, and now hope was crushed again. Well, she would begin a new life. The past was gone.

He shrugged his shoulders and did not offer a defense. He drew into himself.

She looked out the window. The buildings had increased in height, and the sky was changing from black to gray. A river, heavy with barge traffic and spanned by countless bridges, could be seen through the driver's windshield. At one stop, half the people exited. When the door opened, she could smell the river. The newness of the sights returned her happiness. She was free, in a new land. Life would get better.

Beyond the edges of mountain ridges, the trolley ride ended. They picked up another commuter trolley, racing into an empty car while the employee at the station had his back turned. John was afraid the employee might remember them if questioned by police, so they had waited for the opportune time. In the middle of nowhere, they left the trolley and began walking.

The feeling of exertion was new to her. She had never walked more than a few city blocks. She had never liked health clubs and the leering people. The pulsing blood, the expanding lungs, the feel of muscles propelling her was good, though her feet ached. They walked in silence as the pleasure of exertion turned to monotony and some pain. She really didn't need to be walking like this. She noticed his stride, the carriage of his body. He had some indefinable quality of bearing—as if he were a man of authority. He had walked much, there was no wasted motion. She knew he was holding back his pace.

They came to a smoldering wood fire on a back road of dirt. Around the fire, in the trampled grass, were spots of blood. A pagan ritual site, he said.

They walked on. A time came when she was sure she would quit, then that time came incessantly. Two men ran across the road before them and went crashing off into the underbrush of a swampy, forested depression. He didn't seem frightened. Criminals, he guessed. She held closely to his arm, even as she cursed her weakness. She broke the silence; she did not understand why.

"I'm not ready to give myself to a God I don't know." She wondered if those words were the culmination of a subconscious argument.

"Just because you hesitate shows you instinctively know He has the power to take your life away. If you didn't believe He could take your life, you would give permission without hesitation."

"You're crazy. Maybe I don't want to put out the effort to be changed. Maybe that's why I hesitate. Maybe I'm not ready to end up like you—homeless, penniless, hunted."

"There is no effort required to be changed. Christ does the changing for you, through the Holy Spirit. On that point, I am certain. You are right in that there is a price that will be exacted from you if you follow Christ. If you're not willing to give up everything, it is better you don't follow Him." John reflected on his words and saw their possible unkindness, and he spoke. "But stay in America. Gramps and I will help as much as we can."

She let his comments die in the damp air. Then she said, "Thanks." Perhaps his statement about Christ was true, perhaps not. They watched from an ag-land hilltop as the sun rose. In the distance, she saw the white house that was their destination.

CHAPTER 6

Henry sat in the darkness of the kitchen; the rising sun had not yet cleared the wood line. The quietness of the old house was heightened by the sounds of the floor timbers stretching. Henry smelled deeply of the kitchen. Cooking odors, meals from years in the past, permeated the walls. The scent of coffee prevailed over all other aromas. He smelled the woodstove in the corner, unlit, tangy with creosote.

An utter silence was upon his soul. He believed that he could will his soul to heaven now, so detached was his soul from his body. Young men, however pure, still had earthly desires intruding into their walks with the Lord; an old man had none. From the silence, the presence of the Holy Spirit came and filled the room. Henry began to cry as the Spirit talked to him. He had one final work to do for the Lord, one final, crowning achievement. Suddenly an expectancy filled him; someone was coming to help him. John! John was coming. His mind turned to his father's message and that which was yet to come. Visions of the future played before him, were imprinted, then lost to his consciousness. He wept in happiness for the presence of the Spirit. He began to weep for the world that soon would be no more.

Henry saw the figures of two people at his kitchen door, a knock resounded through the house. He quickly wiped away his tears, opened the door.

In the Shadow of Babylon

"Come in, John. Praise God!"

Henry held the shoulders of his grandson and shook. John stared in disbelief; his grandfather seemed distracted, elated, but not surprised. He may have been crying—a moisture was below the eyes.

"I was expecting you."

Henry turned toward the kitchen table as he extended his hand, offering his two guests seats. Diana was perplexed. She turned to John. "Did you call?"

"No!" John's eyes were wide in fear.

"Like he said, he seems to have expected you."

Henry moved toward the table. She spoke before him as if he weren't there, and it seemed disrespectful. It was simply bewilderment. She wondered if they had been seen from the windows; no, the old man wasn't a liar.

Henry, seeing that his grandson was not moving toward the table, turned to face him.

"Gramps, it's me! I came from the Continent. The war!"

His grandfather's reaction had been disturbing. Henry smiled benevolently, took his grandson by the arm, and moved him to the table. "I know who you are, John. I'm happy that you and your friend are here. I know I seem to be acting strangely; I am aware of your perception of me. But angels prepared me to see you. The Holy Spirit told me you were coming."

John spoke in a rapid agitation. "Have I been reported? Have men been here looking for me?"

"No. Should they be?"

Diana scoffed as she sat. The angels hadn't told the old man everything.

"Yes, I'm a deserter and murderer, according to the authorities."

The emotion of the moment and his weariness caused his voice to crack. He could not control his emotions and hoped his distress would impress upon his grandfather the seriousness of his predicament. Diana was composed, even enjoying the novelty of the situation. Angels? Perhaps, perhaps not. The old man had been expecting John. Was a touch of senility involved?

Henry understood John's confusion, grasped him by the arms, and shook him lovingly.

"It will all work to the glory of God, believe me."

Henry smiled broadly. Diana thought he had an honest charm. Then she remembered other men of his type—fit, intelligent, old men with perversity in their hearts.

"You're both tired, hungry. Take showers. Change your clothes, John. I'll get breakfast started. Do the authorities know you might come here?"

The last sentence assured John that Henry had a grasp on reality.

"I don't know. My pursuers could be hours behind me or might not exist at all."

"They exist. If it were simply desertion, there would be no pursuit—the system would catch you in time. Murder? Law enforcement will pursue until you are caught."

Henry's frank words sent a chill through Diana. A part of her had never really believed John was being pursued. If she were caught with him, her hope for a new life would be destroyed. She spoke to John. "Go! Take a shower."

John didn't argue her command. Henry watched John move stiffly, wearily up the steps. The boy looked older than his twenty-two years, not a boy any longer. He needed twenty-five to thirty pounds on his bony frame, days of sleep, and rest, judging by the wide, staring eyes. Henry sensed the hell John had passed through, the intense pressure still upon him. Henry thanked the Lord for John's return.

Henry became fully aware of Diana as he began breakfast. Attractive might be too weak a word. Her hair, makeup, clothes spoke of the world. He saw an emptiness in her, an aching confusion and loneliness. The Holy Spirit was visibly upon her. He also saw the Spirit's foes: bitterness, cynicism, even hate. She had hurt much, and she would love much. She was not aware that she was a chosen one.

"Your name is…?"

"Diana."

"Do you know the Holy Spirit is upon you?"

"The Holy Spirit," she deadpanned. He thought that was good, judging by his intonation. She wasn't sure of what this Holy Spirit was or did. She wanted the old man to leave her alone. Henry sat at the table. The coffee he had poured for her had remained untouched. She sat back from the table, slumped comfortably in the chair, arms on her lap, imperturbable in posture. Secretly she was pleased with his comment—he seemed to esteem the Spirit highly and thus conferred a goodness upon her. She added cream and sugar to the coffee, pulled her seat in, rested her elbows on the table, held the coffee mug. "What is this Holy Spirit?"

"He is the third person of the Trinity, sent by Christ, coming to teach, comfort, defend, live within us, seal us—His children—as we live upon this earth till Christ's return."

Like a crane, her arms swung the mug to her lips. She was beginning to tire. She wished Henry's statement to be true. She wanted a powerful God who would take her with His love. Prove His love by His presence. She wanted to know the Creator of the universe. She wanted a new chance, a new birth. Impossible! Why was she thinking these odd thoughts? Were they truly hers?

Man had invented a god. You did certain things to make this invention real. You built holy places full of light and shadow and colored glass. You wore jewelry and made signs, you sang hymns, you obeyed the major laws, you acted as if He were watching. You induced this invention to become reality. Perhaps you wanted this reality so much that you lived in delusion. Even now she was deluding herself. She wanted a new life and by chance had stumbled upon a philosophy that offered new life. All you had to do was believe, and like magic, life would become better.

She thought about the phone call to Immigration, and a slight panic stirred in her heart. If she did not call, she would become an illegal alien, and in effect a wanderer, a person living outside the system. She could live only day to day, no security, no future. She would not be able, legally, to buy, sell, or work. She would live on the streets, and if she became ill, no hospital would accept her without notifying the authorities. To have your identification number made inoperative was to be outside the world and life itself. Not making the call was a ridiculous thought.

She would call Immigration, and if the police wanted to speak to her, she would deny knowing anything about John Johnson's past. What if they knew she had helped him find a masker? What if they played rough, got a court order to drug her, learned the truth? Saw that her bank account had swelled, almost to the centime, to the amount that had been in Desmit's account. Prison would be her home, perhaps for life.

She didn't owe John or the old man anything. Who had ever sacrificed for her? Her heart was cold to people. Would John and the old man do the same for her? To give up her life, her happiness for two strangers was ridiculous. Why had she entertained the thought?

"You look troubled."

"I must call Immigration within twenty-four hours. I was wondering when that call should be made."

"Wait until you return to Harrisburg and find a hotel, if Harrisburg is your destination?"

"Yes, for now."

"I would offer you a room here, but John and I will both be gone soon. The Lord has work for us. I would invite you, but John is a wanted man, and the work might be dangerous."

Her spirit dropped into the pit of her stomach even as she maintained her smile. She had been hoping…Why bother to hope? Hope was never fulfilled…hope was like a dagger in the heart.

John came into the kitchen; she could smell his cleanness, the scent of soap, hair conditioner lingered. He was dressed in heavy, warm clothes baggy on his lean frame. John spoke to Diana. "Your turn."

"I'll pass." She didn't want the two to talk of her. Besides, she felt clean.

Henry spoke in happiness. "Well, then, let's eat."

***

The flight was smooth, their hostess extremely attractive, the food good. Hanson, reclining in his seat, slept. Borelli stared out the window but saw only the puzzle within his mind. While Hanson slept, Borelli had punched in a query to Federation Travel Security. According to the records, Hanson had placed a hold on Desmit's ID number at 12:30 a.m. that day, which put Hanson in the clear. Yet, the hold had never officially been marked as completed. Registered, yes; but not completed. Johnson could have entered the United States with Desmit's ID number. When Hanson had been told to enter Johnson's ID number that morning, Hanson had done so. But again, the hold was registered but not completed. Johnson had entered the States minutes after the hold and registration time. He could have been caught if everyone in Travel Security had been on his or her game. Did Hanson know a sleight of hand to give the appearance of complying, or did someone of higher authority block the completion?

Why did Johnson change from Desmit to Johnson before entering the Unites States? It was almost as if he knew the name *Desmit* had been flagged first and *Johnson* had yet to be flagged. Yet even *Johnson* would have been flagged in time if the hold had been completed.

John Johnson was just guessing, breaking up his pattern, his method of operation, sensing he was being pursued. He was a clever opponent—a boxer always moving, always feinting jabs. Such incredible luck left a gnawing doubt. Again. Did Hanson trick the computer, or did Johnson have help in escaping at Travel Security? The idea seemed preposterous. But all of Hanson's foul-ups were just as preposterous. An international conspiracy at the highest levels of the bureaucracy to get John Johnson home? This was certainly possible. But why? What was the importance of John Johnson? Borelli needed to clear his mind. He was still the one who needed to catch Johnson.

Borelli studied his computer screen.

Diana Rochembeau, escort/companion, an attractive girl. According to the ticket number, her ticket had been bought by Johnson. She, evidently, was the one who had introduced him to a masker. Her bank account was fat, and Desmit's was empty.

The transaction dates didn't match. He couldn't prove at this time that she had been paid from Desmit's account, an account that had been entered, even though blocked. Good financial computer geniuses could be found in the underworld.

Other prostitutes were on the flight, so many that he thought some type of convention was scheduled for Harrisburg. Or maybe the ratio of prostitutes to population had gone up since he had memorized the figures as a rookie inspector. The others were hardened, experienced, wealthy. Diana, nineteen, might still believe in love.

Hanson twisted in his seat. Borelli was tapping his screen with one finger. Borelli was an irritation even when a man had a rested mind. Hanson spoke through the soft pillow that had formed around his face. "They will part company in Harrisburg."

"If she's legit, she will report within twenty-four hours, and we will pay her a visit."

"Why say *if*? This prostie isn't going to cast her lot with a piece of trouble like Johnson. Ruin her life for a john?" Hanson laughed at his own pun. "Chances are, we can't tie her to the masking deal. She will deny knowing Johnson is a deserter/killer. So, she walks free. Unless we get court authority to dope her. Then we'd get the real story."

"Outsiders attempting to get court authority usually fail. Being we're attached to US law enforcement, we should have no trouble. Why don't you get the work started?" He had no interest in drugging Diana and pinning a charge. He believed in mercy, when it fit. Why ruin a girl's life? He simply wanted to keep Hanson busy and give the appearance of hardness of heart and diligence.

Hanson grunted into the pillow; his seat rose. He pushed the pillow aside in agitation. Borelli spoke. "Both are underachievers, introverts, idealistic, loners. Johnson can barely hide his Enslaver tendencies. She is searching for something."

"Maybe you should work for a dating service after retirement." A glint of laughter sparked in Borelli's eyes at Hanson's comment. He knew it had been spoken in mocking cynicism. He laughed at Hanson's personality, and he actually liked the thought of bringing people together. Life was a cold, lonely trek, and everyone needed a confidant. Hanson spoke again. "I don't see the connections, but he is definitely an Enslaver."

"You believe that Church nonsense—Enslavers, I mean?" Borelli realized *nonsense* had been a poor word choice.

"You don't?" Hanson's eyes held suspicion.

"I believe there is a God. I don't know what an Enslaver is, exactly—I don't keep up with those things. I know the Church has incorporated within it every religion except the one that gave it birth." Ah, he had slipped again.

"I thought you didn't know anything about these Enslavers." Why did Borelli know that Enslavers were once part of the mainstream Church?

Borelli hadn't expected Hanson to be a zealous Churcher. Such men were to be feared. He had to downplay the situation. "I've run across a few in this line of work. I've been at this work a long time. They're harmless people, not pragmatic or intelligent—just harmless."

Had he appeased Hanson? Why did Hanson have such a deep knowledge of Church history? Few but academics knew the Enslavers had once been part of the original Church. Hanson eased his seat back and spoke. "What do you know of the roots of the Church?"

Hanson's voice and demeanor were relaxed, a question for the sake of conversation. Borelli smiled pensively, his seat reclined, the leg rest rose. He felt the weight go off his feet. The relief was such a simple pleasure. Most of his pleasures were simple. He needed to relax around Hanson, to show a personal side. Borelli knew he must subtly cover his true feelings in his discourse; Hanson was seeking a throat hold on his prey. He spoke quietly.

"I didn't always intend to be a detective. There was a time when I wanted to be a lawyer and then a judge. Hard to believe, eh? I've always had a fascination with the law. Not just what it is, but why it exists. Where is its source? What exactly does society want from the law? How did we decide what was so aggravating, disgusting, immoral, dangerous, or unfair that there needed to be a law? How did we decide what punishments needed to be attached to said offenses?

"When you think of the law like that, you've got to touch on morality and therefore religion. I went through two years of law school before my money ran out. My grades weren't scholarship material. I got into police work—at first, just to save up enough to continue my education." Borelli spoke slowly, in a deepened voice. "I found I liked police work, the steady money, the comforts of life. I married. I loved her and never got back to law school."

"Any kids?"

"Two, a son and daughter, on their own, starting families, both doing well."

"You studied the Enslavers in law school?"

"Yes, we studied them. Their law, more stringent than civil and criminal law, is supposedly fulfilled through their Christ concept." He stopped. He'd had doubts since that time—about law, society, the individual—that were best left unspoken.

This was the first time Borelli had mentioned his past. Hanson knew Borelli's past, knew every twist and turn. He had read every file. Yet, it was simple to appear ignorant. Borelli was a weak-willed man, and Bob Hanson hated the weak. Had Borelli pursued his goal, *willed* his success, he wouldn't be a worn-out inspector, a nothing in the course of history. He would match Borelli's tone, speak as a friend.

"I don't understand the history of law. I don't need to. It seems we're on the right track—the government and the Church. The less law, the better—as long as social order is maintained. Isn't that freedom?"

Hanson turned to watch Borelli's reaction. Borelli shrugged his shoulders; his eyes were still in the past. His wife had died years ago.

"So they tell us," Borelli said.

Hanson decided not to press the ambiguous answer. He must be patient. He spoke. "Why do you think this Diana Rochembeau might cling to this John Johnson? Love?"

"Perhaps."

"Perhaps? There is no love, just need. And she doesn't need the aggravation."

Borelli smiled softly. What would a man like Hanson know about love for another? He only loved himself. Probably his wife only loved herself, and that is why the marriage worked.

***

They sat in the living room. Henry balanced on the edge of a worn, heavily stuffed chair. His hands touched a book upon the coffee table and a letter. Diana sat across from him on a couch, warming her hands around the coffee mug. After eating, she and John had napped for an hour. Henry had refused to talk of his plans during breakfast. Now the secret would be revealed.

Her body still held the peace gained from the exertion of the long morning walk. Her stomach was full of eggs, bacon, hash browns, toast. Her mind was expectant, excited, feeding from the keenness in Henry's eyes. John entered the room from the kitchen with two doughnuts and a mug of coffee in his hands. He had been constantly eating since he arrived. He sat close beside her, felt warmth coming from her like an aura. His closeness pleased her; she was certain he had an interest.

John and Diana sat quietly as Henry read from the piece of paper:

I have seen the followers of the cherub and have read their book and know of their ways. The time is near for the birth of his son. See with your eyes and hear with your ears. The stone which the builders rejected, the same is become the head of the corner; this is the Lord's doing, and it is marvelous in our eyes?

Henry handed the paper to John. Diana moved close to John's shoulder. What did he have that she should desire him? The two read the message as Henry continued to talk.

"This note was written by my father seventy-five years ago. Notice the indestructible paper. The cherub is another name for Satan. Their book is the Satanic bible. Satan's son is the Beast, a human being who will rule the Federation in the final days of the world. I believe the last passage, a quote from Christ, who quoted the phrase from Isaiah, is a clue to the hiding place of the Satanic bible and the date of the birth of the Beast.

"What is the significance of this note?" Henry asked. "If we know the birthday of the Beast, then we will know the approximate time, in years, of the Rapture, the time when God's people are taken from the earth. We will know the approximate time of the Tribulation, that seven years of hell on earth, when God's anger is poured out upon mankind. More important than the time of these two events is knowing the time when the World Church of today, called the 'professing church' in prophesy, will be overthrown by the 'harlot church,' the church belonging to the Beast and to Satan. The information my father mentions may be the catalyst for the splitting of the World Church. By bringing this information to light, we may bring many in the World Church back to Christ."

Diana had no prior knowledge of any of these events; she really wasn't certain of the existence of Satan. She spoke. "World Church? Professing church?"

"I apologize. You have no understanding of these terms. The World Church is simply the church you see today—universal and united and not honoring Christ. The Bible calls it the 'professing church.'"

"Maybe this is just a hoax?" she asked innocently.

"My father was a solemn, grave man not given to flippant behavior. He gave meticulous care to the preservation of the message. He died days after writing this message, under suspicious circumstances—a hit-and-run driver. A month later, our apartment was vandalized, the trunk that contained the note broken into. I believe Satan's people broke into the apartment, searching for their bible. They found no bible. They were sufficiently astute to know the note was likely a clue. They left the note in the trunk as a backup plan, hoping someone in the family eventually would interpret the message and lead them to the stolen book—if they had yet to find it. Stupidly they killed my father, perhaps he had given them a false lead they believed, perhaps they did not know he had stolen their book; otherwise, he would have been kept alive, tortured, and drugged to obtain the location of the stolen property.

"What could they do?" Henry asked. "Kill everyone in the family, all his associates—so the book wouldn't be made public? No, they would just wait and see if anyone would lead them to the hiding place or solve the riddle, even as *they* searched and attempted to solve the riddle. Patience was the best plan. Everyone involved is now dead but me. I'm the last. They don't have their book back, but neither does their enemy—the World Church."

John spoke. "How do you know they haven't solved the riddle, recovered the book? They've had seventy-five years."

Henry sighed. "You could be right, John. But is it coincidence that I am the last from that time, in the waning years of life, and that I find the message and understand the content? After all, I read that note many times over the course of seventy-five years and was blind to its meaning. Is it chance that I pray for your return to help me in this quest, and you return—overcoming incredible odds to do so? The Beast has not yet appeared in this struggle for the Church. The message's importance is still valid. The Beast needs the Satanic Bible to wrest control of the World Church to himself."

Diana could not believe God moved men in such fashion—John's coming home at this time was just chance. Just as was her coming to the States.

The whole idea irritated her. She spoke. "Do you think these people are still watching, waiting for someone to solve the mystery so they can retrieve the book? This is difficult to believe."

"What's seventy-five years to Satan? He's been waiting since the foundation of the world for his chance. In his mind, the rule of the world is at stake. The cherubim are the most exalted angels of God, with great knowledge and power, continually in the presence of God, first among created beings. The fallen cherub, Satan, is a joke among mankind—still with a tail, horns, a pitchfork. People laugh at him even as he uses them. Satan is a perverter, a manipulator. He is treacherous, brutal, vicious. Satan glories in fallen man. We are so natural in our sin, so enamored of ourselves and mankind that Satan can now reveal himself."

John remained quiet, immersed in thought. Diana knew he believed his grandfather. Someone had to burst this old man's fantasy. She spoke.

"Getting back to the stolen book. Don't you think Satan's people would have made more than one copy? Are you telling me your father stole the only copy, or that the book was not read by anyone before being stolen? Why couldn't they ask Satan for another copy?" She had once thought Henry might be suffering from senility. He would have to prove his mental competence to her.

"There might be ten copies, all safely in their hands. Satan might have given them another copy. A thousand people could have read the book. It's the copy that might come into their enemy's hands that frightens them. Then, there is the possibility that this original copy has something within it that is unique and necessary for their plans. The final possibility is that, yes, there is only one copy, and they don't have it and have never read it."

A slight frustration had come to Henry's voice. She felt foolish. Of course it was the copy that remained at large that would irritate, frighten. Oh well, she had been called an airhead before. Henry's mind was keen; this didn't mean his premise was correct.

John spoke. "Why would this Satanic bible cause such a commotion if revealed? The world would laugh at it—since Satan isn't real to them."

"There must be something so authentic and true within it that the high ecclesiastical authorities won't be able to shrug it off. Likely, about the Beast and his power play for the World Church." Henry took a deep breath as he leaned back in his chair. He rubbed his hands over his face and eyes. "Once the Beast has dominion over the Federation – political power, and the World Church – spiritual power – all the nations of the earth will be his."

John rose from the sofa, took Diana's mug, raised his eyebrow. She nodded, knowing he was asking if she wanted more. He spoke loudly as he made his way to the kitchen. "All this is just talk unless you tell me you have deciphered the riddle and know the location of the book." John thought on his voice projection—no helmet, no airtight mask to talk through, and a realization stunned him.

He returned from the kitchen with two more doughnuts, fresh cups of coffee. His thoughtfulness pleased Diana, and she thanked him for the coffee. John remained standing until Henry and Diana were both looking upon him. Then, with a with a questioning gaze, John moved his hands and arms around the room in an all-inclusive gesture encompassing the house. Henry searched and caught the meaning and spoke.

"No, it is safe. I have a constant monitoring device. We can speak freely. Now, I believe the book is hidden on the grounds of Colebrook Seminary. That is where my father worked, taught. I have a map of the seminary as it was seventy-five years ago. Another coincidence?"

Diana shook her head imperceptibly. They really believed forces were seeking that book! She smiled in disbelief at the crazy talk coming from these two, and she was beginning to believe, even enjoyed the believing. For the first time in years, she was thinking of something other than what clothes to wear or where to have dinner.

"A seminary is a big place," John said. He sat so near to Diana that he touched her hip. He seemed unaware of the touching.

"The Spirit will guide us. I have ideas. Would you like to hear?" asked Henry.

"Of course," John answered. Diana noticed one doughnut was gone. His presence gave her peace.

"Three meanings are found in the word *stone*." Henry reread the passage. "'The stone which the builders rejected, the same is become the head of the corner: this is the Lord's doing, and it is marvelous in our eyes?'

"Christ is a stone to Israel, a stumbling stone. Because He came as a lowly carpenter and not as a king, they could not hear His message. He was an offense to them. To the Church, He is the foundation stone—the head of the corner. To nonbelievers, he is a stone of destruction, one that will fall upon them."

Henry took his Bible from the coffee table, opened to the New Testament, continued talking.

"Three of the Gospels, Matthew 21:42, Mark 12:10, and Luke 20:17, carry this same passage, which was taken from Psalm 118:22. For our purposes, this stone could be a literal church cornerstone or a large rock formation on which is built a church. It could be an altar, a prayer booth, some symbol of Christ or the Church. Could a rock pedestal to a statue be considered a stone?" Henry asked.

"Now, *stone of destruction*—my mind is left blank, as it is with a stumbling stone. Maybe you two can come up with something or will see something on the campus."

Diana wondered why he had included her in the search. She had a life to live—she was going to become a nurse.

"Let's continue with *stone* as it refers to Christ. Exodus 17:6, 'Behold I will stand before thee there upon the rock in Horeb; and thou shalt smite the rock, and there shall come water out of it, that the people may drink.'

"We may be looking for a spring, fountain, or drinking fountain on the campus," Henry said. "Christ as water, or the rock as water leads us to John 4:13–14, which leads us to a well. A well could be on campus."

John moved around the coffee table to kneel beside Henry. Diana followed. Henry was about to flip to another passage when Diana spoke. "Read it to me, please, that last passage." The angle of the book was too much for her vision.

In the Shadow of Babylon

Henry read, "Jesus answered and said to her, Whosoever drinketh of this water shall thirst again: But whosoever drinketh of the water that I shall give him shall never thirst; but the water that I shall give him shall be in him a well of water springing up into everlasting life."

Diana moved her eyes closer to the written word—she thrust out her hand, her finger a pointer; she pointed at verse ten. "Read that one please, verse ten."

Henry read, "Jesus answered and said unto her, If thou knewest the gift of God, and who it is that saith to thee, Give me to drink; thou wouldest have asked of him, and he would have given thee living water."

"What is the living water?" She studied Henry's eyes as he replied.

"The Holy Spirit. We talked about Him just minutes ago. The Spirit of God working within you, Diana, giving you wisdom—to convince you that Christ is Lord; to conform you to his image; to energize your mind, body, and soul with his presence, His Spirit. Christ's death takes you out of sin; the Holy Spirit guides you in your new life within Him."

Diana said nothing. She placed her hand on the page to stop Henry from turning. Her eyes scanned the passage, moved down the page. Christ was speaking to a woman with many husbands who were not husbands—she understood. She took away her hand, felt a fluttering within her soul. Did God care about her, a prostitute, raised in a state school? A nobody in the scheme of things? Christ had talked to this woman at the well! Henry turned to the next passage.

"Isaiah 8:14. 'And he shall be for a sanctuary; but for a stone of stumbling and for a rock of offence to both the houses of Israel, for a gin and a snare to the inhabitants of Jerusalem.' Nothing new here, although anything to do with Judaism might be worth checking," Henry said.

"Isaiah 28:16. Nothing new, although the next passage refers to justice or righteousness. A statue dealing with justice?"

Henry's eyes took on a luster. "Now to Daniel. Daniel was a prophet, Diana. He knew of Christ, of the political or national events of the future, and he knew of the end. Since we are seeking knowledge of the end times, it is sensible to concentrate on Daniel.

"Daniel 2:34, 'Thou sawest till that a stone was cut out without hands, which smote the image upon his feet that were of iron and clay, and brake them to pieces.'

"That stone is Christ, who destroys Satan and his world system. As it is cut out without hands—perhaps a freestanding stone formation is what we seek. We then read in verse 35, 'Then was the iron, the clay, the brass, the silver, and the gold, broken into pieces together, and became like the chaff of the summer threshing floors; and the wind carried them away, that no place was found for them: and the stone that smote the image became a great mountain, and filled the whole earth.'

"In this passage, the stone, Christ, who destroys Satan, becomes a mountain—which is symbolic for a kingdom. This kingdom then reigns on earth. Could a hill be considered a mountain? Is there a hill on the campus?"

Diana interrupted. "What do the iron, clay, brass...those things symbolize?"

"Past history, the empires of Babylon, Media-Persia, Greece under Alexander, and Rome. Rome divided into two—the legs, the Eastern and Western Roman Empires. Then occurs a division into ten, prophetically called 'toes.' Ten kings, or nations, arise out of the destroyed empire. All this is reaffirmed in another prophetic book called Revelation, which describes the end."

Henry flipped to the back of the Bible. John returned to the couch. Diana remained kneeling by Henry's side even though the position was becoming uncomfortable. Henry began again.

"The son whom my father wrote of in the message, the Beast, is mentioned here in Revelation. 'The beast thou sawest was, and is not; and shall ascend out of the bottomless pit, and go into perdition: and they that dwell on the earth shall wonder, whose names were not written in the book of life from the foundation of the world, when they beheld the beast that was, and is not, and yet is.'"

Diana cringed. The name *beast* unleashed tormenting memories. She knew the meaning of beast, had seen the beast, crazed, irrational, desperate, lusting upon her in stink, sweat, heat while she looked on helplessly. She cried to God for an end of the remembrances, and they ceased.

Bold lettering on the page caught her eyes. "MYSTERY, BABYLON THE GREAT, THE MOTHER OF HARLOTS AND ABOMINATIONS OF THE EARTH."

"What's this about?" she asked.

"That's what the Lord calls the present-day church. She is the mother. Her offspring, the harlots, are the church that will arise when the Beast comes to power and the Federation is under his control. The information we find will reveal fully the mystery that is Babylon. We will prove the Church is the mother of the harlots."

Diana thought it incredible that their actions could somehow be intertwined with the ancient writings. Their actions were connected to the outcome of world history, prophesied thousands of years in the past?

"What is Babylon?" she asked.

"Babylon was the empire that once subjugated God's people, the Jews. Babylon means 'confusion.' It is the spiritual center of the kingdom of darkness."

She felt strange; her body became cold, her flesh tightened. Something was in their presence that John and Henry could not discern. She rose, became light-headed. The presence was ancient, depraved, possessive, and she was its possession to be used, devoured. The cold of its breath ran across her neck. She began to falter; her hand reached out for balance and touched the Bible now on the table. The presence vanished.

John was standing beside her, guiding her to the sofa. "Are you all right?"

"Yes."

Henry understood and said nothing.

John sat beside her, his hand upon her wrist. The pulse was rapid. Her wrist was small, the skin soft. He felt as if he were touching her soul. He gently released her wrist and spoke.

"So that's it. We could be looking for a spring, a drinking fountain, a fountain, a well, a building of justice, a statue or its pedestal, a church, an altar, a prayer booth, a hill or mountain, a rock formation, anything to do with Judaism—even the statue of a war leader who crushed other nations, or something that I have not mentioned."

John's words were tinged with anger. The task was impossible. He lived under the threat of arrest. He was beyond weariness. No one would listen if they did find the information. Who would make the truth known? The media? Their ideology was of the world, firmly in Satan's hands. Would the Church, as Henry suggested, allow the truth to be known? Only if Church leaders saw a threat to their power and privilege. Which was the greater threat to the Church—Christ or Satan? John knew Christ was the threat to that brood of vipers. Regardless, a man's actions must begin in faith, not skepticism.

What if only one person came to Christ as a result of their efforts? Just one man or woman? What suffering should be endured for the salvation of one person? Begrudgingly, John admitted the truth to himself: one person coming to Christ was worth their lives. A simple, brutal truth that people of the world would never understand. He had eternal life; he was expendable. He had been born again to risk, to dare, to boldly serve God. For the man not in Christ, life was eternal hell. He had to go, search, suffer, endure. Satan might have his followers waiting for him to do him harm. He had promised the Lord everything when he first was saved; now the Lord was asking for everything.

"What exactly are we looking for, Gramps?"

Henry smiled. "Ah, the form of the book or documents?" John nodded in affirmation. "An old paper book, mimicking the size, shape, heft of an old paper Bible or scrolls, perhaps? Or did my father have time to create external hard drives for a computer? Those were popular in his day. Before this was the clumsy, clunky microfilm. Micro objects and dots would be easier to hide. Whatever form the book is in, it will be in a strong, element-proof bag or container."

Talk stopped. Henry slumped back into his chair; his eyes focused inward as he thought of the future. John eased back into the sofa. Diana remained on the sofa's edge. His hand reached out spontaneously, touching the middle of her back. He rubbed her gently. Realizing his show of affection, he then patted her vigorously before withdrawing his hand. A friendly gesture of inclusion, of family, loneliness, weariness. She smiled warmly, understood the loneliness within John. She knew his longing for a friend, a companion.

A peace beyond comprehension settled upon her, within her. She turned and studied the face of John. She sat back; their shoulders touched. She saw Henry and John for the first time: an old man not far from the end of his days and a battle-worn kid. Strange, but she felt older than they were and ageless. She sensed their needs. Both were lonely, without the strength for the demands of the coming trials; both yearned to be out of the world. Henry was motivated by a combative spirit, a sense of history, a desire for completion, fulfillment. His final contest, she thought.

John had no motivation but duty; desire was absent. He fought against participating in this mystery. She knew he would go. She had never thought of the word *character* until now. She respected him; he wasn't afraid to suffer, to hurt. He loved his God; of that she was certain. Why wouldn't the Lord allow him rest? Why couldn't the Lord fill the emptiness within him? They both needed her love and care—two little kids.

She wanted the Lord in her life. He was becoming real to her. If this was His peace, if these feelings of love were His, then she would give all to possess Him. Harlot church, professing church, Rapture, Tribulation, Satan, cherubim—words she had never heard before, real to John and Henry. If a mystery existed, waiting to be revealed, it personally meant little to her. Henry broke the silence.

"Let's look at the map of the seminary grounds and pick out some logical choices."

A buzzer sounded from the den; Henry's telescreen had been activated. They heard it snap on. Henry moved quickly to the den, worry upon his face. John and Diana followed Henry, remaining outside the view of the screen. John heard his mother's voice. He ran upstairs to Henry's bedroom, turned on the home's second telescreen, switching off visual broadcast. His mother could not see him, but he could see and hear her.

Her hair was grayer, the fine wrinkles around the eyes had multiplied. Worry and confusion dominated her eyes. John cocked his head to a sound; Diana was beside him. He sat upon Henry's bed. He listened to his mother's voice.

"They say he's in the States, traveling with a girl. Mr. Borelli thinks a good lawyer could win his case—there is no evidence that he killed anyone. You know Johnny wouldn't kill his own captain!"

Henry spoke. "Calm down, Margaret, calm down. I'll help pay for the lawyer—the best money can buy. Find one who specializes in military cases. I'll send John home immediately if he comes here. By the way, who is this girl?"

"A Diana something…Rochembeau. You're not lying? You haven't seen him?"

She had always had that ability, John remembered, to intuitively know when something wasn't right. He smiled sadly.

"I wouldn't lie."

"Mr. Borelli is coming to your place, Henry."

"Who is Borelli?"

"The inspector working on the case. He seems like an honest, goodhearted man, Henry."

"I'm sure he is, Margaret. I'll say a prayer. The Lord will have John do the right thing. You get the best lawyer there is."

Henry looked at Margaret, and Margaret looked into Henry. Henry wondered how he could lie so well. For a moment, he thought of confiding in Margaret. He realized she already knew the truth.

"Good-bye, Margaret."

In the Shadow of Babylon

"Good-bye, Henry."

John held the picture of his mother's face within his mind as the telescreen snapped off. The burden he had cast upon her was heavy. Her anxiety awoke in him a love, a flood of poignant memories that discarded the painful moments of the past relationship. He wished to cry, not for her, but for his life so torn with pain, a life never whole or complete, never knowing external peace. God had cast the burden on him, and so God would lift her burden.

Diana placed her hand upon his shoulder, she sat behind him on the bed. He reached up, touched her hand. His hand became one with hers. She spoke.

"We've got to talk, just the two of us, *mon chéri*."

Henry called up the stairs. "You've got an inspector."

"I know. We'll be down in a moment," John shouted back. He turned to her; the softness of her eyes promised peace.

"What is it?"

"They know who I am," she said. "As soon as I call, they'll be on me. They'll drug me. I'll tell them everything. You will be caught, and Henry too. Aiding and abetting a masking will do me in, and you too—a fact Borelli didn't give to your mother."

She didn't know what else to say. She wanted out, and now it was too late. Or could she call Immigration, make a deal with this Borelli, tell him what he needed to know if he promised not to question her about the masking? Betray John and Henry? Yes, she liked a warm place to sleep, money, a job; she liked buying nice things, she liked living in the world. She wanted a new life, to be a nurse. She had made some mistakes in life, but she was a good person. She had to get out now!

She was beginning to love John. No! No! No! She felt sorry for him, it wasn't love. He wasn't handsome, he had no physique. He had no money, no future. He was odd. He loved this God of his more than he could love any woman. Let them love each other! She wasn't going to be a part of this foolishness. What was love? He had kindness, thoughtfulness. He was loyal. He wasn't the only man with these qualities. He had purpose. So what?

"Call Immigration. Tell them I gave you a ticket in exchange for services. If they ask about the masking, tell them you knew nothing. I could have been masked before meeting you. Tell them I went to visit my brother in New York. They will be satisfied. They don't have time for court orders, druggings. You are unimportant to them. Start your new life."

He had said everything she was hoping he would. Why, then, did he anger her?

"What about this God of yours—will He be happy with my decision? What if I tell them where you really went, under pressure, or because I am drugged? Then you'll never find the book or whatever! And who will teach me about God if you're gone?"

"That's the chance we take. Maybe the time has already passed, and Satan's legions have their bible. Maybe this entire story has come out of Henry's imagination. If it is of God, then it will be accomplished with or without us. As for learning of God, Henry can give you a Bible. That's all you need. Maybe you'll meet another of my kind, a believer. Whatever you do, don't give up on Jesus; He won't give up on you"

"You're one of a kind." Her sarcasm was equally mixed with affection.

What was he supposed to say to her? Her company would be welcomed. He didn't want her to leave, and he didn't want her to ruin her life.

"Look, postpone calling Immigration. Come along. You've only used up a quarter of twenty-four hours."

"Why? What is the advantage? We're just running from the truth. We will be caught. Does it matter if we've found the document?"

"What do you want from me, Diana?" He faced her, grabbed her upper arms with his hands, he shook her. His voice was whispered, deep and sharp, tremulous with anxiety. He wanted to kiss her, hold her close and smell her skin, her perfume, her hair. He wanted his lips to meet hers.

He needed her, wanted her. He could not survive without her. His anger, passion, anxiety touched her own. Her voice tremulous and raging and whispered covered him.

"I want to know what I am to you! Am I some bothersome harlot tagging along? Do you want to get rid of me? Do you want me along? I'm under pressure, too. What does this God of yours want from me? I don't want to go with you—I curse the day I met you." She slapped him, then stood as if to bolt from the room. "I want to be a nurse! I want a new life! I want the good things of this world. I want to be loved! Can you love a fucking whore, shithead? Do I have to spell it out for you? Are you that slow?"

Her voice had been loud, hateful, her face torn in anger. She was certain Henry had heard. She had shamed herself with those awful words. She was just a piece of trash. She had destroyed his picture of her, the picture of the nice girl who had made some mistakes.

Henry called up the stairs, "You have half an hour at the most!"

"Don't lay this burden on me, Diana. If you come, come because the Holy Spirit wants you to come. Yes, I have feelings for you…I don't understand them. I have no future, so I don't think of such things. My mind is burdened by so many thoughts. I've enjoyed your company. You're no whore to me. You've sinned with your body, but the Lord can wash that past away—if you want. Do I look like a man who can do this thing on my own? To say I need you would be to condemn you. I care too much for you to do that."

His voice was pleading. His eyes were wet with tears. He had admitted his need for her—that is what she had to hear. She hardly knew this Christ, this Holy Spirit. How could either of them guide her? If this God wasn't the answer, then maybe there was no answer, and it didn't matter what she did. For the first time in her life, she felt as if she were moving toward something instead of just existing, drifting. Maybe this feeling was worth a few more hours.

She would call Immigration later, learn more of this God. She would like to hurt the Church that had lied to her. She hated the government that loved the Church. She would see how real God was. If He was just the product of man's imagination, then she would hate Him with her whole being. She would gladly call Immigration. This God had eighteen hours to prove Himself.

"Show me where your old clothes are. I've got to dress warmer." She spoke quickly, looked impatiently at him sitting on the bed. "Move it, mon chéri…We're running out of time!"

He jumped up, showed her to his room and dresser, then quickly moved down the steps. He had the feeling that the spontaneous eruption of emotion had been choreographed, and he had been made to reveal what he wanted to keep hidden.

Henry and John were conversing as Diana came down the stairs.

"This will help." Henry handed John a money card. "Ride the trains. If you are in trouble, go to Tim's. Give Diana Tim's address in case you are separated. He can give you advice on where to go into hiding."

John slipped into the rucksack Henry extended at shoulder level. John secreted his army knife within an inner pocket of his coat. Desmit's briefcase had been discarded on the walk to Henry's.

"I have a sword for my journey."

"Pray you don't need it."

"Amen." John's voice was solemn. He remembered with horror the killing of the storm trooper with the same knife. He hated killing. The hunt they were embarking upon was a military mission. Likely there would be death, privation, fear. He would need the Lord of Battle to show Himself; of this he was certain. He intended to conquer, to succeed, and he would not leave the field till his Lord had won.

Henry surveyed Diana's clothes.

"Today's fashions what they are, you'll fit right in with a college crowd."

Henry pulled his Bible from a table at the foot of the steps.

"Though we're pressed for time, I feel led to read to you this passage. Maybe it isn't appropriate or there is one better, but listen:

Therefore I say unto you, Take no thought for your life, what ye shall eat; neither for the body, what ye shall put on. The life is more than meat, and the body is more than raiment. Consider the ravens: for they neither sow nor reap; which neither have storehouse nor barn; and God feedeth them: how much more are ye better than the fowls? And which of you with taking thought can add to his stature one cubit? If ye then be not able to do that thing which is least, why ye take thought for the rest? Consider the lilies how they grow: they toil not, they spin not; and yet I say unto you, that Solomon in all his glory was not arrayed like one of these. If then God so clothe the grass, which is to day in the field, and to morrow is cast into the oven; how much more will he clothe you, O ye of little faith! And seek not what ye shall eat, or what ye shall drink, neither be ye of doubtful mind. For all these things do the nations of the world seek after: and your Father knoweth that ye have need of these things. But rather seek ye the kingdom of God; and all these things shall be added unto you.

A stillness prevailed. Diana knew at that moment she would never call Immigration, never return to the world. How could she have a new life without this God? Food, clothing, a home really didn't matter. Where was His Kingdom? How could He tell her not to worry? Why did she believe Him?

Henry broke the stillness by grasping Diana, hugging her. He pulled back, handed her a purse-sized Bible. "Read this for me. The Lord is with you."

John was pulling her out the door. Her eyes held excitement and a slightly dazed look. John's eyes were moist, his jaw clenched. Henry watched them till they had vanished down the hill, into the trees.

They said nothing. The earth and air were warm, the breeze cool. She assumed Tim was John's brother, the college professor. Her legs were stiff from the morning walk. She felt free, alone, frightened, and she had a strange peace. When they came to a paved road, he stopped, scanned its length. He faced her, studied her eyes, and spoke. "Sometimes I wonder why my heart is always breaking."

She grabbed his hand as they hurriedly crossed to a wooded trail. He needed her, however difficult that need was to express.

CHAPTER 7

Borelli and Hanson circled the old farmhouse by foot. They had monitored the telescreen communication between the mother and grandfather of John Johnson and had learned nothing. Even Borelli had not been able to discern if the old man was lying. No withdrawals had been made from any of the accounts of the principal characters. Diana Rochembeau had yet to call Immigration. She and John Johnson had been placed on the wanted list of law enforcement agencies in the United States.

The two men moved slowly around the house, nonchalantly making use of cover. Borelli sensed the house was empty. Hanson was in awe of the structure.

"Look at that…two chimneys, real wood construction, a huge yard. My wife would go crazy." Hanson was enthused. "Peace and quiet…That's the way I want to live."

Borelli smiled at the talk as if sympathetic. Hanson hadn't mentioned his wife since somewhere on the Continent! Live in peace and quiet! Peace and quiet would kill Hanson. Who was Hanson trying to fool? Borelli spoke the obvious, sensing Hanson wanted a comment.

"You've got to have money to own a country home—more than you make—or have political pull."

"Well, is Gramps rich?"

Borelli shrugged his shoulders. The circle was complete. They walked across the broad lawn to the back porch. Both men scanned windows and doors for movement. Borelli had noticed fresh trails through the high, dew-ladened grass, but the trails could have easily been made early that morning by deer or coyotes.

Borelli knocked on the kitchen door. Hanson stood back from the porch so as to view all exits. Borelli waited a few seconds before knocking again. He knew the old man was gone—now a participant in crime, a wanted man himself. Why would an old man take the risk? It was obvious he could do more for his grandson by remaining, seeking and financing a lawyer. Why would he bolt?

Borelli took his electronic delocking instrument from a pocket. He shook his head in mock disgust. The door had a key lock—the house was an antique. Hanson was circling the house, peering into windows.

"Hey, Bob, come around. Kick this door in for me."

Hanson returned, pulled a log from a woodpile near the kitchen door. He broke a pane of glass and reached in, opened the door.

"That's how it used to be done," Hanson said knowingly.

Borelli had no experience with breakable glass, except as drinking vessels. Hanson had a knowledge of old homes.

The inspectors entered. Hanson's eyes ran over the interior enviously.

"This is amazing. Look! An old woodstove!"

Borelli noticed the kitchen sink was empty; he supposed that's how the dishes were cleaned, as he saw no sterilizer unit. Where would dirty dishes be hidden? He opened the cupboard under the sink and peered in. Sitting in a tub were cups, plates, mugs, silverware. Borelli counted the utensils, three of everything.

"Notify the local police immediately. Have them watch the nearest mass-transit stations."

Hanson gave a respectful but humorous salute, walked outside to obtain a better signal for his hand phone. Borelli leisurely walked upstairs, surveyed the bedrooms. The beds were made but two seemed ruffled, as if people had taken a brief rest. One dresser drawer was half open, the contents in disarray. He opened the hamper that sat in the hallway. He read labels and examined design. Two sets of clothes with French labels, one belonging to a woman. Perfume still clung to her clothes. Hanson was beside Borelli.

Borelli held up the woman's clothes for Hanson, then spoke.

"Diana's clothes."

Hanson shook his head. "Twenty-four hours isn't up yet."

Borelli made no comment. He walked into the study to a huge oaken desk on which sat a computer. He turned on the computer. The first page of a document appeared. Files showed numerous documents, manuscripts by Henry Johnson. The same manuscript titles and author could be seen in the nearby book cabinet: rows of hardbound, old-fashioned, faux paper books.

"Bob, go back to the vehicle, pull it up to the house. Get on the computer and see if there isn't a dossier on this Henry Johnson. I doubt it—he was probably already too old when the law was passed."

Borelli referred to the World Bank and Census Identification System established twenty years earlier. Every child born in the world since that time had a file. Anyone under sixty at the time of the enactment had been given a file.

"Why do you think he bolted?" Hanson asked.

"I have no idea."

Hanson obediently exited. Borelli stared at the screen while he thought. The old man was a writer. There was another bookshelf by the writer's table in easy access of the chair. Books on religion, Bibles, hardbound, very old. Books, antiques, dust, comfortable furniture. Borelli envied the life. To sit and just think the hours away seemed so good. Why would the old man leave with the kid and the girl? To confuse the authorities by leaving a false trail? Or did he leave by himself? Would he meet them later or go to his only family in the area? Timothy Johnson. What an idyllic life he'd left behind—a beautiful home, the peace of the country, an interesting hobby.

Hanson returned to the kitchen half an hour later. Borelli was sitting at the table, drinking coffee, eating a doughnut. The fugitives must have escaped again; the local police had not called in.

"No dossier?"

"No dossier, but I found background information."

"Pull up a chair, have a cup of coffee and a doughnut."

Hanson was surprised by Borelli's conduct. Borelli never took liberties with his position, maintaining a strict code of ethics.

"Why are you so comfortable?"

"He's not coming back. Besides, I think he would want me to make myself at home. What's the information?"

"I made a printout; you can read it." Hanson poured himself a cup of coffee, sat down at the table, changed the subject of conversation. "What was the book about?"

"Nothing important."

"Tell me anyway."

Why was Hanson being so insistent? Borelli sighed; he didn't have the strength for a long explanation.

"He believes civilization is at its spiritual nadir, and God—more specifically, Christ—is coming to clean up the mess and establish his perfect Kingdom."

Hanson leaned back in his chair, laughed. "Civilization is at its peak, spiritually and every other way. Life couldn't be better."

Borelli didn't laugh or even give his trademark smile. Borelli thought the coffee was extremely good—deep in flavor—and the doughnuts were fresh. Plain doughnuts, his favorite. Yes, this was the life—he was thankful retirement was so near. He could write a book about his youth or his career as an inspector. He spoke.

"His standards for civilization are different than ours."

"What are his standards?"

Borelli felt and saw the zealous Churcher in Hanson rising up through his demeanor. Why this interest in the book? Why now for a casual talk? Borelli was wary. "The unchanging laws of God."

Hanson's eyes were gleeful. "When was the last time you coveted your neighbor's oxen or needed guidelines for a stoning? These people want to send us back to the Dark Ages. People change, times change, laws change."

Borelli said nothing. To talk would be to feed Hanson's animosity. The human heart never changed, thought Borelli. You couldn't trust anyone in this age. He kept his distance from people. Only his wife had gained his complete confidence. As his kids matured, he shared more but still he held back. They were a part of their generation, and others—friends—were sometimes more influential than Mom and Dad were. He wasn't a suspicious man; he simply knew what was in the heart of the average person. He had known an Enslaver when he was young, and he would have married her if she hadn't been arrested.

Hanson suspected a more-than-casual Enslaver contact—admitted to through the legal training—perhaps a woman. Enslavers were a disease, born to spread their contagion, the germs of which were the very words carried on their breaths. Hanson wanted debate, argument. He would have his way.

"Let's say this is correct: God's laws are unchanging. What do you want? The government in the business of identifying sinners?"

Borelli decided to create a sense of agreement. "Law is best when it concerns itself with the material, the concrete—property, or an individual's freedom from physical harm." Why had Hanson made the leap in topics from outdated laws to the government identifying sinners? No thread of consistency existed in his conversation unless you knew Enslaver logic. Enslavers believed the law's purpose, in the spiritual realm, was to identify humanity's sinful state. Hanson's knowledge of the Enslavers was deep.

Should he allow himself to be won over to Hanson's viewpoint? He had often thought on the subject of risk. When a man is young, he's not afraid to risk because he has the time and energy to regain what might be lost. When a man is old and death is his future, risk has no meaning. The years between youth and age can make a man a coward. He had become a coward.

He spoke. "I'm not sure we've advanced beyond any law. We've simply walked away from our consciences."

"That is an opinion. Look at the facts. The world has peace, prosperity. Everyone's needs and desires are met or achievable. There is less crime and less law. These are the facts."

"This Henry Johnson believes God measures the prosperity of his creation by how many people obey him." Borelli was tempted to add, "And love him."

"How do you remain obedient to a God who is never satisfied?"

Borelli did not reply; he had already said too much. He knew what the Enslavers would say: Christ's death satisfied God. A man in Christ is dead to the demands of the law, but the law is still true. He didn't understand how this concept worked, but it was their belief.

Borelli held Hanson's eye contact, searched past the gleaming blue conceit for the real man within. Hanson, the Churcher, young, handsome, bound for success. He would be the head of a department someday. This Hanson had not accepted him as a man of more experience and wisdom. The "old man" label was not heard; Hanson eagerly obeyed, but this respect and acquiescence were just a ruse.

Hanson was the type of man who would magnify your shortcomings and deny that he possessed any weaknesses of his own. Hanson would stab you in the back if he could do it cleanly. The spirit of the man was untamed, ruthless. Tell this to Hanson, and he would deny your words. He would deny the truth even as he walked over you. Borelli's last three partners had been Hansons, men of the untamed spirit, the ruthlessness. They possessed manners but no morals. Life always bent to their wills; there were no hardships, no denials, no heartbreak. They were men of soaring egos, iron wills forged by the untamed spirit.

Borelli knew something was desperately wrong with the world. He could not understand why he knew, unless it had been the influence of his father. His father had come from the last generation that had known a core of good men. They were few and far between, but they had existed. His father had been a good man, married for life to one wife, always there for his kids, refusing promotions and advancements to keep his family together. Coworkers, friends, supervisors called him foolish. His father had given guidelines for living. Yes, his father's generation had produced the last good men—so few.

Men were married to men, women to women, they adopted and raised children. Men and women had multiple spouses. Babies were being produced at a phenomenal rate by mere girls, the state schools were bursting, producing unloved and empty clones. Abortion clinics were filled. Everyone was a cutthroat, ruthless, masquerading behind civility. People were honest, kind, faithful, loving, and a hundred other virtues when such virtues were rewarded or worked to their advantage and need. Those virtues were as dead as stone when you could do nothing for them. On the front lines, he had seen civilization's perfect young men butcher, mutilate, torture, rape, destroy with glee and without compunction.

He had been born into this world. He should have accepted its existence, its reality as truth. Everyone else called the world and this life *good, right, natural*. Men had created an illusion; they lived by the illusion. Men dressed as women and women dressed as men. Could you escape the truth when looking into the empty eyes of the children in the state schools? The Enslavers were nearer the truth than anyone else he had heard: God was angry.

All Hanson could see in Borelli's unswerving gaze was a softness. "Are you soft on this kid?"

Borelli knew he should lie. "He's breaking the law. I'll find him and turn him over to the courts. Yes, I admire the kid. He's a rebel to the world, not for the sake of being different or in blind anger, but because he believes in something, some inner code. You read his profile. They gave him the standard questions, and he didn't give the standard answers. He doesn't flaunt his difference; he just lives it. Perfect military record, cited for bravery. One scatterbrained witness to his alleged crime. I like his intelligence, using the priest's ID, passing airport security. Who would have thought he would go this far? Yeah, I like the kid. So what?"

Hanson hid a smirk. Borelli's equanimity had been broken. "Take it easy. Admire the kid. But before this is over, he will have killed someone—maybe softhearted you. When he's cornered, you will see a viper not a good kid who had tough breaks."

Borelli shrugged off Hanson's remarks as he shrugged his shoulders. Anyone would kill when cornered and fighting for freedom. "We will see. As for me, I'm having another cup of coffee."

The calm had come back. Damn him! "It's going to look bad if you don't catch this kid."

Borelli's face remained emotionless as he poured the cup of coffee. What a comfortable position to be in: waiting for the other guy to fail. "So, where to now, Bob?"

"He's got the brother in New York, the college professor. He won't return here or to his parents. I'll call for surveillance at all three places anyway."

"I agree." Borelli threw a schedule printout onto the table. "This was in the trash—not such a good hiding place."

Hanson picked up the printout, read the title: New York State Mass Transit Schedule.

***

He slept with his head against the window. She had offered her shoulder as a pillow, and he had refused, politely. Earlier, their legs had touched, and he had pulled his away. The warmth, need, he had shown at his grandfather's home were gone. The empty car had been ice cold when they had entered; they must have been the first riders since yesterday. The heater motor had hummed to life when she flicked the switch. Half the car was now warm.

Would the coldness in his heart ever leave? This decision to follow had been wrong. Her soul thrashed against an invisible barrier. She wanted to exit, flee at the next station. A good life full of promise still waited for her. She was certain she could make a deal with the inspectors. She knew leaving John would bring no lasting freedom, no fulfillment, no escape from her past.

Her past had now begun to haunt her; why, she did not know. Even as a girl she had never thought of sex as sin or something to be saved for marriage. Sex had been a physical act, a feeling that soon faded but always demanded more. You could no more stop having sex than you could stop eating or breathing. Why the feelings of degradation? She thought of the women who had wanted her, the men with strange requests. Thank God she had some standards. Thank God? She brushed the past aside. Think of anything but that time.

When they had arrived at the station, a small pavilion—a roof raised on one metal girder, a few benches, a ticket machine—hope and adventure had filled her thoughts. The empty cars passing, following the thin track silently on their cushions of air, seemed like life itself, unending, flowing. Then, from the intersecting roads bound by woods and farmland had come the police cars. With the luck Johnny boy was having, they had entered a car unseen, remained on the floor till the police cars were left behind. The adventure and hope had been replaced by fear.

He had estimated they would change commuter cars at least ten times before they reached their destination. An express ticket cost more than thirty dollars, the amount over which purchases were by account and thus traceable. He had hoped to sleep soundly during the trip, but the sight of the police pumped adrenaline into his system. His fatigue and the whiz of the engine eventually pulled him into a fitful sleep. Would other stations up the line have police waiting?

She watched him wrestle in his sleep. She read the Bible Henry had given her, beginning with a man named Matthew. The cover of the Bible said, *Early Theories of Relativity*. She had never seen anyone read the Bible in public, never talked to anyone who had claimed to have read it, never seen quotes from the Bible on the electrascreen, never saw it represented in a movie—maybe there was a law against it? She pulled a half-awake John off the car and onto another at a station with moderate commuter activity. She saw no uniformed police. The car held ten other people, all safely absorbed in themselves.

The countryside consisted of wide fields stretching to distant tree lines or forested mountain ridges in various states of logging and reforestation. The country towns followed the circular plan, one central building of immense size, poking into the sky, followed by a ring of minor structures. Rows of vehicles surrounded the buildings like ants at a food morsel. Finally, a spacious lawn circled the whole, holding playgrounds, athletic fields.

Pressed against the lawns were the agricultural fields. Machines like those John had described to her dotted the fields. She didn't understand why he would have wanted the job—nothing but loneliness. He awoke. She placed two ready-to-eat meals in his hands.

"Thanks. Where did these come from?"

"The last station. Don't you remember?"

He sat upright, activated the heating element of one of the meals. His mind was wrapped in a fog of memories—by his deadened expression, they were unhappy remembrances. She could channel his mind into a place of peace. He found his peace in his God.

"Why did you give yourself to the Lord?"

The soft feminine voice brought a smile to his face. Months in the army without a feminine voice. The three women in his platoon had sounded like foghorns, and then days into the patrol, the foghorns had died. God, how lonely he was. How he could have listened to her voice for the rest of his days. "I couldn't escape Him."

She thought for a moment. "Your natural self resisted, but some part of you wanted God. Why?"

"I was beginning to understand the truth about myself. I saw the truth, and it was ugly. I saw the world, and it wasn't any better. I like truth even when it tells me what I don't want to believe. I don't like delusion. I had always known there was something wrong, but my self, my will, my life kept blocking my vision. The world helped me look inward. Everyone is well fed, clothed, has good housing. You can be anything you want, and yet people are empty…even evil, chasing the wind. I was empty, yes, with evil within, chasing the wind.

"The Church promised many things: eternal life, heaven on earth, freedom intellectually, emotionally, physically. A skeptical voice kept saying, 'God isn't a magic genie. If the Church isn't honest, true, what is left but God?'"

"So now your heart is always breaking and you're happy?" Diana asked. "The God you love and who is supposed to love you does this to you?"

His own words, spoken as they had left Henry's place. A part of her still wanted to make him hurt. She could have asked the same question in another way, with love in her heart. Love was absent; she hated her meanness.

"I love truth more than I love what people call happiness. What else is there but truth? Truth brings joy, from joy comes real contentment. If my heart must break and that is pleasing to God, then so be it."

"What kind of God would break your heart? Or what if it isn't God breaking your heart but your own self-hatred or your own warped perceptions of life caused by the bitterness of your failures and weaknesses?"

"I gave up hating myself the day Christ entered my life. Why would I hate myself for what I couldn't help but be—a sinner? I still hate the sin that was in me, but not at a personal level. Sin so deep I wasn't salvageable. The Lord threw the old me out."

Diana shifted uncomfortably in her seat. "If I were to decide on coming under the authority of God by what I've seen Him do in your life, I wouldn't come. You love God, and you're being hunted for murder. You are despised by everyone—including your fellow soldiers. Now you're running to a situation that will bring more suffering. You have no future but death or prison. You appear empty, unloved, and I don't see any joy. You look like a fool to me."

She saw his soul cringe. How easy it was to hurt him. The words rolled off her tongue effortlessly. Back in Harrisburg, at the restaurant, she had understood that he didn't fit into the world. Then, he had seemed no fool. Then, she had seen kindness, gentleness, respect for life, a forgiving nature. Then, he had purpose even as his life went nowhere. Why couldn't she tell him of the quiet dignity he possessed, or speak of his resoluteness, or the determined focus that was his life?

The price he paid to acquire those qualities was too high for her. Yes, he was a good man and possessed a strange peace, but the price...the price...That was why she was angry, willing to see him as a fool. She feared God was asking her to pay the same price. She was certain! If she destroyed the meaning within John's life, then she destroyed God's request. He was so damned calm sometimes that it irritated her. Even now, he was smiling, ready to chuckle. He should have lashed her with every curse under the sun.

"That was a compliment. I am a fool—for Christ. My foolishness is more glorious than the greatest ungodly life on earth. Do you know that every time my heart breaks, Christ grows stronger in me?"

"Now you brag of your sufferings and failures because they bring loss of control to your life."

"I don't want control over my life. I had control over my life, and it was empty, a lie."

Finally, some emotion in his voice. She had gotten to his temper. Still, he seemed to be talking to, defending himself against some other person, like the words hadn't belonged to her. He continued.

"That is what it means to have the natural man destroyed," he said. "You remember our talk on him. I expect life to be a struggle—walking in the Spirit isn't easy."

He had fallen so nicely into a trap.

"I read where Christ said, 'My burden is light, my way is easy.'"

"When did you have time to read that?"

"Never mind. Answer me."

"He also said, 'If any man will come after me, let him deny himself, and take up his cross daily, and follow me.' Both sayings are true. When sin is lifted from you, you are no longer harried, harassed. Your mind has peace. The way is easy because you're not stumbling over sin. The burden is light, the way is easy. But every day you must deny the natural man. The cross is picked up; the natural man groans, is left motionless under the weight. The new man walks away free and easy."

He had an answer for everything. Now he was talking about the cross. The very thing that held the body of his dead God. But Christ rose! How much of his ego was involved in this knowledge? Now he wouldn't shut up.

"These circumstances that afflict me, crush me, are crushing the natural man. The man most evident to you. Inside I feel the presence of the Lord."

"Don't you think the presence inside should show on the outside?" she asked.

He clenched his jaw. She had found his weakness. If everything he said was true, then he was still resisting the Lord's will. He'd follow the Lord but couldn't fully trust, couldn't fully like or accept the road he was made to follow. He hurt inside, hurt because he really did want more than what he had been given. A bitterness was within him, a resentment she had yet to fully understand. He didn't have all the answers; he wasn't perfect. She would not press her advantage.

He spoke. "Someday you will see the joy on the outside. Someday."

He continued to talk about himself dying and Christ growing within him. Did he want to be all Christ with nothing of himself left? John Johnson existed. The natural man still lurked in the background. She wished to understand completely, rid herself of the confusion. Her will and logic dissolved, and the answer seemed to burst gently throughout her mind.

She understood this God. She sensed the beginning and end of herself. The life force, the animator, energizer of her life, her will lived at a place past the soul. Christ had to have this place, had to destroy her possession of it before His wisdom could live within her. Life would then rearrange, change, fall into place. She would still exist, not as the driver of her life but as a passenger. Christ would drive her life. She laughed; something bubbled within, soothing, refreshing. She remembered the passage Henry had read to her about the woman at the well and the living water. The Holy Spirit! She laughed quietly. The laughter stopped abruptly.

These thoughts were all very nice, but they would end. She had a life to lead, one that was becoming more difficult. The decision to become a companion/escort had been wrong, a mistake. She had listened to a liar and then hadn't had the strength to change. With this part of her life gone, all the other problems would dry up, blow away. God had shown her the mistake, and she was thankful. If Christ wanted to live within, she wouldn't fight Him, but reality was reality. She couldn't make decisions on feelings or even what she thought God wanted. John said Christ grew within under each hardship, but that didn't mean you should seek misery. What kind of God would want you to ruin your life?

He had activated the heating element to his second meal and was devouring the food. He would fall into sleep again. She would babysit him to the seminary and then leave. Her heart ached as she thought this, but one couldn't make decisions based on feelings or vague philosophies.

***

John and Diana arrived at the Colebrook station at dusk. John shuddered with cold as he glimpsed the city from his window before entering the brightly lit, vaulted-roofed train station. The two hundred plus miles north from Harrisburg had changed the weather considerably. It seemed they were in late summer perhaps even autumn. The leaves of the trees were crinkling brown. A strong northwest wind blew signs, flags, trees. Dark clouds were raked over a cold sky. A faded band of orange light clung to the western horizon.

They wore insulated underwear and carried thermal blankets in the rucksack. The night would be cold. They couldn't sleep in a hotel without notifying the Inspectors . They? he thought bitterly. To rest in a public place or near a building would risk contact with police. They were pushed out of the car by a mass of travelers.

John's senses were heightened. Who among the crowd were detectives? Where would the stun stick hit him? In the ribs, the back? Could he fight through the jolt of paralysis? Would he need to kill his attacker? She held his arm. He scanned the people, all young like himself—students within their own worlds, taking no notice of him. No detectives, no police seen. The loudspeaker echoed departures and arrivals, track numbers. The air was bitterly raw even for a train station.

She held his arm, but her face spoke of nervousness, inwardness, betrayal. He had seen the look of betrayal a thousand times as a soldier. She had a right to her life—he couldn't blame her for wanting out. He was a fool, a loser; no woman in her right mind should follow him. He had nothing to offer, no handsome face, no physique, no money, no future, just death or prison for a God who seemed to delight in making him suffer.

He knew a mental breakdown was imminent, his faith had run dry, God was so far away. He did not believe that he would rise from this final despair. Something had broken inside, and life would never be the same. John hated God for what He had done to his life. He didn't want to be despised or hunted. He didn't want to be searching for a nonexistent book. He wanted rest, food. He wanted a wife, children, outdoor work. He wanted to blend into this world, enjoy the good things in life. He could not treat a pet dog the way his Lord had treated him.

He had begun to love her. No! She was the first feminine contact after a year of masculine company. He had been so emotionally starved that he had begun to cling to her. She wasn't the one. She wasn't intelligent. She possessed no conscience—or she would not have become a whore. She had a meanness within her. She was only a shell of a woman—a well-formed body, a beautiful face.

These thoughts meant nothing—he would never marry anyone, never have children, never have external peace—prison was his future. No, not prison; he would die first. Death promised heaven. He spoke. "Let's find a restaurant for the last supper."

Why did he say *the last supper*? The phrase reached into her church days with Miss Ames. She had just read in the Bible of Christ's last meal before he was betrayed and sentenced to death. John knew what she was about to do. She said nothing, fought the guilt so heavy on her conscience.

They passed through the station and onto a major downtown street. The tall buildings lined the street like canyon walls. The street-level floors were filled with nightclubs, bars, cabarets, sex parlors. Lights flashed brilliant colors. Music blared; hawkers called. Naked men and women danced in the windows, mimicked and performed sexual acts. Above street level, the buildings held restaurants, shops, bordellos, health clubs, theaters. Above this level began the apartments and offices. Beneath the street, the ground rumbled with the passing of subway trains. Warehouses, light industry occupied the subterranean city.

The street was crowded with students, out-of-town visitors seeking adventure and novelty. Groups of people talked, laughed, clowned, touched. Most were drunk or drugged on the spectrum of legal intoxicants. Lovers' games were played, lovers' affections were shown—kisses, intimate embraces, touches, whispers, and sexual acts among the range of human sexuality. The odors of food, perfume mingled in the cold air. Yes, life was good to these people.

People the same age as John, people with a future. Good jobs ahead, wives, children, homes. People who weren't hunted, who didn't fear the next moment. He chose a restaurant of moderate prices, near the end of the street where the crowds thinned. As they entered, her eyes scanned the dimly lit room. She clutched her phone. She had already chosen a North American carrier. No doubt the inspectors would know their location by her phone. They took a booth in the rear among empty booths that the bus boys had yet to clear. John sat and said nothing till the waitress took his order. Diana studied his eyes. Never had she seen a man more broken, empty, despairing. It seemed impossible that a man could continue to live in such a state.

"Life hurts, doesn't it, Johnny boy." A taunt clung to her words that shamed her.

"Yes, it does." He spoke sadly.

"Look, a good meal—paid for by me. A warm building on a cold night. An interesting search ahead. Cheer up. Take life one moment at a time. Remember the passage Henry read to us about being anxious?"

"Yes." His eyes lifted in skepticism.

"The Lord didn't bring you all this way to have your life fall apart!"

She remembered the end of the passage. "Seek ye first the Kingdom of God." The peace came again, overwhelmed her, crawled into every recess and stronghold of her mind, throughout every fiber of her body. A wisdom flooded her vision. She had a love for John. Even if they were caught, they could marry, be sent to a penal colony together. What was she saying? Her life was already a wasted wreck and would be again—without the Lord. She would lose the Lord if she turned her back on John.

The food came. He ate hungrily. Strange, how his body wanted to live even as he had no interest. She seemed eager to talk. "You might find the clue, might be responsible for doing something big for God. If not, you can follow your first plan, something about eating insects and drinking honey."

"That was eating locusts and wild honey." He smiled pensively as he remembered first speaking of the subject to her. She laughed; her laughter pulled a deep, weak laughter from him. She couldn't call Immigration. The detectives would ask why she had come to this town. They would suspect John was here. They probably would drug her, and then he would have no chance to escape. Her life wasn't worth his. She wouldn't call—she'd give him an even break, though no one had ever done the same for her. John would do the same for her, of this she was certain. He was a man of character. He was a Miss Ames type—a giver, one who loved, cared.

Had Miss Ames known the Lord? Phrases Miss Ames had used came back to her vividly, phrases that today she had read in the Bible. The remembrances brought tears to her eyes. Miss Ames knew John's God! Foolish Americans, probably only a handful of these believers existed, and she had crossed paths with two of them. God must have a plan for her life; the coincidences were adding up, pointing to a direction. That straight and narrow road she had read about.

She liked this book called the Bible, wanted to live within it. Words, ideas flooded her mind about not living by bread alone but by the word of God, about worshiping Him alone, about repenting. Blessed are the poor in spirit, those that mourn, the meek, those who hunger and thirst for righteousness, the merciful, the pure in heart, peacemakers, the persecuted. She wanted to be salt and light! Where was her treasure? Whom did she serve?

Give it up, Diana Rochembeau! Give up your life! It is worthless without God! Her soul was screaming at her, an inner voice, within every cell of her body. Even if she did become a nurse; even if she had nice clothes and an apartment, even if she ate the choicest foods, she would have nothing—no peace, no direction, no truth. She would not allow herself to hurt this man who sat across from her. She wasn't about to cut his odds. She would stick by him, support him, love him—if he let her. Who cared where it all took her? To an early grave? Prison? She'd spit in the eyes of the world even as she blessed everyone who hurt her. Diana switched off her phone's power.

"Cheer up, *mon trésor*. I'm not going to call. I'm throwing in my lot with the Lord—the hell with the world!" Her voice held determination. She leaned over the table, came within inches of his face. She had never been so alive. "May I come along with you?"

She felt so light, so free. The weight of the past, the world had been lifted from her shoulders. She studied his eyes.

"You're looking at me as if I'm lying! I'm serious!"

The bartender and waitresses heard her, stopped their work and stared. She reached up with both hands and pinched the skin on his gaunt cheeks and shook. He smiled. She saw his disbelief would not depart.

"Sure."

***

They stood at the old gates of the seminary campus; the residential streets behind them were empty. John clutched the seventy-five-year-old map. The main college campus was to their right, hugging an unseen lake. By the absence of light in the sky, John knew ag land surrounded half of the seminary campus. The college campus was separated from the seminary by a steep, wooded ravine. The college spread over the hills facing the lake; the seminary sat on gentle slopes. Large spreading trees dominated both campuses. They could see the lights of the college dormitories through the trees.

The seminary campus was comparatively dark. The high iron gate, hinged in brick, was shadowed by thick-trunked, gnarled oaks. The gate had ceased to be a main artery into the seminary grounds. A new road, hundreds of yards to their right, broke through the high iron fence that encircled the seminary. This new road was well lit, heavily traveled, as it had direct access to the newer facilities on campus.

One lone light shown down upon the old gate. The gate was closed but not locked and gave the appearance of having been blown shut. He peered into the darkness of the campus, saw a few lights, many huge trees, lawns, woods. Rising above the trees, on the high ground, the top floors of modern buildings could be seen, as well as steeples, turrets, towers of an earlier architecture.

The trees groaned in the wind. The clouds raced across the sky. The white light of a full moon imparted an eeriness to the shadows and biting cold.

"I suppose the search starts here. Didn't Henry say something about a gate?" Her words came slowly, fatigue and cold were numbing her mind. If this was the result of less than twenty-four hours of activity and no sleep, what then must John's mind be fighting? A small rill flowed out from the grounds into a drainage ditch that passed under the gate. She listened to the water gurgle.

"I guess he did." His words were slurred through chattering teeth. The cold was effecting him more severely than her—he had no body fat. He scanned the streets of restored single dwellings and duplexes behind them. Probably the same buildings that had stood seventy-five years ago. "I'm seeing the same sights my great-grandfather did."

"I don't see any hiding place." She began a methodical pulling, tugging of the brick column to her left, then moved to the column on the right. She attempted to remove the capstones—no luck. With her feet, she scuffed the earth at the base of each column, moving aside the debris of leaves and turf with determined swings of her legs. The gurgling water reminded her that her body held water wanting release. John was dead on his feet, standing there dumbly; nothing could be accomplished that night.

"Let's get some rest, *mon bonheur*. Where are we going to sleep?"

He pointed with his chin, his hands deep within his pockets. He was bending at the knees, rising on his calves, attempting to keep his feet warm. "Back there, near the ag fields." He looked sheepishly at her. "What's a booner?"

She laughed delightedly. "You're my happiness. We'll work on pronunciation later." She returned her mind to the implications of his statement as to the sleep site. Looking across the campus, she suddenly was aware of the presence of evil. An unease stole over her, like that present when Henry had talked of the Beast. Oppressive, draining, malicious, and gloating were her first thoughts. The evil sat waiting. Should she tell John? Did he need more worry?

John was aware of movement along the iron fence, within the shadows of the partially leaved oaks. The wind abated for a moment, and he heard the gentle footfalls on the brick sidewalk.

"Come here."

She had never heard him talk in such a tone—demanding, authoritarian, uncompromising. She came to him expectantly and reluctantly. He unzipped the top portion of his jacket. The knife was waiting by his heart. He seemed taller, more rigid; the stupor of fatigue was gone. He grabbed her coat by the collar and pulled her tightly to him. He gazed directly into her eyes.

"A man is coming. To our right. Kiss me, embrace me."

She tried to pull away from him. His tone frightened her. He would not allow her to pull away. If she kissed him, he would know she needed him, she would be a burden. She didn't want to love him in this way—sexually.

Why was she resisting him? Foolish woman! He didn't need her, didn't want her; his future was set, misery was his course. The beautiful face; the green eyes misty, frightened; the soft lips; the smell of perfume upon her neck. She didn't want to be kissed, and he would kiss her. Her back stiffened as his lips met hers. She pushed at his chest. His lips were upon her chin, her neck, the small ears, her eyes.

The man was alongside them now; he slowed his walk, he passed. She was limp in John's arms. Her breath was sweet, her exhalations pulsing in his ear. He needed her—loved her.

She whispered. "John…John…let me go…please. Oh Lord, please…"

John glanced at the passing man. Diana took a step back. A huge man, solidly built, a shock trooper? A calf-length coat, a wool-brimmed hat. The carriage and stride of the man held something alien, not human but animal, not earthly but sub-earthly. The man caused John to shudder as if a high ordnance shock wave had passed through his body.

He had not released her collar. He pulled her into himself again. Looking into her eyes was life. He had never seen her vulnerable. She had spoken his name with a longing. Love, fear, confusion played in her eyes.

"You love me, don't you, *mon coeur*?" Her voice was soft, helpless, playful. Her lips begged for his. The scent of her sweet breath, hair, perfume pulled him toward her. He resisted. "I don't love anybody."

Why couldn't he admit it? What bitterness clung to him? "It's me you love."

She looked deeply into his eyes, smiled a soft, faint, knowing smile as she zipped up his jacket, smoothed the fabric upon his chest. The tears streaming down his checks told her the truth she needed to know.

He took her by the arm, opened the gate. Walking the old brick road, they toured the seminary of the past. The man had been no casual pedestrian. He walked the fence line with a purpose. A security guard? No uniform. A former shock trooper by the build. A killer of men, John was certain. Had that been Satan's man? Was Henry correct? Were the forces of evil waiting patiently for someone to uncover the hidden satanic bible? He knew he had reentered the world of violence he'd left on the front lines of Eastern Europe.

"Who was that man?" She saw him retreat into himself.

"Just a man." Why worry her? He saw Jones dying, men falling, from knife, laser, shrapnel. He saw corpses hanging from trees, lying on the earth, rotting in sunlight and shade. How men liked to kill. He felt the last despairing struggle of the knifed shock trooper. How many men had died under the laser fire of John the Baptist? He didn't want to enter the violence. That state of being where no mercy, no love, no meekness were allowed. That place of brutal logic, where life had no value, where men exalted over the suffering of others. Once he entered, he could only ultimately lose, however many battles he won. The state would crush him.

The lights were far between and blocked by thick branches. The moonlight hid and was revealed as the clouds wished. They turned from the brick walkway before they came upon the buildings of the old seminary campus. At the base of a bluff, where a small creek flowed, they saw a raccoon feeding in the water. They passed a power station, were behind the seminary buildings. In the reemerging moonlight, they easily followed a nature trail into a wooded area.

Somewhere within the woods, he left the path, moved down the slope of a hill. They stopped near the bottom of the slope, when through the trees they could see nothing but endless, flat fields.

"We're out of the wind. That must all be ag land." His chin pointed to the fields. She had never slept outside before, better not to bring up her fears. He used his hands like a broom, gathering up leaves into the shape of a rough rectangle. He threw sticks and rocks from the rectangle. The blankets were spread on the leaves, the chemical-heat release cords pulled. He stripped to his insulated underwear. She turned her head. He snuggled between the blankets.

"Come on. You'll stay warmer in your underwear."

"One false move, and I'll smash your face."

Her voice held no venom.

"No false moves."

His tone was dry. He turned his back, heard her move off in the woods—nature was calling. She returned and within minutes was between the covers, her back against his—the width of the covers left no choice. He chuckled.

"What?" she questioned defensively.

"Lucky I have these blankets, because you don't give off much heat."

"Go to sleep." She spoke in mock annoyance. No retort came—he was asleep.

Her twenty-four-hour deadline would pass as she slept. He seemed unaware of what she had given up. She would not remind him; remembering she was a fugitive would add to his burden. He wasn't insensitive, just worn to a frazzle. He was definitely worried about that man who had passed. Strange how she had thrown her life away, all its hopes, expectations, comforts, and felt no remorse—only joy.

She had purpose—to follow God, to help John. She had peace. She had given up everything for these. She had lost her life, and she had found it—Christ had said this is the way it would be. Everything in that book was coming true. Why did God love her? This was the mystery that puzzled her. She was a mean-spirited nobody, worse in conduct than the woman at the well. Henry had known the Holy Spirit was upon her. What did it all mean? She slept.

CHAPTER 8

He awoke with her head nestled upon his neck, his hands around her waist. Her heat, her scent soothed him. She seemed so small in sleep. Her hair was soft against his cheek. He smiled as he noticed her brown roots appeared. He lifted his head; hers fell gently, turning toward him.

He studied her face, the firm but delicate jaw, the soft flawless skin. The lips that hinted of fullness smiled. He enjoyed the pattern and placement of each hair within her eyebrows. She must call Immigration. With a start, he realized the end of her twenty-four hours had passed in the night. His mental acuity was far worse than he had realized.

Why had she thrown her life away? She had incredible beauty, a natural intelligence—he thought of how quickly she had grasped his talk of God, the new terms thrown at her. She could improvise, she had readily adapted to wearing his clothing, sleeping outside. She knew how to read the moment, as witnessed by her fainting spell at the airport.

She was a gambler, a risk taker, or she would not have come to the States, would not have followed him. She was physically tough, had pushed her body on the long walk and subsequent journey and never complained. Her humor appealed to him—her use of personas, the nicknames *mon bébé, chéri, trésor, bonheur, mon coeur*. He thought *bébé* was baby and *coeur* was heart—he knew that from somewhere within the mind. She was loyal, faithful, and somewhere deep inside, she was giving, loving. This woman with so much potential had followed him. What a wasted life!

If she had deserted him in the restaurant, he would have given up. He kissed her gently on the lips. Her legs moved; her hands grasped his waist. The iridescent green eyes opened, smiled. She kissed him upon the lips, searched his eyes for his thoughts, said nothing. He spoke softly. "Why did you stay? Why did you throw your life away? Why did you waste yourself on me?"

She turned her head quizzically, his voice had quavered, cracked, and a tear had come before he had willed control over his emotions. Her eyes gleamed happily—he loved her. She spoke carefully, slowly. "You were kind to me and honest, treated me as if I had worth. You showed me your God, and He gave me peace and purpose. You're a good man, John Johnson. You threw your life away when you followed your Lord. I had to do the same for you. Didn't Jesus waste His life on us?"

"To the world, we're trash," he whispered.

She studied his eyes, wondering why he had brought up such a subject. She stroked his face with her free hand. She spoke determinedly. "Look, mon coeur…that means *my heart,* if you have forgotten. You're my heart, John. The future is going to be rough. The world didn't give Christ any breaks, and we can't expect any either. But we have each other, and we have God."

He studied her face and eyes and felt her determination. "Let's rise and shine, then," he said, smiling. John was in love.

***

They sat in a student lounge at a long table designed for eating or the piling of backpacks, computers, water bottles and lunches. Few people were in the lounge so early; custodians sat on a sofa and drank coffee. One lone student read in an easy chair. John and Diana had bought their breakfast from a wall of food vending machines. Diana had finished, John continued to eat. Both thought upon the church and cemetery they had passed on their way to the lounge.

"What do you think?" he asked as he began eating from the last food container.

"The church was a blank to me. Lots of statues and a prominent cornerstone. How could your great-grandfather put the book in or behind a cornerstone without an involved and noisy process? The statues seemed clean—you'd have to lift each one from its base to be sure. In the cemetery, the statue of the general looked promising, but the connection was vague, and the statue was all in one piece."

He leaned over the table as he ate. "I don't think the general has any possibilities—no biblical connection. Still, we could check the paving stones around the monument, maybe under one of those?"

Her hands were upon the table; he touched her fingers. She grasped his hand firmly as she spoke.

"I don't know, something seems wrong—we're missing the key. We've got one more church, a fountain, your great-grandfather's office, and a general look around."

She slid the map that was beyond his food tray over to herself. She silently studied the map. He spoke after the final spoon drags over the bottom of the food container.

"The key, in my opinion, are the Daniel passages. They refer to the future coming. Daniel saw the world's end. Daniel—"

A man sat at their table, directly across from them. He had come upon them when they had both been concentrating on the map. A cold wave of shock passed through John: this was the man from the night before. The calf-length coat, folded once, and brimmed wool hat had been placed on the table as he sat. The man stared at them, waiting to make eye contact.

John looked up. The face was wide, the eyes piercing blue, the hair blond, cut short. The jaw was massive, solid. The right ear had been severed in half. The eyes penetrated, with no hint of intelligence or of dullness, only a mirroring blankness.

The man was pushing forty, broad shouldered, bull necked, barrel chested. Even sitting, he loomed over John. Storm trooper? The size, the musculature devoid of fat said, "Yes, storm trooper." Some other undiscernible quality in the posture, the musculature hinted of an untampered natural size and strength.

The man was a killer. John had stood beside many such men on the front. These men had an aura about them of invincibility, arrogance, confidence that dominated, suppressed, drained the power of lesser men. A deranged soul lived within the body, one that delighted in broken bones, rent flesh, tortured minds. The soul fed upon the fear of its victims, the dazed moist eye, the quivering flesh, the muscular weakness, the stuporous movements, the cries. Unlike most men who killed, this man did not need the frenzy of the pack, the legitimacy gained from the group. Nor could he be bounded by fear or remorse. This man was of Satan's legion.

John glanced at Diana; she was unaware of the man's evil and his power.

The man spoke. "Hello."

The voice was not guttural or heavily masculine. The limberness of the tongue hinted at a facile mind, a mind that could torture with words, ideas as easily as the body could with strength.

"Hello," John answered cheerily.

"Need some help? I noticed you looking at that old map."

Diana spoke. "We found it in a downtown antique shop and thought it would be interesting to see how the seminary has changed."

John glanced at the hands of the man upon the table, fingers interlocked, relaxed. The hands were huge; muscles bulged between each joint. Scar tissue flecked the knuckles. Such hands could pull a living body apart.

"Are you students here?"

"No, just visitors—thinking of becoming students. Are you security?" asked Diana.

"In a sense." The man smiled as the top half of his ear moved imperceptibly. The blank eyes suddenly focused, pierced the gaze of John and Diana. John believed he perceived a smile. The man rose slowly, gathered up his coat and hat, spoke. "What antique shop was that? I would like to see if they have another."

Diana answered, "Somewhere on the main street. We only saw one map in the store."

"I understand." The man turned to leave.

"Who are you?" Diana spoke loudly, hiding her demand in a friendly tone. He turned back to her, stared into her eyes.

"By name I am Cain. But I am what you make of me."

Cain walked across the lounge and out the doors. John noticed the litheness in the muscular legs and hips and the doglike gait of power and stamina. A man of his age, with a body that evidently had seen hard use, should have had a stiffness, a weariness. Cain had the suppleness, agility of a boy, the strength of a man. The body exuded an incredible internal power.

"What was that about?" Diana's eyes narrowed in worry as she looked at John.

"He's the guardian. Satan's man waiting for us to appear and show us where the book is. He's the man who passed us at the gate last night—a guard dog patrolling. But why would he make himself known?"

"Why not? Perhaps he wanted a good look at us? Or maybe he wanted to assure himself we are the people he has been waiting for?"

John did not respond. He wondered what this man would do to them once the satanic bible had been located. Diana stood.

"Come on, let's go and get it over with."

She moved behind John, rubbed his neck muscles deeply. She knew a dangerous man when she saw one, and Cain was dangerous. John would have no chance against him; she prayed a confrontation would never occur. How incredible that Henry had been right about the message! How incredible that she was a part of this search!

***

The fountain was located in the center of the original seminary plaza, from which lecture halls, classrooms radiated. In the center of the now empty pool was a bronze statue of Michael, the archangel. His sword was raised, a host of angels were circled around his feet, engaged in a battle with serpents and dragons. The figures wrestled, stabbed, and slashed with swords. The serpents and dragons bared fang, teeth, claws; they writhed and bled. The plaque on the fountain's rim read:

And there was war in heaven: Michael and his angels fought against the dragon; and the dragon fought and his angels,

And prevailed not; neither was their place found anymore in heaven. (Rev. 12:7, 8)

"What do you think?" The words came stiffly from his mouth, his jaws and lips impaired by the cold. His condensed breath formed a gray, smokey trail lost quickly in the wind. The wind had already robbed him of the heat that had collected in his clothing from the lounge. The coffee he had drunk only minutes before was cold in his bladder.

"I don't know." Diana leafed through her Bible as watery mucus dripped from her nose. She wiped away the mucus with the back of her gloved hand. Her nose was red.

John spoke. "The passage seems to fit Daniel."

"Look! Daniel 10:21. 'But I will shew thee that which is noted in the scripture of truth: and there is none that holdeth with me in these things, but Michael your prince.' Who is Michael?" Frustration clung to her words.

"He is an angel of the Lord. A soldier of the Lord. The dragon is a symbol for Satan, as are the serpents."

"Here is Michael again. 'Michael, one of the chief princes, came to help me; and I remained there with the kings of Persia.' I don't know what this all means—you know more about the Bible than I do—but the location on campus seems too obvious."

"But an easy place for a desperate man to reach. So obvious as to be unsuspected?" queried John.

"No. Fountains are serviced; pipes are dug up; cracks repaired, especially over the course of seventy-five years. Your great-grandfather would have had to come in the middle of the night to hide something here. They had security back then. He would have had tools, made noise. Besides all that, I don't see any hiding places. Not on the statue or in the fountain, or even around the fountain."

He took her jacket by the waist and shook her playfully as he pulled her close. "You're so smart. 'Ears to hear, eyes to see.'" Her presence allowed him to joke, to cast away the anxiety and weariness.

"'Eyes to see, ears to hear.'" She repeated the words plainly, slowly, attempting to hear in a new way. "Let's go to your great-grandfather's office."

John studied the map as they began walking. They left the plaza, went down a gentle slope, and emerged on the old roadway. The building sat at the bottom of a shale cliff. The cliff was covered in ivy, honeysuckle, scrubby sumac trees. The brick of the building matched the old roadway and the brick of the buildings of the plaza. He surmised all had been built in the same phase of construction.

Many of the building's windows were boarded. Four turrets rose from the angles of the rectangular shape. They saw no evidence of human activity, except for a new lock on an old door. The lock was open. A squirrel scampered into a cracked window above the door. Diana pulled at his arm.

"I don't see any reason to go in. If there had been something hidden, it would have been found. You don't even know what room the office was in."

"Number 315. End of the hall on the left."

She shook her head in annoyance at this thoroughness. He understood she anticipated danger. He had the same foreboding. They entered. The ground floor had been gutted and turned into a maintenance storage area. Mowers, snow removers, and blowers sat. White light filtered through the unboarded, dirt-streaked windows. Mixing with the smell of grease, oil was the musty odor of mice and squirrel nests. He heard a squirrel gnawing somewhere in the rafters.

The second floor consisted of rooms used for storage. Stacked chairs, tables, boxes were glimpsed through cracks in doors or walls. The cold lay in the building; the smell of dust was heavy. The floorboards creaked.

On the third floor, the rooms were intact, the room numbers still upon the original doors. John looked into the first room at the top of the stairs. A few boxes were stored; the walls, floors, ceiling appeared to be original. He sensed a person on the floor—perhaps he caught the slightest scent of human odor, beyond where his conscious mind could identify. He moved slowly, quietly to the end of the hall.

He opened the door slowly; by the increase in light, he knew the room had a window. Diana was at his shoulder. His hand was within his jacket, clasped upon his knife.

Cain began laughing at the frightened faces of his guests. He sat in a straight-backed chair that was angled to face both window and door. On a far table sat electronic equipment. The laughter held no anger. Cain seemed pleased at their presence; an aura of friendship was exuded. Diana pulled at John.

"Come on, let's go."

Cain smiled, spoke. "You are in my home. You are safe. Stay."

John eased. Cain would not harm them—they had yet to find the book. Cain had anticipated them searching the former office. All doubts were gone as to Cain's identity and purpose. Diana ceased pulling John's arm.

"What do you do here?" She could think of nothing else to say.

"I do my master's work."

"Your master is Satan," said John flatly, with no tone of accusation. John methodically took inventory of the room. Cain had no weapon upon him, but on the table of electronic gear John saw a dagger and a laser pistol.

Cain laughed again. "He gives me freedom. Allows me to be what I am. He never casts me away from his presence or takes his spirit from me. The god you worship is the evil one."

John fully realized Cain had been expecting them, and that Cain must have other men watching their movements. John recognized Cain's words to be a mockery of the words spoken by King David in a Psalm. John knew he was being pulled into a debate, yet he felt powerless to remain quiet. "You withhold from the true master your life. Who atones for your sins?"

"I have no sin. I am who I am. What is mine is mine." Cain's eyes gleamed with haughtiness and anger. "Tread lightly on the ground you walk. It is not your time to die, but I can give you pain." Cain analyzed the stratagems welling in his mind. He could hurt both of them or one—just enough pain to frighten or even to produce a spilling of their thoughts on the location of his bible. The anger and hatred they would then have would only hurt their clarity of mind in the search. He needed them mildly carefree and confident.

The threat sent chills and a weakness through John. His body began to tremble. Cain's voice had come in a deep, reverberating tone totally different from what John had considered his normal voice. John realized, with a calm alarm, he had heard the voice of Satan speaking through Cain. Cain was possessed. This fact perfectly fit the strangeness of events and seemed unworthy of further thought.

What had been said that aroused the anger? Had Cain sensed the absence of fear? Or was the threat to place them in a state of anxiety, emotional imbalance? Cain, again, had mocked the scripture—the very name of God, I Am, spoken to Moses. Cain appraised John, moving his eyes slowly from feet to head. The goodwill, friendliness of his opening words were gone. Disgust and mockery gleamed in the eyes as he studied the thin form. He stared at John's crotch and smirked.

Diana saw and understood the stare; she had seen men in their games many times. The tactics, the mind behind the stare, were not new to John; still, he had difficulty remaining poised.

Cain spoke again. "What do you have that I don't have in abundance?"

"Eternal life."

"I have eternal life. Is it not written in your book: "If anyone slays Cain, vengeance shall be taken on him sevenfold"?

Was Cain claiming to be immortal? Diana pulled slowly, determinedly at John's sleeve. Cain recognized the surprise on John's face.

"Yes, I'm immortal, though it was not your god who made me thus but the true God—the one who accepted my offering. Cain's eyes became soft as he turned inward to the past. Satan seemed to have retreated, leaving Cain, the man. "I've been a soldier in the struggle. You should understand—a soldier yourself."

Cain's tone embraced John as a brother, a man who knew war, shared the same experiences of hardship, misery, victory, and exaltation. John thought it strange that Cain, the man, knew loneliness. How much of the life of John Johnson did Cain know?

"I've crushed Jew and Christian." Cain's words were not a boast—only the musings of the past. "Nothing on this earth can withstand my Lord." Exaltation was missing from his voice, as if somewhere deep inside he wished someone could withstand his god. "Join the winning side and taste victory." Cain searched John's eyes, seeking a brother.

"Christ is the winning side. Your master has never beaten Him, and He is in me."

"Christ?" Cain, the man, was gone; Satan spoke. "How many times must I slay His people for you to understand He can't help you. I've seen men with ten times your faith, and they died by my hands. I've slain Christ's men while they read their holy book, while they prayed, in their churches, as they fought. If this parasite Christ is in His people as He claims, then why do I destroy them? Am I not destroying Him? If God protects me and destroys Christ, then who is God?

"Doubtless, you have read: 'Every Kingdom divided against itself is laid waste, and no city or house divided against itself will stand,'" Cain said. "'If Satan casts out Satan, he is divided against himself. How then will his kingdom stand?'

"I ask you. If Christ cannot create victory in His people, then how can His kingdom stand? The Jew performed a few magic tricks while He lived. He died and has no kingdom. But look at *our* kingdom—the world united, prosperous, men free!"

John answered quietly. "Free from truth, free from God. The perfect kingdom is coming."

"What coming kingdom? The earth continues as it has from the beginning. We see the fullness of our kingdom now—Babylon has arisen." The challenging, aggressive tone died, and the implorings of a man began. "Stop denying yourself and live—live like you were meant to live since the beginning of creation. What pleasures could be yours, John! Women to thrill under your body—of all types, all personalities! Realms of thought—theology, sociology, any that you wish—so deep, powerful, beautiful, flowing like rivers through your mind. Power, wealth, strength..." Cain's eyes held an ecstasy.

"My pleasure is in following the Truth. The True God owns me, and that is enough."

Cain locked his eyes upon Diana, who was peering over John's shoulder. She had seen lust many times; her stomach turned in revulsion.

"I know a thousand ways to give pleasure to the flesh," Cain said to her. "In the cult temples, women worshiped me as a god. What do you want with this worn, lifeless, effeminate boy?"

Cain waited for an answer as he studied John's reaction to his words. John remained impassive. Inside he raged. He could not escape the world of violence, violent men. He had met the first challenge in the war, only to have it reappear again. When would God give him a moment of respite? Why did the same challenges come to haunt him? When did the struggle end?

"If it is my pleasure, I will take your woman and abuse her before your eyes," Cain said. "She will know a man truly a man and never want you again. And if she still wishes to cling to you, I will take her apart piece by piece till there is nothing more to take. You will do nothing. You will be paralyzed in fear. Look! Even now you have no strength. You tremble in my presence!"

John remained silent. He had no strength; he was trembling in fear. He knew Cain was stronger. John raged at the Lord for allowing his weakness. Cain watched curiously. Recognition flashed in John's mind. How clever and subtle was Cain—his outpouring of bravado, arrogance, dominance, his threats had been meant to raise from the dead the natural man. To make a man rage against God, that was Satan's deceit, and it would only result in a man's defeat.

Cain wanted confrontation on his terms; he wanted raw emotion, wanted a response. Raise that earthly man, that man who wanted to conquer by physical power, who wanted to hurt. Abuse the man who had hurt and abused him. Cain wanted to see himself mirrored in John—then the flesh would have won. The truth was that Cain could destroy John Johnson acting in his natural strength. Submit to the truth! Trust God! John laughed as he found the key: submission.

"You are right, Cain. You could do all that you say—if the True God was not upon His throne. If Christ weren't within me."

Satan's voice in Cain raged. "I've told you what I've done to Christ's men!"

John ignored the anger. "I'm leaving now. I'm sure we will meet again. There is still time to give your allegiance to Christ."

John turned his back on Cain, took Diana by the arm, and left.

Cain laughed mockingly. The eyes of Cain glowed with immeasurable hatred, loathing. The Enslaver, the parasite, would never have his soul—never!

John trembled as they hurried out of the building. Diana had never seen him afraid, and his fear caused her to fear. He had stood before Cain calmly, but the calm had disappeared the moment they walked out the door. John knew he had spread his fear to Diana. She had never seen the flesh mutilated, mangled, never seen men in their death throes. The flesh was capable of great agonies, excruciating pain. Cain's threats were real. She had not lived and fought with such men, had not seen the brutality within man.

She understood John's fear of Cain; the fear coursed through her body. Nothing could be gained by dwelling upon Cain's threats. She spoke. "There's the church."

She thrust her chin toward the long brownstone structure. Even her mannerisms were becoming like his, she thought, not at all displeased. The church roof had great height, increased markedly by the tall steeple. Two huge beech trees with gnarled branches, the smooth gray bark scarred with initials, anchored the entrance of the church. The red wooden doors, heavily reinforced with iron, were overshadowed by a bas-relief of angels, gargoyles, the faces of saints.

They studied the bas-relief without exchanging a word. Diana drifted to the cemetery hugging the side of the church. Pines and hemlocks shadowed the worn tombstones, and moss splattered northern exposures. Tombstones from the early seventeen hundreds. The wind whipped the evergreens. John spoke. "Let's get out of the cold."

John moved toward the doors. She ran up to him playfully, then pulled back suddenly from the doors. He scanned the campus, searching for Cain's men, who were, without doubt, watching. He placed his hand on the massive iron door handle as he studied her eyes. She had a premonition of danger. He watched her breathe deeply as her body shook. She smiled weakly. He opened the door.

The sanctuary was long, narrow; columns lined the sides. Stained-glass windows began high on the walls. Shadow and darkness were broken by beams of blue, red, yellow light stained from their penetration of the colored glass. The light seemed to carry an electricity within, as if it were living. Candles burned on a massive and ornate altar. The busts of saints stared down

In the Shadow of Babylon

from the columns. Incense burned by the altar; the smoke formed layers in the undisturbed air. The stone building held only the warmth of the candles.

A black-robed priest, facing and kneeling at the altar, had gone undetected until he rose. As they walked forward, they heard his chanting. Diana moved into a pew and sat. John followed. The chanting echoed through the stillness. A timelessness was within the sound, an antiquity, a reverence, a holiness that lulled the senses into peace, serenity. The sound was hypnotizing. The chanting built in speed and volume, the priest signed before the host of candles and small statues. The candles flickered with the movement of his arms. The incense soaked into the clothing, skin of John and Diana. The chant ended. The priest turned, spoke.

"You have finally come." The words, given in a conversational tone, echoed loudly down the aisle to John and Diana.

"We are here." A humor was hidden in John's matter-of-fact reply. The priest walked toward them with a smile on his face, a hidden displeasure in his eyes. The echoing sound of his heels on the stone floor spoke of determination. He stood before John and Diana. The eyes seemed slightly glazed.

"Come with me." The tone was warm. The priest was a small man with a heavy, dark growth on a round face. Incense clung and hid within his dark robe. "Come." The priest offered his hand to Diana. John stiffened as he noticed Diana leaning forward as if to rise. She sank back, responding to John's movement and her own common sense. The priest smiled. "Remain here if that is what you prefer."

"That is what we prefer," John said gruffly.

"You've come to find the book," the priest stated.

"If you say so." John studied the priest's eyes.

"I do. And what of the Lord of this earth? Why do you refuse his sovereignty and work against him?" The priest's head twisted as he spoke, as if attempting to pull out the objecting thread of dissension with his teeth. The priest faced Diana, his countenance and tone became fatherly. "You know him well. You are yet free. Don't bind yourself to a god who can only bring you pain and hardship."

John felt Diana's body trembling. The priest continued. "You will serve us in the end. We will allow you to search for the book; perhaps you will find it. Then, we will take it from you. We've already searched those places you've gone and others besides.

"'The stone which the builders rejected, the same is become the head of the corner: this is the Lord's doing, and it is marvelous in our eyes?'" The eyes of the priest bored into the eyes of John and Diana; their discomfort brought him happiness.

"For seventy-five years we've searched, and with the aid of the greatest minds, the most advanced equipment. You're wasting your time," the priest said. "In the end, you will have nothing to show for your effort—nothing but our wrath. But if you cooperate, allow us to help you understand your foolishness, then we will reward you generously."

The priest focused his benign eyes upon John. "You want a woman, John. I sense your loneliness, your emptiness. Why hasn't Christ filled your need? He can't. You want a caring woman, full breasted, warm, loving, to give you children. A home…" The voice was so persuasive; warmth came from every word. "Quiet, woods, streams, a farm. No one seeking your life, no one. Time to think, to read, then outdoor work. That is your paradise. My lord can give you those things."

John shook his head. Forced his mind through the warm haze that had enveloped him. The peace was like a drug within him…he was drifting into the priest's words…it seemed so good. Why couldn't he resist? His tongue would not move. He must deny these feelings. God had given him a woman—Diana.

The priest turned to Diana.

"Young woman, you want a man to love you—your mind, your thoughts, your very being. If I can read your thoughts, how much more one of our men can meld into you. You don't have to go back to your former life. You were in the wrong profession—that was a mistake, an error. You did not sin, and you are no sinner for not knowing what you wanted. Don't turn your back on life, on our god, just because of a mistake.

"Why allow them to bind you with their laws? The law of life is happiness, not struggle, not guilt, doubt, slavery to a demanding god. You are what you are—that is god's promise to you. He can make you forget the past without a single confining law to bind you. I can feel you coming to him."

He spoke with such eloquence and emotion. Love exuded from his voice. His warmth was probing her soul. She felt so relaxed, weak. The warmth penetrated. She stiffened. He wanted to rape her soul. Power and anger flooded her body. She would never go back, never! He was a liar. A damned liar who only wanted to possess her soul. He wanted power over her like so many had wanted in the past.

"No," she said weakly, in a whisper. "No!" she shouted. The warmth was engulfing her, fighting to enter her soul. She lunged forward, her fist shot out, caught the round face solidly on the cheek. The priest, recoiling from the heavy blow, slipped off the pew to the floor. Diana was up, pulling John from his seat. John was on his knees, crawling toward the door. What had happened to him?

The priest stood, red faced, embarrassed but made no effort to follow. "You belong to him; don't resist. I am always here for you."

John had gained his feet. She pushed open the door; the cold air hit them. She was sobbing, still shaking off the invisible demon that clung to her. "I'll never go back. Never! Never! They will never have me."

John's eyes were opened wide. He watched her pacing. The stupor was leaving his body. He inhaled deeply of the cold air. The incense still clung to his clothing. He realized, with confusion and then certainty, the incense was an airborne drug! The effects of the scent had been magnified by his weakened condition. A fury had been unleashed in Diana. She paced stiffly, her muscles hardened, her movements agitated. She broke her pace, turned toward the doors. He thought it not impossible that she could kill the priest.

He placed himself in front of the doors. "Nothing good can happen if you enter."

Her eyes were hard, steely. Her words burst angrily into the cold air. "Why won't they leave me alone? Why do they haunt me? Why do they try to pull me back? He doesn't know me…what I want. He wears a black robe and thinks he can do and say anything. I don't want any more of this world! I've had enough of lies and liars."

She tried to force her way past John. He held her arms in a bear hug. She struggled, twisting, her head whipping, attempting to strike him. The explosive anger died in his confining arms. The struggle ceased; the body went limp. He held her. She spoke as she sobbed. "I'm no good, John. So many men have entered me…so many…Oh God, forgive me! God, forgive me! I'm so filthy…Don't love me! Don't…"

"Christ wants you." John spoke calmly, slowly, as he attempted to place his eyes to hers. "Christ wants you. He can make you clean! Give you a new life! I love you, Diana! Give yourself to Christ!"

"I can't."

"Do you love to hate yourself? Or do you truly hate your past? Give yourself to Christ!"

"I can't."

"You can't or you don't want to?"

Her sobbing was deep, she mumbled words. He heard. "Louder."

"I want to…" Her voice was weak. "I want to. I want to. I want to. I want Jesus! Oh God, help me!"

She raised her red, tear-stained face to the sky. Her hands went to the heavens as if she could reach up and touch God. God was not in the heavens; He was beside her; He was within her. God touched her. It began within her torso—a bubbling, a gushing volume, continually welling up, flooding her soul, her mind, her heart. The living waters, the living waters

Henry had read about! What Jesus had promised the woman at the well. The Holy Spirit! Given to her!

She stood dumbfounded, enraptured as the cleansing rinsed through her body. The past was gone, washed away, no more guilt or shame. She felt such pity for the dead Diana, the Diana that was. Now she belonged to God. He really did love her, cared about her—He had died for her. He would always be with her, the Living God within her, beside her.

The joy and the peace would not stop flooding her soul. Her hands came down. John had said he loved her? Hadn't she heard that through her tears?

"This is glorious! Wonderful!"

She grasped John by his jacket and shook. She looked into his eyes. How worn he was, yet the eyes gleamed—he knew what was happening. She searched the campus. Far across a broad lawn she saw someone walking. She began waving her arms, ran toward him. He was too far. She turned to come back to John. He was running to catch her. His arms were opened wide. She hugged and kissed him. She was crying tears of joy as she laughed. He laughed and cried with her, tasted the salt of her tears. He loved her.

***

They searched the entire campus, hand in hand, had lunch in the student center, then went back to all the likely locations and searched again. They blended easily with the student population. The wind and cold did not abate. She was changing before his eyes. A reserve had been dropped; the hard exterior was gone. An emotion, an agape love was upon her face and in her voice. She became playfully coy, a girlishness long suppressed emerged. He willingly was drawn into her. He laughed at her witticisms and unending stream of comments. Her tongue had been unleashed and spoke of the joy within.

They stood in the foyer of the library unable to enter the library proper for lack of a student card. The heat soaked into their worn bodies. John went to the restroom. Diana walked the wings of the foyer. She studied the collection of old books, Bibles, trophies, memorabilia, displayed in the glass-enclosed cases. Pictures of alumni, professors, administrators hung from the walls. The cases had been dedicated the year John's great-grandfather died.

John returned to her.

"Let's go eat and call it a day."

She held his arm, her arm twining into his pocket, where her gloved hand touched his. She sensed his mood darkening. They walked out of the library; the sun was close to the horizon. He spoke.

"There's something wrong."

"How could that be?" Everything was wrong externally. Inwardly, she had peace.

"This is serious."

"I know, but so is God. We will find the key."

He smiled at her faith, but the disturbance didn't leave. "They had seventy-five years. They would have found the book."

"Why didn't they lie and say they had? You see, John, they have confidence in us—their enemies! Why can we find the documents, and they—with all the time, technology, and brains—can't? There is something about us that is different," she said. "We have a different perspective that allows us to see and to hear."

"The Bible, please," John said.

She rummaged in her pocket, handed him the book. He found Matthew 13:14 and read aloud, "And in them is fulfilled the prophecy of Esaias, which saith, By hearing ye shall hear, and shall not understand; and seeing ye shall see, and shall not perceive.

"'For this people's heart is waxed gross, and their ears are dull of hearing, and their eyes they have closed; lest at any time they should see with their

As he ate his meal, she neatly undressed to her thermals, folding her clothes to use them as a pillow. She opened a meal as she sat on the leafy mattress, pulled a blanket over her. He gazed into the dark woods. The wind whipped the treetops. He wondered about the future. Even if they found the book, could they escape Cain's men? And where were the inspectors, the police? The Lord knew the answers. He had not brought them this far to watch them fail.

John undressed to his thermals, entered the blankets sitting upright, bringing his clothes along. He faced her, looked into the green eyes, as he gently held her arm from reaching for another spoonful of food.

"You know I love you."

She smiled sweetly. "I know you do. I heard you say it at the church. I love you, John, and always will. You're my buddy, my man. The best that's ever happened to me. You are my heart, mon coeur. I trust you."

He leaned into her ear and quietly spoke. "You're my pal, my woman. The best that's ever happened to me. My treasure, my heart. I trust you." She placed her finished meal aside and put her arm around him, kissed his cheek. She had never felt such contentment and love. She sank into the blankets as he remained sitting, eating. "Good night, my heart, my treasure, my happiness."

"Good night, my blessing."

CHAPTER 9

She awoke with a deep sense of calm. Cain prowled the edges of this calm but could not penetrate. Her God was greater than Cain. The answer had been given to her; all she had to do was bring it to light. The leaves on the ground were white with frost. The highest tree limbs, those that caught the wind rushing over the hill, were creaking, clashing, tossing. The wind was a dull roar in her ears. The temperature was lower than the day before, the sunlight brilliant, the sky clear.

She studied John's face as he slept. She loved everything about him now. His face was handsome, his physique noble. His arm was about her waist; this made her happy. A penal colony with her treasure was sufficient hope for her. He had seen a goodness in her when her mind was still wrapped in darkness. A goodness she had not understood but to which she had been destined. She had to be his strength, his mind, his heart until this mystery was resolved. He would be her authority, her leader. She wanted him to need her so that she might give back to him the love he had given her.

She leaned over him and with a small leaf taken from her clothing, traced his ear. His hand went to his ear twice, his eyes opened slowly to see her smiling at him. Her voice came smoothly, syrupy with love.

"Good morning…my treasure.…beau…"

"Stop," he said sheepishly. She liked his shyness.

"Day," she said firmly. "You didn't let me finish. Good morning. Beautiful day! You think you're beautiful?"

She burrowed her face into his neck and shook. He lovingly grabbed her hair with both hands, steadied her face before his. "But I am your treasure?" he asked.

"Yes, you are."

"Do you have an answer to the puzzle?" he asked.

"I will as soon as you give me a Bible," she said with confidence.

With one hand he reached into the rucksack, pulled out the Bible, and gave it to her.

"If we look at the passages, Christ will give us the answer. Think about it, John. The words of the Bible cling to the Holy Spirit because it was the Spirit Who spoke those words."

He wondered where she had gotten this wisdom. With a schoolteacher's purpose and tone, she continued talking.

"Let's read the stone-which-is-rejected passages. Matthew 21:42. 'Did ye never read in the scriptures: The stone which the builders rejected, the same is become the head of the corner: this is the Lord's doing, and it is marvelous in our eyes?'

"Now Mark 12:10. 'And have ye not read this scripture…'

"And in Luke 20:17. 'What is this then that is written…'

"Let's go to John 4 to read of the well and the living water." She scanned the text, her brow furrowed. "No mention of scripture."

She skimmed through chapter 4 to chapter 5.

"In 5:39 Christ says, 'Search the scriptures; for in them ye think ye have eternal life: and they are they which testify of me.'"

John slowly reached for the Bible. "You've gotten off the track, maybe? Jesus as stone—remember the rock at Horeb?"

By using the margin notes, he was given the list of supporting scripture for Jesus as stone.

"John 7:37…" He turned the pages and read, "'In the last day, that great day of the feast, Jesus stood and cried, saying, If any man thirst, let him come unto me, and drink. He that believeth on me, as the scripture hath said, out of his belly shall flow rivers of living water.'"

He looked at her triumphantly. She smiled modestly. "You are right," he said quietly.

His face clouded with perplexity. "Where is the scripture we seek?"

She clapped her hands gleefully like a child and laughed. "In the library—old Bibles, made of paper. Thick, huge Bibles in enclosed cases. The cases were dedicated the same year your great-grandfather died. The book we want is in one of those Bibles." Her wide eyes stared into the narrow, slitted eyes of John. He squinted to penetrate her truth revealed. "Yes, yes, I see…"

She began again. "That's why the Satanic forces couldn't find their book. The scripture is a blank nothingness to them, an impenetrable wall. Their senses are dead because they don't have the Spirit. But we, who know Christ, are driven by the Spirit into the scripture. The word of God is alive to us, in us. They couldn't think of looking literally into the Bible, even though it is tangible, real, like any hiding place must be. Their minds couldn't break the barrier to true hearing, seeing."

She flopped on top of him and mussed his hair before rising to her knees. John smiled softly; her affections were like living water to his soul. He spoke thoughtfully, "Those cases are probably vacuum sealed. Chances are they haven't been disturbed in seventy-five years. The perfect hiding place. All we need is a plan." He kissed her on the cheek repeatedly, rapidly, impulsively, in an outpouring of euphoria. He jumped to his feet. "Let's go to the library."

and never will be. You will make wrong decisions, and you will hate God sometimes. Tell Him what is bothering you instead of holding it in." She laughed. "Look! He's given you me, mon chéri! Your prayers are being answered. He has a good life planned for you."

"Yeah, I'm sure." His voice was emotionless even as he smiled.

She stopped suddenly, stomped her foot in annoyance. "But you don't really believe. Be honest."

"No, I don't really believe that I will see any goodness on this earth. But I am thankful for you."

"And I am thankful for you." She grasped his hand tightly. She moved ahead, pulling him along when she saw desire in his eyes.

"John, don't you understand? God has trained you for this task since you were a child. You are the only one who can pull this off. He had to train you hard. You were a soldier. You know what it means to train."

Where was she getting these ideas? They came straight from the Bible, but she had only read one book: Matthew. Or had she? Her words were those of Paul in the Epistles. The Spirit had given her all knowledge. Her words comforted him, even as he resisted the comfort. Yes, if there was a plan, a reason, if it really mattered, then there would be peace, accomplishment, fulfillment. Oh, God, the hurt seemed unbearable.

They passed joggers, walkers on the nature trail. The campus was bustling, busier than the day before. Students were moving quickly to their first classes or into the student lounges and cafeterias. They saw the doors of the library open; a throng of students gathered before the doors began entering. John and Diana entered as the last of the crowd moved inside. Diana went directly to the lavatory. John used his phone to make a call, then, seemingly bored, strolled along the cases in the wings of the foyer.

The three Bibles were in one case. The oldest was from the 1600s and printed in German. The next Bible was dated 1852; the last, 1952. She came up to him as he studied the case. She smelled of lavatory soap. Her face was clean, her hair combed, with a hint of wetness along the temples. She placed her arm in his. He was aware of the circulation desk employee watching him. He thought the woman's interest more than casual. He whispered to Diana.

"We have to take all three."

"But they're so bulky."

"I'll empty the rucksack in the lavatory. We can search through them tonight."

"Tonight!" She thought there would be at least one day of planning. He smiled at her.

"Are you ready to run?"

"I could…I guess…Why?" Certainly, he wasn't about to steal the books now, at this moment!

"The simple and direct approach is sometimes the best. The more spontaneous the action, the more bungled the reaction." He paused and took a deep breath. His heart was pounding. He felt weak, anxious, frightened. Yet he would fight through these obstacles as he had done so many times as a soldier. He had to tell her his fear, a frightening truth, a revelation that might destroy her confidence. "If we are wrong—if there is nothing hidden within these Bibles—we are done. Captured. Failures. Likely, no second chances." Her breath caught in her throat. She did understand. If they escaped with the Bibles and found nothing, they would be unable to return and search again. Either the police would capture them and charge them with theft, or Cain would capture them and torture them for any clues they might harbor.

"I want you to walk to the entrance gate—the old entrance gate, the one we entered. Wait by the gate if I haven't already caught up to you. Someone may be following you or guarding the gate. Don't let them get close to you. Run back toward the library if they try anything."

His voice gripped her—a man's voice having authority, talking of a game played before. She knew he was experienced in situations of life and death. His voice demanded uncompromising understanding, clarity. They weren't cleaner went into the rucksack, so the hand cleaner would come out of the rucksack—if your mind is focused. Remember, God is on your side.

He calmly freed a wedged corner, lifted out the hand cleaner. He placed the books in the empty rucksack and walked out of the library.

He began to run easily, as if a student late for class, a smile on his face. The books were incredibly heavy. He glanced behind. A man ran after him from across the plaza. Ahead, a crowd of students was moving toward the new entrance; they walked in groups of twos, threes. He left the main road, jogged the old road down the hill, toward the old gate. The frozen ground was hard under his feet. He could see Diana near the gate, walking slowly.

No one else was by the gate. A young man, moving at Diana's pace, walked behind her, keeping his distance. This man glanced over his shoulder apprehensively but did not turn completely around. John assumed this man had just been warned of his approach. John shifted to the man's lazy side, the side unwilling to turn.

John glanced over his shoulder, the man trailing him was fading, not able to keep the pace. John was running at full speed when Diana's trailing man chose to take seriously his compatriot's warnings. He turned fully, reaching inside his coat for an object. John's body slammed into the man's chest, knocked him down, ran him over. A stun stick went skipping across the ground.

Diana was running as John caught up with her. He barely broke stride. Where was Cain? He grabbed her arm, they swung out the gate and into the street. The pace lessened. No one was following. He turned down a quiet residential street. They began walking, attempting to normalize their breathing, straighten their clothing. John studied the addresses of the homes.

"Here we are." He stopped before a home just as a taxi hummed down the street and stopped before them.

"Here is our taxi." They entered the taxi. John spoke into the intercom to the robo driver, who was separated from the passengers by a see-through plastic shield.

"Station Nine, please."

"You mean Ten? Downtown?" The soothing voice inquired.

"No. Nine, please."

The driver said nothing as it pulled out onto an intersecting street. Why did it care if they wanted to go miles out of their way to a suburban station—the more fare for the company.

Diana's face was flushed red from exertion and the cold. Her eyes laughed with excitement. "You called the taxi when I was in the lavatory, but the address?"

"Got that the first night we walked through town."

She kissed him on the cheek and whispered into his ear, "Where's Cain?"

"I don't know."

She heard the apprehension in his tone. He believed, like her the theft and escape had been too easy. Both wondered if the books in the rucksack contained the Satanic bible. The thought of returning for a second search was best left unexplored and unspoken.

Station Nine was small—a terminal building with one ticket counter and a restaurant wedged into a corner. John placed the money card in the ticket machine. Diana scanned the benches. Her eyes came back to an old man with a large satchel, sitting alone. What was familiar about him? John noticed the smile of recognition on her face.

"Don't say a word. You don't know him."

John pulled the tickets from the machine. Henry came to the same machine and bought his ticket as John and Diana walked away. Henry kept his distance from the two. They waited only minutes before their commuter stopped. The three entered; they were alone in the car.

John set the rucksack on Diana's lap. She held the fabric with her fingernails as he pulled out the tight-fitting books. John handed the heavy books to Henry, who set them upon his lap. Henry began with the German Bible, leafing through the stiff pages. The binding crackled. They found nothing. Henry leafed through the 1852 Bible; the rag paper was stiff but not brittle. Nothing. Henry's eyebrows arched.

"Well, this must be it, or we have to go back." He added as an afterthought, "I never guessed it would be in a Bible. Where were the Bibles?"

Diana answered, "In the library, in an enclosed case. Turn to Matthew 21:42."

By long practice, Henry opened the Bible directly to Matthew. (He could do this with any book of the Bible). The New Testament had cut within it a shallow well containing a thin black cylinder. The cut began on the page where verse 42 began. John smiled, chuckled. Diana gasped. Henry whispered a chant of "Praise God! Praise God!" that trailed into a silence.

John, shaking his head in wonder, spoke. "So it is all for real."

Henry's eyes were wide from weariness as well as amazement. "Probably microdots—my father had a microdot machine. It makes sense. He took the book home and reduced it." Henry lifted out the pen-shaped cylinder and examined it. "Fireproof, waterproof, indestructible. The technology was outdated then—probably by a hundred years. He placed it in a display case with the same qualities of indestructability. Many times in the past I walked right by those Bibles."

A quiet, borne of weariness, awe, the completion of their task, came over the three as each in turn held the cylinder. In the quiet, an incredibly overpowering sadness hung. A sadness of resignation, shame, pity, of betrayed potential in the race called man. The Holy Spirit grieved with an intensity and depth that passed their understanding or emotion. They sensed a finality in the grief.

The cylinder held the culmination of man's rebellion, his perversity, lust, pride of life, all that is meaningless and empty, all that is separate from God. The weight of humanity's history, its strivings, accomplishments, boasts rested in the small container. Humanity had yearned, from birth, to cast off, overthrow its Creator, and had succeeded.

Henry, John, Diana grieved with the Spirit for the world gone mad. They knew the nearness of the end of the world's folly. The world in which they were born, had life, hopes, dreams was coming to a swift close. They would have wept for all those who had been a part of their lives—from parents, family, friends, to the store clerk, the repair person, the teacher, any who had ever touched their lives, if only through a fleeting glimpse. The Spirit veiled the future, restrained the sadness. They wished to weep and could not.

Diana was the first to recover, perhaps because she hated the world more.

"How long have you been waiting at the station?" Something had to be said.

"I left home a few minutes after you two. Yesterday, I relaxed in a hotel room. Today I've been sitting since early morning."

"This was all arranged back at the house," she stated assuredly.

"While you were dressing for the trip. This station seemed safer than Colebrook—where they would be looking for you and are."

"The authorities are looking for you by now," Diana said.

"Yes, I suppose they are." Henry's eyes twinkled mischievously.

Behind the twinkle she saw the beginnings of senility, an inability to grasp the danger? Perhaps it was good that Henry had no fear, had not weighed the consequences of their actions.

John said nothing, absorbed in his own thoughts. She could read his moods; he was worrying. John harrumphed loudly as an awareness came to him. He took a pen and pad from Henry's coat pocket and wrote, "We're bugged—sound and/or location!"

No questioning arose in Diana's mind; she had sensed something was wrong. John thought someone could have prowled the woods with night-vision goggles, came upon the glowing blanket edges, planted the devices as they slept. Or in a crowd, someone could have attached a device, or even sprinkled electronically charged powder on their seats or on door handles. Devices were so numerous and varied, from invisible powders, paints, and dust, to tiny metal shavings, to transmitters the size of an ant. Only by throwing away all their clothing and bathing could they be certain of being untraceable.

The three travelers listened to the silence of despondency as the train car ran smoothly toward Colebrook Station. What had first seemed a brilliant plan—to pass through the enemy at Colebrook Station—was now a brilliant blunder. They were riding to their capture and perhaps torture and death. Had they been allowed to escape so they would lead Cain to others? If so, Cain's plan had worked—Henry was here. Or had they truly escaped only to be snagged by Cain's contingency plan? Did it matter now?

They sat with blank eyes as the car automatically slowed to enter Colebrook Station. John slumped in his seat; Diana followed his example. Henry, sitting by the window, acted as a partial screen. The car entered the high-ceilinged station. John saw Cain standing before the row of small shops that sold magazines, fast food, souvenirs. People parted around the tall, broad figure. The face was stoic, the hands were thrust deep into the pockets of the long overcoat. Another man stood beside Cain—shorter, younger, carrying a briefcase. John saw a receiver in Cain's ear.

Cain knew his quarry was close.

John slumped from view as Cain's eyes grasped the car moving at walking speed. Henry spoke. "The eyes are burning with anger."

John knew that Cain had never planned on his quarry's escape.

"He's walking with the car."

John knew they were bugged with a location sounder. Cain's walk with the car had solidified the pulsing signals coming into his ear. The car stopped and would remain only for a moment—unless a ticket had been purchased at the station.

"A little man with a brief case is running…He's got a…"

John was in the aisle, crouching, scurrying to the opened door. He heard the man's footsteps, the noise of the station. He heard Cain yell a warning.

The man filled the doorway. John rose, kicked savagely. Only a glancing blow to the chest. The man lost his grip on the handrails, fell backward, a stun stick in his hand. Cain bounded, was before the door just as it closed.

Cain's eyes locked onto John's. Cain's eyes held no anger, only a bemused confidence. The fallen man rose with fear in his eyes for Cain's reaction to the bungled job. Henry and Diana were up, standing beside John, as the car sped away. Henry placed a hand on John's shoulder, Diana held his arm. Henry spoke.

"Good work, John!"

Diana bragged. "My man's rough and tough."

John laughed as an emotional release. Henry continued talking. "This car will make one more stop a mile further—at the edge of town. I scouted this area yesterday. There's a natatorium nearby. Strip there and bathe. I'll carry the clothes away." Henry rifled through the large satchel beside him. He pulled out two bags. "Change of clothes. We have to move fast."

The three waited by the door as the city rushed by. They rocked forward, tensed as the car automatically slowed. John studied the crowd on the platform of the outdoor station—no one suspicious, just commuters waiting for their trains. Inside the station building, two men stood, their eyes searching the entrance doors, the ticket machine. Cain's men, who had yet to be notified their quarry was on the train. John, Henry, Diana slipped away to a nearby entrance to the subterranean levels, screened by the crowds moving toward the commuter cars. Henry took the lead. John and Diana anxiously searched the crowds jamming the spacious hallways. Henry stopped; John smelled chlorine. They stood before the entrance to a natatorium. Henry drifted off to a bench before a public electrascreen. John and Diana were already through the doors to the pool.

They bought tickets and throw-away suits that would never be used. Within minutes, Henry was walking away with their old clothes under his arm. He walked hurriedly. He wanted to dump the clothes as far from John and Diana as possible without himself being captured. When was that perfect time to drop the clothes? Only the Lord knew. He trusted that the Lord was not only capable of choosing the right time but also cared enough to tell him when that time was. Wasn't the Spirit of God walking with him this very moment?

He moved up to ground level, crossed a street, went down a narrow alley, over a pedestrian bridge. The trains passed below him. Smooth, silent, clean, they ran. A freight train moved slowly under the bridge. The Lord didn't need to speak; even an idiot would have dropped the bundles. He watched the clothing fall. He had a brief moment of worry when a shirt trailed out of the bundle and began to drift away from the cars. Henry willed the shirt into the cars and it fell with the bundles. He smiled contentedly; that train would give Satan's men a ride.

He took a circuitous route back to the business district, saw no one following or lying in wait. He went into a drug store. Hair dye might help.

**

Tim Johnson walked up the four flights of stairs to his office and lab. The steps were part of his daily exercise regimen, designed to lessen the strain of field work and to prep him for the workday to follow. His step had a spring; he carried little excess weight; his health was excellent. He had a noteworthy physique, a handsome face. Life was good.

The university professorship was exciting. He was respected by his peers and students. He had opportunities to travel and as much field work as he wanted. He loved to interact with the students, not only sharing his knowledge of geology but also listening to their dreams, the problems and victories of their personal lives. He had loved rocks and the earth since a kid digging in the backyard, so a geologist he had become. He had two fine children, a loving wife, and he and God understood each other perfectly.

He also had an AWOL brother accused of murder and a missing grandfather, presumably an accomplice to his brother. Both of whom would certainly turn up at his doorstep. Life was still good. His schedule was tight, and he didn't need the aggravation of an old man and a young kid running from the law. But he loved them both; they were more important than his schedule, and with the lawyer his mother had hired and his political and Church contacts, whatever mess they were in would work out.

The door to the fourth-floor hallway opened automatically. He saw figures down the hall, their features hidden by the bright sunlight streaming in the window at the hall's end. He walked confidently. Three figures sat on the floor, leaning against his door. Exhausted figures by their postures, two men and a woman.

John, Gramps, and a young woman. Mom had mentioned something about a woman. He sighed with relief and vexation. They tensed as he approached. He wasn't recognized. He saw the tension leave; they rose to greet him. All three sets of eyes were wide. First impressions: weariness, anxiety, happiness, unkempt but clean.

Tim hugged Gramps and John, shook the hand of the woman, Diana. He had prayed for John nightly while John had been in Europe—well, he had thought deeply about him and God heard. John was so thin, gaunt cheeks, bearded, tired eyes. His hair and beard were blond! The ribs could be felt through the jacket. He could have passed as a chemically dependent person. He saw no health or vitality within the body. A tear came to Tim's eye.

"Well, let's go into my office and talk." The door swung open.

"Who told you to expect us?" asked Henry in a voice tinged with nervousness and curiosity.

"Mom."

"Not the police?"

"No police. Mom mentioned two inspectors."

John had opened a refrigerator behind Tim's desk. Tim was pulling up window shades. John's hair had been dyed to avoid the police, thought Tim.

"Help yourself."

"Thanks, Tim." John pulled out a carton of milk. He held it toward Henry and Diana; they shook their heads. John gulped from the cartoon.

The office was lined with rock displays. Tim sat at his desk, motioned John and Henry to the chairs before the desk. Diana curled her feet under her on a couch behind the chairs. Her legs ached, and her feet hurt. All three kept their jackets on. Tim studied his brother—John had changed. They were ten years apart in age, but John could have passed as the elder.

More than the appearance of age was the brokenness that hung upon his brother, speaking of a life crushed, a heart aching. Here was a man who could not be surprised by life. John had seen evil, seen the extremes of life. This worldliness, instead of enhancing life had destroyed him; he would never trust people again. Yet, he wore this air, this aura like a badge of honor, with a certain confidence—faith, perhaps?

"Why are you running? Mom and Dad are worried sick. Our lawyer could straighten this out if you'd turn yourself in."

John heard the absence of accusation, judgment, or panic. "My being AWOL and accused of murder are only incidental to why we are here, Tim."

Henry continued John's conversation. "We need you to listen carefully."

Tim's posture stiffened attentively. Henry waited, hoping the wait would bring a gravity to his words. Tim looked past Henry to Diana. How did she fit into this mess? She was an attractive young woman. She had a certain look in her eyes he could not define. Henry began.

"Your great-grandfather uncovered some information. He was killed before the theft of the information was known. He left a clue to where this information was hidden. John couldn't turn himself in because I needed him—and Diana—to find the information. They found what your great-grandfather hid, and with the help of your visual equipment, we're ready to read it."

"Great-grandfather murdered?" Disbelief and incredulity crowded Tim's face. He watched Diana for her reaction; she seemed to believe what was being said.

"Yes, John found the material that was the catalyst for his death."

John added, "That's why we're being followed."

"By the law?" Tim heard his voice rise in pitch with disbelief and resolved to regain his composure.

"No, by others who don't want this material to come to light. But it wouldn't surprise me if your home has been under surveillance by the police—looking for John." Henry was pleased that he had not used the term *Satan's men*, knowing Tim's antagonism toward the belief in a Satanic being.

Tim studied John's eyes. Gramps was old; senility could be a determining factor in this story. John's mind had always been sound, but now, worn and stressed, gullibility was possible. John stared back as if this were all the gospel truth. Diana seemed the least weary; the eyes spoke of intelligence, soundness. What was that other quality in her eyes? She offered no resistance facially or verbally to what was being said.

"What is this information about? Why is it so valuable? Even after seventy-some years there are people who still want this information?"

"Yes! Exactly!" shouted Henry. "My father stumbled upon the Satanic bible and plans for Satan's church, which is within the World Church. These plans concern the coming of the Beast and his regime on earth. They don't want these plans to become known. They are afraid a revealing may arouse opposition and rob them of complete victory."

Tim shook his head sadly, spoke calmly but with an undertone of sarcasm. "Revelation, isn't it? Daniel? The Holy Spirit leaving the earth! The Church is corrupt! The Rapture is coming!" He sighed in exasperation. "Gramps, I've heard all this from you before. I thought you had laid it to rest. How convenient that you're writing a book on the subject, and mysteriously, these plans are presented to you."

Tim looked at John. "Doesn't that strike you as odd?"

John's dull mind, drifting away, heard but could not answer. He wanted to list for Tim all the workings of the Spirit—from the mutiny of his platoon to finding the microdots. He uttered a word.

"No."

Tim leaned back in his chair, threw his hands up and kept them up. "I give up, Lord. I give up. What did I do to deserve these people?" He looked up at the ceiling. His outburst of frustration embarrassed the trio. Diana readily discerned the war within Tim's soul. Tim continued. "I've said it all to Gramps before in countless religious, cosmological, philosophical arguments. Listen: The world's never been better. Christ said feed the hungry, clothe the poor, heal the sick, and it's being done. Bless the peacemakers: the world has never been so peaceful—one minor European conflict soon to be resolved. That's it, all over the world! So how could the Holy Spirit be leaving the earth? Life is good, and we are in control.

"And all this crap about the Church being corrupt. The Church has never been more powerful or done more good. How can you get good fruit from a bad tree? There! That's some scriptural proof against you."

Henry spoke quietly, with anguish. "The Gospel message has been perverted. Christ's atoning death has been made obsolete. The world lives for itself."

"Why has this happened?" Tim demanded. "Because men no longer believe they're totally evil? Because we have advanced, with the help of God, to be better people, a better society? We've outgrown the archaic laws, evolved out of sin. I give God the glory! What is the problem?"

Tim's eyes were wide with disbelief. Tim saw in John's eyes a mirror, and he realized he had lost his temper. "I'm sorry, John. This seems new to you. But Gramps and I have had this same discussion for years now, ever since you joined the army."

Tim turned back to Henry and spoke calmly. They heard his will concentrating upon calmness with each word he uttered. "You want to tell me that all I have mentioned are external material advances or a change in the environment and not in the basic character of people. You want to tell me I need to be born again because the Holy Spirit isn't in me. How can I be more in the Spirit? I ask. I go to church, believe in God. I make mistakes, I have problems, but I keep going, just as you do. Why do you want me to feel badly about myself and my fellow man? I can't understand.

"To bind ourselves in self-hatred seems perverse to me. Christ is my partner, my friend, and He frees me. Why does He bind you?"

Tim's voice had become accusing, bitter. Anger came to John. He wished to speak from that anger—from his own bitterness. He said nothing. Christ could speak if He wished. From the weariness, words came. "Tim, we are not partners of Christ. We are slaves, subjects of a King, bondsmen to a Master first. Then friend, then child. We must die with Him and be raised with Him, walking in His Holy Spirit. If it isn't Christ energizing our minds, then it is ourselves. If it isn't Christ leading us, then it is ourselves. If we rid ourselves of sin by human will, then it is delusion. If we rid ourselves of the laws that show us to be sinners, then we can never know our Savior. He must show us what it means to be dead to the law, through His power. We must deny ourselves and abide in Him."

Tim silently, impatiently waited for John to finish. He had listened only enough to snag an offending thought, and his mind drifted to formulating objections and justifications.

"Well." Tim spoke resignedly and as one who had the upper hand. "Then it is a circle: because there is no *you*—you only do what Christ wants and Christ energizes. Christ is loving Christ, obeying Christ. You don't really exist. God loves God. You're not in the picture."

"I'm in the picture. I still have my individual life, experience, memory, abilities, sensations, soul, spirit. I'm in the picture because each day, each second, I refuse me, myself, my carnal nature, my control by looking to my Lord. I'm a tool, a slave. I admit it, and it is right and proper, and God is worthy."

"Enough. Enough," Tim said wearily. "You always have another argument—we could go on forever. Somehow, we pass by each other like two ships in the night, and whatever lifelines are thrown are never are picked up."

What had happened to his brother while in the army? Tim wondered. Had the stress made him relinquish his life? If it worked for him, fine. But it wasn't working. John was wanted for murder, evading the authorities. Tim would say no more. He didn't want to argue. He was happy, content, and he wasn't going to think thoughts that would make him discontented and unhappy. Unhappiness, discontent, even guilt were evil. The proper way to rid oneself of evil was to ignore its presence. Was there any other way to rid oneself of evil?

Tim's eyes drifted to Diana. Attractive, yes, but not a stunning beauty—well, maybe. Something about her gave her a radiance. Was it a quality of character—strength, patience, love? Or did her weariness give her an unnatural calm? She was content to sit on the couch and not enter the conversation. Her eyes were tired, worn, but she was not nearly to John's level of exhaustion. What was it about her?

"What do *you* think, quiet one?" Tim asked her.

"I think Jesus wants you."

Tim smiled in kindly surprise. John had found one of his own. "God bless you." Sincerity marked his voice, and satisfaction. He was happy for John, and maybe she was the key to his salvation. He knew his position was sound and right and these people before him were deluded, lost. He could help them before their lives were irreparably ruined. He would need patience, kindness, and God was giving him these very qualities.

Henry spoke of conciliation. "Let's forget the old discussions and arguments. I want John to tell you how we found this information and what we're up against."

John tilted the milk carton, pressed against his lips, to the ceiling. He leaned his head back for the last drops. The entire gallon was now finished. He began to talk, beginning with the mutiny. He did not mention Diana's past. The words were halting at first, then became a torrential narrative of concise, unembellished fact.

Tim listened attentively, and as he listened, he realized his younger brother was a man. He remembered a boy, and here was a man. The brokenness clung to him even as his words had fire, determination. John did not talk of himself, but Tim clearly read the man of the narrative, a man with resolve, purpose, daring, an incredible endurance.

Tim was proud of his brother; his account would have made a best-selling book. To be in his presence was ennobling, which sounded melodramatic but was nonetheless true. John was one of those rare people who believed in an idea and had the courage to live it. Whether the cause was true was not important to Tim; the belief in something other than oneself had worth.

The caveat was that the cause had to have good embedded within. Tim was having trouble finding sufficient good. This Diana, behind John, seemed to melt into him, fit like a missing piece of a puzzle. He wondered if sex was a part of the relationship.

The story of the clues, Cain, the priest, the bugging devices were no doubt true. John could be trusted; Diana was his witness. The situation was tense, but these Satan worshippers were just a cult, a fringe element of the pagan religions now flourishing. These were groups that had given themselves over to shortsighted ideas, practices that were socially unacceptable and incapable of sustained growth. Sex orgies, spells, chants, demons, blood sacrifices of animals were all childish practices he associated with these people. That was Satanism, and only the extreme fringe elements had ever killed anyone.

Had his great-grandfather been murdered? A hit-and-run accident seemed like the truth. Why doubt? John's AWOL and murder charges were serious and needed prompt attention. Nothing could be accomplished till John turned himself in. Tim knew his first task was to downplay if not discredit this religious mystery they had presented. John would then feel justified to concentrate upon his own problems. Tim spoke. "I believe you, John. I'm interested in reading this microfilm. Can it wait till my lecture is through? I'll be down in the lecture hall on the first floor for an hour. You're welcome to hide out in my office and use my equipment. Gramps can be a retired professor and you two, students."

Tim found the hard drive of lectures, which he had planned to review that morning, on his desktop. The students would just have to bear with his pauses. John watched, wondered if he could trust his brother not to contact the police. Yes, he could trust his brother, and to ask for a promise would have been insulting.

"Okay. We'll be waiting."

CHAPTER 10

When Tim returned to his office, he found the blinds pulled, an antiquated projector in place, the screen down. The new hologram projector that had been occupying the table was on the window shelf. Where had they found the antique? The couch and chairs had been turned to face the screen. John was asleep on the couch, Henry, on a chair. Diana was pouring coffee. His brand, fortified with the mild caffeine boost in vogue, would wake them. He went to the projector to examine the light setting; the old dots would burn in a whiff of smoke even with this fifty-year-old reproduction machine. The light setting was already on low. He noticed the copying component of the machine contained blank film and was ready for use.

He picked up the black cylinder sitting by the machine. Certainly made to withstand any environment or catastrophe—some type of titanium alloy. His curiosity was aroused. This might be fun, even if it were a hoax. Tim switched on the power. Words appeared on the screen.

"We read the first dot and stopped. Coffee? I hope you don't mind us using yours."

Diana spoke quietly. He smiled; she had a pleasant voice that spoke of a soul at peace.

In the Shadow of Babylon

"No thanks. And no, I don't mind."

He sat by the projector and read:

My name is Jeremiah E. Johnson. I am a doctor of divinity, a professor at Colebrook Seminary. The year is 2165, June 15. The following documents came into my possession through mistaken identity. These documents have made me aware of a false church hidden, coexisting, feeding upon the present Church. This false church will devour the present Church in the last days. I have always known the Church to be corrupt, yet by the will of God, I was placed within the Church. Perhaps, to be a witness of this coming perversion of the perverse. I believe I do not have long to live. I trust in the Lord these documents will fall into the proper hands.

Jeremiah E. Johnson

The signature above the name appeared to be authentic. Tim had books signed by his great-grandfather and a picture of him in his family's den. His daughter, Katie, and her brother, Matt, as little children, had both mentioned how they liked "that man" in the picture. A kindly looking man with gleaming eyes, who had loved children, the outcasts and misfits of society, the aged and frail of body and spirit. He had been a powerful speaker. It was said he had the boldness to deliver sermons on the topic of hell, though no one believed, and everyone scoffed.

This was the only writing on the first dot, evidently added hurriedly to complete the package. No mention of specific names. Did he know the passage of time would take this letter of introduction past his own lifetime and the lifetimes of those who sought his life? Had Jeremiah been murdered as Henry suggested? Jeremiah thought he would be murdered. Why did a sense of desperation and hope cling to the words, unremarkable words, not polished or eloquent? Maybe it was simply truth that clung to the words and gave them power. He had a responsibility to this dead man who had given him his blood, his name.

"You're in charge of the projector. Keep the dots rolling."

Tim looked behind; Henry and John were both awake, had been for some time by their postures, the coffee cups in their hands. Diana was beside John on the couch, cuddled up against him. Tim unscrewed the cap of the black cylinder and removed the next dot. He read:

Faithful ones, renew your hearts, minds, strength. Be zealous in my work. The Holy One will be born soon after the year of the exploding sun, and he shall grow amid wealth and prosper in splendor. He shall have all knowledge of good and evil. Wisdom will flow from his mouth in an everlasting stream. He will grow strong among you to be a blessing upon the world. He will sever the false god's restraining hand and lead my legions to victory.

He shall reveal to you what is mine, and you shall possess all that has been denied you since the founding of the world. It is my good pleasure to give happiness to those who honor me. I shall sit upon the throne of the world with my son at my right hand. The wonders of Babylon shall be your inheritance.

In that day, which is soon, Christ and his slaves will be cast away into darkness, men shall be free, my Church whole, without blemish. In the thirty-third year of my son's life, he shall set his bride free.

Well done, faithful elect. You have worshiped my name since Eden. I have cast away the sin of the world. I have removed the chains that bind. I feed the hungry, clothe the naked, make well the sick. Behold my world which you are creating, rejoice in it and know fulfillment is nigh. I am worthy of praise. My son is worthy. The prophet yet to come is worthy.

Tim turned off the projector, faced his audience. "Do you expect me to believe these are the words of the devil—Satan?"

"Are they the words of God?" asked John.

"No."

"Are they the words of men?"

"Certainly."

"Then they are the words of Satan."

Tim shook his head. "Man is a mix of good and evil, his own independent entity. Good and evil are concepts. We don't have to belong to one or the other."

"If you're a mixture of good and evil, you belong to evil," John said. "Tim, the evil will always triumph, always in the end have its way. That is the way of the flesh. That's reality. That is why you need to be born again from above."

Tim remained silent. Satan had spoken through a man, the writer of the words. Plausible, if there was a force of evil in existence. John was telling him that he—John—had no evil within, which was a lie. This debate would get them nowhere. Tim looked at Henry, who was strangely quiet. Gramps's color was poor: ashen white. He was now coughing periodically. The left hand was twitching. Gramps was killing himself with this adventure. For Gramps's sake, he would try to keep the fireworks to a minimum. Stick to provable facts. Tim spoke.

"When is the year of the exploding sun? The time of this man's birth?"

Henry's eyes became alive with intensity, burning into Tim's mind.

"It was thirty-two and one-half years ago."

His stare continued, caught the momentary passing of fear, uncertainty in Tim's eyes. Henry continued. "I remember it well—speculation that the earth would be knocked from its orbit and this would destroy the world as we know it. This, of course, didn't happen. But gravitational, magnetic fields were affected, mostly around the arctic regions. No one died."

Diana shuddered. "Thirty-two and a half years ago. Six months, and this man, the Beast, will be in power?"

Tim spoke. "Soon after the exploding sun…that gives a range." Tim remembered and recalled information on the exploding sun incident, had studied the effects on the magnetic alignment of certain geologic formations. Astronomers could have been predicting the event seventy-five years ago, forty-some years before it occurred in 2208. Only six months from now, when the thirty-third year had begun, could the prophecy be proven valid.

"We don't have long in this world," Henry said quietly.

"Of course, the Rapture!" Tim announced sarcastically. He hadn't wanted to be sarcastic or hostile. Why had he been?

"Even Satan says it will happen. I quote, 'Christ and his slaves will be cast away into darkness.' Only Satan is claiming the act as his own and the destination as darkness. The destination is heaven. A time will come soon when you will look for us, and we won't be found." Henry wagged his finger at Tim and immediately realized the gesture could only alienate.

"If it is true, I'll be with you." Tim was hurt and indignant. "I'm a Christian."

John's tone was flat. "He's not talking *Christian*, Tim. But those who are in and of Christ, who have given Him everything."

Henry added, "You always laughed when I said the Holy Spirit would be leaving. This document says the same thing. 'He will sever the false god's restraining hand, lead my legions to victory.' Only the restraining hand is Holy and leaving of His own accord. The Heavenly host will have the victory."

Tim quietly, unobtrusively shook his head and spoke deeply. "None of this is odd, if both sides are using the same source to prove or disprove this futuristic scenario. The sides interpret the same projected events differently, almost as opposite."

"Don't you see that they agree with us more than your own Church does?" John asked.

Tim regained his composure. "I see two polar extremes feeding off each other to make conflict where there is none."

John understood that Tim could not hear, the Holy Spirit could not penetrate Tim's self. A wise man would not force Tim to hear. Strange as it seemed, John could understand Tim's skepticism, unbelief. He understood the reasoning, the logic of the world as Tim saw it. If Tim was to be convinced, the work must begin in his heart, and only God had that power.

Henry spoke. "Tim, the Church for hundreds if not thousands of years has taught that Satan is the destroyer. That all his actions through people end in almost immediate death, violence, and ugliness discernable to all. But that has never been the truth. Yes, Satan is the destroyer, but he isn't anxious to destroy because he has no power to create. He, himself *was created*. He wants to take what is God's and claim it as his own. He is a liar, a deceiver, a mesmerizer, an illusionist. He uses these qualities to keep people within their sinful flesh. Mankind, confused or satisfied, it doesn't matter to Satan as long as they remain in their flesh.

"Satan isn't against virtue, character, loyalty, faithfulness, or the entire range of good qualities that humanity admires. He needs those qualities for his world. He simply wants to be in control of these qualities. He has always energized, controlled, motivated people *secretly*. Now he wants the glory and the praise. He wants to be worshiped openly.

"He's puffed up the world with pride, pride in their humanity, their intellect, their will. He has spoken what it is most convenient to speak, what it is easiest for a man to do, and men have called it truth. You're so proud of your life and yourself that you could never humble yourself before Christ."

"I am in Christ! I am a Christian! The Church is Christian and in Christ!" Tim's voice was tight, throttled by emotion. Why did they keep pounding him with the same phrases, the same information, as if he were a moron? Where did they get their conceit? These two who were supposed to love him.

Henry listened to his heart racing. The heart was straining; death would be coming soon. Tim was of his flesh, blood. He wanted his flesh and blood in heaven as if there was something special in his flesh and blood. Did he love Tim too much and Christ's blood too little? What was it to him if Tim rejected the truth and burned in hell for eternity? God was sovereign, yet He forced no man to give allegiance. What did God owe Henry Johnson? Nothing. The fate of his grandson was in the Lord's hands.

Tim separated himself mentally from the three. Too much emotion; a man could lose his objectivity. He knew from experience that stubborn belief could pull others into that belief regardless of evidence. The bottom line was that he loved these people—even Diana had become precious to him. The best plan was to go along with them. The most they would want him to do would be to hand some papers to a high-ranking member of the Church. He would embarrass himself, but he had embarrassed himself many times in the past for family. For John, Gramps, and even Diana, he would willingly suffer shame.

"I'm going to help you with this mystery. But it is up to you to tell me what I am to do. In exchange for my help, you must promise to turn yourselves in at a time of your choosing. Stay here tonight. I'll call in food, tell the custodian you're here. I'll expect a concrete plan of action tomorrow."

"It's a deal." John spoke quickly, confidently.

"I'm going back to work. I've got a lab class in another building." Tim rose, shaking his head. He gathered up some papers from his desk, placed them in his briefcase, and closed the door behind him.

Resigned laughter bubbled weakly from John. "Tim's considered a radical conservative in the Church. If he can't believe, what hope is there? Time is short—six months to a year, maybe. Let's call it quits. I've got to warn Mom and Dad. I've got to know they believe. The uncertainty is tearing me apart inside."

Henry's eyes were focused on the floor. His soul ached. "No, we've got to stick to our work—God's work given to us. We're to make this information known before we leave this earth. God has intervened too many times for us to fail now. We know when the Beast will assume power over the Church. This information is a catalyst. We will initiate an awareness. We must persist."

"What for? To accomplish what?" asked Diana. She remembered, vaguely, having been told at Henry's home. So much information had been given her at that time.

"The Bible tells us the professing church or World Church will become the harlot church. As I told you back at the house, this information might be the catalyst for a schism in the World Church. By presenting this information to the World Church, we may open the eyes of many—save their souls."

"Why is it called the harlot church?" She needed to know, even if the answer shamed her.

"Because this church plays for the favors of men, taking its holiness, its virtue, its vow to the Lord and denying it, degrading itself for wealth, splendor, the allures of this earth," Henry said. "Whatever men wish to do to her, she does; whatever men wish her to be, she is. She claims to be the bride of Christ, but from the beginning, she was tainted with her own lusts and desires."

Diana heard and felt no shame. Christ had washed her clean. She remembered, clearly, the conversation at Henry's home. This son, the Beast about to come to power, would reign over the harlot church and the European Federation. "This Rapture is soon, and then seven years of hell on earth. Then, the end of all this futility?"

Henry nodded sadly. John smiled at Diana's use of the word *futility*. The apostle Paul had used the same word to describe life in this world. John gently moved Diana's head from his shoulder and stood.

"Let's go through these microdots and find the information we need. Tomorrow we must have a plan."

***

Tim stood in the aisle of the commuter train—the seats were filled, no standing room remained. Someone had propped an ebook upon his back. He was jammed so tightly between people that he could not turn to complain, had he wished. These people were his neighbors, friendly, well educated, and they enjoyed life. He was glad to be on his way home—just on the other side of the campus—to peace, sanity.

He hadn't been able to concentrate on his work after the events of the morning. He had attempted to lecture but found himself constantly wandering from his discourse, even staring off into space. Later, he had willed himself to review the next day's lesson plan but found himself bitterly formulating arguments against the logic of John and Gramps. His imagination and emotion had run wild during these imaginary debates. He caught himself talking aloud. Anger, even hate were in his words. He wondered at his mental soundness. His satisfaction was that Gramps and John had been completely thrashed.

He had gone to work a respected geologist and professor and had walked out of his office somehow responsible for the end of the world! The Church taught that the millennium was now, and it was continuously renewed if humanity obeyed God. What if people weren't obeying God? That damned thought kept haunting him, though it had no basis in fact.

He loved God, went to church, gave money to charities, raised his kids to be responsible citizens. He gave God the credit for all the good that had happened in his life. He never purposely did anyone any harm—though there were times when he wanted to. He wasn't perfect; no one was, not even Gramps or John. They seemed to have overlooked that fact.

What was it about him that assured them he wasn't going to heaven and didn't have Christ in his life? Maybe he did think of Christ as a partner and of God as a concept of good. So what? What if Christ wanted to be more than a partner? All right! Christ was God, Lord of Tim Johnson's life, and Tim Johnson wanted to obey. There, he had said it. Strangely, his annoyance departed.

It would be good to hug the kids, place his hands upon Mary, touch her so that she knew he desired her. He'd call Mom and Dad, tell them John was okay, and see what the lawyer had come up with. No, he'd hold off on the call until tomorrow; then he'd have solid news to report.

He was poured out of the commuter with tens of others. He walked through the neighborhoods surrounding his own development. All apartments, five-story jobs, on tree-lined streets. The fewer the stories, the higher your status, unless you were talking about downtown skyscrapers. These were "fivers," middle class…upper middle class almost. Kids were playing on a recreation field. He heard their laughter. Life was good; people were happy, prosperous. What more could God want?

He came to the streets of single-dwelling homes—the lower upper class. The university owned his home, an old single dwelling—one of the perks of his professorship. He liked to think he could afford such a home without the university's help. A single made a man feel solid, substantial. Father Winkler's car was in the driveway. It wasn't uncommon for Wink to stop in; they were good friends. Usually he called in advance. Tim wondered what the surprise visit meant.

He entered his home. The familiar surroundings soothed him—the large foyer, wooden floors, throw rugs, space. The kids came running to greet him as they often did. He hugged them with a greater-than-usual appreciation and love. Life without them wouldn't be worth living. He could smell an alien odor in his home—of priestly incense, aftershave, heavy black suits that held a person's personal scent. Mary was by his side, her perfume arousing a familiar desire, her shapely form exciting him. He thought the kids had forced a promise from him—for what, he didn't know. He placed his hand around Mary's waist, squeezed, then grasped her bottom. Her eyes lit with love, desire, and playfulness. She spoke softly.

"I'll take care of you later. Right now, we have company. Father Winkler and Archbishop Gilroy. I invited them for supper. They want to talk to you."

He kissed her and whispered into her ear. "You're a good wife. Did they say what they want?"

Most wives flipped at unexpected company; Mary enjoyed the challenge, loved to share the warmth of her home with others. Winky would lift the burden from him, as he had so many times in the past, with common sense and wisdom. The archbishop probably wanted a donation to some special fund or wished him to serve on a board. Why an archbishop? Where was Bishop Jennings?

***

Hanson watched Tim Johnson enter his home as he had watched for the past two days. Borelli entered the vehicle in which Hanson was sitting. Borelli had been following Tim Johnson to and from work. Borelli had allowed Hanson to believe that Hanson had conned him out of the easier home stakeout. Borelli knew the fugitives would go to the lab first.

Borelli had seen the fugitives enter Tim Johnson's building; the office had been bugged. The custodian, Sam, informed him of their movements within the building. Yes, he had heard everything, knew John Johnson's entire story—from his escape from the Continent, his search of Colebrook, to Cain, the priest, the stolen Bibles, the microdots now in his possession.

It had slowly seeped into Borelli's consciousness that John Johnson may not have been as lucky as first surmised and that Hanson's errors were likely purposeful, either by Hanson or this evil element of the Church, who wanted Johnson at Colebrook Seminary. It was possible Hanson was connected to the evil element. Hanson was a Churcher, and Hanson was ruthless. The initial act, the killing of the captain, which triggered Johnson's escape, must have been an act of the times and circumstances. Or were God and Satan contending? Yes, if you believed the premise of this mess. For even if, somehow, the murder of the captain was contrived and purposely presented to Johnson, who could have assumed he would have fled? Who could have assumed he'd flee to the United States and get help along the way? Not impossible. Perhaps whether Johnson showed his ID or that of Desmit was immaterial—if bureaucratic manipulators had allowed both codes to work because they wanted John Johnson searching for that Satanic bible. The logging in of the ID codes, which would have shown as complete, were never completed.

Unbelievable! Simply unbelievable! This case could be the crowning achievement of his career or his doom. The kid hadn't killed anyone, but now this Church intrigue could lead him into serious problems. Only fools butted heads with the Church. Who was the Church now if this information they believed they had could divide the Church? What was that information?

This is why he would give them one more night to uncover the information in the microdots. He had a curiosity that could lead to his firing, the loss of his pension, a jail sentence, even his death at the hands of Church assassins. Oddly, these possibilities produced no anxiety. He had a peace about the situation: it was going to work out. He just had to keep a straight face before Hanson for one more night. Borelli spoke. "What's new?"

"A priest and an archbishop visiting. What's new at the lab?"

"Nothing." A priest might be a normal visitor; an archbishop was not. And visiting the same day the fugitives made contact with Tim Johnson? No coincidence. The Church, or a part of it, knew just where to go to find the microdots. This could mean Cain and his element were tied to the archbishop and were in the vicinity.

"The dining room light is on; the living room light is off," said Hanson.

"Let's give them time to eat, then pay our respects. But let's listen in on the conversation." Borelli inwardly cursed his blunder. What if Tim mentioned the arrival of his brother? Hanson would see his partner's lie. Hanson grunted in acknowledgment. Borelli began searching for a plausible alibi then prayed that Tim would protect his brother and not reveal the secret.

***

The dinner party retired to the living room after dessert. Tim had not asked why the archbishop was present, and the archbishop had not volunteered the information. Their meal conversation had been general, compliments on the food and to Mary, talk of the weather, national and world events. There was something about the archbishop that Tim did not like, a vagueness of character, a slyness—wonderful traits for a politician.

Tim felt they were engaged in a contest of wills: who would first bring up the reason for the visit? The archbishop should have stated his reason for visiting sometime during the meal. Etiquette had been breached. Tim wished to think the best of the man, any man, and placed his negative thoughts aside. Wink began the conversation.

"Tim, I know you're curious as to why the archbishop is here."

Tim wondered why the archbishop couldn't speak for himself. Why hadn't Wink, at dinner, stated the reason for their visit? Unless, Wink had been ordered to remain silent.

"I guessed you want to appoint me to an important post, and only an archbishop can impress upon me the importance of that position."

Tim laughed unaffectedly at his own humor. Wink smiled wryly, as was his nature. The archbishop's eyes twinkled, not in merriment, but in self-possession. Tim thought the eyes twinkled because the eyes were expected to twinkle; sincerity was absent. What were they setting him up for? Why was surprise important? Why was the archbishop tense? The archbishop spoke.

"Not exactly. Though I am aware of your great service to the Church—from altar boy to numerous committee chairmanships—and we will certainly call upon you in the future. But at the present, it is your brother who concerns us."

Tim felt relief and elation. Between Wink, his trusted friend, and Archbishop Gilroy, who had political power, John could be helped. Yet he was unable to utter a word. A force stilled him, held his emotions back, and told him to be wary. He owed an allegiance to his grandfather and brother, if only to keep silent for a short time. Tim saw that Gilroy was studying his eyes, his emotion. Tim's tone held a real confusion.

"How could John concern you?"

Gilroy searched for Tim's true depth of awareness.

"He has stolen some very valuable books from our seminary library at Colebrook. We think he will come to you. If he hasn't already."

The archbishop's eyes penetrated Tim. A jolt of fear entered Tim's body. He was angered by the stare and the fear. Wink noticed the archbishop's gaze; he did not like the man. He had done his duty to the archbishop and the Church and would do no more.

The archbishop was a small man, slight of build, less frail than weak, neither effeminate nor manly in bearing. His silver hair gave the appearance of wisdom. His eyes held the superiority that comes with power, with intrigues won, dogma enforced. Tim noticed a momentary calm about Gilroy, but he suspected the revealing of his purpose had released some of his inner tension. This Gilroy had nothing within that should inspire fear. Tim could crush the man with his hands or his intellect. Gilroy had the strength of the Church behind him—was that where the sense of superiority had its origins?

"Why would he steal books when he's wanted by the authorities on murder charges?" Tim asked. "What books did he steal? Are you certain it was John?"

Tim thought his voice carried just the right amount of shock and surprise. Gilroy seemed skeptical.

"How did you know he was wanted on murder charges?" The voice hissed.

"Why, my mother called me the first day he entered the US. Inspectors had called her." The accusation was unnerving—disrespectful. Tim clenched his teeth to bridle his tongue. Angry? No, rage came when he thought of his dutifulness to the Church, the sacrifices in time, money, energy he had freely given. Now the Church accused and morally rejected him in his time of need.

Gilroy ignored Tim's defense. "Three Bibles—very old, worth a good deal of money, besides having great historical and sentimental value."

"Why would he steal Bibles? What if he returns them?"

"We may be satisfied if they are returned intact."

Gilroy had not answered the first question. He was certain Gilroy knew of the microdots. Tim spoke again, in a submissive, confused tone. "I would like to ask again…Why would John steal three Bibles?"

Gilroy's countenance grew smug. "The motivation of your brother is not my concern; the return of the books is."

"How do you know it was my brother?"

"The police were called, of course; facial recognition."

Tim sensed a lie. John's name had been known before the theft as a deserter. Only police files could have put a name to the facial recognition data. Had the Church tapped into police files? The two inspectors who had talked to Mom had not mentioned Church involvement. Or had the harlot church files on John and Gramps as John and Gramps believed? More questions were being raised than answered. People high in the Church hierarchy wanted the microdots, of this Tim was certain. The microdots were authentic—but what did *authentic* mean?

Mary stood in the doorway. Tim knew by her slightly crooked smile that she was uneasy. Two men stood behind her.

"Tim. Inspectors Borelli and Hanson wish to talk to you." The young, blond-haired inspector stepped around Mary boldly, brushing her arm.

"I'm Inspector Hanson; behind your wife is Borelli."

Borelli, chagrin upon his furrowed brows, moved next to Hanson. Tim stood, as did Winkler and Gilroy. Tim spoke. "You're here about my brother?"

"Yes." Borelli, the older man—large, heavy, with dark eyes, wrinkles, and graying hair—offered his hand. Tim grasped the outstretched hand. Some men shook your hand firmly, looked you in the eyes, and then at the first opportunity crossed you. Borelli had the firm shake, the sincere eyes, and something more: honesty clung to Borelli like an aura. A fatherly, concerned warmth exuded from the man. Hanson offered his hand. Firm shake, perfect eye contact. Hanson was not to be trusted.

Borelli continued speaking. " I spoke to your mother. Has she informed you of your brother, John's, plight?" Borelli noticed the archbishop attempting to leave. Gilroy and Wink had slipped around Tim and were thanking Mary for the meal. Tim's voice was forceful as he stepped in front of Wink.

"Don't leave yet. I insist. We all have someone in common—my brother."

Gilroy pushed past Mary; Tim grabbed him by the shoulder, felt the hate emanate from under his hand. A haughtiness and rage lingered under Gilroy's smile as he turned back to the room. Tim escorted Wink and Gilroy to their seats, and the inspectors took the remaining chairs.

"You're the only authorities working on this case?" Tim asked.

"Yes," answered Borelli.

"If my brother committed a crime, and it was reported, you'd know of it? That's why you are here, right?"

Borelli answered, "We are seeking your brother on the original charges, we're not aware of any others."

"We'd know instantly. We're programmed into the crime network." Hanson wanted to appear the eager young detective. He watched wrath flare on the face of Gilroy.

"So what gives, Your Grace?" Tim's eyes pierced Gilroy with scorn.

"I don't like your disrespectful tone, young man. I kept the theft from the authorities to save our institution some negative publicity as well as saving your brother from another charge."

Gilroy had lied about the facial recognition. Were his people illegally tapped into police files, or had John Johnson been expected all along?

"You didn't want to add another charge to murder?"

"One more disrespectful word from you, and you can do without my help. You forget these are valuable books; robbery on seminary grounds appeals to the news media."

Tim hid a wry smile. Gilroy's tone had been laden with depraved wrath. If any man could be Satan's disciple, it was Gilroy.

"I'm sorry, Your Excellency. My brother's plight has deeply affected me. I thank you for your concern in this matter, and I will help recover the books if at all possible. I will turn my brother in as soon as I know his location or speak to him."

Tim knew Gilroy's kind: slippery, without integrity, lusting for power. Why aggravate a man who had the power of the Church? The archbishop hid his skepticism and spoke curtly.

"That's better. I'm on your side. You will see."

The archbishop rose; Wink stood and spoke. "I know my way out."

He winked at Tim with the eye not visible to the archbishop. Tim, feeling betrayed by Wink, did not smile. Tim heard the door close. Through tensed lips, he smiled at the inspectors.

"As you witnessed, you're not the only ones who want my brother. He's stolen some books from a library. The archbishop said the Church was working with the police."

Tim thought it possible that one or both of these inspectors were tied to the Church. Borelli's seeming honesty could mean nothing as to his allegiance.

Hanson spoke. "Very curious that a fleeing man, wanted for murder, would go to a New York seminary and steal books. Perhaps under the influence of your grandfather?"

"Possible. Gramps has some strange ways and even stranger thoughts."

Borelli took a chance and spoke. "Any idea where your grandfather or John are at the moment?"

"No…My mother told me the government doesn't have much of a case, as far as the murder. She was told this by you?"

"That's correct, and I stand by that position. There is only one eye witness to the supposed killing, and he was occupied with remaining alive during a firefight. What could he have seen? Discredit his testimony, and your brother is free. If the murder charge is invalid, then his subsequent escape, masking are justified. Though he might have to furnish information about the masking…name names, locations, procedures. Stealing a few books, if returned, won't carry a heavy sentence, maybe no jail time at all, just parole. The best place for him now is in custody."

Tim thought on Borelli's words. He was tempted to turn John in—for John's good. Could the police protect John from the Church? His brother wouldn't go willingly. Maybe this information supposedly so destructive to the Church was all a hoax, or of less importance than his brother supposed. He had made a promise to John and Gramps and would not break it. One more evening and tomorrow, and it would be over. He owed them this evening.

"If you know something, tell us. We might be able to help." Hanson's voice was soft with concern. Borelli prayed Tim Johnson would keep his word to his brother.

"I did receive a note from my brother; found it in my pocket on the way home. Someone must have slipped it in while I was walking to the commuter." He marveled at how well he lied.

"Where is it?" asked Hanson, doubtfully.

"I threw it away. He said he'll make contact tomorrow afternoon. When he does, I'll turn him in." Lying was like breathing now.

"Okay," said Borelli as he rose. "We can't ask for any more than that. Here's my number. Call anytime, day or night."

Borelli handed Tim a card. Borelli respected Tim for the lies that had protected his brother. Lies abounded, but none came from love, only self-interest. What was a man if he did not protect his family? Tim led the inspectors to the door, watched them leave. Mary was in the hallway. She recognized his lying face was on. He had a number of faces, all equally readable by her and by no one else.

"Honey, I'm going to the lab."

She came to him, hugged him. "Anything wrong?" He was going to lie again.

"No. I've got some work that needs to be done, and I'm restless."

She knew Tim had seen John. "All right. Be careful."

She knew every lie he had ever told and never challenged him. He only lied to protect her or the children from the pressures of life. Eventually, whatever problem couldn't be solved was shared with her. She never let on that she knew, didn't want to rob him of his misguided nobility and manhood.

He picked up his coat, opened the door a crack, saw the inspectors drive past. He slipped out when a home blocked their view. Borelli expected Tim to leave for the lab. He thought when the corner house blocked their view, Tim would exit.

Tim walked quickly in the cold night air. The mutiny charge was in the hands of the lawyer. The stolen microdots were the danger. Had the Church killed for them? Would the Church kill again? Gilroy had gotten under his skin; he detested the man. He hadn't liked being treated like a wayward child. The question was, what was in the microdots that had certain people excited, even panicked?

***

Cain stood in the recessed entranceway of an office building. The sidewalks were packed with pedestrian traffic, the streets crowded with vehicles. It was convenient that the university buildings brushed a commercial district; easier to go unnoticed. The darkness was a blessing. He'd had men posted since midmorning when Tim Johnson's shadow had reported. Tim Johnson had had a shadow for the past four months, as had his brother, John. The natatorium had briefly covered their whereabouts, but they soon turned up exactly where expected.

The wind gusted on the street, blew past the recessed entrance. Even without the wind, he was cold. He had been cold before. The Russian Front of the 1940s had been cold—the coldest. Why hadn't Christianity remained in the Middle East? He smirked at his humor.

He had been to this area before, when it had been fields and woods, and his Iroquois brothers roamed free. They had loved the crying flesh, the hysterical soul, men reduced to charred stumps of whimpering humanity. He had raped a woman near this place as her husband lay scalped, dying in his pitiful cornfield. He had countless times given the god that had scorned him the blood and flesh of men in a mockery of sacrifice. Blood and flesh upon crops had a special irony. He looked into the windows of the university building across the street and lusted for Diana.

A street police officer walked by—a former shock trooper. Cain spat in disgust; he hated the genetically engineered steroid men. Satan's power gave him strength; these synthetic men could not stand against him. He watched Tim Johnson stealthily glide into the building. He saw the inspectors, Borelli and Hanson, arrive in their car and discreetly hide it slightly down the street.

He waited for his orders. He could have taken the microdots in the morning or the afternoon—just walked in and forcibly taken the canister. But the fools above him were still debating, still seeking a subtle solution when brute strength would have been more appropriate. He admired his quarry's ability to find the microdots after seventy-five years of intensive searching by his people. He admired Johnson's boldness in breaking into the bookcase in full view of everyone, then simply running off the campus. Boldness and simplicity were the rules of all successful undertakings.

He would have captured them on campus if not for one weak-lunged man, who could not keep pace and who had hesitated in calling reinforcements. John Johnson, you aren't so clever. I could have slit your throat that evening while you slept with your whore and the chem blankets dazzled with their heat. It was all the same—he would bring to bay his quarries, all three—and all three would suffer, praising Satan as they died. He could wait; he had been waiting since Eden.

***

Hanson sat; Borelli reclined. The heater had warmed the inside of the car to a comfortable temperature, their coats had been discarded. Hanson was eating; they had picked up an order at a drive-through restaurant. They had a clear view of the entrance to the university building. Borelli lay his coat over him. He had erased the copy of the fugitives' conversation with Tim. This gave him a feeling of security. Hanson had no possibility of knowing the truth.

Borelli thought upon what he had heard in that conversation of the morning. Was the world only seven or eight years from destruction? Would this Satanic leader soon come to power? Would those in Christ leave before the world fell apart? He knew he did not belong to Christ. Not even at Tim Johnson's level of doing good works, of looking toward God for direction.

He had lived his life as best he could, always wanting to do the decent thing, always attempting to treat everyone, even criminals, with respect. Treat others as you would want them to treat you, had said his father. In the far past, within the context of American history, this sentiment had been called "the Golden Rule." He even knew the Bible had introduced the concept. Borelli had taken the concept a step further than actions at a civil level. He tried to apply it to his thought processes concerning strangers before him, in the thoughts, motivations, and behaviors he attributed to the strangers. Simply, he attempted to think well of others and apply empathy in judging their actions, dispensing mercy when appropriate.

Oddly enough, the few Enslavers he had met—those so anxious to bind—believed in the best of an individual. The Enslaver philosophy had depth; he had known this since a student at law school. It was easy for him to believe the world was wrong—there were too many Hansons; everyone was a Hanson.

The question now seemed to be was *he* a Hanson? He had never believed he was until he heard Gramps—Henry—talk of Satan. "He's a liar, a deceiver, a mesmerizer, an illusionist. He uses these qualities to keep men within their sinful flesh. Mankind, confused or satisfied, it doesn't matter to Satan as long as they remain in their flesh," Henry had said. Borelli thought he might be satisfied and in the flesh. He'd always prided himself for his good qualities—understanding, consideration, tenacity. But Satan could use and perhaps control those good qualities. How could he know for a certainty who controlled him? He did not believe like Tim that man was both good and evil. Like John, he knew that if you were a mixture of good and evil, the evil would always triumph. That's what men were—evil—and he was a man. How could he belong to Christ? How could he give Him everything, know for certain?

He didn't want to know because he was afraid of the end, of a hell, though he felt the end of time pushing him. He wanted to know he was acceptable to this God, the only God, the Creator. He just wanted to be acceptable. He had always wanted to live right, do right, have no illusions. Since a child playing cops and robbers, he had always wanted to be one of the good guys, he wanted to wear the badge.

Hanson broke the silence. "I saw a program awhile back that said at one time, night, by custom, was a time for sleep. Everyone slept at the same time; everything closed down; the streets were deserted."

The unending stream of people on the sidewalks seemed to mock Hanson's words. A police officer walked by—a former shock trooper. His eyes were keen for violence.

"It's difficult to believe that's the way it was." Borelli paused. "What do you think of this case, Bob?" Borelli thought back to Hanson's treatment of Gilroy—he seemed to have animosity for His Grace. Just an act by Hanson. Borelli could read the man now.

"I think we would be wise not to speculate. It's gone on long enough. Let's find them and pick them up. You and I both know our trio stole something other than books, and the Church is embarrassed or afraid that whatever was stolen may be made known." Hanson picked up his phone. "I've got to call my wife. It's been days." He opened the door and slid out of the car, peered in at Borelli as he swung the door half closed. "I need privacy and some fresh air."

"Sure, I understand." Borelli understood. Hanson was probably calling higher authorities either in law enforcement or the Church. Were the Church's spies listening in on the conversations within the lab? Would they tell Hanson what was said? Did Hanson know his partner had been lying to him? Borelli nestled into his coat and seat to escape the blast of cold air that had entered. The wind had picked up and was buffeting the car. He wondered if John had found a moment to nestle with Diana? To be young again, to love another more than one's self. She was a beautiful girl. She had tagged life correctly when she had called it futile. They were two good kids; life had thrown both some curves. He thought of his own grown children. What if he viewed John and Diana as his own kids? How would he help them? He admired John and Diana. They were faithful, honest, clever, enduring. He would not allow them to kill or be killed. They could still have a life worth living in a spousal penal colony.

Borelli scanned the streets. Somewhere, the archbishop's men were in position, waiting; or Cain and his men, whom John had tangled with at the seminary. When seen, he wondered if Cain would live up to John and Diana's description. He was certain of their presence even though they had been quiet for quite some time. He had electronic eyes on all exits of the lab building. He should warn the local officers, stationed in a van, that they could be under surveillance by the Church's men. This case was turning into a free-for-all.

He had kept the lab sound unit under his authority for security. He had a bud in his ear. He told Hanson there was no sound.

***

Tim entered his office. Diana was curled on one end of the couch, minus shoes, a book in her hand, his office desk light pulled close to her. John lay on the remainder of the couch in a fetal position, his and Diana's coats upon him, fast asleep. Diana smiled at Tim. She hadn't even tensed when he came in. He whispered.

"Where's Henry?"

"In the lab, sleeping."

"*Early Theories of Relativity?*" he asked, glancing at the cover of her book.

"It's the Bible."

Tim quietly picked up a padded chair, placed it before Diana, and sat.

"Are you and my brother...?"

He held up his two fingers, crossed, the slang for sexual activity or sexual involvement.

"No, that has never happened." She appeared shocked, hurt.

"You would be the perfect wife for him."

She blushed. "Thank you."

He paused and wondered if he should begin the next topic upon his mind. He could foresee the uncomfortable outcome. "Do you think I'm in Christ?"

"No."

"That means you are?"

"Yes."

"Don't you think that is highly conceited?"

"It would be if I were boasting of something I earned or deserved. It would be conceited if I didn't want to share being in Christ with you."

Her voice was soft and loving, the green eyes moistened. He witnessed a deep peace and satisfaction envelope her.

"Why has He come to you and not to me? I've known of Christ since my youth. Never left the Church." He was deserving, perhaps more than she was. "How long have you known Christ?"

"Two days? I've lost track of time. But I've wanted Him since I was a child. I just didn't know who He was."

"So what happened to you?"

She smiled a peculiar smile. "I was empty inside—bitter, hateful, breaking God's laws with every breath—and I thought that was a normal life. I was like everyone else. That was the way life was; it was reality. But I sensed something more. Then your brother came into my life. He was different than anyone I had ever met." She laughed quietly, thankfully. A tear came to her eye, and she shyly wiped it away with a finger. "He saw life differently. He was kind, good. He told me of God, of Christ. The Holy Spirit began working on me, and I resisted."

"Why did the resistance end?"

"I went too far to turn back. I don't know what that means. The Lord presented me with choices: my life, or His life. I kept following Him till I had left me behind. Then, He just burst into my being. The Holy Spirit took control."

"The taking control is another way of saying you are born again?"

"Yes."

He didn't doubt the validity of her story—to her; it was her reality. She'd evidently had a hard, lonely life. She couldn't handle the pressures, and she cracked. Her concept of God filled the crack, the void. He would never crack because his life had been fortified with God, the Church since his youth.

"You think I'm weak and that's why I need a crutch like Christ?" Diana asked.

How did she know his thoughts?

"Well, since you brought it up, yes. I have my weaknesses. I sin, I'm not always perfect. But there is no reason to throw all of my life away because I make an occasional mistake."

"Were you born a sinner?"

"No, I have sinful tendencies that God helps me overcome."

"You're missing the point. You were born a sinner; that is your nature. You have good tendencies that society rewards, strengthens. That is what your Church has done—rewarded your good tendencies, strengthened them. At heart, you are apart from God, and therefore you sin."

"No. No. No." Tim's voice increased in volume, and John stirred restlessly. She was like Gramps and John—weak. They had fallen apart under the stress of life. Well, he would always be strong, and so Christ didn't need to fill him. God's guidance was enough. He had three times the education she had—and, most likely, three times the intellect—yet, she was basically saying he couldn't understand her? He hated his conceit, but the truth was, *she* couldn't understand *him*.

Diana opened her Bible. "Listen to this, Tim."

"'Verily, verily, I say unto thee, Except a man be born again, he cannot see the Kingdom of God,'" she read. "Here's another passage." She saw his frustration and anger mounting.

"'But as many as received him, to them gave he the power to become the sons of God, even to them that believe on his name: Which were born, not of blood, nor of the will of the flesh, nor of the will of man, but of God.'

"Even if you could lead a sinless life apart from God, you could not say you were born into his family. You could not be a son of God," she said. "Tim! You don't *want* to give up your life. You like controlling it, deciding its course, enjoying its pleasures. You don't want that life to die." She paused to reflect. She saw her own miscommunication and needed to clarify. "You know there are good people who sin and bad people who sin. It isn't about our actions. It's about who our Daddy is. He decides our genetic code. He gives us life."

John was moaning, tossing, spitting out unintelligible words. She left her seat, knelt beside him, stroked his hair, his forehead. She studied Tim's eyes as she comforted John.

"He's seen too much, Tim, and still he goes on for his Lord. He dies each day. Each day, his dreams go unfulfilled. Each day, he faces death or imprisonment. Each day, he smiles at me and loves me. God is a Living God, Tim."

In the Shadow of Babylon

Tears streamed down her cheeks. "You can't share your life with Him. He can't be a guiding principle. He must be within you, and you must throw all of your life away, no matter how much it hurts to let go."

Her tears brought tears to Tim's eyes as he witnessed her love for his brother. With startling clarity, he realized the sufferings of his brother and the bleak future ahead of him.

"You evidently have a wonderful life, Tim, but it is worthless. It serves you, and it serves the world. Where is the Jesus who died for you? On the outside looking in."

Tim stood, wiping the tears from his eyes, and walked away. He didn't care for emotional displays. He didn't see why he should throw away a successful life, a life that did much for Christ—through the Church. If what she was saying was true, then, yes, he would give his life to Christ. If Christ wanted his life, Christ must take it; not because he wouldn't give it freely, but because he had to be sure it was of God. He just didn't believe God was asking. He sat by the projector, turned it on, began to review the microdots.

CHAPTER 11

Tim awoke on the couch; jackets had been placed over him. He could feel the darkness lurking behind the pulled blinds. The projector light illuminated the center of the room. John and Gramps sat by the projector, staring at the screen, reading and commenting to each other in low voices. He assumed Diana was sleeping in the lab. He had no remembrance of moving to the couch. Henry caught movement from Tim's awakening and spoke. "Good to see you up, Tim." The voice was strained from overuse, a cough followed the words.

"What time…"

"Is it? Four o'clock in the morning," said John. "Have some coffee."

"Oh, my Lor—"

"Don't worry. Mary called ten minutes ago," John said as he held up Tim's personal phone. John had texted back, impersonating Tim's written mannerisms, assuming the phone transmissions were being intercepted.

"Good. Good…"

In the Shadow of Babylon

Tim rose, grabbed his coffee mug from his desk, moved to the coffee machine on the lab table and poured a cup.

Henry spoke, a triumphal tone underlying his words. "We found documents after the Satanic bible that should interest you. By the way, Satan's bible is simply amazing, the most complete work of disinformation ever done—it's just pure lies. The serpent is the hero. God becomes the evil one—withholding from humanity what is rightfully humanity'. And Christ is portrayed as a trickster."

Before falling asleep, Tim had only gotten through a quarter of the Old Testament on the microdots before skipping to the New, where he read another quarter of the text. The account had been interesting, carefully woven from the original Bible, though his knowledge of the original Bible was scant. Many points seemed to be well made. "What did you find?" He was surprised by his relaxed tone. His neck ached from sleeping without a pillow. He was hungry; his stomach growled at the coffee.

Henry answered. "We found the plans and timetables for subverting the World Church. The methodology, everything. A nine-point plan, four of which they completed over seventy-five years ago. I don't know of all the inner workings of the Church since then—statements of theology and doctrine—but on major issues, it seems their timetable was met."

"What does that mean to me?" Tim's curiosity dominated his cynicism.

John replied. "It means the World Church you're so willing to defend is being subverted by the very people you don't think are real. Their subversion has been done so well so far that if you look at the plan and at what you believe, you will see no difference."

"Insults so early?" Tim exhaled a laugh from his nose. He couldn't be angry at John. Diana had made him appreciate the cost of his brother's beliefs. Tim continued. "You know, I thought about what you said concerning evil—what it is, how it manifests itself—and you made sense. But now you're telling me these people actually have an organization to coordinate and accomplish Satan's purposes? Since the beginning of time, they have been working through an organization, and no one has caught them until now? Witches, demons, incantations, spells, covens, blood sacrifices everywhere," Tim stated flatly.

Diana entered the room from the lab, her hair disheveled, her eyes soft and sleepy.

"Hi, Tim."

"Hello, Beautiful." Tim spoke tenderly. He liked her for the love that was in her heart, and for the love she gave his brother. Henry took up Tim's challenge.

"The world, the flesh, the devil, they work independently of each other and in combination. I'm not saying there has been an organization of evil controlled by man since the founding of the world, and it has had continuity all these years through human planning and effort. But Satan has his church, Babylon—confusion; his administration of fallen angels as otherworldly and determined as he is. He twists and subverts the word of God, becomes part of the church that professes God. Jesus likened Satan's influence to leavening in bread. It mixes in until invisible then rises through all ingredients, until it is the bread."

"In the past, Satan's church was noted for a virgin who conceives a son," he continued. "He was the promised deliverer—Tammuz. All the Old Testament prophets—Ezekiel, for one—railed against this lie. The religion of a mother god, always popular, and a child was introduced. A secret priestly cast was always part of Satan's church. All that God declares, Satan mimics, from Genesis onward. The more closely Satan adheres to God's truth, the better his subversion. Satan's church even had a cross, the letter *T* for *Tammuz*.

"From Babylon, Satan's church went to Phoenicia, where Jezebel worshiped him. In Egypt, the names changed to Isis and Horus; in Greece, they became Aphrodite and Eros; in Italy, Venus and Cupid," Henry said.

"The lies, subtle, clinging to elements of truth, were cleverly introduced to Christendom. The leaven was added, and the World Church has risen. This leaven is the fermenting soul of the natural man—the man who likes being cut off from God, who likes the pleasures of disobedience, the sensuousness of the flesh.

"But forget history, forget the World Church. Even corporations are subverted, power shifts occur, and ideas contend. It's all because men draw sides to seek advantage for themselves," Henry said. "If you can believe it happens to worldly organizations, then why not the false World Church, which has been worldly since the beginning?"

"Simple black and white? Night and day?" Tim asked sadly.

"Why shouldn't it be simple?"

Tim ignored Henry's question. He didn't want a debate. He turned to Diana, who had come to the coffee machine. "What about you?"

"I don't know. I'm no scholar like Henry. I just know the World Church told me to live free, presented me with rituals, made me a whore, and said I had all I needed. Your brother came and told me I was a sinner and filled me with the Living God. Now I'm truly free."

She smiled, wondering what he would do with that confession of her past. It didn't matter what he thought; God loved her. Tim noticed a presence was upon her again, of love. It had to be her emotion welling to the surface. Had she been a whore? Did she exaggerate? Perhaps she had slept with a few boyfriends; that wasn't being a whore. He would say nothing. She spoke again, and Tim had the sensation of viewing her face through a swirl of translucence.

"He lives within me! Can you imagine? Me! He loves *me*, a sinner of the worst kind!" she said. Her sincerity forced a belief into his heart.

"Let me see these plans," Tim said determinedly as he pulled up a chair. Henry flipped back through the film and then stopped. Tim read aloud from the main points of an outline.

"'Deny: God, Christ, Christ's return, faith, sound doctrine, separate life, Christian liberty, morals, authority.' It doesn't sound very profound or systematic. To deny Christ is to deny His return."

"It is possible to accept Christ as a man or God and deny His return," Henry said. "Besides, subversion doesn't have to be systematic or profound;

it just has to isolate various tenants, then break them apart by any means necessary—without regard to logic or continuity."

Henry began slowly scrolling through the text. "Stop here."

Tim began reading. "'To deny Christian liberty is to deny Christ's death as the freeing agent from mankind's natural, carnal self. The awareness of man's natural self and the need for Christ's death is created by the condemnation inherent in moral and spiritual law. These laws must be proven contradictory to rational thought, social evolution, and individual freedom by stressing the mystic and supernatural, the unscientific premises of Christ's death. The Christian-to-be must be made to understand that man cannot free himself through the multitude of self-suppressive and psychologically damaging techniques that would necessarily need be applied to his personality and psyche through the Christ concept.

"'It must be shown, through rational thought, that the law's intent was to hold man within bounds until mankind could achieve the spiritual perfectibility necessary to control the excesses of his nature. This process of control is evolutionary. Through time and knowledge, man sheds his unwanted spiritual baseness, until law becomes obsolete.

"'Example: Fornication and adultery were forbidden by the law because the sexual act was used to aggrandize the self or demean another. But any sexual act done in love, with respect and sensitivity, is a glory to God. Man, through social and spiritual evolution, can now objectively identify his motivations, control them, and thus fully understand the freedom of God's creative act. The law has become obsolete as man's knowledge of self is completed.'"

A puzzled expression covered Tim's face. "It seems right."

John spoke. "But it isn't. What if your wife had sex with another man? This reasoning says that would be right and good. As long as she wasn't doing it to demean you or aggrandize herself."

"No, it would break the bond of trust that Mary and I have. Our love for each other would be like the common property of mankind."

Henry spoke angrily. "If that is all the deeper your trust and love extends, then perhaps you shouldn't be married. Why do you bind Mary to yourself? Why can't you share her with others? Maybe she could find greater sexual satisfaction with another? Why deprive her of being fulfilled?"

Henry knew the priestly lines of logic. Henry thought his acting had been quite good. Tim stared with a bewildered and angry snarl.

"You'd be jealous to the point of rage or murder," John said, chuckling softly.

"Those feelings of betrayal and hurt wouldn't be wrong," Henry added. "To attain this freedom they talk about, you would have to deny the institution of marriage ordained by God—where two become one flesh. That's a scriptural verse the enemy has purposely overlooked. What the enemy is proposing is freedom for the natural man, love reduced to the level of the animal world. We can use that line of reasoning to any law God has set forth. What you get is mankind hiding from his true nature. By changing the law, circumventing the law, he can pretend to be within God's will. By controlling his own passions, he justifies his independence from God and nullifies the need for the Lord's control over his life."

Tim looked blankly at Henry. John realized that Tim simply wanted to be told what to do, which had been their agreement of yesterday morning.

"What we want you to do, Tim, is turn copies of these microdots over to a certain cardinal whom Henry believes is still listening, hearkening to the Word of the Lord. We believe many of these subversive plans were implemented within the last twenty years by people within the World Church. Those who opposed the plans, or the people with the plans, would take a real interest in these documents."

"Sure. I'll be glad to. I promised I would." He paused and then said emphatically, "You promised to turn yourselves in."

A fist pounded upon the office door; rough commands were heard. The lock was electronically picked within a second, and into the room burst two thick-bodied men, followed by Archbishop Gilroy and Father Winkler. The thick-bodied men smirked. The men were known as Gilroy's goons within the higher echelons of the local Church. Gilroy's eyes sparkled in victory even as the face remained grim. Winkler stood behind, embarrassed, ashamed. Gilroy, parting his men, faced Tim.

"This will be a brief visit." The voice was cold steel, disdain glowed in the eyes.

"What can I do for you?" Tim found it difficult to be submissive. He assessed the thick-bodied men: strong martial arts skills were displayed in their bearings and stances. He could incapacitate one, perhaps, with some luck. He was lying to himself.

"We know you have the information we seek." Gilroy peered at the screen just as John turned off the projector. The room held the gray light of dawn and streetlights edging around the blinds. John moved around the corner of the couch, as if wishing to join Tim. He let out a stifled grunt, and while bending over to assess his stubbed toe, deftly pulled his knife from the corner of a cushion. The knife slipped into his waistband at the small of his back.

"What information?" Tim asked.

"Stop playing dumb. The microdots. We want them."

Tim shrugged his shoulders dumbly. Gilroy needed a fist in his face. He wondered if Gilroy truly knew what was on the dots. Surely, Gilroy didn't fear this information.

"I don't think you really want it."

Gilroy shook with emotion. His eyes burned hatefully into Tim. "You will understand where the power lies. The Church wants the information. You have no legal right to keep us from our documents. If you think you can toy with the power of the Church, then call home."

Winkler stiffened in apprehension, shock, betrayal. Tim stared at Gilroy in perplexity. The image of a frail, silver-haired saint worthy of respect contended with the image of the weak-bodied, ruthless, egocentric man flaunting power. The archbishop snorted in disgust and impatience. He went to

Tim's desk and punched numbers into the telescreen. He didn't like this Tim Johnson—though Winkler had nothing but praise for him. He was too cocky, too clever. He was smart mouthed and contentious. The archbishop sneered as he turned the screen toward Tim.

A man appeared on the screen. He sat on a sofa within a home. He sat in Tim's den.

"Cain," gasped Diana.

A wave of nausea passed through Tim. Cain said nothing, simply stared at the screen moronically. A strange dullness, an evil emptiness clung to the face.

"Where's my wife?" Tim wanted his voice to project strength, confidence, aggressiveness. Instead, it was weak and quavering. The man named Cain barely fit on the screen.

Cain answered. "She is here, safe—so far—and being well treated. If the time comes, I can make her hurt and bleed; your children too." The moronic smile remained. His voice had been strangely pliable. Tim had hoped the kids had gotten off to school. The screen turned to Mary, sitting on a sofa.

"Are you okay, honey?" Tim was overcome with conflicting emotions of grief, hope, anger, self-control.

"Yes." She spoke quietly.

"He'll be leaving soon."

Tim's voice held a calm as he raged inside. He saw Mary's agitation, her fear, and the strength of will, the animal fury she would use upon the man who would hurt her children. This was all a dream, wasn't it? The screen went blank. Tim faced Gilroy. The rage died; a submissiveness swept through his soul. He would beg on his knees, if necessary. He spoke. "What do you want besides the documents?"

Gilroy's stature increased, his chest rose, a smile covered his face as he gloated over Tim's submission. "That is all. These three are free to go."

John gathered up the dots, placed them in the canister, threw the canister to Gilroy. Gilroy spoke. "What of copies?"

"We didn't have time to make copies. Search us if you don't believe me. Besides, we know you're not going to let us go free. You'll follow us, thinking we might have copies. You'll kill us," John said flatly.

Gilroy smiled. "Well, if you don't want to believe my word is good."

"You abide not in the truth, because there is no truth in you." Henry's voice was harsh. He pursed his lips in anger. Gilroy's eyes narrowed to slits.

"You know some scripture. Congratulations. Now, back away from the projector so I can verify the material."

The four moved away as ordered. Gilroy was apparently familiar with antiquated projectors—no moments of hesitation or confusion. Tim wondered at his deftness. The machine was an antique to the point of being an historical relic. Such deftness came only by long familiarity. He ran through the dots quickly, stopping at various places. He knew what proofs of authenticity he was seeking. Unconsciously, Tim shook his head in disbelief at this high-ranking member of the Church who, evidently, had immersed himself in the minutia of John and Henry's claims long before the claims had even been made. The dots were inserted back into the canister, placed into his pocket as he spoke to Tim.

"You are to go directly home. Cain will be gone."

A fist pounded on the door, immediately followed by the entrance of Borelli and Hanson.

"Gentlemen." Borelli's voice was cordial as he flashed his inspector's badge to the big men with Gilroy. He held the badge while their eyes focused upon it and identified it. He locked onto their eyes until he was satisfied that he saw submission.

"Good morning," Gilroy said cordially as he attempted to pass the inspectors.

"You always want to leave when I'm arriving. What is it about me that offends you?" Borelli touched Gilroy's chest with his outstretched hand.

"We're in a hurry," Gilroy said gruffly.

"I won't take long."

Hanson was silent. Borelli understood Hanson had no desire to cross the Church; he just wanted to watch as the "old man" dug his own grave. Well, let him watch.

"We had a listening device aimed at this office window. Even telescreen conversations are picked up." Borelli moved close to the archbishop, into that space men think of as their own. A physical fear emanated from the man who was so eager to instill fear in others.

"I heard your man threaten Tim Johnson and his family. That is a crime. A man of your intelligence—breaking the law. I want you to call your man now. Tell him to report to the Southside Police Station. You will be escorted there, along with whichever of your men broke into this office. Then, we will fill out some arrest forms—if Tim Johnson is willing?"

"Yes, I'm willing."

The archbishop's gaze burned into Tim's eyes, seethed with hate. The hate was returned tenfold. The archbishop straightened; his small chest puffed. He stood as if he wasn't the weak, small man he was, as if some higher power strengthened him. Borelli turned the screen to Gilroy.

"Now, to the screen."

The archbishop did not move. Borelli lay his arm around the little man's shoulders, gave a firm but friendly grasp with his hand, and gently moved the archbishop to the screen. The archbishop balked, attempted to force his heels into the ground. Borelli pressed with greater force; the heels stuttered across the floor. Borelli saw the eyes wince at the indignity, then recover composure. Gilroy's men smirked silently; they hated their little boss. Gilroy glared at Borelli and then smiled—he had the power, and Borelli would pay. Revenge was always sweet. Cain appeared on the screen. He had both of Tim's children sitting by him on the couch. He held a children's book in his hands.

"Report to the Southside Police Station immediately. I'll be there shortly." Gilroy's voice was curt. The screen snapped to blankness.

Horror welled in Tim as he thought of the perversity of Cain, befriending children he might torture or kill. Hanson had enjoyed the confrontation. Borelli's anger was the first display of raw power and emotion he'd witnessed since their partnership began. Borelli was true to his kind, possessing that indignant anger, that rage against injustice and cruelty—a man's family had been threatened! What a fool! What a comic!

Borelli spoke. "Now, about the stolen microdots and the books. A formal complaint has yet to be made to the police. Now is your chance, Archbishop."

"There is no need." Pressing charges would alert the media, members of which scanned the police blotters. The four might inform the news media, but if the Church seemed disinterested, the media might think there was no story. Besides, the three would be dead before long. Borelli would find trouble in his future, if not death. "Close to retirement, Inspector Borelli? I suppose you plan on a pension?" Gilroy smiled.

"Threatening an inspector. That's another charge. Hand back the canister."

"What of these people? One is an illegal alien, another is wanted for murder. The old man has aided and abetted both."

Gilroy had no fear of returning the canister; his men would soon retrieve it. Better that Borelli thought he had a fear of relinquishment.

"Hanson, escort the archbishop and his men to the police station."

Hanson gazed at the fugitives. "What about them?"

"I'll bring them along in a few minutes." Borelli wondered if Hanson would object.

Hanson turned to his charges. "Let's take a little ride, Archbishop; you and your men."

Borelli's voice boomed. "Hand me the canister."

Gilroy complied disdainfully as the party turned and left the room.

Borelli stood silently before the fugitives. He had scrambled the sound units prior to entering the office. No one could hear their conversations. He had also initiated a defensive sound disrupter in the eventuality that Cain had his own sound system. He reviewed the events. Were all his probabilities covered? He hoped the answer was yes. He seemed to be waiting. A faint smile came to his lips as he studied John and then Diana. Nothing remarkable in the appearance of John Johnson, except his hair was now dyed blond. Diana's hair was black—her computer photos had showed her as a blonde. She was a beauty, and she was in love. The old man was near death—pale, weak. Tim Johnson looked confused and disheveled. Satisfaction enveloped Borelli. The chase had been long and arduous; the quarry was at bay. He heard the elevator door close down the hall.

"Let's move into the next room."

John tensed, thinking Borelli, who could be the Church's man, might have murder on his mind. Borelli laughed at John's tension.

"Relax, John. I'm a friend. I just want some conversation."

John did relax, entered the room at peace.

"Sit." Borelli obeyed his own command, and the others followed, glancing quizzically at each other. Borelli focused his gaze on Tim, who seemed to be brooding. "You could claim the canister as your property or Henry's, even though it was found in stolen property. The media would see that on the record and have great fun with it. A grievance against the archbishop would also help. That would go all the way to ecclesiastical court—a perfect vehicle for making the contents of the microdots known."

Borelli noticed a collective breathless pause and sigh. Borelli bored into Tim's eyes.

"Unless you think civil court is enough punishment for Gilroy."

Tim's eyes hardened angrily. "The queer little man isn't going to escape so easily. I'll expose him and all his kind. Even Winkler, my friend, didn't utter a word on my behalf. If Cain ever gets close to my kids again, I'll atomize his moronic brains into the wind."

Borelli saw a rage coursing through Tim—the jaw jutted, the face flushed, the eyes could have cut diamonds. Tim continued. "They will find there is one man among their sheep!"

Borelli noticed John nodding his head in affirmation, smiling at his brother's righteous anger. Strange that he felt as if he were with friends. These people were different than the world's people. They weren't out for themselves, weren't protecting their egos, had no mask upon the intentions of their hearts. He realized that he belonged with them. They were the good guys of his childhood games. God, life had been lonely. He hadn't realized it till this moment. Should he ask them? Should he relax his guard for one moment? What did he have to lose? They sensed something; they were waiting.

"How can I know that I am acceptable to God? One of his men? I've always wanted to be one of the good guys, upholding law and order. Now, I'm not so sure I'm the real thing."

Diana was the first to recover from the surprise of Borelli's question. "You were made acceptable when Christ died on the cross for your sins. He died for you, took the penalty of your sin upon himself. You are acceptable…"

John spoke when Diana faltered for words. "Yield your mind and body to the Holy Spirit, God's Spirit, His very self, and the reality will grow. Then you will know for sure."

Wisdom was passed to Henry. He spoke. "Under the authority of God, who is all that is good, you can't help but be on the right side, one of the good guys. Say this now, aloud: Father, I am a sinner."

"Father, I am a sinner."

"In need of a savior, your son, Jesus."

"In need of a savior, your son, Jesus."

"Forgive me and take me into your love."

"Forgive me and take me into your love."

"Amen."

"Amen."

A peace came to Borelli, and an assurance. He had thought all along that it was simple faith. No tears came to his eyes, no softness entered his gaze, no weakness penetrated his voice as he spoke. "Henry Johnson, I can let you go and, of course, Tim. But John and Diana, you two must be arrested."

"So be it," John said sadly.

The kid would allow himself to be taken without a fight, without clever words or arguments. Diana would obediently follow him.

Borelli knew Gilroy would settle for nothing less than the microdots in his possession and the Johnsons and Diana Rochembeau dead. If Gilroy could not have exclusive possession of the microdots—if they were put into his enemy's hands—then having the principals dead was still advantageous. An old man like Henry could easily be poisoned, given a heart-stopping drug, hit by a vehicle, or pushed from a high place or down a flight of stairs. John and Diana could just as easily be murdered in jail by one of the inmate population or by a guard. Tim Johnson's family could be threatened again or kidnapped. For all Tim Johnson's indignant anger, he would become docile, subservient if that were required to save his family.

The opportune time for Gilroy to kill would be before the microdots were delivered to higher Church authorities. Briefly, he thought he might be overstating Gilroy's evil, but then he thought of Cain. Cain was a killer. Men like him were brought into a situation to kill; coercion and intimidation were secondary. Borelli focused his gaze on John and Diana.

"You know that if I arrest you two, Gilroy will probably have you murdered. You'll be helpless, without a weapon or a friend while in police custody."

Borelli noticed Tim Johnson wince.

"There is a better world waiting," said John.

Borelli smiled. "Besides, this world hasn't much longer." He laughed as he watched the faces light with surprise. "I've heard some conversations, read some of Henry's book."

He wondered if Gilroy would or could take away his pension or if the shoving incident would be forgotten. Gilroy wasn't the type to forget. Borelli could live with his kids; he had savings. Would Gilroy think it necessary to kill him?

"I'm going to leave the room for two minutes. In that time, decide if you would prefer to flee or to be arrested."

Borelli stood, walked out the door.

"Is he serious?" asked Tim, his voice rising in pitch. Fear possessed Tim. Could Borelli be trusted? If he could, was the situation that grave? An inspector allowing two fugitives to flee? What was happening? Everything seemed upside down.

"I think he is..." John said reflectively. "Tim, that place in the drought zone—springs in the middle of nowhere. We've only got six months to a year at the most."

Tim smiled to himself. Then they would float off into space. Why not? Let them believe it.

Henry spoke. "I'll stay with Tim till the grievance is settled. I'll do what I can for our family, John."

Tim spoke earnestly. "This place is in the mountains—barren, dry. Only at the upper elevations is there vegetation other than cacti and mesquite. Some deer, panther, bighorn sheep can be found. Springs so small they are no good for commercial use. A geology station sits fifty miles to the north. It's packed with provisions for rescue crews, seismologists, geologists. Probably enough food to last two people six months.

"Take the university van out in the parking lot. Ditch it somewhere, walk to the station, pick up your supplies, head to the springs."

Tim drew a map on a small pocket notebook pad as he talked. He handed the map to John.

"The van's operating number is at the top. Do you think Borelli is honest?"

"Yes," Diana said forcefully.

"Expect the worse. Cain will not give up." Henry's voice trembled even through his efforts to maintain a confident tone. "Remember, we're worn and beaten—perfect people for God to use to exalt His power."

John spoke flatly. "Christ is more than a match for Cain, regardless of what Cain believes." Christ must defeat Cain, for John knew that in the flesh, he could not. In the flesh, before Cain, John had felt nothing but weakness, no livening of his spirit, no strength, just physical deadness. A man couldn't survive on feelings. The word of God, taken in faith, brought victory. An anxiety hovered about him that he rejected through the name of Christ.

Borelli reentered the room.

"What's your preference?"

"We're going to flee," John said.

"Hanson and I will try to track you down. I can't give you any more breaks. I will arrest you the next time we meet. Hanson doesn't have my sympathies. Be wary of him."

A kindness and a sternness were seen in Borelli's eyes.

"Just don't kill anyone, son."

"I won't. Unless it is the Lord's will."

"Unless it is the Lord's will." Borelli repeated the sentence. Perhaps it would be the Lord's will, and who could argue against the Lord? "Just don't ruin my retirement status—unless it is truly the Lord's will."

Henry spoke. "I retired but I never retired. How soon is it?"

"Within the year."

John stated, "I will pray that you have peace, for I don't think anyone will have retirement in the coming destruction."

"Thanks," Borelli said. "And one more thing. You do have a copy of the microdots, right? Henry or Tim must have something to show to start the court proceedings. I need a copy to place into the evidence room, where it will be promptly stolen by Cain. John, you hold onto the originals." Borelli looked deeply into John's eyes. Would John and the others see this as the closing of a trap? Once the Church knew of the location of the original microdots and the copies, death could freely be administered.

"We're good as we are." John smiled as he spoke.

Borelli digested this comment. John was telling him two copies had been made. The original was already with John, and he, Borelli, was holding a copy as were Tim and Henry. Borelli smiled. "Just to be sure, everyone has what they need?" John or Henry were always one step ahead.

"Yes," answered Henry as John nodded his head.

Borelli motioned to John and Diana. "Let's go. John pushes me to the floor, you escape."

John understood. The physical act of pushing Borelli to the floor must occur if Borelli was to be able to pass a drugging test for truth. John rose, grabbed Diana by the arm, bolted for the door. With the strength he possessed, he shoved Borelli in the chest. Borelli's eyes widened as he tumbled backward onto the floor. John and Diana were gone.

Tim offered Borelli a hand, helped the aching inspector to his feet. Borelli noticed the utter confusion in Tim's eyes.

"You don't understand why I am doing this?"

"No. No, I don't," Tim said. "I don't even know that you did the right thing. I don't understand anything about this situation anymore."

"You understand your family was held hostage by a murderer, don't you?" Borelli's words came with a trace of contempt and anger.

"Yes…"

Borelli wondered if his confidence in Tim had been misplaced. Well, it was too late now. Henry had joined the two standing men. "God bless you, Inspector Borelli. God bless you."

Borelli smiled. At least Henry understood. Borelli placed his arm around the old man. He hadn't placed an arm around a man since that time in the hospital when his father had been on his deathbed. Henry would be going soon—he had the death look. Henry reminded him of his father.

"I have a question that has intrigued me since law school, and I think you might be able to answer it."

"I will give it my best," said Henry as Borelli moved to a chair.

"We need to give John and Diana time, and I am woozy from my fall." Borelli sat down, and Tim and Henry followed his lead.

"Where does God's law separate from the laws of government?"

Henry's eyes smiled. He coughed deeply and spoke. "That is the last question I expected to be asked. My answer is: in God's eyes, there should be no separation. 'Love thy neighbor as thyself.' Men of normal intelligence, men not under the sway of perversions, can agree to a standard for that precept. A command from our Judeo-Christian heritage—so simple, and yet parts of the world have never known it. The flip side is, 'I wouldn't want that to happen to me or my loved ones, so I won't inflict it upon you.'"

Borelli thought back to the words of his father—to treat everyone as you would want to be treated. His father had somehow found this rule of life and clung to it and taught it to his children. "My father taught me the golden rule. Why was it never taught in the schools? Why do so few know it?"

Henry breathed a barely audible laugh. "Because it comes from our God. Someone decided that religion, especially Christianity, should not be taught to all. Why would they do that?" He laughed, knowing why. "To free rebellious humanity. The amendment of 2100 outlawed the free speech of true Christians. Remember, I mentioned men of normal intelligence not under the sway of perversions. There is no greater perversion than to reject the God who created you, redeemed you. How easy to ignore His truth. The world, the flesh, and the Deceiver are near to winning. Governmental law was only meant to keep a semblance of order among mankind for the sake of those who will know Christ and for those who follow Him. God restrains man through the law—all men, even those who are not His children.

"Though man has cut himself off from God, the memory of truth still lingers in his soul. By conscience or training or fear of punishment, he obeys the law. But the absence of moral absolutes and conscience has allowed laws enacted by perverse men to slowly strangle the world. Anarchy will reign."

"Do you truly believe that God's restraining arm is leaving the earth?" Borelli asked.

"You have read my book!" Henry was startled.

"Just passages. While at your home. I ate some of your doughnuts, too." Embarrassment was in the tone. "That subject caught my eye."

"What are a few doughnuts among friends?" Henry's laughter turned into a cough. "Yes, the Restrainer will soon leave. Humanity obeys the few remaining laws through will—will motivated by fear of punishment. Soon God's restraining force will let go of humanity's will and the fear of punishment. Then, the earth will see the full manifestation of the evil in people's hearts, the full range of sin within each individual. The sad thing is, not one person will realize how far he or she has fallen, for their consciences died long ago. For the sake of the elect, God will shorten that time." They sat in silence.

Eventually, Tim rose and started a new pot of coffee. In silence, they listened to the percolation. In silence, they sat and drank one last, slow cup before rising.

They entered the street; a police car had remained to transport them to the station. Borelli opened the door for Tim and Henry. "Let's file charges. Put that canister in a safety deposit box as soon as possible. Or better yet, Tim, keep it on your person. Make more copies, as many as you can. Post the book on the web. Find a conservative web site – give them a copy. Hire private security guards for yourselves till you have your moment in ecclesiastical court." Borelli followed his charges into the back seat. He spoke to the robo driver. "Southside."

The car sped away.

***

The archbishop entered his private sanctuary. He was possessed of an anger, a rage. The humiliation of the arrest process at the police station, the physical degradation of Borelli's treatment were a pollution within Gilroy's spirit. The sanctuary room was dark, save for the burning of two candles on the altar. The altar was clothed in black, the silver cross shone, not for Christ but for Tammuz. Tammuz, who was the Beast. A beast who was needed to destroy the parasitic Christ. A beast of a man to deliver men from bondage.

The archbishop knelt before the altar. His prayers began, and the naturally flowing strength of Satan rushed through his body. With Satan's help, the threat to the true church would be crushed forever. The World Church, whole, undefiled, would be given to the Deliverer, the one called the Beast. The bridegroom would receive his bride. Then the mysteries of Babylon could be revealed. Man would live fulfilled and happy upon the earth. Lords, they would be, with no pleasure denied them, no material object withheld, no bonds upon their thoughts, consciences, souls—freedom. How sweet the word *freedom*!

He must bring out the demon within. The demon within could war against these Enslavers. The demon would take their strength, empty their minds of Christ. Then the thoughts of the flesh would come—to distract, hinder, confuse. The demon would separate them from the parasite within. They would come home to the true god, and he would destroy them for their infidelity.

Gilroy breathed deeply; he held his breath and pushed. He repeated this process again and again. He could feel the demon rising to a rhythmic pulse. Like a woman in labor, he felt the demon separating from his soul. Like the tropic sun coming over the horizon, he felt the demon's size and heat. The archbishop reached into the font of holy water and sprinkled himself. Heat and water; his flesh, the earth. He began to cry, controlled sobs at first that turned joyous and spasmodic as the demon came out and stood before him. Flesh but not flesh, substance but not substance, a vassal to the prince of darkness.

Gilroy whispered in reverence.

"Holiness of my flesh, guide me. Do my bidding. Death is yours. Death I desire to give these monstrosities of humankind—dead flesh upon the earth, maggoty with Christ. Exorcise this Christ from the souls of John Johnson and Diana Rochembeau. Punish them for their infidelity. Grant me these things in the name of Satan, lord of the earth."

The demon vanished; he had heard. Gilroy rose, shuffled, bent at the waist. He hurt inside. He was a shell of himself; that which energized his being was gone. He was living on the residue of his spirit still trapped within the flesh, still imprinted within the mind. Few could call the demon from themselves; few could withstand the pain of separation. He entered a side room of smaller size, slowly eased onto a cot, covered himself with a heavy quilt. He would remain on the cot till the demon had done his work and returned home victorious.

CHAPTER 12

Hanson drove, and Borelli sat, passively watching the monitor. The monitor displayed a road and rail map, a flashing dot pinpointed the van of the fugitives. Every vehicle produced was linked to a satellite identification system. Hanson had correctly deduced that Tim had access to a university van, and that the van had been taken. Borelli had offered no input into this deduction. Their quarry had an hour and a half head start.

Borelli had been surprised by Hanson's lack of anger when told of the escape of the fugitives—he had only smiled and shaken his head. Borelli thought back to the beginning of the case. The beginning seemed years ago, not days. Borelli remembered his reasoning. One: Hanson wanted John Johnson to escape because of some unknown connection between the two of them. This theory had been dismissed. Two: Hanson wanted John Johnson to escape for personal reasons. These were obvious at the time. The longer John ran, the longer they would be out in the field, the more incompetent Chief Inspector Borelli would appear. The second line of reasoning was dead—an inspector couldn't be any more incompetent. Hanson should have reported to superiors long ago; by letting the case run, Hanson now could be under suspicion for incompetence. The incompetence theory was no longer viable.

The first reason, a connection between the two, had become real that night in the vehicle, waiting outside Tim's office. The Church was the connection between Hanson and John Johnson. Hanson was the Church's man. The evil element of the Church had the Satanic bible or portions of it. The evil element knew the approximate time of the birth of the Beast. The Church had known that Jeremiah Johnson knew also. Had Jeremiah Johnson had time to tell others? Those he could have told quickly and easily were colleagues or family members. Jeremiah only had his wife and son, a mere boy. But that boy, Henry, grew and had a wife, who'd died twenty years ago. They in turn had produced one son, who had produced two sons, Tim and John.

Think about this, Borelli. Markers had been placed on the living files of Tim and John, their parents, and Henry. These markers would explode in red warnings when any untoward event happened—say, going AWOL from the military. Perhaps the incident had been provoked by the Church and was not the coincidence it appeared to be. That is why it was eight hours before the inspectors were notified. Eight hours for the Church to decide on strategy and manpower. The strategy? Give John Johnson space, even help with his escape. Allow him to pass through airport security. Satan may have given John Johnson the absence of restraint through the mutiny. But God Almighty moved John Johnson home. Satan likely laughed as God did Satan's work. The enemies of God, Satan and his earthly church men, knew God would act! Incredible! God moving a man without a man's knowledge or consent, a willing man, following in faith even as Satan marked his course. Borelli shook his head in disbelief and in humility—for he had been allowed to witness this event and understand. God moved men toward conflict and victory irrespective of Satan's plans. This understanding had implications for his own life lived and the lives of all humanity. Maybe at some future time he would have the peace and quiet to think it through.

Hanson broke the silence. "We aren't gaining much on them. Let's have a state trooper make the stop."

"No, the chances of violence are less with us. I don't want anyone hurt. We can wait."

Borelli hoped to apprehend the fugitives on the drought zone's fringe, at a rest stop or on a wide shoulder. Borelli clearly saw that Hanson was his enemy. How far would Hanson go? Certainly, Hanson would have no qualms about killing his partner. What was Hanson's next move? Borelli wondered if Cain had made bail and was in pursuit. What did Hanson want from John Johnson—his immediate death? Or did he want to capture and torture him for all the information in the canister? Borelli knew he would not be allowed to witness either option.

Hanson hid his glee. Not even a smile came to his face. He had counted on Borelli refusing the suggestion of involving a state trooper. "I guess we're going west," Hanson said flatly.

***

John sat in the driver's seat and watched the flat land, weighted with buildings, stream past. Speed, destination, even deacceleration and braking were programmed before the drive had begun. He was a backup, should the computer system fail. Diana slept. She had offered to drive so that he could sleep, but he had postponed her suggestion.

He knew they were probably being tracked by satellite. Hanson didn't appear to be incompetent. Hanson had already, or would shortly, find out about the van. Who would make the stop? State police or the inspectors? Borelli would do everything in his power to make the arrest. On a positive note, maybe the vehicle could be ditched before Hanson even suspected the van had been taken.

Borelli. John smiled as he thought of the inspector. John understood perfectly what the man had given up so that two strangers might have a chance at life. No doubt, Borelli had his retirement planned, had been thinking about it for years upon years, perhaps all his working life. The dreams of retirement that had made the tough times livable, the reward, the prize at the end of the race. The man had a capacity for love and sacrifice in his heart.

John felt an unworthiness of that love, that sacrifice. Christ would pay back the price of the debt to Borelli—Christ, who owned the world and all in it. Christ of unlimited wealth would give Borelli his reward. John prayed that they would remain free so that Borelli's sacrifice would have meaning. He prayed Borelli would collect his pension from the vaults of heaven for eternity.

In the Shadow of Babylon

His heart was deeply touched. To think a stranger would have such kindness. This act of kindness fortified John. How many more good people were in the world, and yet not of it? How many good people waiting to know the God who was the source of their goodness? Good people still existed! For so long he had not believed this to be true. For so long he had viewed every person with skepticism, wariness, perhaps even contempt. The army had done this to him. No, it was the time in which he lived. Maybe this struggle was worthwhile. Maybe the information they had uncovered would identify and gather the good people of the world.

A sense of elation, aliveness, happiness came upon him suddenly. He was free! He was going into the drought zone—to live like John the Baptist! He had a woman beside him, and he would soon consummate his love for her. Men were after him, but he was young; his strength was returning. These emotions, thoughts were good. His life had been a depression, a blackness since entering the military. The hope and confidence was pleasing to his soul.

He wondered at the source of these feelings. Were they from his flesh or from the Spirit? Perhaps he didn't want to believe God would give him anything good? Yet, these thoughts, feelings reminded him of the man he once was, before Christ. Was the flesh awakening? He was angered at the constant vigilance needed to remain in the Spirit. Why couldn't life be easy, simple? Why was it necessary to study, probe every feeling that passed through his mind?

He studied the form of Diana curled up on the spacious front seat. He had a sexual desire for her when he thought the need for sex had died in him. He loved her with an agape love. He loved her for what she was in Christ—uncomplaining, supportive, caring, loyal, physically tough, intelligent, buoyant…the list didn't seem to end. The Spirit possessed her, filled her with a joy and peace that was seen in every gesture, word, attitude. To touch her was to touch a part of God. He was reminded of the time when the Spirit had first come to dwell in him.

He liked most her habit of crawling into his mind, playing with his perceptions, his words. She toyed with his every utterance. He was touched by her attention, her wanting to know him. He couldn't believe anyone would be interested in his thoughts or welfare. She lifted him out of his loneliness, she took his bitterness away, she made him feel unique, she made him understand he had been trained by the Lord for this very work.

Her touch, her breath, her scent, her form, her movements excited him. He lusted for the warmth of her body. He loved her for who she was, for her womanhood. There was another love within him, an admixture that he knew was wrong—not holy. Sex had been created by God and was good—in marriage. He wished to love her properly. His physical and mental weariness allowed him no victory in the struggle of conflicting thoughts. He doubted if he had slept four hours straight in months. He wanted, his body *demanded*, sleep. He could pull over now and sleep. Pull over, make love to Diana, and sleep.

Now he began to have doubts about his role in this work. How important were the microdots? The world wasn't going to be saved by his efforts. The professing church was predestined to be corrupt; the harlot church was supposed to pervert the professing church. He seemed to be living a preordained script. Did he have any control, any say in this drama?

His own brother, radically conservative in church matters, didn't understand. How could anyone else? And the Rapture—people being lifted off the earth, even the dead—for some reason this was straining credibility. He believed he was going to heaven, but in that manner? How could the world witness this Rapture and not repent? If the Rapture did not occur, his capture was assured. He couldn't hide forever. He would either be killed or imprisoned.

He knew all these doubts were foolish. How could he believe so strongly one minute and then minutes later, scoff at the truth? Or was he simply questioning the truth? Why should he question? He knew God's power intimately. Why couldn't he consistently hold to what he knew was the truth? His thoughts were tainted; at the same time, he knew the substance of his faith. The corpse of the old John Johnson was stirring. He had no energy and very little will with which to fight this new battle.

He touched her hair, ran the back of his hand along her temple. He bent over her, kissed her ear, caressing the outer edge with his lips. She awoke but didn't move.

"What are you doing?" Her voice was soft and dreamy.

"Kissing you."

"Why?"

"You're beautiful."

She raised herself to her elbows and looked into his eyes. He stared into her eyes and spoke. "Kiss me."

She kissed him on the lips.

"Not like that!" He moved closer to her. They kissed and their tongues met. She gasped quietly. His hands were upon her, around her waist, upon her chest.

"No, John!" Her voice wavered from firmness to weakness.

"No? You love me, don't you? You've done this before."

She pushed herself away as she studied his eyes. "Something isn't right. You're not the John I know. Who are you? The John I know wouldn't have said that. Jesus knows I'm clean, a new person. Why are you trying to make me filthy?"

He slammed his fist into the dash. "Damn it! Damn it!"

He was in a rage of confusion. He was angry at her words and at himself. She had loved a hundred men. Why now did she deny him? He truly loved her, and those men had not. Why was he attempting to pull her down? Simply for his own sexual needs?

She had never heard him swear. Even in unguarded moments, in situations of extreme stress, he had never cursed. One of the first works of the Spirit in her was to rid her of the desire to curse. She had never seen him exhibit violent behavior. He was outside the Spirit. He looked at her in anger and distress.

"Something's wrong, Diana." He spoke to her in confusion. "God, help me," he said calmly as he forced himself under control. "The man outside of Christ has returned. I want to use you. I'm so tired. I want to live while I'm still on this earth."

She saw the frustration and desire in his eyes.

"You know being outside of Christ is not living, no matter what your body says. Are you going to hold onto what you know or give in to what you feel?"

She placed her hands firmly around his neck and massaged slowly. He seemed to be listening deep within himself, attempting to judge the direction of the battle within. She spoke.

"I've been having strange thoughts, too, within the past few minutes. Something is trying to pull me from Christ. Doubts are coming into my mind. Do you see me as clean, pure, or as I once was? I want to love you as God wants me to love you. But how can an act that made me unclean now be righteous and pure? I don't want to touch you, and I want you to consume me. I have the same thoughts of wanting pleasure now because time is short, and there might not be another chance. I know I love you…"

The other man was growing within him. He shuddered as his veins were filled with the old, almost forgotten spirit of the carnal man. His body felt so alive, so good, under that man's control. He had power, and God was but a memory. He flipped the vehicle's automatic controls off. He writhed within his soul as he struggled to remain on the highway. She flipped the automatic controls back on.

His face was taut as he spoke. "Read from the Bible." He chuckled evilly. "I can say that to you, but all I want to do is throw that book out the window. No! Rip it page by page. I want to be free."

His tightly clenched hands left the steering column. He grabbed for the book in her hands. With a superhuman strength, she held onto the Bible as he attempted to slap the book away. She tried to pull the Bible into her bosom, but he gripped the book and pulled her to him.

She seemed to relax her hold. Suddenly, she slapped him hard across the face, then pulled the book back to herself. She lunged to the far door, quickly opened the book, began reading an Epistle. John was breathing deeply.

"'This I say then, Walk in the Spirit, and ye shall not fulfil the lust of the flesh. For the flesh lusteth against the Spirit, and the Spirit against the flesh…'"

As she continued reading, he began to calm.

***

Archbishop Gilroy was upon his cot, when, with one violent blow he was upon the floor. He had a moment of confusion, then the realization that his demon had returned in terror, fleeing into him. He writhed upon the floor, kicking and screaming in agony. The demon had not returned alone but rather, the demon was locked in combat with the Spirit of the false God. He begged for mercy as the God of Truth pinned him to the floor, subdued him, and tormented him.

***

The land had become progressively drier, emptier, more inhospitable as the fugitives went west. By late afternoon, a bleakness clung to the flat land; the sky was leaden. Occasionally, a single structure of great size would rise from the flatness, sometimes surrounded by smaller buildings. The smell of a food-processing plant or a slaughterhouse would enter the vehicle. The sparse grasses were brown, ponds were frozen, the wind was stiff—buffeting the vehicle. The traffic was light. Diana continued reading the Bible, her voice had become thick and cracked repeatedly.

A hundred years ago, the land they crossed had supported farms that grew wheat, corn, soybeans, cattle, hogs. Now only raggedy grasses grew, which supported scattered herds of cattle. A few isolated farms drew water from the last puddles remaining in the once-expansive aquifers.

The map indicated one last rest plaza before the barrenness of the drought zone. The drought zone knew only desert vegetation. Volcanic activity had coated vast areas with thick ash, which in turn had been coated with a thin plastic binder meant to keep the ash stable. The plastic-glazed land collected water from the occasional storm into catch basins, where a few wild animals would come to drink. Replanting desert vegetation was still an ongoing project. The drought zone was vast and uninhabited except for communications stations, road and rail-maintenance villages, rescue personnel, land management employees. A few holiday resorts managed to survive as places where people could feel alone, could feel openness, wideness.

John marveled at the devastation wrought upon the land by the volcanic eruptions. The temptation to sin seemed to be gone, and he thanked God repeatedly for his deliverance. He prayed their pursuers were far behind. He prayed the geology station still had provisions. He prayed they could remain hidden till the Rapture came. He would marry Diana. The Lord would be their witness, and it would be right and holy. He hadn't begun to penetrate the surface of her soul, her thoughts. He smiled. She loved him. He had never had anyone love him. He thanked God for Diana and prayed he would never hurt her again.

The final rest plaza was before them. He pulled into a huge parking lot that was only a quarter full. The great throngs of summer travelers moving toward or from the West Coast were gone. The plaza had drive-through windows where food could be purchased, but he needed the stretch and to feel the cold wind on his face and solid ground beneath his feet.

He parked on the edge of the mass of vehicles. He knew the stop was dangerous. They had to eat and buy some provisions for the coming days. The van should be ditched near the highway to mislead their pursuers into believing they had hitched a ride and were heading west. A substantial walk to the geology shed would have to be made; food was needed to maintain their strength. What if the shed was empty? They had to buy food, just enough food for a few days.

Some travelers were sleeping in their vehicles. He saw bodies stretched out on spacious seats and fold-down beds. Many vehicles had the shades drawn. People were arranging seats, luggage, putting jackets, sweaters on or taking them off. Groups entered and exited the plaza station. Lights were on, the edge of the horizon reflected an orange hue from the set sun.

When they exited the building, their arms and rucksack full of provisions, the natural light in the west was gone. The overhead pole lights shone brightly on the parked vehicles. John had been cramming food into his mouth till the provisions in his arms began to spill to the ground. Diana picked up the fallen items, fed John the remainder of his food, then placed her drink to his mouth and heard the straw sucking liquid.

Borelli and Hanson crouched behind the van and watched John and Diana move toward them. Borelli smiled as he studied the two—no traveling disagreements; they were still deeply in love. Diana walked close to John, attentive to his every desire, feeding him like a baby. Borelli remembered the hope and optimism of his own youth when life had been an adventure. He was disappointed their freedom had been so short. Hanson seemed anxious to apprehend them. The letting-it-all-play-out period was over. Their freedom might soon be gone. He sensed Hanson had chosen this isolated place for murder. Snap out of it, Borelli! Your partner intends to murder you! John and Diana will probably be taken alive for interrogation. He had never killed anyone with whom he had close contact. Even as he detested Hanson, he understood Hanson. He even sensed what was missing from Hanson. What if the missing piece could be found? No, it was too late; the man was hardened to change. Hanson was a killer without remorse. Borelli didn't value the little that was left of his own life, but the kids—John and Diana—they needed to live, to experience love. Borelli whispered.

"Remember! No violence. We protect ourselves if it is necessary, but no more force than is needed. I'll take John, you take the girl." Borelli's heart was pounding as he fingered the antique snub-nose revolver in his jacket pocket. Hanson knew nothing of the antique and could only have known if he had searched Borelli's private luggage. The antique was just as effective as a laser at close range. The laser at his hip remained in place. Perhaps, this ruse would give him more time to draw down on Hanson, who would be expecting a move toward the laser when he made his play. Hanson was keyed up, impervious to the words just spoken. It was as if he had heard nothing. He had never seen Hanson agitated in mind and body. Hanson couldn't hide the murder in his heart.

The two men moved to the center of the van's rear door. When would be the time to kill Hanson? When? Just coldly send a round into his back? Should he confront Hanson? How do you murder a man? They heard the footsteps, her laughter, the locks clicking open. Hanson rushed around the van to the driver's side, laser drawn. Borelli swore. He hadn't expected Hanson to make his move in the parking lot. Borelli was attempting, with his left hand, to reach for Hanson's jacket as he followed around the taillights of the van. His right hand was reaching for his revolver.

Hanson recoiled back into Borelli and lost his footing as he trampled on Borelli's feet. Borelli stumbled backward, turned his body, and landed on his left side. Hanson's laser clattered on the macadam as his arms went out, seeking balance. He fell onto his buttocks. The laser slid under the van. Hanson rolled onto his hands and knees, moved closer to the van, and extended himself under the vehicle. He cursed wildly. John and Diana were gone. Borelli saw blood smears on the macadam. He saw the two moving between parked vehicles. His memory recalled a black object, a knife upon Hanson's sleeve. John had struck so swiftly that Borelli didn't remember the exact moment of impact.

Hanson hadn't had time to fire. Or had the laser been just a bluff? A means to coerce submission until he moved them to a quieter place? This was not the place to shoot Hanson. Borelli released his revolver in his pocket. Borelli spoke angrily, yet softening the tone in afterthought, not knowing the extent of Hanson's injury. "What in the hell were you trying to pull?"

Hanson said nothing as he emerged from under the van, holding his laser with one hand; his other hand, attempting to stop the flow of blood, was wrapped tight around the wrist of his gun hand. His eyes were angry and crazed with determination. He ran toward his quarry, eyes riveted upon John. Borelli trailed behind, keeping his vision on John and Diana, who were now fleeing for the desert to the right of the buildings. Borelli saw the blood dripping from Hanson's jacket sleeve. Borelli yelled urgently, "Hanson, let me bandage your wound. You'll bleed to death!"

He hoped the words would redirect Hanson, buy some time. Hanson turned and fired, aiming at center mass and the heart. Borelli dodged, and Hanson's shot went into Borelli's thigh. Hanson readjusted for a head shot, even as Borelli ducked his head and fired his laser at Hanson. The shot caught Hanson on the outer torso. Exasperated, Hanson closed upon Borelli, who had fallen on his back. He stripped the old man of his laser and the weight within his pocket, an old revolver. He must get back to his quarry. He withheld the fatal head shot. The leg shot was high and inside the thigh, adjacent to the crotch. Borelli wasn't going anywhere. The old man would slowly die.

John and Diana were on the coarse sand, beyond the parking area, clawing their way up a slope of jagged shale. The loose debris moved in slow avalanches, shooshing in their ears. The cold was intense, a wind cut through their clothing. John felt powerless and weak as he had so many times on the European front. The Lord would be his strength.

He turned and saw Hanson reaching the apron of the paved area. Borelli was struggling to follow, using his arms as legs and dragging his body. Hanson fired. The rock exploded two feet to the left of John. John pulled Diana as she began to slip downward. Diana was hyperventilating. John rolled over the crest of the slope, dragging Diana by her arm. Hanson was at the base of the slope, steadying his shooting arm on his knee as he squinted to find his fluorescent bead. The dot was upon Diana's leg. The leg vanished over the crest.

John was upon Diana, pulling her to a sitting position, her head tightly in his hands as he forced her eyes to his. "I want you to go down the backside here." His voice was determined as he pointed out the route she should take. "Circle wide around this ridge and go for the van." His voice was patient, spoke of confidence in her. "Start the van and wait. I'll be along."

She knew he had played these games before, in the army. She had heard the same tone of voice, felt the same strength when he had made their plans in the library at Colebrook.

He wasn't frightened, he would prevail. She could obey him; her breath was flowing normally now. He had done all this before, she trusted him. His presence gave her strength. She ran.

Hanson yelled up to the crest. "I want the microdots!"

He had moved back from the base of the slope so as to have vision of the ends of the ridge. He could now see anyone circling back to the van. His quarry could only go deeper into the desert, using the ridge as a screen. Hanson yelled again. "You can go free!"

John spoke cynically to himself. "That's why you fired at me—so I could go free."

John moved fifteen feet to his right before peeking over the ridge. Hanson saw John, pointed his laser below John slowly, in a nonthreatening manner. John held the microdot canister in the air, wishing to buy time for Diana. Borelli was now beside Hanson with his trademark penknife in his hand. Borelli had scanned the parking lot; no crowds had gathered, no one was in the lot. He thought he had heard a laser as he turned to scan the travel plaza.

Hanson saw Diana run from the far end of the ridge and across the macadam—she would wait for her love at the van. Hanson saw Borelli's bent-over form collapse into a sitting position on the cold earth. Hanson knew Borelli was done. Too decent, too honest for this game.

John yelled down the slope. "Borelli! Hanson is going to kill all three of us here at this rest stop!"

"You don't believe that, do you?" asked Hanson as his eyes and laser remained on John.

"Easily. You were sent to Europe to watch John Johnson." Borelli had gasped his words.

John remained in sight, not moving. Hanson laughed deeply: the old man finally understood. Hanson's voice burned with arrogance. "When did you suspect?"

"Lost on the way to Desmit's billet…head start…no…luck. You aren't… clever, Bob." Borelli thought the first name would rankle Hanson.

"But I am." Hanson turned his eyes from John, still on the ridge, to Borelli. For a fraction of a second, Borelli's eyes left Hanson and moved in the direction of the ridgeline. Without a change in his posture or his gaze, Hanson pivoted his laser and fired. Borelli slumped forward, fell, his penknife dropped into the sand. Sarcasm dripped from Hanson's voice. "A fuckin' penknife." Hanson jumped from his position, turned quickly, fired at John and missed. John ran down the backside of the ridge. Hanson glanced at the prone Borelli. The old fool played by an antiquated set of rules—he should have fired the moment he knew his death had been planned.

"What in God's name…?" Borelli gasped in shock as his hands felt frantically for the hole. The hands stopped. He knew effort was useless. He was dying. He had always wanted to die bravely. He asked the Lord to allow him to die like a man. A peace came to him.

Hanson backed up from Borelli, his eyes still on the end of the ridge. He had seen John move to the left, the same direction in which Diana had bolted, but that movement could have been a feint.

In the Shadow of Babylon

"Why, Hanson?" Borelli called out weakly. Distract Hanson, keep him near, give John a chance. The arrogant bastard liked to talk. He was hit somewhere in the torso. He couldn't sit up to look. He spoke again. "Money? Country home?"

Hanson sneered. How much Borelli resembled the pictures of the dying Christ on the cross—weak, conquered, a failure. "You fool! My lord is fighting for his kingdom, and you talk of money, a country home?" Hanson was enraged. He strode to Borelli, kicked him in the side, spit in his face. "You old, stupid man!"

Borelli smiled as Hanson wasted time. Borelli, with his last strength, held up his middle finger, knowing Hanson would waste more time in his rage. Hanson kicked again and again, even as he saw John break fifty yards up from the left flank of the ridge, running at a sprint for the parking lot. A smart move, extending himself from the ridge—a pistol couldn't make the shot. Hanson began running for the vehicles. Borelli lay looking at the cold sky. He had no feeling in his arms or legs. The blood was pumping onto the dry, cold earth.

John felt warmth returning to his body as he ran. The cold air burned his lungs. He moved into the mass of parked vehicles; many had their internal lights on, curtains drawn. Most were dark, their owners within the plaza building. Once among the vehicles, he sank to the ground, crawled back to the last row of vehicles on the edge of the parking area. Hanson had to die. No other options were available. Though only armed with a knife, he was still in this fight, and he would win. Was Borelli alive?

Hanson, nearer the parking area, entered the collection of vehicles before John. He fell to his hands and knees, scurrying like John, on hands and feet, hoping not to be seen. Both had the van as their destination. The two men darted, crouched, scampered. Wariness clung like an aura, the eyes moved rapidly, searching all directions. The ears strained.

Diana sat nervously behind the wheel. She should be outside the vehicle, so no one could surprise her. John had told her to start the van, not necessarily to wait inside. She began to open the door. The door flew from her hand. She was spun around. The gloating face of Hanson was before her. The eyes laughed at her fear and shock.

Hanson's pistol arm was struck from behind. The laser, pulled from his fingers, fell. The crease of John's arm wrapped around Hanson's eyes and nose. He yanked the head sideways; his foot went into the crease of Hanson's knee. As Hanson's body momentarily collapsed, John bent the body backward. The knife penetrated the kidney and was jerked back and forth as the arm covered the mouth. The two men crumpled to the ground. John inserted the knife behind the ear and shook the blade inside the skull. Hanson was dead. John ran at a lope to Borelli. Borelli's glazed eyes opened as John felt for a pulse in the neck. The skin was cold, the pulse weak.

"I'm dying."

Borelli's assessment was correct. Silence bonded the two men. John knew the presence of the Lord was upon them. Borelli's eyes cleared. He had so much to say, but his lips would not move. He was taken to Europe; the events of the past days were reviewed; the sounds, sights, thoughts came vividly. The Lord, as guide, showed him the events behind the stage of history. That moment as a child when the Spirit of God had entered him and guided him to this moment. He had been chosen to be Hanson's partner. He had been chosen to hear of the coming Kingdom. He had been chosen because he was a decent, a loving man in a world of indecency and hate. He had chosen to distract Hanson just minutes before so that John could live.

He knew Christ! What was His name? The Alpha and Omega. Christ the Lord was beside him, a friend, taking him to a new place, to eternal life. He yearned to tell John of the peace he had, the visions of the future. John knelt beside Borelli, touched Borelli's forehead with his hand, and prayed. The hand would remain until death.

He noticed spittle on Borelli's cheek and wiped it away with his free hand. It seemed he wiped the spittle from Christ himself. Oddly, he felt a sadness for Hanson. Hanson, in eternal torment, Hanson who had believed a lie and lived it, deluded, deranged, bound with hate. The hand on the forehead felt the holiness emanating from the body of flesh. God was present. Still, dying must be a lonely thing. It was pleasing to God for a man to touch the dying.

"You're one of the good guys, Borelli." Borelli did not hear.

He thought back to Borelli's manhandling of the archbishop. Of Borelli's deeming his pension a small thing compared with justice. Borelli, who had allowed two fugitives to escape. Borelli, who only wanted to be acceptable to the God he had always known existed. God had not forgotten Borelli. Borelli gasped, smiled as the waning light of his spirit left his body.

John had watched men die in combat and had never cried. Those men had died for the hope of glory, or a paycheck, or to better their earthly lives. They loved nothing but themselves. Tears came to his eyes. He had never seen a man die for what was good and honorable, had never seen a man die for Christ. Borelli had listened to the decency of his heart in simple faith and because of that, had died.

Diana was beside him. She studied the peace on Borelli's face. She took John's arm, rubbed her hand in his as they walked back to the van. Her touch gave him strength. She gave him a reason to continue. Few cars were entering the parking area. People were entering and exiting the plaza building. His eyes were pulled to the movement of one figure. He could only see the back of the man, and it was only a fleeting glimpse. The man had a strange spring to his walk—Cain! John said nothing to Diana.

John ran toward the van. Why wasn't Cain in ambush by the van? Had he posted men? Had Cain seen the empty van, surmised his quarry was in the plaza? He wouldn't kill in the plaza, would he? Perhaps Cain needed food, drink from the plaza and had not yet checked the parking lot. Or had the van been missed?

Hanson's body lay under an adjacent van. The supplies that had been scattered during the initial confrontation were in their van. Diana saw John's puzzlement at the location of the body.

"I put him there, and his laser. Borelli's laser and an old gun are in my purse."

"Good for you." He smiled. She had a coolness. He reached into the van, grabbed Borelli's laser and slid it under the adjacent van. "Probably has a tracker. Borelli likely never told anyone of the antique revolver." What of Cain? John had an impulse to kill again. Cain had to die. Why not now? With Cain dead, there could be peace. It was an opportune time; Cain was unsuspecting while his own adrenaline, courage, were at their peak. Slay him as he walked out of the plaza, in the midst of people. Cain would feel secure with people around. Just slip up behind him. Stick the knife in his back.

Then, there would be peace. It seemed right, logical, and yet it wasn't right. He sensed his flesh speaking—sensed that God did not want Cain's death yet. Had enough men died for today? No. God had slain thousands in a day. Who could understand the reasoning of God? God's timing was always perfect.

"Let's get out of here."

***

Cain smelled the scent of blood as he walked out the plaza door into the cold night. The wind had shifted direction. He drank from the coffee cup, took another bite of his newly purchased sandwich. He knew the fugitives had entered this rest stop along with Hanson and Borelli—his vehicle was equipped with a monitor. He had entered the plaza building to give Hanson time to kill or capture, a professional curtesy. If Hanson had made the kill, fine. Why were the bodies left in the open? They had to be in the open—the blood smell was so strong. He suspected Hanson had failed. He circled the parking lot, his nose sniffing the air.

He found Hanson, pulled him from under the van, smiled fiendishly, admired the clean knife work. The laser pistol was in his holster. He could smell Diana's perfume on the handle. He had told Gilroy that Hanson wasn't necessary and couldn't do a professional job. Gilroy had insisted. Another pistol was nearby. Borelli's? Cain's eyes caught a dark form on the light desert earth. The earth reflected the light from the parking area and seemed to lift the figure from the earth. He went to the form.

Borelli, dead. Hanson, dead. The two inspectors. He had known their faces intimately but only by picture, though he had seen both at a distance and in poor light. Hanson had shot Borelli before himself being killed in the parking area. He bent down to the body. He saw the smear of dried spittle on Borelli's cheek. Borelli could not have spit on himself—Hanson had the hate in him. It was well enough to hate if you had the cunning that allowed it to survive. Hanson was a loser. The bodies were only minutes dead. Borelli's weapon was gone, thus accounting for the laser under the van. John Johnson likely did not possess a laser—unless his brother had given him one. It was common knowledge that lasers had trackers imbedded within.

Cain shifted the lightweight body armor that encased his torso; cold air was creeping underneath. The armor was sometimes annoying, as at the moment, but it had saved him injury many times—especially from knife thrusts. It seemed John Johnson could use a knife. He was tempted to follow the tracks leading up the slope, simply for the pleasure of reading the story. Wisdom said to press Johnson, pursue him before the gap widened.

Cain ran back to his vehicle. Within seconds, he was on the highway, monitoring the screen with its pulsing dot that was the van. He raced at twice the legal speed limit, heading west, looking into every vehicle he passed. He thought his quarry was still in the van, but this Johnson was clever—the satellite responder could have been taken off the van, placed on another vehicle, while Johnson and his whore rode undetected. Or they could have stolen a vehicle or hitched a ride with some lonely traveler.

***

John pushed the van's engine to maximum speed. In a few minutes they would reach the dirt road that led to the geology station. He could feel Cain in pursuit. John shook in terror. Cain's arrogance was backed by a fear-inspiring physique. What man could stand against him? He attempted to wipe the blood from his hands and sleeve. The blood had become sticky and was drying.

He had visions of the past, dead and dying men and women, Jones injected, ambushes, birds of death hovering, dead and decaying flesh, laser fire from unknown sources, storm troopers in the night. The visions crowded his mind; he could not rid himself of them. He couldn't control his shaking. This assault was far worse than the sexual temptation. How many more beatings could he take?

Diana found a rag in the back of the van and wiped the blood from John's hands and his sleeve. The waves of shaking frightened her. She had seen the same fear displayed after the meeting with Cain in the old office at Colebrook. She pulled out the Bible and began to read aloud.

John spoke. "Cain was entering the plaza as we left."

"So?" she said defiantly. "The Lord hasn't brought us this far to watch us fail. The Lord gave you victory over a storm trooper and over Hanson.

Why won't He give you the victory over Cain? God only deals out victories, mon trésor!"

She was right. God was consistent. Man was the inconsistent one. She continued. "Cain has himself convinced he's been alive since the beginning of mankind. Maybe he's been brainwashed, hypnotized, or maybe he's psychotic. Whatever the case, we know he's deluded. Only God has the power to give eternal life, and God would not give Cain eternal life, or even life outside the span of mortal men. Mortal men can be killed. Don't let Cain's delusion become yours."

"I'm having visions of the war. I can't rid my mind of them. I'm afraid of pain, of death." He shrugged his shoulders in confusion.

She answered calmly. "I should think so—if you are in the flesh, then what happens to the flesh should make you worry. But you are not in the flesh—you're in Christ, in the Spirit. Memory is making you fear. Satan has stirred up your memory—it's an illusion. He's trying to awaken the carnal man. You don't have to fight your memory or Satan—you couldn't win. And you can't hold onto Christ, either; so stop struggling. Offer yourself to Him, present yourself—that is what you told me was the key to victory. Have faith that God has done everything He has promised. The old you is dead, John."

She began reading again, calmly, methodically. His body ceased to shake. The past horrors were gone. Cain would be defeated. They passed a mileage sign.

"This is it. I might have driven right by it during that mental attack." He squeezed her knee gently and held the pressure. She was indispensable. "Thank you."

She smiled. He appreciated her, needed her; they were partners, buddies; a satisfaction came to her. He was her purpose in life, and it was good. He took the van out of automatic drive, switched off the generator, and went to rotor power. They slowed; there was no traffic in sight. They came to a dirt road, barricaded to traffic. He pulled well off the shoulder of the road.

John sighed. "Look for the heaviest boulders you carry and place them on the driver's seat."

In the Shadow of Babylon

    They gathered rocks and placed them on the seat. John restarted the van, placed the controls on automatic. The highway was empty as he ran beside the van and directed the van onto the implanted guide rail. The vehicle picked up speed and was gone from sight.

    They gathered their clothing, sleeping gear, and provisions, crammed it all into two rucksacks, the one they had brought from Henry's and another found in the back of the van. He cut a mesquite bush, walked backward down the service road for half an hour, wiping their tracks as he went. Then, they faced the desert and walked into the cold night. The stars were thick above them. The wind sang a desolate song over the sand.

CHAPTER 13

The temperature outside the cave was below freezing; the wind gusting to at least fifteen miles per hour, John guessed. The blowing sand crystals seemed to shatter on exposed skin, bursting into pricks of heat before the skin went numb. With one more trip back to the geology station, he could assure their survival, in comfort, for a year. He would, at the least, like to bring back the station's thermometer.

He would not go back. Not because of the sandstorm—he had made one trip in the storm—or because of the cold or fatigue, but because he knew a greed was possessing him. He would be content with what the Lord had allowed him to retrieve. He would trust his future to the Lord and not to a collection of material objects. John wondered if Cain was at the station by this time, waiting, and that is why the Lord told him to be content.

Surely Cain had found the van, called in help, and was searching the area. They had pushed themselves that first night and second day to escape Cain's likely search radius. Tracks on every piece of sandy ground had been erased. Somehow, they had gotten the jump on Cain and had maintained that lead. No drones, no aircraft overflights, no distant dust columns from all-terrain vehicles. Then again, satellites could have tracked their every move.

The absence of Cain was frightening or freeing, depending on your opinion of Cain's ability. Cain, once the university van had been stopped, had probably begun with a twenty-five-mile radius around the highway, retracing the van's course. No doubt, where the service road branched off from the highway, another radius would have begun, following the road to the geology station. Simultaneously, Cain could not have ruled out that his quarry had entered another vehicle and was continuing west on the highway. Surely, at the station, Cain had discovered the missing provisions. But who had taken them and when? In time, the serpent would come to their Eden. John shrugged off the fear, kept his faith in the Lord.

John studied the cave from his bed of lightweight blankets spread on the cave floor—God had been good to them. The cave was spacious, yet the ceiling was not so high that they lost heat in the expanse. The sandstone walls were smooth; they had the feeling of being in a tent. No crevices for rodents, bats to shelter within. The cave had a dampness, due to a spring, but they had a heater, chemical blankets, sufficient clothing, and a hearth would be built.

The spring bubbled clear, pure water from a fissure at the back of the cave. A number of pools had been scooped out of the rock by the passage of the water. John deepened the pools with rock dams, fed the small minnows in the pools, wondering how much he could increase their size. The spring water supported a number of bushes and scrub trees at the naturally small entrance to the cave, thus providing welcome camouflage and acting as a windbreak.

John and Diana knew they had found their rock of Horeb, thanks to Tim. The spring had been given to them through the love and grace of God. The water ran free, abundantly, of pure taste, and sustained them. At no other place could they have found such an abundance of water, certainly not within a livable cave. The cave and water seemed a miracle. Prior to finding the cave and the spring, John had doubted the Lord's wisdom in bringing them to this desert waste. He had wondered if Christ was truly within them, guiding them. Their rock home was Christ; the water, living water. In the bosom of Christ they lived, in the rock that had clefted for them.

John watched Diana as he rested. The one-hundred-mile round-trip hike to and from the geology station had left him exhausted. He estimated he had carried a load of one hundred pounds. Seven days since the completion of the trek, and the weariness was just lifting. Diana had worked assiduously, cleverly to make a home in that week. He longed to love her physically. Each day she brought him nearer her soul, her Christ. It was impossible not to think of her. Perhaps she was his reward for the struggle, the pain of the last weeks, if not years.

She swept the stone floor with a broom she had made of brush. The handle was short, she was bent awkwardly. Her awkwardness made him love her more. She was determined to overcome any obstacle, determined to have a clean home.

He must stop thinking of her. Think of fire. Wood was plentiful, some of it dead a hundred years, preserved in the arid climate and volcanic ash. Live trees grew at higher elevations. He could vent smoke to the back of the cave. He could rig up a pipe to the outside to provide a draft, a clay pipe, as clay was plentiful. Once the hearth was built, he would shoot quail, and they would feast on fresh meat.

Because there were deer and bighorn sheep in the higher elevations, he thought hunters might come. Then the cave would become a sanctuary. He had seen no hunters, no signs of hunting in the past, and this encouraged him. Diana had finished sweeping. She was at her calendar, an area of the rock wall flat and smooth. She picked up her chalky sandstone rock. She had been counting days. She added another stroke to the wall. It was five months and two weeks till the thirty-third year of the Beast. Would he come to power at exactly age thirty-three or at the end of that thirty-third year? Five months, then the Rapture could come at any moment within the year. They had to plan for a year.

He wanted the Rapture, but life was good now. A hard life was ahead, but free, and with a woman he loved. A year and five months was too short for the physical desire he felt for her. They were in their Garden of Eden, communing with God in peace. Why end an idyllic life? He knew men would neither be married nor given in marriage in the resurrection world. The one flesh of marriage would end on the day of Rapture. A resentment came from that knowledge.

Diana entered John's blankets, snuggled up beside him. She studied his face, ran her finger down the length of his nose. She spoke softly.

"When are we going to consummate our marriage?"

"I didn't know we were married." His eyes widened in mock puzzlement and shock, as if the thought had never occurred to him.

"You love me, and I love you. We're married." Her voice was soft with contentment.

He felt odd joking of his love for her. He loved her deeply, didn't want her to have the smallest doubt of that love. "Yes, I love you." He studied her eyes for confirmation to his words, her peace was the answer.

Her lips held a soft smile. "So, we're married. It isn't our fault there is no one to marry us. It would be better to have a ceremony, make it known to your family and society—such as it is—but we are here alone until the Lord takes us."

He didn't need to be convinced. The Lord made marriages; ceremony affirmed legitimacy and commitment. "What if you become pregnant?" His tone was grave.

"I'm sure the Lord made provisions for children, even the unborn, in heaven."

"We don't know how long this peaceful life will last. We could be running for our lives days from now, or a minute from now. Being pregnant won't help."

Indignantly she sat up. "Nothing is for certain but the love of God, John!" Her anger penetrated his heart. There was only the love of God—the only guarantee in life. Strange, when she said *John*, he felt like a somebody, a man of God's own choosing. Through the day, he would yearn for his name to come from her lips, to hear the respect and love in the utterance. She spoke. "If we're found, let's not run—not into that wilderness in the winter. A spousal penal colony wouldn't be so bad."

"Maybe you're right." He spoke assuredly. She didn't understand the power of the Church. Even the government authorities were corrupted; money had been paid to have two fugitives killed. Better to allow her to think a life existed after capture. He pulled her legs, she eased back onto the blankets.

She lay still. He kissed her slowly at first, then rapidly, passionately. He whispered into her ear.

"You make me feel whole, complete."

She laughed at her power. He had the same power over her.

"You are life to me, John." She spoke a flat, submissive statement of reality.

"Will you marry me?" he asked.

"Yes. Yes. Hold me, John." The tenderness in her voice was absorbed within his soul. He held her firmly.

"Tomorrow, we will marry. I have to make a ring. We will have a ceremony, scriptures will be read, a prayer said in reverence. We won't marry prodded by lust."

Tomorrow would be time enough.

***

John awoke long before first light. The day held a newness, an anticipation. He was thinking of her from the moment of waking. He had made two rings from the plastic pull top of two juice bottles; they were crudely fashioned but had meaning. He put them in his pocket. His restlessness desired physical movement. He had planned to begin a daily morning scout, before sunrise, the next day. He would start today.

He dressed warmly. Diana was opposed to the scouting, thinking he was exposing himself to unnecessary risk. He felt it was more dangerous to hide in the cave, forced to make the needed forays for materials without knowing if someone was in their Eden, watching. Fourteen days since they had abandoned the van. He had to assume it was safe. Manpower would have been pulled out, had there been a search. Even Cain's resources must have limits.

He tucked his knife into his belt; he left the powder gun in their bedding—for her protection. He studied their home; all safe and secure. He pulled back the blanket that was their door, entered the cold air. He heard the wind moving through the canyon. The morning star was visible, along with many others. He moved up the canyon to the plateau, and from the plateau he moved to the highest hill. He draped a heat deflecting blanket over his sitting form. He had total visual command of the area.

To the east lay flat, poly-bound desert, flat till his eyes could see no more. To the west were the mountains—cold, gray, forbidding. Traces of snow shone on the mountains. To the north was a continuation of the desert; to the south, the same. Occasionally lights could be seen on the band of highway thirty some miles to the south. Immediately surrounding him were plateaus, canyons, covered in mesquite.

The country was beautiful in its desolation. The absence of man is what he liked best. He would press the landscape into his memory, so that even a deer miles away would be noticed—not so much by sight but as an object out of place on the memorized backdrop of unmovable permanence. He saw no signs of human life, only three deer, a coyote. The east was turning an orange hue. Time to leave, check access points into his stronghold for forms or tracks before the sun was up. He moved on all fours down the hill. A satellite would think him a deer.

***

Cain remained motionless. Silently he praised the name of Satan. By what he thought had been error, he had bedded on the hill adjacent to his quarry. He had moved to the hilltop in the darkness of the previous night, thinking he was upon the highest hill—the hill where his quarry now sat. If he had gone to the highest hill, his tracks surely would have been discovered, or his presence seen. Satan was watching over him.

He had slept with his night-vision goggles in place. He had awakened when a chill entered his lightweight sleeping bag, a rip had formed from an abrasion with a sharp rock. That is when he had seen the movement up the hill. The sighting might have been luck, but hard, patient work and Satan's hand had brought him to the moment.

He thought back on the hunt. He had found the university van humming along on the highway, empty. Thinking his quarry could have rendezvoused with accomplices or unwary travelers and were still moving west, he moved west, searching vehicles with his scanning equipment. He wasted twenty-four hours searching moving vehicles, then wasted more time at the next plaza, searching, waiting. A day later, he began backtracking along the highway. He had wasted time gathering rugged clothing, provisions, a laser rifle, and search teams. He had wasted three days searching the highway in three twenty-five-mile radii. He meticulously searched a gravel service road for miles, then continued searching the highway.

Only upon accessing a different mapping program on his computer did he become aware of the geology station on the service road. His search teams returned to the access road. He found the station missing half the emergency food supply. The security camera was broken. He had wasted three days checking legitimate users entitled to the supplies as he waited for his quarry to return to the station for the remainder of the supplies. Another day was wasted in a twenty-five-mile radius search around the station. He had not thought this Johnson capable of a longer trek, loaded with probably a hundred pounds of supplies.

He sent his teams back to the highway, expanding the search to the east and to the west. He remained at the geology station. The supplies could have been stolen by Land Bureau employees, or by youth from the few families still employed in the desolate area. Or John Johnson could have taken those supplies. No fingerprints, no DNA evidence was found. The search had spread outward, toward the plateau country. Each night, he inserted himself on a high piece of ground. The men above him wanted drones, air platforms, satellites, and he refused. He was the master of his craft, and they listened.

He loved the desolation, the hunt, the anticipation. He tired easily of civilization—weaving through the clutter of flesh was annoying. He had loved the earth since man was just a struggling species controlled by the forces of nature. He had pleasant visions of the past killing times; the killing times were too few now. He remembered the lush grasslands that once existed, carpeted with buffalo; the Plains tribes in their ritual warfare of coup counting; the deadly, brutal clashes between entire bands. He missed the carnage, the emotions gone wild, the smell of fear and blood. Soon the killing times would come again—as never before witnessed by the world.

He was content for the moment in the suffering he would give today. They both would die slowly. He would rape her, unravel her bowels as she watched, set parts of her afire. Piece by piece, he would dismember her mate—fingers, toes, eyelids, penis, slowly, oh so slowly. To have mastery over another, that was the essence of life. To give pain and receive none, that was the victory of life.

Cain watched Johnson crawl from the hilltop. Clever, being on hands and knees. Johnson entered a ravine and was lost from sight. Cain followed his quarry's trail till another trail intersected the path. Cain surmised Johnson was scouting his domain. The faint trail was most likely the one to his hideaway and his woman. He wanted the woman first; she would give him the microdots quickly. She could be used as a tool, a hostage.

The trail followed a cliff face. A cave was a likely possibility for a hideaway. He was surprised to find water, small springs, oozing the smallest flows—cupfuls, but still capable of sustaining life. He inspected the rock face carefully. He searched for booby traps. He became apprehensive of Johnson's location.

He moved into a collection of shrubs and small trees. Here, he saw a narrow entrance to a cave, no wider than a man's hips. Below the entrance, water issued from the rock. He smelled the entrance for the fetid odor of cat urine and dung. No odor, no cougar's den. He smelled humans.

This was the hideaway, the perfect shelter; in a remote location, immune to probing satellites, with a self-contained water source, hidden entrance, difficult access. John Johnson's brother, the geologist, must have picked the area, if not the cave. Cain had an admiration for John Johnson, for his stealth, for his stamina—moving the provisions so far—for his skill with a knife, for his daring and resourcefulness. They were brothers at heart, serving two different masters.

Cain crawled through the entrance. He was forced to angle his shoulders; his hips rubbed. He scraped by a metal reflector in the crevice-like opening, used to bring sunlight into the cave. He brushed past the hanging blanket. His laser pistol was drawn. She was at the entrance, standing still, calm, staring at him without surprise or shock. Inwardly, he raged, for she seemed to expect him and had no fear.

"The microdots."

"We have no microdots."

He knew a copy would have been made, kept in Johnson's possession, while the original went with Johnson's brother. Or did John have the original? All the same in the end. She wished to play dumb. He liked such games.

She had gone to the entrance when she heard the reflector move, expecting John. Her emotions for the man she was to wed had been wild within her. Her affection drained in a rush when she saw the flat face, the massive jaw, the severed ear, the laser pistol aimed at her heart. The pistol was in the bedding at the far side of the cave. She must, by speed or trickery, return to the bedding. He rose to full height, moved nearer to her. She backed away.

"Stay where you are."

"You're going to kill me. Why should I make it easy for you?"

He hadn't witnessed such calm in a woman for hundreds of years. She reminded him of the Saxon woman in the Thirty Years War, and the Spanish slave girl in Rome, when Christians lit the roads with their burning bodies. His adversary, Christ, was in her body. Abel had been calm, too innocent to fear. No, she knew the fear of violence. It was the magician Christ blocking her memories of the past. Cain leaped at her, caught her by the arm, lashed her face with the butt of his pistol. A moment of pain came to her face, only a moment, and then the calm returned.

He was enraged. "You're as foolish as Abel. Death is easy. It is the time between life and death—the suffering of the flesh—that is difficult. I'll take your eyelids first so you will see everything, then a breast."

Words were so important. He had to enter her with his words, explore her fears, her hopes. He would know her soul intimately. He grabbed her breast. She did not flinch. She just stared at him.

"Christ will not give me to you."

He released her breast. "Christ?" Fear seemed to mingle with arrogant pride. "Christ? When we last met, I told you of your Christ—how He stands by while His sheep are slaughtered. The cowardly shepherd will not defend you. He boasts of His meekness, His lowliness."

She saw the lust come to his eyes. She began to back away, toward the bedding. He allowed her to go, still holding onto an arm. She knew the Lord was with her. He tripped her to the bedding, tore her shirt from her. She did not resist. She spoke as he gloated over her.

"You are so sad, so empty. What pleasure can this be? You don't know what it is to love."

Her free hand was within the blankets, searching for the pistol. Or should she depend solely on the Lord? The Lord had given her the pistol; this was not a game of faith.

Her words infuriated him. He couldn't love. He knew self-love, and he knew hate. He ripped open her baggy pants, mounted her. Still she looked at him calmly. Damn her! He could not make her fear! He went berserk with anger and rage.

"I'm Cain! I give death, and I never die. I've killed thousands! *Thousands*! And you are foolish enough to be unafraid?"

He began striking her across her face. "I am filled with life, and my power is like fire upon the earth."

His rage overwhelmed his sexual desire. She bucked, squirmed, even as she searched the bedding for the pistol. With a fury, he attempted to pin her hips to the floor. He wished to enter her, and his flesh could not respond. He felt the Restraining One, the Holy Spirit, pulling the life from his body. He leaped from her, screaming, gyrating.

"Satan, come to me! Satan, come to me! Satan, be my strength!"

She pulled a blanket over her half-clothed body, sat up with the pistol in her hand, hidden under the blanket.

She screamed at the maddened Cain. "You have not lived forever! Only Christ can give eternal life. You believe a lie! The demon in you has passed from memory to memory, and now it is in you." Why hadn't she fired? Why did she debate with him? She should end this foolishness.

"No! No! No!" He battled the air, swinging, dodging, fighting the constraint upon his flesh, fighting to regain his strength.

"You have not lived forever."

He cringed at her words. He could not look at her, yet his eyes were pulled to her face. She spoke again as his motions ceased. "You are in bondage to your flesh. You will die, whoever you are."

Cain's torment ceased. He stared at her dumbfounded, unable to comprehend the stillness that had come over him.

"In the name of Christ, come out of him," she demanded.

He slumped to the ground, shuddering in weakness. He mumbled to himself, "Satan lives. Satan lives. Master of the universe, Satan lives."

The shuddering stopped. His gaze was strangely lucid. A smile came to his lips as some thought was whispered to his consciousness. He whispered to her. "You are impure." He rose to his feet. "He will never want you. You were a whore from the beginning. In a whore's body, you live. You are alone."

She was not alone! She had a moment of remembrance; she felt her former filth, the corrupt flesh within her, all the men who had entered her. In that second of doubt, he sprang upon her. She fired three rounds. A shot grazed his arm, another entered above his right lung and passed cleanly through his body. The final round entered the soft cavern wall. He snapped her neck. Diana died. He slit her throat, played in her blood, wallowed in the stickiness. He mocked the Lord, drank her blood.

"The blood of Diana, shed for the remission of sins." He looked upward and laughed at God.

***

In the Shadow of Babylon

John stood in the entrance, watching Cain. A premonition had seized him. He had run to the cave. He heard three muffled explosions. Before entering, he knew Diana was dead. He had felt his soul break in two. He had died with her and knew he would never be whole again. Alone, as he had been his entire life, alone with Jesus.

Cain turned, saw his adversary. John could not feel contempt or anger or hatred for Cain. He saw her bloodied body. Cain's bloody visage, dark red, except for gleaming eyes, stared back. Cain appeared so pitiful, a grown man playing in a childish mess. No, less than a man, a dog at a kill.

They stared at each other. Cain's pistol had been placed in his holster on his belt; his laser rifle was slung tightly upon his back. John had his knife in his hand. He saw Borelli's revolver laying on the stone floor. In three bounding steps he had secured the pistol and aimed at Cain's torso. Cain had watched. Cain could not find emotion in the man before him, no life, nothing to feed upon. John had no desire to live, or to struggle, or to talk.

Cain approached his quarry warily, his body tensed, light, agile, searching the eyes for a sign, a clue to what was happening within the mind. His head twisted as he walked as if attempting to corkscrew into John's mind. Cain smiled and spoke. "There's still some of Satan in that flesh. You want to hate me, kill me, don't you?"

Words. Cain had many words. John knew Cain wished to draw him into debate, distract his attention. Cain laughed as he spoke. "The flesh has power."

John responded by pulling the trigger as the fluorescent dot touched Cain's heart.

Cain had seen a thousand triggers pulled, had made a study of eyes, facial muscles, body postures, hand movements. He dove toward John before the trigger struck; the bullet skimmed his back as one last shot echoed on the ceiling. He somersaulted, a savage kick went into John's ribs, propelling him into one of the pools of water.

The thought "living water" passed through John's mind.

Cain leapt upon John, a knife in his hands, his pistol still in its holster. John pulled his own knife as he lay submerged. His hand went numb, the knife dropped. He couldn't feel his hand. John, possessed of a frenzy, slithered from Cain's hold. A knife raked over his back in a burning streak as he collapsed on the small dam of rocks. He clamored over the rock wall, knocking it down. Cain hesitated as he wiped water and Diana's blood from his eyes. Her blood was thick in his eyes. Cain attempted to pursue but was hindered by a numbness in his legs, John's shot had caused more damage than first realized. Diana's shots had caused his knife arm to weaken. Her damned blood in his eyes burned. John turned suddenly, a large rock in his hands. The rock flew into the head of Cain. Cain fell into the pool in a sitting position, dazed. John pulled another rock from the dam as Cain began to rise, grabbing his pistol from the holster. The rock came down, missing Cain's blocking arm, catching the back of his skull. Cain fell into the water, dead.

John sat on the edge of the pool, listened to the agitated waves slapping the rock as the pool turned pink from Cain's blood.

John began to calm. He spoke to the silence. "Everyone who falls on that stone will be broken to pieces; but when it falls on any one, it will crush him."

***

He cleaned the blood from her face and body. Her face was cold, waxy white, so beautiful—even in death. He ran his fingers along her nose and lips. He studied each hair of her eyebrows, each indentation in her lips. She only slept; they would soon meet again. She had made his life on earth worth living, the pain worth enduring. She had been a gift from God, and God had taken her back. John buried her.

He could understand no reason for her death. No good could come from her absence. Had he loved her more than God? The thought was powerless to convict. He would have hated God had he any strength for hate. He would have hated God if there was no heaven, no resurrection. He would see her again, and the wait for that meeting, insignificant in the stretch of eternity, would be so short.

Yet, time had slowed, as if to mock him, to prolong his agony. He had wanted to physically love her. Why had that been denied? The Lord did what

He wished; to argue against Him was to argue with the wind. Would God spitefully hurt His children? In time, he would know the reason why.

In the lonely, empty days that followed, the Comforter was with him. He fought with the Comforter many times. He found the bitterness to hate God and life. His soul wrestled, cursed the Truth, and then his strength would ebb, the tears would come, and the silent emptiness. He lived with the Holy Spirit in him, upon him. He read the Bible—sometimes with faith, sometimes with sarcasm. He prayed—sometimes with hope, sometimes with cynicism. He looked upon the earth and waited.

***

On the fortieth day after the death of Diana, airfoils appeared in the desert, rugged vehicles of the land-management service. Four vehicles coming out of the southern flatness. He watched them from the highest hill on a frigid, cloudy day. They were coming for him, and he was indifferent. Cain had not reported, or the satellites had recognized a human form upon the wasteland—what did it matter?

The vehicles came to his hill, parking at the base. Three men began the climb to the summit. A knot of men remained by the vehicles. He saw the glint of laser rifles from the knot of men and knew he was within their sights. He faced them so they would have a clean shot. He had a contempt for life. He saw the men stop before the desiccated flesh and bones of Cain. He had left the bones to the beasts of the desert, the coyote, the vulture, the cougar. One man continued toward him—his brother.

Tim was breathing heavily from the uphill climb, as much from emotion as exercise. He had put on some weight—that would be expected if he were in seclusion with time on his hands. Tim glanced at the bronzed, haggard face. The skin was stretched over the bones, devoid of fat. A silent overwhelming grief clung to his brother. The spirit was almost extinguished, cringing in sadness and loneliness. John peered into Tim's soul. He saw the weariness of a man who begins a journey he cannot finish. Had the pride within Tim been broken?

They had loved each other once. Neither could feel that love returning from the other. Perhaps they had no love to give. They did not embrace or think to do so, their hearts were within themselves.

"May I sit, John?"

"Yes, of course."

Tim sat on a nearby rock. John sat cross-legged on the earth. They studied each other in a moment's glance.

"Where's Diana?"

"Dead. Murdered." The reply was flat.

Tim had guessed as much. He asked another question to which he suspected the answer.

"By whom?"

"Cain."

"I'm sorry."

John shrugged his shoulders. He had no words.

Tim wondered at the total absence of emotion. His brother seemed to have fled from life, his body. His heart broke for his brother. If Mary were taken from him, life would cease. He needed to be blunt; John liked honesty.

"I need your testimony, John. We have a trial date, men on our side. A power struggle is taking place. Other incidents are involved. In our case, we have no one to tell us how this incident came about and no microdots."

"How was Grandfather murdered?"

"Pushed in front of a commuter train." Tim's eyes searched the earth.

"The microdots?"

"Stolen from the police evidence room."

Tim's eyes remained downcast. Gramps's death had hurt Tim. John spoke.

In the Shadow of Babylon

"Why do you persist?"

"I have no choice!" The words were embittered. "Like Gramps said, men were eager, willing to take up our cause, and I'm caught in the middle of a power struggle. I'm the ball they're playing with. I'm trapped."

"Mary and the kids?"

"They're safe, but we're prisoners. We can't live normal lives."

John allowed the sentence to die in the quiet, and then he spoke.

"What of Christ?"

John didn't wish to begin the old arguments again. Truthfully, he had no concern for the state of his brother's soul. At the moment, John cared little for God or His earthly plans. He asked from curiosity. Tim shook his head, pursed his lips.

"The same answer you've heard before. How can I give more than what I have given?" An urge seized Tim to begin the old arguments again. He needed to prove his position, justify his thoughts, pull John out of his bleak existence. He hadn't the energy or desire; perhaps John had the truth.

John spoke. "Let's go."

"The microdots?"

John smiled at Tim's worried tone. The microdots were all that mattered. He knew he had been betrayed. The Church didn't need him; perhaps a brief statement for appearance's sake. They wanted, needed, the original microdots. He would be handed to the civil authorities for the charges of mutiny, theft, for the slayings of Hanson, Borelli, Cain. He would meet with a fatal accident. Tim knew these things, hid them from his conscience. He was only thinking of his family. His family came before his brother. John accepted his betrayal, for he loved Tim's family more than himself.

"I carry the canister with me." John rummaged in the pocket of his coat, handed the canister to Tim. "Take it." It was over, the struggle.

Tim stood, took the canister. It was happening so quickly. Was he being insensitive? They should have talked more, said or done something to reestablish their love for each other.

"John, I am sorry about Diana's death. She was special to me."

Love had been like an aura on Diana. He had never seen a woman cherish a man more than she had cherished John. He would remain silent on these thoughts; John's eyes had winced at her mention. Remembering could only hurt more.

"Yes, I know." John rose with an agitation in his soul, began walking toward the knot of men. "What of Mom and Dad?" He spoke as he walked past Tim.

"They're fine. Worried about you—but that worry will soon be gone."

Tim spoke to John's back. They descended the hill, Tim trailing behind John. Tim wondered if John would struggle when the handcuffs were applied. He didn't like turning in his brother, but there was no other way. John went nimbly down the hill. He held out his hands, his wrists touching, as he approached the group. He turned and brought his hands behind his back, locking his fingers. Two of the men looked at each other in surprise. The older man spoke as he brought the fugitive's hands back in front of his body, placed the handcuffs securely.

"You are under arrest for the murder of your commanding officer, mutiny, theft, the murders of Inspector Borelli and Inspector Hanson. These handcuffs can be exploded, severing your hands from your body and causing death from blood loss."

The handcuffs snapped on heavily as the elbow bands were secured. John wondered what actions would be necessary on his part for the detectives to explode the cuffs. No, he would go to trial, go to prison. Christ had been obedient to the Father's will the day of his humiliation and death.

John walked in silence to the vehicle that would transport him. He saw men coming out of the rock of Horeb, carrying clothing, supplies. They would find Cain's laser rifle and pistol, Borelli's pistol—he had carried no weapon since Diana's death. Would he be charged with the murder of Cain or was Cain a phantom man, hidden by the Church? They would never find the grave of Diana. John turned to his brother.

"You did this for Mary and the kids?"

His voice sought reassurance, so that he could believe the best of his brother.

"Yes, John. The Church needs the microdots. The case will fall apart without the original evidence. Copies carry no judicial weight. How could I retrieve the microdots from you without someone knowing? I'm being watched constantly by friend and enemy. I've gotten you one of the best lawyers in the country."

"Nothing matters now. Gramps, Diana, and I did what we set out to do."

An understanding could have been worked out with the Church to retrieve the microdots and allow him his freedom. The Church didn't need him. Had Tim attempted to push an understanding that included freedom, or did Tim wish him imprisoned? Were Satanic infiltrators in the Church responsible for demanding his capture so that murder could follow? Or had the Church not wished to offend the state authorities over a fugitive and murderer? The state authorities were likely controlled by the Satanic forces.

The two detectives stood close to John. One opened the door, the other physically turned John from Tim. John paused in his movement into the vehicle. Strangely, the detective allowed him the pause. He studied the two detectives, early forties, healthy, muscled, with cynical, compassionless eyes. John spoke to them.

"This may mean nothing to you, but Inspector Borelli was the finest man I have ever met. I did not kill him."

"Tell it to the judge, Chief." The two men grunted a laugh as John was shoved into the vehicle.

***

They imprisoned him in a cubicle two feet longer than his body height. He had a basin on the toilet and a cot to sleep upon. Subversion against the state, that is what they were now calling his crimes. They demanded harsh treatment, but rapists and murderers lived in private homes in penal colonies. He was not bitter. He thought it odd they believed they could crowd and worry his soul.

His defense attorney met with him on his first day in jail. This aggressive man of keen wit and impatient manner had no intention of fighting the government or a part of the Church. He thought it his duty to obtain life imprisonment when the state clamored for the death penalty. The lawyer didn't exist who would cross the state and the Church—especially for an Enslaver. His presence on the witness stand was short. He offered no memorable lines, no theatrics. His part had been played.

John spent his days and nights thinking of Diana and the life they might be able to share in the new world coming. He speculated on Christ's reign on earth. What work would Christ have him do? Where would he live? He hoped to have some free time just to think. He would like to understand the nonbelievers, their place within history, enter their consciences and thoughts. He wished to see each denial of the truth of Jesus and understand the reason why. But he knew the reason why: a former cherubim named Satan had come to earth.

John hoped to travel with Diana at his side, walk over the earth, delighting in nature restored and in God's people. In all these thoughts of Diana, the love they had not shared ached in his soul. He kept his faith in a loving God and looked forward. He had moments of depression, wondering whom he would not see in the next life. Would God excuse those of an honest heart who hadn't known to give themselves to Christ? How much knowledge did a man need to have before God could righteously condemn him for ignoring Christ? Thoughts of the coming Tribulation filled him with anguish for Tim and his family. He loved the kids, Matthew and Katie. What pain was coming to the earth as the prideful illusions of men collapsed?

He was allowed electronic magazines but not an electrascreen. He read of the Beast, whom the world embraced, idolized, fawned upon. A handsome man, with dark-brown, caring eyes. Strange to look upon the man who had unknowingly but purposefully caused so much pain to the ones John had loved.

In the Shadow of Babylon

Each day John wondered if the food was poisoned. Each day he was surprised when a passing guard or inmate did not murder him. He waited quietly for the Rapture, his Bible in hand.

CHAPTER 14

Tim Johnson watched the electrascreen from his gently vibrating recliner. The kids were playing quietly on the floor, absorbed in a computer game. Mary was cooking in the kitchen. An element of the Church had been steadfast in its promise of protection, providing the luxurious country home, surrounded by electronic surveillance and security patrols. Three armed men lived within the home—they were good men, unobtrusive, friendly to the children, highly professional in their duty as bodyguards.

Since his recorded statement and that of his brother, the Church had disappeared from his life. No calls, no questions. Tim worried about his brother. Could John cope with life in prison? He would have exhausted his food supplies in the desert or broken a bone in a fall or even died from a fall. Turning John in had been the right course of action, he was certain; his conscience was clear. Even John had admitted he didn't want Mary and the kids to suffer because of him.

The original microdots and all copies had eventually been stolen but not before being widely disseminated to Church personnel and the news media. The story had been quashed in the media but not before a sizable number of congressional representatives and senators were made aware. The story was circulated throughout the European Federation's administrative and legislative bodies. The original microdots that had been in John's possession had been needed for the trial to continue. Only a few people had read the entire text. John's original had been necessary, and how could you get John's original without the authorities capturing John? Satan's men—he hated the term—on finding John, would have killed him. The authorities had stressed John's capture as being vital. He was a witness. John had no will to live—in the drought zone—he would have perished from loneliness. Life would be good again.

Tim had pity for John over the loss of Diana but even more so for the warped religious fervor that had caused so much heartache. John lived in a world of pessimism and cynicism. The war must have been the cause. He didn't hold John responsible for breaking under the strain of combat; John had always been a sensitive kid. An alternate source of strength should have been found other than Enslaver doctrine, one more rooted in reality and God's plan for man. The truth was, John hadn't belonged in a combat unit.

Perhaps, he could bring John back to reality once the Rapture did not occur. The nonevent would destroy John's faith, a dialogue could be established. Then, the loving Christ, who only wanted humanity to be happy and find satisfaction in life, could be accepted. Christ as a guide, developing the inherent goodness in man. Christ as an historical figure, not a personality within.

The telescreen buzzed, the electrascreen automatically reduced its volume. By remote control, the telescreen pivoted toward Tim. On the screen was the stolid, lifeless face of a balding man, a bureaucratic face. Name and place of call appeared in small letters at the bottom of the screen. Warden Sims.

Warden Sims spoke.

"We met two months ago, Mr. Johnson."

"Yes, I remember. Is my brother all right?" Tim tensed. What trouble had John caused? Or had someone attempted to kill him? The latter possibility had weighed heavily upon his conscience, despite repeated assurances by Sims at their initial meeting.

"We don't know. He was reported missing this morning. We held off contacting you, thinking he would turn up. He hasn't."

"What do you mean *missing*?"

"It must have been an inside job—no breakout occurred, the cell was locked, no sign of escape. We're questioning men now."

"Don't harm him."

"No, we won't." Sims smiled. "He hasn't left the grounds; of that we are certain."

"You're telling me he has just disappeared?"

"He is hiding within the building; men don't disappear," Sims scolded.

"Has anyone else been reported missing?"

"One man, but the incidents are unrelated." A panic came over Tim that turned to terror.

"Was that one man an Enslaver?"

Sims turned away from the screen with a blank face and began punching the keyboard of a computer by his side. He swiveled around to face Tim. "As a matter of fact…How did you know?"

"Just a hunch…just a hunch…" The voice was dull, trailing off into a deep depression. "Thank you, Warden Sims."

"You will be hearing from us. Don't worry; we will find your brother."

"Sure."

The screen snapped off; the electrascreen returned to normal volume.

Impossible! Simply impossible! A nagging thought asked, What is impossible to God? Others would be missing, at least hundreds of thousands from the world! He and his family would be missing. Damn it, and they were right here in their temporary home. John! Crafty John had escaped. Perhaps the Church had arranged the escape, needing him for more detailed and sensitive information? Or perhaps they wanted to hide him where he would be completely safe? Or had he been kidnapped? Would he be tortured? Had he been murdered?

Tim thought of calling someone from the Church, then decided against it. They would contact him. He would wait it out—that was always the safest and most productive course of action in such a situation. Don't tip your hand too soon. Allow the situation to develop. Supper was almost ready. Life was good. The kids had finished their game, run off to a bedroom. Time for the news, the familiar face of the top-rated anchorman was on the screen. The face was one you could trust, one that was a part of the pattern of life. Tim listened.

"Here is a news bulletin just received. Last night, scattered outbreaks of mass hysteria were reported within the United States. Those afflicted spoke of sightings of spirit beings rising from the earth. The hallucinations were brief, less than seconds, and no discernable long-term effects have been noted. Possible causes of the outbreaks center on contaminated water supplies—as in the incident of 2105, when thousands hallucinated. Now another story."

Tim turned the electrascreen off. No live bodies were reported missing in the newscast. No one vanishing from the office or the construction site. No mass transit vehicles left driverless, no doctors missing from the operating room. No living bodies seen floating off into space. Contaminated water, that was all. No Rapture. Maybe so few live bodies went that no one noticed? Was the state suppressing information? These thoughts are ridiculous, he assured himself. He and his family were still there, and that was all the proof he needed that there had been no Rapture.

Hallucinations. He remembered studying hallucinations in college, in a psych class. In the hysteria of 2105, no one saw the same hallucinations. As this incident was reported, however, everyone saw the same phenomenon, spirit beings. "In the twinkling of an eye" was a phrase that came to his head. Another sentence came: "One shall be taken and the other left."

He began to have difficulty concentrating. His stomach was uneasy. An emptiness grew in him, and a chill. He ran to the den. Somewhere on the bookshelves was a Bible—somewhere!

He pulled books from the shelves, they scattered on the floor. He found the Bible, searched for and found Matthew, chapter 24. He read furiously, then reread, attempting to slow his racing, unfocused mind.

He passed by the kitchen on the way to his room. Mary noticed Tim was distraught, she followed. He walked in a peculiar manner, as if about to collapse. She glimpsed the side of his face as he turned into the bedroom. His skin was pale. She called to him; he did not answer. The door was closed, locked. She knocked on the door—had John died?

"Mary, leave me alone, just for a while. I'm fine. Just leave me alone."

She walked away from the door. Something was terribly wrong. Had John gotten into trouble? No, Tim would have told her. She went back to the kitchen; the kids had to eat. She couldn't concentrate on her tasks.

He pummeled the air. He quietly cursed God a thousand different ways. He knocked over chairs with feet and hands. He tore the bed apart, ripped the mattress from the bed; he furiously punched and savagely kicked the mattress slumped against the wall. He cursed himself. He hated himself. He thought of what he had done to Mary and the kids, and his self-hatred exploded into one long, paralyzing ache. His soul screamed to God for forgiveness, for help. No answer came, no peace. His family would suffer. He was desolate, forlorn. In his stubborn pride, his unbelief, he had doomed his wife and children. Oh God! John had been right. Gramps had been right. Why hadn't they fought harder to win his belief? The door had closed, and Christ was on the other side.

Stunned, he lay on the wood floor. In the ache that was his soul, he had visions of the things to come: war, pestilence, famine, love grown cold. Deep within him, the future was being read to his spirit. He had failed miserably. All that had once been important—success, money, the admiration of his peers and neighbors—meant nothing, had never meant anything. All that he had held as foolish, the struggles of his brother, the rantings of his grandfather, were now truth. The weight of his pride and ego crushed him. The weight of the truth broke him into a thousand pieces. He died inside, wept beyond tears, wept in heaving convulsions that had no end. He had doomed his family. He lay in the coming darkness alone.

EPILOGUE

The shades were drawn, no lights were on. He had placed a towel against the door to keep the sounds of his children from invading his solitude. Morning. His small downstairs study had once been their den. He had liked coming back to the university home, the perk, the two-story single home. The country estate was no longer needed; the Church trial was over. No obvious shift within the Church that a layman could perceive. That was all he was now—a layman. Even Wink had stopped coming around. He was a nobody in the Church. He was not wanted for committees, not wanted for work on the Easter celebration, not asked why his wife and kids weren't in Church. Familiar friends turned their backs on him. He sensed, on the other side of the shades, the sun was unfettered by clouds. Spring, somewhere near Easter? The question: What did John and Gramps know that he did not know? Every day, the same question until weeks had collected and time had been forgotten.

It had not been in vain. Hope had been found, and yet the hope was so very small. This line: "But he that shall endure unto the end, the same shall be saved." Matthew 24:13. The long discourse on the end of the world as it was known in this present age. If he and his family could endure for seven years of hell on earth, they would be saved for eternity. Or was it until their own ends, within the seven years—if they endured in faith until events took

In the Shadow of Babylon

them? He had another passage that offered the key, or at least this was John and Gramps's contention. Found in John 3:3, "Verily, verily, I say unto thee, Except a man be born again, he cannot see the kingdom of God."

Somewhere within those passages was hope. He must find that thing—that experience of rebirth—and live it, teach it to Mary, Matt, and Katie. Once found he must live it within a world gone mad. He knew it would take time. He knew his family must have time—perhaps all seven years would be needed. Christ's words showed that the course of events would only wish to kill them. In a sense, he could deal with the concrete nature of the problem—staying alive. Basic thoughts: food, water, shelter, clothing. Weapons to defend against man and beast. Medicines to protect against the unseen world of disease. He had a head start by knowing what the world didn't know. He knew learned men, men of science, geologists, volcanologists, climatologists, agricultural experts. Find a place or places to make his family's stand as they searched for the elusive secret—the experience. Gather supplies and earnest people of character. Really, like ancient mariners on the seas of storms, seeking that new world to find their peace.

Today he would begin. Within seven years, he would know if his family had won the prize—life.

REND THE HEAVENS

Moving Heaven to Shake Earth

By GLENN MELDRUM

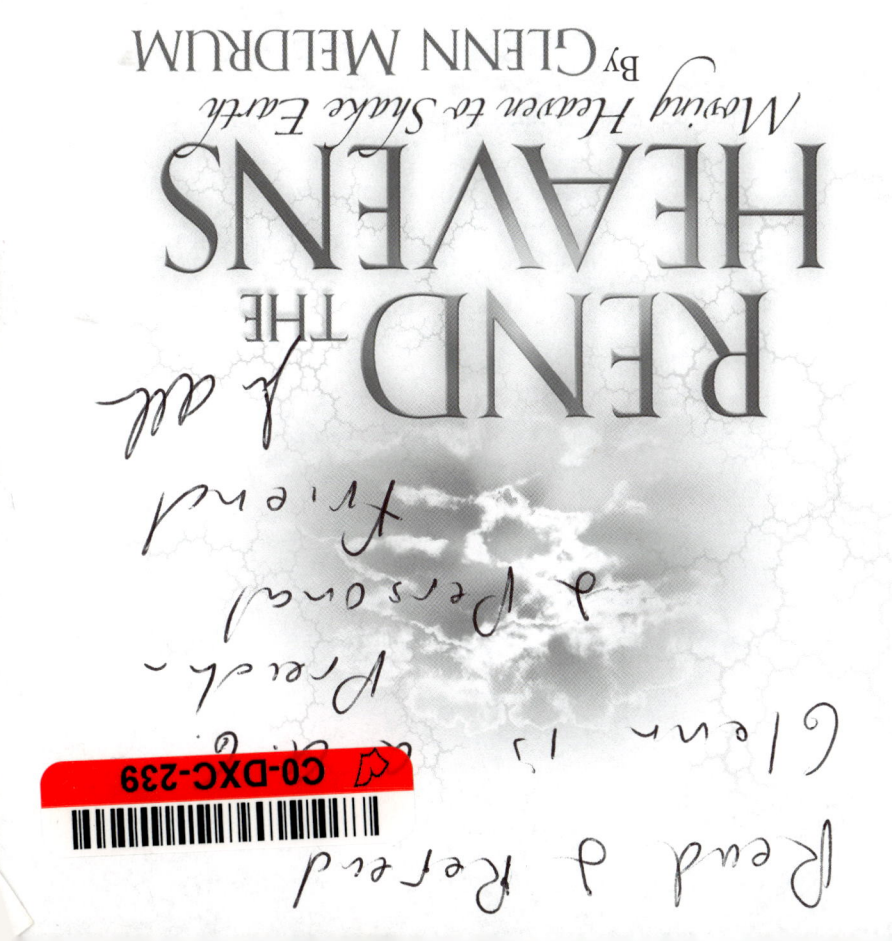

Published by
WISDOM'S GATE PUBLISHING
www.WisdomsGate.com

ISBN 0-9728139-1-8

Copyright © 2005 by Glenn Meldrum

All Scripture quotations in this publication, unless otherwise noted, are from the HOLY BIBLE, NEW INTERNATIONAL VERSION® NIV® Copyright © 1973, 1978, 1984 by International Bible Society. All rights reserved.

The "NIV" and "New International Version" are trademarks registered in the United States Patent and Trademark Office by International Bible Society. Use of either trademark requires the permission of the International Bible Society.

ACKNOWLEDGEMENTS

My deepest thanks and appreciation goes to those who helped in the editing of this book: my wife Jessica, Steve Bruce, Darla Gray and especially Pastor Mike Sanders who did the majority of the editing.

I would like to give special thanks to Steve and Kathy Gallagher. Their friendship is an irreplaceable gift from the Savior. They have encouraged me in countless ways, both in this project and in building Christ's glorious Kingdom. Thank you.

Dedication

This book is dedicated to my wife, Jessica.
Her passionate love for Jesus, her faithful love to me,
and her consistent enthusiasm for the ministry
has been a priceless encouragement to my life.
Through the grace of God
she has helped me become all that I am.
She is the most precious earthly gift God has entrusted to me.
Words cannot express how much I love you!

REND THE HEAVENS
Moving Heaven to Shake Earth

TABLE OF CONTENTS

ACKNOWLEDGEMENTS	2
DEDICATION	3
FOREWORD	5
INTRODUCTION	6
1. Concepts of Revival	11
2. Defining Revival	22
3. By My Spirit	34
4. Prepare the Way	45
5. The Work of Preparing	55
6. The Beauty of Brokenness	65
7. Repentance: The Gift of God	77
8. Passion for Holiness	87
9. Holiness to See God	98
10. Revival Praying	110
11. Spiritual Warfare	120
12. Destiny of the Damned	133
13. Rescue the Perishing	146
14. The Word and Faith	158
15. Unity	170
16. The End of the Matter	181
BIBLIOGRAPHY	185

Foreword

Would to God every believer in America would read this book. It addresses the greatest need of the Church in this critical hour of history—a Heaven-sent revival. The prophet Isaiah cried, "Oh, that Thou wouldest rend the heavens and come down, that the mountains might quake at Your presence." What a difference the presence of God makes. Mountains, those seemingly immovable obstacles that defy the advance of God's Kingdom, suddenly melt before the presence of a holy God.

Every year the American Church spends multiplied millions of dollars on various types of evangelism and yet, in the words of the apostle Peter, "We have toiled all night and caught nothing." Peter was a professional fisherman with a lifetime of experience and he knew all about the tides and seasons. He knew how, when and where to fish. He was committed to his task, having toiled throughout the long dark hours of the night, and yet in the end, had little to show for his efforts. Likewise, the twentieth century church is continuing the same pattern. Only when Jesus became involved in Peter's fishing business did his nets begin to break under the weight of the fish. This book is filled with examples of Jesus stepping down from eternity into time, and forever changing lives, cities and nations. I have had the privilege of sitting under the anointed ministry of the author. He is a true "revivalist" with a burning passion for God's glory to be revealed again, in and through the Church. Glenn and his wife, Jessica, are a rare breed these days. They have gladly relinquished the normal luxuries of life to travel throughout the nation by motorhome, ministering wherever God opens doors. Their lifestyle is simple, their message powerful, and their lives humble. I recommend both this book and their ministry to you.

David Ravenhill
Author and itinerant teacher, Lindale, TX

INTRODUCTION

"Oh, that You would rend the heavens and come down, that the mountains would tremble before You!"

Isaiah 64:1

The promises in the Word of God concerning revival are seeking to be fulfilled. These promises are waiting for people who will live out their conditions so the glory of the LORD can be unleashed upon the church and a perishing world. The Creator is timeless—the same yesterday, today and forever. He is not a respecter of people, nations or times. What He has done in the past He can, and will, do again. The spiritual awakenings of old are prophesies of what the Almighty intends to do again.

Isaiah prayed that the LORD would rend the heavens. He yearned for mortal men to see the holiness and majesty of God. To "rend" the heavens means that the King of kings rips open the veil between Heaven and earth and steps down among mankind to make His glory known. His holy presence causes men and nations to tremble by disturbing their world and upsetting their lives. God's self-disclosure exposes the hearts of men by revealing the depths of their sinfulness and their tremendous need for a Savior. The psalmist recognized this when he prayed, "O God, do not keep silent; be not quiet, O God, be not still" (Ps. 83:1).

Why would Isaiah pray such a dangerous prayer for God to rend the heavens? He knew that once men, women and children encountered the presence of the LORD in such a manner they would stand in awe of His magnificence and taste of His goodness. The prophet understood that in response to the cry of the repentant, the Savior would stoop down to heal the sin-sick soul with the balm of sweet forgiveness and mend the shattered heart with tender grace.

This book is my heart cry for revival. It is a plea for the church to awaken from her spiritual slumber and return to her New Testament foundations—those timeless truths that transform men and nations. Our efforts to reach non-Christians have produced little results and it is not God's fault. We are not bringing our countrymen to Christ; they are bringing us into the world. Oh, how we desperately need the Holy One to rend the heavens and come down!

Many dear saints have taught that revival is almost a science. Others have declared that spiritual awakenings are God's sovereign responsibility. Some take a middle-of-the-road approach between the LORD's sovereignty and our responsibility. In the end, we must face the unsettling fact that we only "know in part" and "see through a glass, darkly" (1 Cor.13:9, 12). We are like men who look through a frosted window or gaze into an ancient mirror. You can see the outline of the form, not the distinct features.

In truth, there is only one authority on revival and that is the LORD. The rest of us are amateurs, grasping for a divine Being Who is greater than the mind itself. This simply means that there is no definitive work on the subject. To our eternal benefit, we have the gift of His eternal Word. Through the Scriptures, we can understand the truths of salvation and the mysteries of His self-disclosure. Yet we know very little about the Ancient of Days and His moving, actually, far less than we think. Our experience is extremely limited, and history—which is full of marvelous accounts of divine visitations—can never fully express the awesome wonder of the LORD rending the heavens to reveal His presence to frail humanity. Our knowledge desperately needs to be coupled with experience before we can begin to comprehend the force and wonder of the Spirit being poured out upon a people.

The Bible reveals many powerful, timeless truths about how the church can prepare the way for the LORD to rend the heavens. Most of these promises are contingent upon conditions that believers must first meet. History clearly demonstrates these promises are attainable. Although the Savior cannot be forced or manipulated to pour out His power, He can be moved to shake the earth when His people passionately cry, "Part Your heavens, O LORD, and come down" (Ps. 144:5).

When the Almighty breaks into our world, He awakens the church and saves the lost in such great numbers that secular society is transformed. The transformation of society by the power of the Holy Spirit is the only sure proof of revival. The outpouring of the Holy Spirit was never intended to be reduced to pop-

Christian movements or mere clichés. Regrettably, we are far too quick to call something revival that is not. This grave error lulls Christians to sleep by making them feel they have somehow obtained the prize. Some believers reject the concept of revival, or particular historical accounts, because they do not line up with their narrow understanding of spiritual awakenings. The Redeemer acts in human history according to His good pleasure and is never subject to opinions or doctrinal positions.

The LORD desires His people to walk with Him in unbroken fellowship. This is the place of deep, abiding intimacy with Jesus. This is where people come alive in Christ as they live and move through the Spirit's power. Here saints operate in a state of divine usefulness because they are full of faith and full of the Holy Ghost (Acts 6-7). "God's purpose for our lives is continuous revival," stated Stephen Olford, "and continuous revival is equated with the continuous fullness of the Holy Spirit" (Olford, 98). Few Christians know this kind of relationship with the Lover of our souls.

Experience teaches us that there are seasons to revival. The decline of revival is the fault of our sinful nature that is prone to wander from the Living God. Our natural propensity to stray is always a willful choice. The human condition necessitates that the Holy Spirit rains new and afresh upon each generation or whole generations are lost.

We need to be honest with ourselves. We have no revival in our land because we are content to live without it. Most ministers and congregations are ignorant of what authentic revival looks like. Scores of Christians who do believe in the necessity of revival are unwilling to pay the price for it to come. Many are not convinced that a spiritual awakening is the only answer for the church and nation. Nonetheless, revival is far more than our only hope. It is a Biblical mandate!

At times, the fruitlessness of our churches drives ministers and congregations to their knees aching for the presence and power of the Holy Spirit. Unfortunately, many end up adopting the latest church growth marketing strategy or Christianized secular philosophy. They mistakenly believe that they can heal the spiritual diseases of our land with what is little more than secular solutions to sacred needs. Such "answers" are like putting band-aids on cancer; they cannot bring true healing to the human soul. Before nations can change, men must change; before men can change, hearts must change; before hearts can change, we must comprehend our need for change. King David boldly prayed, "Test me, O LORD, and try me, examine my heart and my mind" (Ps. 26:2). Paul admonished the saints to, "Examine yourselves to see whether you are in the faith; test yourselves. Do you not realize that Christ Jesus is in you—unless, of course, you fail the test?" (2 Cor. 13:5).

During the oil shortages of the 1970s, the Japanese were exporting to America inexpensive dependable cars that got great gas mileage. The Japanese automakers began taking more and more of the U.S. market. Concern about major layoffs became the catalyst to the "Buy American" campaign that followed. However, this did not correct the root problem. Then the auto companies came to a point of crisis. One American automaker went bankrupt and a second was soon to follow. This motivated the auto-executives to do something very bold: they judged themselves. They asked the difficult question, "Why are people buying foreign cars instead of ours?" After admitting that their products were inferior due to poor quality control, they changed their manufacturing process. When the quality of their automobiles increased so did their sales. They never needed the "Buy American" campaign.

A similar dilemma faces the church today. The Western world is rejecting Christianity for other religions and philosophies because we have failed to demonstrate the validity of Christ's exclusive claims. We have been too arrogant and frightened to judge ourselves. Some of the first-century churches suffered under this same malady. Since they were not willing to judge themselves, Jesus took up the cause and evaluated seven churches (Rev. 2 & 3). His judgment was based upon their true spiritual condition. Their only hope of survival was to repent.

The Savior reproved five of the seven churches because they were producing a distorted form of Christianity. They had become irrelevant to the lost and dying world they lived in. If they had judged themselves, the LORD would not have had to. Instead, Christ's rebuke made them tremble, "Remember the height from which you have fallen! Repent and do the things you did at first. If you do not repent, I will come to you and remove your lampstand from its place" (Rev. 2:5).

Christians begin to die spiritually when they stray from their relationship with Jesus. Revival resurrects the spiritually dead by infusing them with Holy Ghost life. D. M. Panton defined revival as the, "... inrush of the Spirit into a body that threatens to become a corpse!" (Pratney, 287). This is a gift of God to dead and dying saints, an act of grace to undeserving sinners.

Rend the Heavens was written to help believers comprehend what constitutes true revival and of its necessity in our time. It is a challenge addressed to Christians and churches to examine their faith and return to the New Testament pattern of Christianity that turned the world upside down. Moreover, it is an appeal to live the Biblical principles that can bring about a national awakening. These principles need to be freshly applied to the present needs of our postmodern world. Whole generations are at stake! Eternity hangs in the balance for multitudes. This should break our hearts! Western Christianity has predominately become irrelevant to a spiritually dying culture. We do not need a new message, but a new anointing!

This book does not lay out plans, programs or strategies, but deals with the issues of the heart as they relate to revival. I believe there are many practical helps in this book to aid Christians on how to prepare the way for the LORD to visit His people. This book was designed to help believers draw closer to Jesus through deep repentance and intimate fellowship, for this is where revival springs forth.

Each chapter, along with many sub-points, brings out Biblical truths that are vital components of genuine revival. Think of each principle as a piece to a puzzle that, when correctly assembled, reveals a beautiful picture. Every piece is an irreplaceable part of the whole. Each authentic revival will paint its own picture due to certain dimensions that make it unique. Yet every Holy Ghost outpouring will have essential elements that are common to all, such as "... prayer, brokenness, repentance, confession, restoration from backsliding and radical conversions" (Roberts, *Scotland*, 325).

Throughout history, many precious saints have written about revival. This book contains quotes from a number of believers who have personally experienced the glory of the LORD's presence. The bibliography at the end of this book offers a wonderful resource to investigate further this vital subject.

Rend the Heavens is for people desperate for a spiritual awakening. My prayer is that the hearts of many Christians will be stirred to seek the Savior's beautiful face until He rends the heavens—transforming our homes, cities, nation and world. This is our only hope!

CHAPTER ONE

CONCEPTS OF REVIVAL

Revival is a sovereign, supernatural work of the Holy Spirit. It is God breaking into human history and revealing His holiness and glory. When the church is awakened from her spiritual lethargy she begins to see the world anew as her God-given mission field. Men, women and children are converted in such large numbers that secular society is dramatically changed. One of history's wonderful accounts of revival is the Hebrides Awakening that began in 1949.

The Hebrides (heb´ri-deez´) are islands off the coast of Scotland. This awakening predominately remained within the traditional Church of Scotland. Although the LORD used many ministers in the spread of this spiritual outpouring, Duncan Campbell from the Faith Mission became the primary evangelist.

The first communities radically transformed were Barvas and Shader, which are located on the big island of Lewis. News spread over the island of what had happened in Barvas. Soon busloads of people were coming to the meetings from several villages. Other churches on the island also began experiencing the power of the Holy Spirit. Work and normal activities were set aside for people to get right with God and for Christians to seek out those who had not yet met the Savior. Campbell held services in many villages for the next several years.

In August of 1951 he commenced preaching in a village called Bernera. He was having little success in the services due to the absence of prayer meetings so decided to send for the praying men of Barvas to assist him through intercession. The evangelist specifically asked that they bring with them 17-year-old Donald MacPhail. Donald was dramatically saved in the revival. Two weeks later, he received the baptism in the Holy Spirit on the side of a hill. God imparted to this young man a powerful gift of prayer.

One night as Campbell preached in Bernera, he felt that the powers of darkness were doing all they could to stop the spread of the revival. In spite of this, Donald sat in the front of the church weeping. The evangelist knew that this young convert was closer to God at that moment than he himself. This compelled him to stop preaching and ask Donald to pray.

Donald prayed for about five minutes then declared, "I seem to be gazing into an open door and see the Lamb in the midst of the throne and the keys of death and Hell on His waist." Then he began to weep. When he finally composed himself he looked towards Heaven, lifted his hands and proclaimed, "God, there is power there. Let it loose!" (Campbell, *When The Mountains*). The Holy Spirit instantly fell upon the entire congregation with an overwhelming demonstration of power.

"When I said amen," Donald later recalled, "and looked around me, I was amazed, for people were on their faces in the pews. Many were bent over the pews. There were also those who went into trances or fainted. The power of God was intense. It was a wonderful evening of the revelation of God's presence and power. That night, and during that time of divine visitation, a number of people came to Christ in the little village of Kirkabost a few miles away" (Peckham, 236).

This awakening wonderfully reveals the Biblical principles of revival. First God stirs a hunger in a few faithful saints. Then He moves them to pray by filling them with compassion to see the church set on fire and the lost saved. Their impassioned prayers move Heaven to shake earth. Revival first breaks out by awakening the church. Then the Holy Spirit descends upon the unsaved, bringing them to life-changing repentance that produces genuine salvation.

The word revival carries with it a vast array of definitions, opinions and emotions. This can make a discussion on the subject extremely challenging. Two people can use the same word and have very different definitions. In this chapter, we will define revival from a Biblical and historical point of view. From there we will examine some of the general fruits of revival and finish with its necessity in our time.

OLD TESTAMENT REVIVALS

The Hebrew word *chayah* is translated in the King James Version as "revive," "revived" and "reviving." *Chayah* is used 262 times in the Old Testament and is translated 153 times as "live," 12 times as "revive." The word is also rendered "alive," "save," "quicken," "surely," "life" and "recover" (Strong's number 2421). A strict definition of *revive* means to bring back to life that which is dead, or to resuscitate that which is dying. *Chayah* directly speaks of God reviving, or bringing back to life, a person, people or nation that is spiritually dead or dying.

In one sense, the Hebrew concept of revival presents the idea that a person, or people, previously had a relationship with the LORD. Through compromise, indifference or persistent rebellion they turned their backs on God, thus reaping His wrath and incurring spiritual death that would have national consequences. Since the dead cannot raise themselves, it required a divine act to resurrect them.

The revivals of the Old Testament do not hold to the narrow rendering of *chayah*. Many of the people who were transformed by the move of the Spirit were not actually "revived" in the strict sense of the Hebrew word. Because they never had a personal relationship with the LORD, they were being "saved" for the first time. The reason so many Israelites thought they were right with God, even though they were not serving Him, resides in their understanding of salvation. Though the Old Testament does present a clear concept of personal salvation (Ps. 109:26), the Israelites also believed that the LORD was saving His people on a national basis (James Orr, *ISBE*, vol. 9, 502-503).

This concept of national salvation comes out of the many covenants God made with Israel, beginning with Abraham. The LORD promised to save His people if they wholeheartedly walked before Him in truth. In time, the Israelites distorted the covenants by thinking that since the LORD was saving the nation as a whole, individual lifestyles were not as important. John the Baptist dealt with this issue when he preached, "Produce fruit in keeping with repentance. And do not think you can say to yourselves, 'We have Abraham as our father.' I tell you that out of these stones God can raise up children for Abraham" (Mt. 3:8-9). The people thought that the Mighty One of Israel was obligated to save them on the primary basis that they were descendants of Abraham. Yet, being descendants of Abraham brought upon them an even greater responsibility to walk in fellowship with the LORD. "You only have I chosen of all the families of the earth; therefore I will punish you for all your sins" (Amos 3:2).

Whenever the Israelites turned from God to worship idols or resorted to dead religious traditions, they in turn taught their children such practices. This allowed whole generations to live and die without personally knowing the LORD. For Israel to turn to the LORD as a nation they would have to turn to Him as individuals. If many of those who turned to Him in times of national revival never knew God in the first place, then the Old Testament demonstrates that genuine revival both awakens the spiritually dead and saves those who never served Him. Those Jews who never had a personal relationship with the LORD were Israelites by birth, but not by faith (Deut. 10:15-16; Jer. 4:4; Rom. 2:25-29).

The Old Testament gives at least seven accounts of revival.
1. Jacob and his household returns to Bethel (Gen. 35:1-15)
2. Asa's reforms (2 Chr. 15:1-15)
3. Joash's limited reform (2 Kings 11-12; 2 Chr. 23-24)
4. Hezekiah's reform and reinstitution of the Passover (2 Kings 18:1-8; 2 Chr. 29-31)
5. Josiah's reforms (2 Kings 22-23; 2 Chr. 34-35)
6. Two revivals under Zerubbabel in which Haggai and Zechariah play a prominent role (Ezra 5-6)
7. Ezra and Nehemiah (Neh. 9:1-6; 12:44-47)

There are other Biblical events that could be construed as revival, such as Elijah confronting the prophets of Baal on Mount Carmel (1 Kings 18). When fire from Heaven consumed the sacrifice, the people fell prostrate in the worship of the LORD and rejected their idolatry.

There are common characteristics to the above-mentioned revivals. They always occurred in times of spiritual backsliding, moral declension and national rebellion. As with all spiritual awakenings, they began with a consecrated servant, or servants, who awaken the people to follow the LORD with all of their heart. In many of these accounts, the king and people entered into covenant with the LORD. God's Word was an integral part of these revivals and in some, powerfully proclaimed. Whenever the people consecrated themselves to the LORD, they destroyed their idols, returned to the worship of the LORD and turned from their wicked practices. Finally, these revivals produced seasons of personal and national prosperity.

THE ASSYRIAN REVIVAL

The Old Testament revivals stayed within the nation of Israel and Judah with one exception—Nineveh. Some scholars claim that this was evangelism, not revival. However, it keeps in line with the above stated truth that during times of revival, the unconverted turn to the LORD in vast numbers. This is consistent with the New Testament accounts of revival that continues to our very day.

The book of Jonah presents the story of a prophet who the LORD sent to the Assyrian city of Nineveh to warn them of divine judgment and call them to repent. Jonah rebelled against the call and fled from his assignment. This reluctant prophet typified the inwardness of Israel who refused to be evangelistic. God intended Israel to be a blessing to the world by bearing His message of salvation to all people.

When Jonah finally preached God's message to the large pagan city the results were astounding. Repentance spread like a wild fire as both king and subjects cried to God for mercy. They prayed and fasted for three days under tremendous conviction of sin. The LORD poured mercy upon repentant Nineveh instead of wrath. This is the fruit of revival and serves as an example of what has happened throughout church history.

THE NEW TESTAMENT PATTERN

The first years of the church were not unlike the revivals of the Old Testament. The move of the Spirit predominately remained within Israel. It awakened the God-fearing and saved many Israelites who never knew Him. It was only after the stoning of Stephen that persecution grew intense enough to force the church beyond the borders of Israel. Even so, for the time being, the gospel mostly stayed within Jewish communities.

With great reluctance, Peter ministered the Gospel to Cornelius, a Roman centurion. Cornelius and his household were marvelously saved and baptized in the Holy Spirit. This forced Peter to accept the fact that God would save and fill Gentiles who did not adhere to the Mosaic Law.

The disciples criticized Peter for reaching out to the Gentiles (Acts 11:2). Peter presented a thorough account of the events and demonstrated how God saved and filled these non-Jews just as they themselves had been. Only then did the objections cease. The brethren confessed, "So then, God has granted even the Gentiles repentance unto life" (Acts 11:18).

Though God used Peter to prepare the way for the conversion of the Gentiles, the apostle Paul became the champion of revival among them. Paul began his ministry by going to Jewish synagogues to minister the Gospel. Two situations arose that changed his early approach to ministry and compelled him to pursue aggressively the conversion of the Gentile world. The first was the rejection of Jesus as Messiah by the majority of the Jews. The second was the Gentiles' joyful acceptance of the Gospel.

The power of the Holy Spirit working through Paul made him a controversial figure. Wherever he traveled there was revival, riots, or both. The fire of God consumed him and everywhere he went the fire spread. His reputation preceded him as the man who "turned the world upside down" (Acts 17:6; KJV). Though he passionately reached out to his own people, he became the apostle to the Gentiles. Paul is a beautiful example of how the church must move beyond her comfort zone to reach a perishing world.

In the New Testament, revival began with the preaching of John the Baptist, was furthered by Jesus, and spread around the known world through the early church. The New Testament incorporates the Old Testament pattern of revival that awakens the people of God and saves those who never knew Him. It makes common the dynamics of the Assyrian revival in Nineveh that transformed secular society by radically saving vast numbers of people in a short period. As Dr. F. B. Meyer stated, "There has never been a great religious revival without social and political reforms" (Olford, 64).

FRUITS OF REVIVAL

An honest examination of the fruits of revival will inevitably lead to the conclusion that there is no other hope apart from God rending the heavens. The profound effects of revival upon the world are not new. Local awakenings change the character of a community, national ones the course and nature of a nation. "Revival does more than wash away moral impurities and pull drunkards out of the ditch. It determines the type of government under which we live and the polity of the churches ... The Colonial Revival was the determining factor in the formation of the government of the young nation, as well as the religious coloring of the people" (Autrey, 22).

For example, the 1904 Welsh Revival changed the character of the nation and stirred saints around the world to seek the same blessing for their own land. It began with a handful of intercessors that paved the way for the conversion of over one hundred thousand people in Wales alone. The percentage of converts that kept the faith was over 85%. "Drunkenness was immediately cut in half, and many taverns went bankrupt. Crime was so diminished that judges were presented with white gloves signifying there were no cases of murder, assault, rape or robbery or the like to consider. The police became 'unemployed' in many districts" (J. Edwin Orr, *Evangelical*, 101). The people even abandoned their national obsession with football (soccer) for chapels full of the Holy Ghost.

The Christmas of 1904 was the happiest Wales ever knew. When the miners came to Christ, wives received as back from the dead their husbands, and children their daddies. Their conversion caused domestic abuse to drop dramatically. When the men ceased their immoral practices, even the economy was affected. They brought the money home, began paying off long-standing debts and purchased things that the families had been forced to live without. The God of revival radically transforms individuals who then change the character of their home, city and nation.

STATISTICS

Listed below are some statistics of revival. Nothing can compare to the wonder of God revealing Himself in the beauty of His holiness. Because these statistics come from a wide variety of sources, only a few references are given.

On the day of Pentecost 3000 were saved (Acts 2:41). The church quickly increased to over 5000 men, the number not including women and children (Acts. 4:4). Converts were added to the church on a daily basis. Before long the early church swept through large portions of the Gentile world, even entering Caesar's household (Phil. 4:22).

Though revival has been a reality throughout the history of the church, the statistics prior to the seventeenth century are hard to establish. Chrysostom (A.D. 344-407), called the "Golden-Mouthed" because of the eloquence and power of his preaching, saw true spiritual awakening. Attentive hearers thronged the church where he ministered. They hung on every word that came from the preacher's mouth. "Numberless were the conversions in his day; God was exceedingly magnified, for sinners were abundantly saved" (Whittaker, 20).

Florence, Italy experienced revival in 1496-98 under the ministry of Savonarola. The Spirit of God poured through his preaching as he "denounced the sins of the people." They came from all walks of life to hear him preach. Deep conviction gripped their souls as they wept over their sins. They walked the streets "half-dazed and speechless" under the Spirit's influence. The tremendous moral change was demonstrated when a great pyramid of worldly possessions were burned in the town square. "It towered in seven stages sixty feet high and 240 feet in circumference. While bells tolled, the people sang hymns as the fire burned" (Duewel, 45-46). The Catholic Church sought to silence him by cruelly taking his life, yet his voice and influence powerfully lived on.

The Great Reformation of the sixteenth century presents an enormous difficulty in determining the vast numbers converted. In Scotland alone, church historian Richard Owen Roberts maintained that, "While the effects of the Great Reformation were partial in Europe, 'in Scotland the whole nation was converted by lump ... Lo! Here a nation born in one day; yea, molded into one congregation, and sealed as a fountain with a solemn oath and covenant'" (Roberts, Scotland, 15). The results of the Reformation are so profound that virtually every born-again believer today is the byproduct of that revival.

The Great Awakening in New England began in the 1730s and added roughly 50,000 people to the church in a population of only 340,000. The camp meeting era began on New Year's day, 1800, in Logan County, Kentucky and produced an increase in the church of 300%. Overall, between 1825 and 1832, 200,000 were added to the church in America.

Charles Finney saw 500,000 people come to Christ. In 1830, one hundred thousand came to the LORD through the far-reaching affects of the Rochester, New York revival that began under his ministry. By the end of the Rochester Revival, every doctor, lawyer, and businessman in town was converted (Towns, 103). Dr. Henry Ward Beecher commenting on this awakening stated, "That was the greatest work of God, and the greatest revival that the world has ever seen in so short a time (one year). One hundred thousand were reported as having connected themselves with churches as the results of that great revival" (Finney, *Autobiography*, 164-165).

The laymen's Prayer Meeting Revival of 1857-1858 is an indirect result of the Spirit's work through Finney. One million people in America came to Christ, 50,000 from New York City alone, which then had a population around 700,000. During the height of the revival, 50,000 were saved weekly (Duewel, 131). The awakening jumped the ocean in 1859. Over 1,000,000 surrendered to Christ in the British Isles; Ireland had 100,000 saved out of a total population of 1,000,000; Wales saw 110,000, Scotland 300,000 and Britain 500,000. A conservative estimate for the 1859 revivals in Sweden and Norway rests at 250,000.

There were over 5 million saved through the worldwide revivals between 1903 to 1910. Evan Roberts prayed for 100,000 souls and the 1904 Welsh revival produced near 150,000. England alone saw 300,000 added to the body of Christ. Church membership in seven major U.S. denominations increased by more than two million in five years. This does not include the gains in the younger Pentecostal and Holiness denominations whose dynamic rate of increase was dramatically higher. The Christian church in India increased by 70% while the Korean church quadrupled in size, 80,000 being added to the church in the city of Pyongyang alone. The church in Indonesia grew from 100,000 to 300,000. The island of Nias won two-thirds of the population and Malagasies increased 60%. In Africa, the church grew from 300,000 to 500,000 (J. Edwin Orr, *Evangelical*, 99-105). "When John G. Lake departed Africa after five years of ministry, he left behind 125 white congregations and 500 native ones" (Lindsay, 53).

During the 1965-66 Indonesian revival in Timor, 200,000 where saved, 100,000 from animism. The Latin American churches during the 1960s formed 47,000 churches, 35,000 prayer cells, trained 160,000 workers, and won 140,000 to Christ (Cairns, 242-243, 336). Today, the church is increasing at a rate of three times the growth of the population.

The revival in Almolonga, Guatemala won 80% of the population to Christ, and of the thirty-six bars that the city had, only three are left. Moreover, they closed the city's four jails because they are no longer needed. God has also abundantly blessed the land, which is now producing three crops a year (Otis).

This statistical overview of the fruits of authentic spiritual awakenings would not be complete without noting the explosive growth of the Chinese underground church. In 2000 Brother Yun, one of China's underground church leaders, claimed that believers in the house-church movement numbered 58 million. Current information now amazingly places the numbers upwards of 80 million.

These are just a few of the results of genuine revival. Volumes of books could not contain all the eternal and temporal benefits of God rending the heavens.

NECESSITY OF REVIVAL

We pay a fearfully high price when there is no revival in the land. This is most cruelly seen in the moral and spiritual condition of our children. They have followed the example of their parents. Only they have taken the wicked practices they learned to deeper depths.

- Our children are being robbed of their innocence through the flood of sexual immorality that is sweeping the land.
- Venereal diseases have increased from three in the 1960s to over 30 today. By the end of the last millennium, one in four high school students were infected with one or more of these diseases, the majority of which are not curable.
- Children are either birthing children, or they are killing their unborn babies.
- Homosexuality is sweeping through our schools. One charter schoolteacher in the southwest was overwhelmed with the lesbianism that swept through her class of 11- and 12-year-olds. A pastor in that same area lamented the fact that bisexuality has become vogue among middle and high school students in his town.
- A growing number of teens consider oral sex no different from making out. Girls as young as eleven have been found in oral sex parties. Venereal diseases are just as contagious through this form of sexual perversion.

- Incest is at epidemic levels with conservative estimates that thirty-eight percent of American children are suffering under its wicked curse.

- Pornography is destroying individuals and homes as adults and children literally become addicted to the vile material. Children and teens then practice the sexual perversions they view on pornographic sites on the internet.

- Cyber-sex has recently become America's greatest adult past time, surpassed only by TV viewing.

- The break down of marriage is a scourge upon the land. More disturbing are the newest statistics placing the church's divorce rate above that of secular society. Even atheists are less likely to divorce than evangelical Christians are.

The American dream of prosperity consumes the minds and hearts of Americans at the expense of the family. Gambling has become a plague loosed upon the land, with even our government lining its pockets through this evil industry. The pain of hopelessness in the land of prosperity has propelled suicide to the eighth leading cause of death in our nation (2nd cause among Anglo-American youth and 3rd among African-American youth). There has been a 400% increase in teenage suicides over the past decade. Eighty-five people die each day as a result of suicide, over 30,000 each year, while 500,000 are hospitalized every year due to an attempt (Crosswalk.com; 10/2001). Professionals are more prone to attempt suicide. Doctors and dentists have an attempted suicide rate of 6½ to 1, while lawyers have a rate of 5 to 1 (LogosResourcePages.com; 10/2001). All this demonstrates that prosperity has not satisfied our desires nor has our depravity gratified our lusts. Where has the church been through all of this?

These statistics are just the tip of the iceberg of our nation's moral and spiritual plight. Until Christians are convinced that revival is the only answer for our country we will not desperately pursue it. We need to see what God has done in the past, is presently doing in many parts of the world, and plead with Him to make it a reality in America. It is time to passionately, and persistently pray as Hosea did. "LORD, I have heard of Your fame; I stand in awe of Your deeds, O LORD. Renew them in our day, in our time make them known; in wrath remember mercy" (Hab. 3:2).

CHAPTER TWO

DEFINING REVIVAL

Revival broke out during 1859 in Ulster, formerly a northern province of Ireland. In the city of Coleraine, a young boy fell under deep conviction of sin while in school. The schoolmaster observed that the lad was unable to do his work so he sent the student home to seek the LORD in private. The teacher had an older boy, who was recently converted in the awakening, accompany him.

On the journey home the two schoolboys came upon an abandoned house and went inside to pray for the younger boy's salvation. They prayed through until the lad was gloriously saved. Joy flooded his soul and he exclaimed, "I must go back and tell." After entering the classroom he said to his schoolmaster, "I am so happy; I have the Lord Jesus in my heart."

Suddenly, boy after boy left the room and fled onto the playground. The schoolmaster looked over the schoolyard's stone wall and found them on their knees seeking God for salvation. The teacher asked the young man who had just prayed the lad through to assist these other boys in prayer. Shortly after he began praying, the boys' silent weeping turned into bitter wailing. The sound of their deep lamentation reached the remaining boys in the classroom. The Holy Spirit was overwhelmingly present. Those students also dropped to their knees in desperate cries for God to have mercy on their sin-sick souls.

The girl's school was on the second floor. The moment they heard the loud wailing from the boys they too were overcome with concern for their souls. Before long, the weeping filled the entire school. The volume was so great that it could be heard in the streets. Concerned neighbors came rushing into the building when they heard the commotion. As they crossed the threshold, grief gripped their hearts over their own sin. "These increased, and continued to increase, until first one room, then another, then a public office on the premises, in fact, every available spot, was filled with sinners seeking God."

Clergymen labored through the evening leading the repentant to the Savior. "Dinner was forgotten, tea was forgotten, and it was not till eleven o'clock at night that the school premises were freed from their unexpected guests" (Gibson, 49-51).

Such an encounter with the Living God will do more for our children and grandchildren than immense wealth, superb educations and organized sports could ever begin to accomplish. This is the greatest legacy we could pass down to subsequent generations.

WHAT REVIVAL IS NOT

Revival is never a random act of God. Everything the LORD does is purposeful, timely and according to His perfect order. Since the Ancient of Days does not change, and the need of sinful humanity remains the same, there are certain characteristics that are consistent throughout every revival. Though these characteristics may vary in intensity and focus, they remain an integral part of an authentic awakening.

In the last chapter we examined some Biblical concepts of revival. In this chapter we will deal with those basic characteristics that are consistent in every revival. Sometimes it is easier to define a term, or idea, by telling what it is not, rather than what it is. Consequently, we will first define revival by examining what it is not and then look at what it is.

REVIVAL IS NOT A CURE-ALL

Revival is not a cure-all to church problems. When a spiritual awakening comes, church pews will be filled, offerings will increase, but everyone will not accept or approve of it. Revival is messy business. It awakens dead saints, angers the self-righteous, it rescues the worst of society (who bring in years of painful baggage) and changes the priorities of families and churches. Though pews may be filled and offerings increased, the challenges and problems will multiply as well.

God designed revival to accomplish specific goals–to awaken the church and save the lost. The church must continue the work through evangelism, discipleship and discipline. Holiness, prayer and evangelism are normal to Christianity and must be taught to the new converts by mature saints. New believers need to be discipled by those who have the fire of God since, spiritually speaking, children will act like their parents. When discipleship is neglected during times of revival the backsliding rate increases.

The enemies of revival are often those who claimed they wanted a move of the Spirit, but found that it did not fit their theological opinions or compromised lifestyles. When God shows up, He exposes the sins of the people, many of which grow angry. Some church goers do not want to be inconvenienced by newcomers taking their seats and parking places. Others complain that the services are too long or the preaching is too confrontational. Numerous churches and ministers may condemn the move simply because it did not begin with them. Critics will seemingly come out of nowhere to pass judgment. One way or the other, revival upsets the status quo. Those who desire an awakening must be ready and willing to deal with the trials and opposition. Problems and abuses are not the fault of revival, only of the unrefined characters of men.

RENEWAL IS NOT REVIVAL

Spiritual renewal is a move of God that brings life to the saints but leaves secular society untouched. It brings spiritual healing and refreshing to many saints and churches that have long been spiritually dry. There is a difference between renewal and revival. Renewal is blessing-oriented, whereas revival is repentance oriented. Renewal emphasizes what you can receive from God, while revival awakens the church to transform society.

Within the renewal movements of the 1990s, God touched His people in wonderful ways. Though it predominately stayed within the church, many Christians were profoundly changed. Some of the experiences were overwhelming and left behind irreplaceable memories that are impervious to the arguments of men. Still, it was not revival. Only when the move of the Spirit transforms secular society through the conversion of the lost can it be said that revival has come. This is the single sure proof of revival.

REVIVAL IS NOT A SERIES OF MEETINGS

A series of "revival" meetings does not produce the genuine artifact. In certain parts of the country when an evangelist ministers in a church or a brush arbor, they call it "Revival." Some may erect a tent or put up a "Revival" banner and still never experience an authentic spiritual outpouring.

Churches that claim to be in revival, though they in truth are not, can be lulled into a spiritual sleep. This can be a major obstacle to obtaining a legitimate awakening. False claims of revival can spiritually stagnate a church. This in turn may cause the people to become resistant to a bona fide move of the Spirit.

REVIVAL IS NOT EVANGELISTIC CAMPAIGNS

Evangelism is not revival. Yet when revival comes, evangelism explodes. There is a difference between the two. Biblical Christianity teaches that EVERY believer should reach out to the unsaved no matter the spiritual climate they live in (Mt. 28:19). Evangelism is the loving, obedient response of Christians to the lordship of Christ and the needs of a perishing world. A successful evangelistic campaign does not constitute revival. This does not diminish the importance and necessity of evangelism in all of its various forms. Yet evangelism cannot compare to the incredible results produced when God rends the heavens.

The presence of the Holy Spirit in revival creates a divine magnetism that sweeps hundreds, even thousands into the Kingdom in a moment. Without revival we plead with men to yield to Christ and struggle to see them walk with Him. When the Spirit is poured out, men flee from the wrath to come by running to the foot of the cross.

The 1859 Ulster Revival in Coleraine is a perfect example of the converting power of revival. One twenty year old man with his face to the ground was "uttering a peculiar deep moan, sometimes terminating in a prolonged wailing cry." The pastor enquired as to why he cried so. In misery of soul he bawled out, "Oh! my sins! my sins! Lord Jesus, have mercy upon my poor soul!" The young man was "filled with one idea—his guilt and his danger." There was no comfort a mortal could offer.

After the minister arose from praying for the man he began going from person to person, to pray the repentant through to Christ. It was late at night when he was finally able to head home. He soon discovered that the work which began in the market square was rapidly spreading through the community. People were watching for him to come by so he could help pray the "stricken ones" through. His mission was still not completed when the sun began to rise. The minister testified, "I was wandering from house to house, on the most marvelous and solemn errand upon which I have ever been sent" (Davis, 33-35).

Rev. John Stuart from outside of Coleraine stated, "Hundreds have been converted to the LORD; some 'stricken' down when the Spirit came upon them like a 'rushing mighty wind'; others converted when He spoke to their consciences by the 'still small voice.' The first effect of the revival was that 'fear came upon every soul.' Then our church was filled to suffocation, and we were obliged to take to the open fields to declare the message of mercy to a hungering and thirsting population. Of all the stricken ones, I do not know of one backslider" (Davis, 37, edited).

In the city of Ballymana, "... worldly men were silent with fear. Careless men sobbed like children. Drunkards and boasting blasphemers were awed into solemnity. Languid believers were stirred up. Ministers who had often toiled in heartfelt sorrow suddenly found themselves beset by inquirers, and wholly unequal to the demands which were made" (Davis, 36). Though evangelism is a necessary part of Christian life it cannot compare to the awesome force of revival.

REVIVAL IS NOT AN EXPERIENCE

We were created to experience God, but experience does not constitute truth or revival. Some Christians have become self-absorbed with seeking new spiritual experiences and then define Christianity according to those experiences. There is a grave danger here. The prize of Christianity is Jesus, NOT experience. We were created to know the LORD on a personal basis. He commanded us to love Him with all of our heart, mind, soul and strength. Jesus went to the cross to make us God seekers, not experience or blessings seekers.

To seek spiritual experiences can become a form of idolatry. How tragic when we reduce relationship with the Living God to little more than another spiritual or emotional high. It is far easier to chase after the latest movement or experience than to seek God's face and cry for Him to pour out the fires of revival in a local church and community.

When the LORD steps down out of Heaven people will experience His presence in profound ways. The spiritually dead will be raised to life and the lost will be found. The effects can even be terrifying. Men and women may tremble and weep under the convicting power of the Holy Spirit. Some will cry out with agonized pleas to the Savior for mercy as the reality of their sin overwhelms them. Yes, revival does incorporate experience; it is impossible for it to be otherwise. However, experience does not equal revival. As stated earlier, the proof of revival is the transformation of secular society through the power of God, not spiritual experiences.

REVIVAL IS NOT ABOUT MANIFESTATIONS

We can develop a nice, neat theology of what it means to do everything decently and in order until God shows up. Then He blows all of our order and theories to pieces. What is decent and in order in an earthquake differs greatly from the normal, daily routines of life. Genuine revival always produces some form of physical manifestation. Those moves of the Spirit that are less emotional will have weeping or trembling. Others have included more intense experiences such as falling, shaking, groaning, trances and visions.

Whether or not physical manifestations fit into our theological framework is for the most part irrelevant. The LORD is God, and He does as He pleases, whether we like it or not. In addition, individuals can react differently when supernatural power falls upon them. Revival is about the revelation of God's glory, a divine invasion into the lives of frail humanity. Spiritual awakenings are not about manifestations; however, when the Holy Spirit falls upon these bodies of flesh, there will be some form of outward response.

Dr. Schofield accurately addressed this issue when he said, "One thing to be borne in the mind is that since the days of Pentecost there is no record of the sudden and direct work of the Spirit of God upon the souls of men that has not been accompanied by events more or less abnormal ... We cannot expect an abnormal inrush of divine light and power, so profoundly affecting the emotions and changing the lives of men, without remarkable results. As well expect a hurricane, an earthquake, or a flood, to leave nothing abnormal in its course, as to expect a true Revival that is not accompanied by events quite out of our ordinary experience" (Jonathan Goforth, *By My Spirit*, 9).

Those who concentrate on manifestations miss God. Whether a person is a critic of them or an experience seeker, they both are in error. The critic will be judgmental of the spiritual outpouring no matter what takes place because his theology leaves no room for a God of signs and wonders. The experience seeker takes his eyes off of Jesus by being consumed with manifestations and judges spirituality according to experience.

Manifestations are NEVER proof of revival. Nor can a move of the Spirit be discredited because they are evident. As Jonathan Edwards wisely wrote, "A work is not to be judged by any effects on the bodies of men; such as tears, trembling, groans, loud cries, agonies of body, or the failing of bodily strength (Scripture gives no support for them or against them)" (Edwards, Revival, 91).

CRITICS AND ABUSES

Critics of revival can be like armchair athletes: they ridicule those on the field while never playing themselves. It is one thing to have opinions about revival and totally another thing to experience it. People can judge according to their own experiences, or lack thereof, and then manipulate the Bible to agree with them. Such an approach to understanding and explaining the work of the Holy Spirit is thoroughly flawed.

Some of the greatest foes of spiritual awakenings are religious people who walk in self-righteous pride. They point the finger at others while never examining themselves. Jonathan Edwards faced this problem during the First Great Awakening. He wrote, "There is a great aptness in persons to doubt of things that are strange; especially the elderly persons, to think that not to be right which they have never been used to in their day, and have not heard of in the days of their fathers" (Edwards, Revival, 90).

Many critics have attributed revival to the work of the devil because of abuses, whether perceived or genuine. Even Jesus was accused of doing miracles through demonic powers by the Pharisees of His day (Lk. 11:15-19). "There are some of these things which the devil would not do if he could," Edwards penned. "Thus he would not awaken the conscience, and make men sensible of their miserable state by reason of sin, and sensible of their great need of a Savior; and he would not confirm men in the belief that Jesus is the Son of God and the Savior of sinners, or raise men's value and esteem of him: he would not beget in men's minds an opinion of the necessity, usefulness, and truth of the Holy Scriptures, or incline them to make use of them; nor would he show men the truth in things that concern their soul's interest; and give them a view of things as they really are. And there are other things that the devil neither can nor will do; he will not give men a spirit of divine love, or Christian humility and poverty of spirit; nor could he if he would. He cannot give those things he has not himself: these things are as contrary as possible to his nature" (Edwards, Revival, 118).

Abuses can take place in revival, but God is not the cause of them—people are. This is due to our flawed nature and lack of understanding about the move of the Spirit. Because some people exploit and misuse such spiritual phenomenon does not invalidate its authenticity. The benefits exceedingly outweigh any abuses. Far better is it for a church to have the organized chaos of a hospital emergency ward than the tranquil order of a cemetery. Better to have some wild fire in the midst of having the real fire than to have no fire at all. This is why a revival needs pastoring so abuses are kept to a minimum.

WHAT REVIVAL IS

Charles Finney defined God as "one pent-up revival" (Ravenhill, Why, 139). The LORD is aching to manifest His grace through the wonder and power of spiritual awakenings. When saints live in the reviving power of God's presence, the world takes note that there is a God, we have been with Him and His name is Jesus.

Revival demonstrates the LORD's desire and ability to save sinners from the power and love of sin. Spiritual awakenings are the positive work of the Spirit that deals with the negative character traits of sinful humanity.

Revival is God's self-disclosure. It speaks of a Savior who yearns to dwell in the midst of His people. Hosea prophesied, "After two days He will revive us; on the third day He will restore us, that we may live in His presence" (Hos. 6:2). To live in His presence is the prize of Christianity and the purpose of an awakening.

We now turn to five points that will help further define authentic revival.

REVIVAL IS A SOVEREIGN ACT OF GOD

There is a great tension in Christian theology over the sovereignty of God and man's free will. God's sovereignty means that He has the absolute right to do anything He desires and superabounds with the power to accomplish His good pleasure. "The LORD does whatever pleases Him, in the heavens and on the earth, in the seas and all their depths" (Ps. 135:6).

The struggle we face with this issue lies in our understanding of man's free will and how that free will works in conjunction with a sovereign Being. The Creator, in giving mankind the gift of a genuine free will, does not cease to be sovereign. How this works is known only to the mind of God. This is a mystery that no man or denomination will ever solve.

Revival is a sovereign work of God. No one can force His hand to act or else He would not be the Almighty. "All the peoples of the earth are regarded as nothing. He does as He pleases with the powers of Heaven and the peoples of the earth. No one can hold back His hand or say to Him: 'What have You done?'" (Dan. 4:35). Yet the LORD has chosen to place the responsibility of revival in the hands of men (2 Chr. 7:14). This means that we have a legitimate ability to move the heart of God so He will act on our behalf (Heb. 4:16; 10:19-22).

This is the great mystery of revival: the LORD sovereignly moves and yet acts in accordance to the prayers of His people. To say that revival is exclusively the act of God implies that man can do nothing to bring revival. This reduces His commands to pray and seek His face to meaningless acts. However, to assert that revival is solely the responsibility of men places too much upon the shoulders of flesh. This degrades the magnificence and infinitude of the King of kings. The LORD is able through His infinite wisdom to make His sovereignty work with and through our humanity.

For revival to come we must comprehend that in and of ourselves we can do nothing (Jn. 15:5). Yet, our responsibility is real.

This means that a cooperative effort between God and man takes place for the Spirit to be poured out. The Logos of God has given us the privilege and responsibility of securing revival through those means He has established in His written Word. The Spirit moves the hearts of men to move the heart of God—a mystery indeed.

REVIVAL IS A REVELATION OF GOD'S HOLINESS

God is holy! His self-disclosure means that people will encounter His holy character. Time and again the Scriptures unfold the response of men to divine visitation. Isaiah said, "Woe to me" while the apostle John fell at Jesus' feet "as though dead." When Moses saw God descend on Mt. Sinai, the sight was so terrifying that he proclaimed, "I am trembling with fear" (Heb. 12:21).

Revival is a "person or a community saturated with the presence of God ... an invasion from Heaven which brings to man a conscious awareness of God" (Olford, 60). This awareness of God includes the revelation of His holiness. The beauty of His holiness will always illuminate our sinfulness, which subsequently produces tremendous conviction of sin. When we look at our sin through the presence of God, we begin to understand how hideous our transgressions actually are. This is Christ's goodness revealed to a race of rebels (Rom. 2:4).

While preaching during the First Great Awakening in Lyme, Connecticut Jonathan Parsons described the scene: "... many had their countenances changed; their thoughts seemed to trouble them, so that the joints of their loins were loosed, and their knees smote one against another. Great numbers cried out aloud in the anguish of their souls. Several stout men fell as though a cannon had been discharged, and the ball had made its way through their hearts ... people had to be carried from the meeting house" (*America's Great Revivals*, 19). This has often been the result of the revelation of God's holiness to unholy people.

REVIVAL PRODUCES DEEP HEARTFELT REPENTANCE

When the Holy Spirit descends He convicts the "world of sin, and of righteousness, and of judgment" (Jn. 16:8, NKJV). Tremendous conviction of sin brings masses of people to repentance, which transforms individuals who then transforms society. Heartfelt repentance produces a change in character, and a change in character produces a change in lifestyle. History demonstrates that according to the depth of conviction will be the depth of repentance and according to the depth of repentance will be the depth of the revival.

John the Baptist told the people to "Produce fruit in keeping with repentance" (Mt. 3:8). What is the fruit of repentance? It is holiness and love for God. Revival is always a move of the Spirit that produces repentance and personal holiness. It cannot be otherwise.

REVIVAL IS NEW LIFE

Heartfelt repentance and a passion for holiness imparts new life to the saved and unsaved. When the spiritually dead come alive, babies can be born. The river of living water that pours forth from the throne of God gives life wherever it flows (Ezk. 47). When that river flows through the church there will be power and desire to reach the unsaved. When it sweeps through the streets of our cities, radical conversions will abound.

New life produces new priorities. The light of God's brilliance illuminates the meaninglessness of worldly pursuits. Compromise falls off as love for the Savior replaces the depraved love of the world and the twisted love of self. Vibrant worship and prayer become the norm for those who have tasted of that heavenly river and are now alive in Christ. There is no room for dead and worthless formalism. The self-righteousness that possessed many professed believers is exchanged for a holy zeal that is the love of God ablaze in the soul.

New life in the soul means new life in relationships. When men and women abandon themselves to Jesus, the result will be transformed lives that affect every relationship they have. Marriages and families are restored as godly virtues replace wicked character traits. When rebellious teens are genuinely converted, their rebellion ceases. The power of God delivers the fornicator, adulterous spouse or homosexual from their demonic sexual addictions to live in pure and holy freedom. Revival is literally new life for individuals, families, churches and nations.

REVIVAL IS A SPIRITUAL REVOLUTION

"Revival is a divine method of operation in human history … an instrument of spiritual revolution" (Autrey, 14, 16). This spiritual revolution is birthed through radicals and martyrs who reproduce after their own kind. They see the world through the eyes of Christ and are willing to lay down their lives for the One who laid down His life for them. This is the place of desperate love and surrender to Jesus, where sacrifice ceases to be a burden.

An explosive missionary spirit is always a byproduct of revival. The LORD uses common saints who live in the light of eternity to turn the world upside down. They comprehend that people are eternal creatures that will live forever in Heaven or Hell. So they joyfully abandon themselves to the cause of Christ to rescue a self-destructing world no matter the cost. This is normal Christianity! Since "revival should be the normal condition of the church. A church that is not in revival is a sick church" (Wright, 21).

The radicalness of revival is demonstrated through the transformation of nations. "To the extent that the Spirit of revival prevails, mercy, justice and righteousness sweep over the land" (Coleman, *Dry Bones*, 16). Some of the most profound and compassionate laws that have ever been passed were the results of far-reaching and deeply penetrating revivals. Gerhard Lohfink asserted, "It is true that Jesus never called for a political, revolutionary transformation of Jewish society. Yet, the repentance which he demanded as a consequence of his preaching of the reign of God sought to ignite within the people of God a movement in comparison to which the normal type of revolution is insignificant" (Brown, *Answer Book*, 272).

Radicals begin and advance revival. Without these radicals to press forward Christ's Kingdom, nations fall deeper and deeper into rebellion. The manifest glory of God is the greatest hope for the salvation of our loved ones, the most effective means of restraining the wickedness that is sweeping America, and the only power that can transform cities and nations.

CHAPTER THREE

BY MY SPIRIT

The Holy Spirit is the Creator of revival. Approximately two thousand years ago, a small band of believers gathered in prayer on the day of Pentecost and learned this truth. They discovered that giving preeminence to the Spirit was essential to the growth and life of their newfound faith. Three thousand were gloriously saved on that momentous day. It could even be reasoned that the church would not be in existence today if the first Pentecostal outpouring never occurred.

An examination of the history of the church unfolds the reality that whenever the people of God exalts the Holy Spirit the fires of revival burst forth. The 1904 Welsh Revival is a perfect case in point. Prompt obedience to the Spirit's leading was one of the governing principles of that awakening. When the Holy Ghost was exalted to His rightful place, He swept through the country like a fire in a drought-stricken land.

The presence of the Holy Spirit in Wales was tangible, affecting Christians and non-Christians alike. People flocked into Wales to partake of the revival. "One man and his daughter went to the railway station and bought train tickets to attend revival meetings. When they asked the porter at the station how to find the meeting, he responded, 'You'll feel it on the train. Go down that road and you'll feel it down there'" (Towns, 34).

William Stead, the famous London editor of the *Pall Mall Gazette*, was interviewed after visiting this awakening. He stated, "A revival is something like a revolution. It is apt to be wonderfully catching."

The interviewer, sensing an apprehension in his voice, commented, "You speak as if you dreaded the revival coming your way."

"No, that is not so," Stead quickly corrected. "Dread is not the right word. Awe expresses my sentiment better. For you are in the presence of the unknown ... You have read ghost stories and can imagine what you would feel if you were alone at midnight in the haunted chamber of some old castle and you heard the slow and steady step stealing along the corridor where the visitor from another world was said to walk. If you visit South Wales and watch the revival, you will feel pretty much like that. There is something there from the other world. You cannot say whence it came or whither it is going, but it moves and lives and reaches for you all the time. You see men and women go down in sobbing agony before your eyes as the invisible Hand clutches at their heart. And you shudder. It's pretty grim I tell you. If you are afraid of strong emotions, you'd better give the revival a wide berth" (Pratney, 193-194).

When the Spirit unveils His glory to mortal men, there will be no question that they have encountered the Living God. This means that people can literally experience the glory of His presence. Equally as much, when the Holy Ghost is absent from the church it is painfully known and felt.

Every revival throughout history has been the result of the Spirit being exalted to the place He rightly owns as God. The 1904 Welch revival compelled G. Campbell Morgan to testify that the Spirit moved from "day to day, week to week, county to county, with matchless precision, with the order of an attacking force" (Roberts, *Glory*, 172). A truly yielded church becomes a powerful tool in the hands of the Holy Spirit. Then He will do "awesome things" that we have not expected. He will come down and cause the kingdoms of men to tremble before His splendor (Isa. 64:3).

The Korean and Chinese revivals during the early twentieth century are wonderful examples of what happens when the Spirit is given preeminence in the church. The missionaries and national Christians had come to understand the heartbreaking reality that they were grieving God by not granting the Spirit His rightful place in the churches and mission stations. Presbyterian missionary Jonathan Goforth honestly confessed, "That which weighed most heavily on the consciences of all was that we had so long been grieving the Holy Spirit by not giving Him His rightful place in our hearts and in our work. While believing in Him we had not trusted in Him, to work in and through us. Now we believe, we have learned our lesson that it is 'not by might, nor by power, but by my Spirit saith the LORD of hosts.' May we never forget that lesson" (Rosalind, *Goforth*, 97). Revival swept through those two nations when the saints fully surrendered to God and gave the control of their lives and ministries over to the Comforter.

The value of embracing the lordship of the Holy Spirit can be seen in an interesting story Goforth shared of a minister who wisely relinquished the control of the service over to God. "Mr. Swallen, along with Mr. Blair, visited one of the country outstations. While conducting the service in the usual way many commenced weeping and confessing their sins. Mr. Swallen said he announced a hymn, hoping to check the wave of emotion that was sweeping over the audience. He tried several times, but in vain, and in awe he realized that Another was managing the meeting; and he got as far out of sight as possible" (Jonathan Goforth, *When*, 8). Mr. Swallen humbled himself before the Almighty. By yielding to the Spirit a work was accomplished that infinitely exceeded the abilities of mortal man. How few ministers and churches today would allow the control to be taken out of their hands and be placed into God's.

THE PROBLEM OF OUR AGENDAS

The Word plainly teaches that the Kingdom of God advances through the ministry of the Holy Spirit. This means that Christ's Kingdom progresses through men and women who are filled with, and thus moved by, the Spirit. R. A. Torrey noted that, "Two passages of Scripture might well form the watchwords of every true revival, watchwords that should never for a moment be forgotten. The first is a portion of Zech. 4:6, 'Not by might nor by power, but by My Spirit, saith the LORD of Hosts;' the second is, 'It is the Spirit that quickeneth (gives life), the flesh profiteth nothing' (John 6:63). In the conduct of any real revival, the Holy Ghost must occupy the place of supreme and absolute control. Revival is new life, and only the Holy Ghost can impart life" (Torrey, 11). True spiritual life comes only through the Spirit. The flesh life, or sinful nature, is hostile to God and cannot fulfill His will (Rom. 8:6-7).

When Christians walk in the lusts of their flesh, they grieve the Holy Ghost and hinder His outpouring in our world. Paul told us that, "the sinful nature desires what is contrary to the Spirit, and the Spirit what is contrary to the sinful nature" (Gal. 5:17). This is why he warned us not to, "... grieve the Holy Spirit of God, with whom you were sealed for the day of redemption" (Eph 4:30). He further counseled, "Do not put out the Spirit's fire" (1 Th. 5:19).

Far too often our goals and agendas are nothing other than the works of the flesh which the Scriptures call "self-ambitions" (Gal. 5:20). What lies at the core of this issue is who will be god—the Almighty or the individual? We must move beyond Christian clichés in answering this important question. Whoever defines the life and worship of the church is the god of that person or people—whether it is the LORD, man or Satan. In essence, if the Counselor is not guiding our lives then what is directing us is something sinisterly evil.

We must ask ourselves another challenging question. Who has the preeminence in the church on the issue of evangelism? Whoever holds the reins of the church will define how evangelism will be done (if it is done at all). Either evangelism will be done through the power of the Spirit or through our programs, campaigns or Christianized secular marketing techniques. The truth of the matter is that God does not need our programs or church growth strategies in building His Kingdom. The LORD of Hosts is not looking for our abilities, talents and agendas, just our loving abandonment and faithful obedience. This truth desperately needs to be grasped by pastors and church leaders or genuine revival will be kept from the land.

Our agendas can be extremely detrimental to the move of God. Even our desires for revival can be mingled with pride and self-will. The Biblical principle that it is "Not by might nor by power, but by My Spirit, says the LORD Almighty" must be more than a pop religious phrase. Giving preeminence to the Holy Spirit must be a way of life, a principle that defines how we worship, live our daily lives and fulfill our ministries. J. Hudson Taylor addressed this topic when he said, "We have given too much attention to methods and to machinery and to resources, and too little to the Source of Power, the filling with the Holy Ghost" (Brown, *Revolution*, 294).

Churches that give preeminence to the Holy Ghost are very rare in America. This includes the vast number of Pentecostal and Charismatic churches. Scores of ministers and church folk have never been taught the Scriptural mandate of relinquishing the control of the church to the Spirit. A large number of church leaders are afraid of the Holy Spirit and the holy chaos that could happen at a modern day Pentecost. This leads them to control the spiritual atmosphere of the church or denomination. Though they may offer a vast array of arguments as to why they do not allow the move of the Spirit, they none-the-less grieve God. Alice Reynolds Flower, wife of J. Roswell Flower, an early Pentecostal leader said, "We were taught to court the Spirit's moving, and through the intervening years the urgency of this has greatly dominated my personal life along various lines of ministry. There were no ruts to our training, no spiritual habits; we were encouraged to expect a fresh working of God in any service, noting whichever direction the heavenly winds blew and learning to trim our sails accordingly" (Gardiner, 33). Oh, how we desperately need ministers today to understand and apply this foundational principle that defined the early Pentecostal movement.

Smith Wigglesworth, another early Pentecostal, saw many revivals because he endeavored to live yielded to the Comforter. He wisely asserted, "Any assembly that puts its hand on the working of the Spirit will surely dry up. The assembly must be as free in the Spirit as possible, and you must allow a certain amount of extravagance when people are getting through to God. Unless we are very wise, we can easily interfere with and quench the power of God that is upon us ... If you want an assembly full of life, you must have one in which the Spirit of God is manifested. In order to keep the boiling point of that blessed incarnation of the Spirit, you must be as simple as babes; you must be wise as serpents and harmless as doves" (Wigglesworth, 199-200).

If we grieve the LORD through sin, unbelief, control or dead traditions, we hold back His transforming power in our own lives and our nation. Only when the Spirit is given His rightful place will His glory and power be known in the church and to a perishing world.

THE WORK OF THE HOLY SPIRIT

The Scriptures reveal many dimensions of the Spirit's ministry to humanity. Understanding His work is of enormous value in helping us to be open and sensitive to His leading. Briefly listed below are seven essential ministries of the Spirit that are dynamically evident in revival.

THE SPIRIT GLORIFIES THE SON

The Bible teaches that the Spirit will always glorify Jesus. "When the Counselor comes, whom I will send to you from the Father, the Spirit of truth who goes out from the Father, He will testify about Me" (Jn. 15:26). Theologian Thomas C. Oden said it this way, "All that we understand of the Father and the Son, we understand through the illumining work of the Spirit" (Oden, 3). Revival is a work of the Spirit that brings glory to Jesus by drawing vast numbers of people to love and serve the King of Creation. The degree to which the crucified Christ is revealed will directly relate to the depth of the Spirit's outpouring.

The Moravian Revival that began on August thirteenth, 1727 in Herrnhut, Germany is a perfect example of how the Holy Spirit glorifies Christ in an awakening. John Greenfield wrote, "Their spiritual vision became so keen that they could 'see Him who is invisible' (Heb. 11:27). The form in which He appeared to them most frequently was when He was 'led as a Lamb to the slaughter,' wounded for their transgressions and bruised for their iniquities.

"In this divine presence of their bleeding and dying LORD they were overwhelmed with their own sinfulness and with His more abounding grace. Hushed were their controversies and quarrels; crucified were their passions and pride as they gazed upon the agonies of their 'expiring God' ... Their prayers, their litanies, their hymns, their conversation and their sermons had one theme, viz., the wounds, the blood and death of Jesus" (Greenfield, 44).

GUIDES INTO TRUTH

Because the Spirit of Truth is the embodiment of truth, all He says and does is absolute truth. "The Counselor, the Holy Spirit, whom the Father will send in My name, will teach you all things and will remind you of everything I have said to you" (Jn. 14:26). Revival is an invasion of the Spirit of Truth upon a people. It is impossible for the Holy Ghost to make mistakes in leading His flock. He always leads them into truth and empowers them to live the truth. Errors in doctrine, character and actions are always the fault of men and women, for there are no errors in the character and acts of God.

THE SPIRIT OF SURRENDER

Jesus taught His disciples, "But when He, the Spirit of Truth, comes, He will guide you into all truth. He will not speak on His own; He will speak only what He hears, and He will tell you what is yet to come" (Jn. 16:13). Notice that the Spirit of Truth is in perfect submission to the will of the Father. There is no rebellion in the Holy Spirit, only submission and loving obedience to the Father. In like manner, those led by the Spirit will live surrendered lives to Christ.

The work of the Spirit in revival empowers people to live abandoned lives to Jesus. Through radically surrendered saints, the Holy Ghost can turn the world upside down. One historian commenting on the Moravian Revival explained that the extensive influence of this move of the Spirit related directly to their profound surrender to Christ. "Everyone desired above everything else that the Holy Spirit might have full control. Self-love and self-will, as well as all disobedience, disappeared, and an overwhelming flood of grace swept us all out into the great ocean of Divine love" (Whittaker, 193-194). The extensive missionary endeavors that the Moravians undertook demonstrate their surrender to Christ. They abandoned their lives to the service of their King to reach unsaved people throughout the world, often at the expense of extreme personal sacrifice.

CONVICTION OF SIN

Mankind is powerless to convict of sin. Only the Holy Ghost can bring a person to see the reality of his sins and then empower him to flee from them. When the Spirit comes, "He will convict the world of guilt in regard to sin and righteousness and judgment" (Jn. 16:8). "Pleading does not produce conviction," stated C. E. Autrey. "The Holy Spirit works conviction. Evangelists always call upon sinners to accept Christ, but in revivals sinners beg Christ to accept them. Sinners never do this unless they realize their condition ... Revival brings men face to face with their actual need" (Autrey, 21).

The conviction of sin is always followed by the Spirit's empowerment for repentance. The 1857 Prayer Meeting Revival clearly demonstrated the power of the Holy Ghost to convict multitudes and lead them to genuine repentance. "The fires of revival spread up and down the eastern seaboard and then moved westward into the heart of the country as the Great Spiritual Awakening of 1857-1858 burst full force. City after city received the testimony of God's mighty convicting power as the consuming fire of the Holy Spirit purged the church of the dross of unconfessed sin. As God's people began to pray, the heathen began to respond to the holy conviction of the Spirit of God, and the churches were filled as never before" (King, 19).

FAITH AND REGENERATION

Faith is a work of the Spirit that enables people to place their trust in Jesus as Savior (1 Cor. 2). Left to ourselves we would remain in our sin, trusting in the philosophies and idols of our own creation. "But God demonstrates His own love toward us, in that while we were still sinners, Christ died for us" (Rom. 5:8; NKJV). This means that God pursued us, not we Him. The Holy Spirit is the Hound of Heaven that chases after us, moving us, even driving us to the foot of the cross. Only in light of Calvary can we begin to comprehend our desperate need and deep rooted wickedness. Then He opens our eyes to the only remedy for our sin-sick souls—Jesus Christ. The Spirit leads us to the foot of the cross so we can place our trust in Jesus.

Regeneration, or the new birth, is the imparting of new life to a person who was dead in trespasses and sin. Paul proclaimed that salvation is, "Not by works of righteousness which we have done, but according to His mercy He saved us, by the washing of regeneration, and renewing of the Holy Ghost" (Tit. 3:5; KJV). After regeneration, the Holy Ghost gives the assurance of salvation by the inward witness to the spirit of the believer that he or she is a son or daughter of God (Rom. 8:16). The assurance of salvation is alone the work of the Comforter, never our responsibility. If we tell a person he is a Christian when the Spirit of God has not, we could damn that soul to Hell by lulling him into a false spiritual confidence when he is still at war with the Creator.

HOLINESS AND SANCTIFICATION

Sanctification is a ministry of the Spirit that has a twofold meaning. Firstly, when an individual is born again, he is sanctified, or set apart and made holy by an act of God (Rom. 15:16). For a person to be a Christian the Holy Spirit must take up residence within his being. A man can only be holy according to his relationship with the Holy God.

Secondly, sanctification is a progressive work (1 Pet. 1:2). After a person is made holy by entering into relationship with God, he is commanded to practice a lifestyle of holiness according to God's righteous standards. This dimension of sanctification is a cooperative work the Spirit does with, and through, the believer. As a man grows in holiness he will grow more humble, selfless and sensitive to the sin in his own life. According to his longing desire to draw near to God will be his striving after personal holiness.

BAPTISM OF THE SPIRIT

The purpose of the baptism in the Holy Ghost is to empower Christians to be witnesses through the power of the Spirit. John the Baptist prophesied that Jesus would "baptize you with the Holy Spirit and with fire" (Mt. 3:11). Our LORD told the disciples that it was needful for Him to return to the Father so He could send the Comforter to make them powerful witnesses of His resurrection (Jn. 16:7). He commanded them to, "tarry in the city of Jerusalem until you are endued with power from on high" (Lk. 24:49; NKJV). After His resurrection He told them, "you will receive power when the Holy Spirit comes on you; and you will be My witnesses in Jerusalem, and in all Judea and Samaria, and to the ends of the earth" (Acts 1:8). The great emphasis and commands that Jesus placed upon believers to seek and receive the baptism in the Holy Spirit are still relevant for us today.

More than anything, the church in America needs a fresh Pentecost. How can we expect to see revival if we are not yielded to the Spirit, nor desiring to be truly filled by Him? Evan Roberts, the primary evangelist of the 1904 Welsh Revival preached, "The baptism of the Holy Spirit is the essence of revival, for revival comes from a knowledge of the Holy Spirit and the way of co-working with Him which enables Him to work in revival power. The primary condition of revival is therefore that believers should individually know the baptism of the Holy Ghost" (Whittaker, 108).

Only the Holy Spirit can make us useful to Christ's Kingdom. Wigglesworth declared, "Beloved, if God lays hold of you by the Spirit, you will find that there is an end of everything and a beginning of God. Your whole body will become seasoned with a divine likeness of God. Not only will He have begun to use you, but He will have taken you in hand, so you might be a vessel of honor" (Wigglesworth, 130). The Spirit-filled life is far more than speaking in tongues. Though the gift of tongues is an initial evidence of the baptism in the Holy Spirit, it is not proof that a person is full of the Holy Ghost (there are a tremendous amount of worldly Christians that speak in tongues). Being filled with the Spirit also means giving Him the preeminence in our lives through intimate prayer, a passion for holiness and fully yielding to the purposes of God. The Spirit baptism was given so we can be saints full of the Holy Ghost as was Stephen.

The power of Calvary and Pentecost are irrevocably united. To be Spirit-controlled we must understand, and identify with, the cross. Jesus shed His blood on Calvary to save us from our sin so we could intimately know His love and be filled to overflowing with the Spirit. Arthur Booth-Clibborn forcefully wrote, "Any cheapening of the price of Pentecost would be a disaster of untold magnitude. The company in the upper room, upon whom Pentecost fell, had paid for it the highest price. In this they approached as near as possible Him who had paid the supreme price in order to send it" (Bartleman, 56). True Pentecostal power is very costly. It costs us our sin, our will, our ambitions, our very life.

The cross was the starting point for those who partook of that first Pentecost. This is still true today! Those who want a Biblical Pentecost must embrace Calvary. Arthur Booth-Clibborn further declared, "Do we ever really adequately realize how utterly lost to this world, how completely despised, rejected and outcast was that company? Their master and leader had just passed, so to speak, through the 'Hangman's rope,' at the hands of the highest civilization of that day. Their Calvary was complete and so a complete Pentecost came to match it. The latter will resemble the former in completeness. We may, therefore, each of us say to ourselves: As your cross, so will your Pentecost be. God's way to Pentecost was via Calvary. Individually it must be so today also. The purity and fullness of the individual Pentecost must depend upon the completeness of the individual Calvary. This is an unalterable principle" (Bartleman, 56-57).

The power of Pentecost is alive and well throughout the world. What it did 2000 years ago it is accomplishing today, and even more. Dr. Michael Brown revealed an astounding statistic on the present Pentecostal outpouring: "Around the world, the fastest-growing religious faith is not Islam, nor is it some cultic New Age ideology or some atheistic philosophy. Not at all. Rather, on every continent on the globe, the fastest-growing religious faith—far and away!—is Spirit-empowered signs-and-wonders Christianity ... Or, to put it another way, the largest Protestant group in the world today consists of those who would call themselves Spirit-baptized, tongue-speaking believers" (Brown, *Answer Book*, 153). The LORD of Pentecost is revealing Himself around the world through those who give Him the preeminence that He justly deserves.

Since the Holy Ghost is the author of revival, and since revival is the unleashing of the His power upon humanity, all the works and ministries of the Spirit are manifested in incredible ways in the throes of revival. It is true that the works of the Spirit are present to some degree apart from spiritual outpourings. Unfortunately, what we have called "normal" in many of our American churches is an atmosphere void of His presence. Biblically speaking, "normal" is being "full of faith and full of the Holy Spirit" (Acts 6:3, 5, 8; 7:55). Nothing can compare to the Spirit breaking forth in powerful, earth shaking displays of His glory.

The answer to our church problems is not a new building, a new pastor or a new pastorate, a larger budget or the latest church growth strategy; it is the tangible presence of the Holy Spirit. The early church exploded because they were Spirit-filled and Spirit-led. This is still true today! Only those who have yielded to the Spirit will be agents of revival. Those simple souls that came out of the upper room brought tremendous glory to their resurrected LORD. When the tangible power of Heaven fell upon them the world could not ignore that ragtag bunch of believers. So the infant church grew astronomically. It can happen again if we will only return to the upper room until we are "... endued with power from on high" (Lk. 24:49b; KJV).

CHAPTER FOUR

Prepare the Way

Whenever God's people grow desperate for His manifest presence, they return to the simple truths that govern revival. One of those unalterable truths is that preparation always precedes revival! Preparation begins with a passionate heart for God that is lived out through prayer, repentance and holiness. A desire for revival that does not produce action only generates a profitless fantasy.

The Hebrides Awakening is a wonderful example of the passionate preparation that births revival. This move of the Spirit was conceived through many praying saints. "Two such prayer warriors were Peggy and Christine Smith of Barvas on Lewis Island. They were 82 and 84 years of age, one blind and the other arthritic. Their poor health did not allow them to be in church as often as they liked but their home was a sanctuary, a place where they daily met with God in prayer" (Meldrum, 8).

One day while the Smith sisters were in prayer, God gave Peggy a vision that revival was coming to their spiritually dead church. The sisters contacted their pastor and compelled him to begin praying for the glory of God to be revealed. The pastor, Rev. James Murray MacKay, secured seven other men to pray two nights a week in a local barn from 10 o'clock at night until four or five in the morning. They covenanted with God, and each other, to seek His face until He stepped down out of Heaven. The LORD heard their cry and revealed Himself beyond anything they ever imagined.

"The remarkable thing about this visitation of God was that simultaneously as God moved in the church, the Spirit also swept through the town and areas around. Everywhere people came under great conviction of sin. Atheists and Communists, slain helplessly under awful conviction of sin, prayed for hours that they might find peace of mind. Drunkards, standing at the saloon bar, trembled, dropped their beer upon the floor and cried for God to save them. Businessmen, who never darkened the doors of a church; schoolteachers, correcting their papers; housewives in their homes, even the herring fishermen out upon the sea—were all gripped by deep conviction of sin. People felt some strange, internal compelling to go to the church where they could find relief. They felt wonderment and misery alike. The hills were soon black with people streaming to the church from all directions" (Murphy, 9).

The much earlier Moravian Revival of 1727 is another example of preparing the way for divine visitation. One little church in Germany, awakened by the Spirit's holy fire, did more in the evangelization of the world in twenty years than the entire evangelical church combined did in 200 years (Pratney, 306). Dr. Kenneth Pfohl pointed out their diligence in seeking a new Pentecostal outpouring: "The great Moravian Pentecost was not a shower of blessing out of a cloudless sky. It did come suddenly, as suddenly as the blessing of its greater predecessor in Jerusalem, when the Christian Church was born. Yet, for long, there had been signs of abundance of rain, though many recognized them not. In short, the blessing of the thirteenth of August 1727, was diligently and earnestly prepared for" (Greenfield, 86). This move of the Spirit was not the product of time and chance, nor were the results that followed.

The New Testament is a book of revival that demonstrates the principle that preparation precedes spiritual awakenings. Revival began with John the Baptist who prepared the way for the Messiah. Through signs and wonders Jesus took the spiritual outpouring further and prepared the way for the revivals of the early church. He established revival as the basis for normal Christianity and sent the Spirit after His ascension to accomplish it. The revival that originated on the day of Pentecost and continued as narrated in the book of Acts is the standard by which the church is to judge her spiritual life. The New Testament Epistles are letters written to churches birthed through revival. Considering the church's humble beginnings, it was only the power of the Holy Spirit that caused the gospel to spread like wildfire throughout the Roman Empire.

Preparing for the Messiah to come to His people can clearly be seen in the life and ministry of John the Baptist. John was the fulfillment of the prophecy proclaimed in Isaiah 40:3-5 which Luke quoted:

As is written in the book of the words of Isaiah the prophet: "A voice of one calling in the desert, 'Prepare the way for the LORD, make straight paths for Him. Every valley shall be filled in, every mountain and hill made low. The crooked roads shall become straight, the rough ways smooth. And all mankind will see God's salvation'" (Lk. 3:4-6).

We will now examine the first three points of this prophecy and how they relate to preparing the way of the LORD in our day.

A VOICE OF ONE CALLING

The LORD has chosen to use frail people to advance His Kingdom through the power of the Holy Spirit. For revival to come there must be a holy instrument that the LORD can use. Someone must be the voice crying in the wilderness to a sleeping church and a perishing world. How can a person repent if he does not comprehend he is a sinner, or be saved if he does not know that he is in danger of Hell? How can a man live a holy life if he has not been taught what holiness entails? In addition, how will the church know that God desires to revive her unless she realizes that she is spiritually dead and in need of reviving? A person who is spiritually comatose will never be able to discern his own situation. So it is with the church. Someone must have the courage to warn a lukewarm church of her sin. Otherwise, she will suffer the consequences of her transgressions.

Jesus heralded John the Baptist as the greatest prophet (Mt. 11:11). He said, "From the days of John the Baptist until now, the Kingdom of Heaven has been forcefully (violently, KJV) advancing, and forceful (violent, KJV) men lay hold of it" (Mt. 11:12). In other words, only men aggressively moved with the heart of God, by the Spirit of God, can advance the Kingdom of God. A watered down gospel may build large congregations, but never Christ's Kingdom.

The cry of every believer, and especially every preacher, should be "Prepare the way for the LORD!" We are called to unashamedly stand among our families and neighbors, in the streets of urban decay, and even in our churches and cry out, "Prepare the way for the LORD!" The critical need of the hour is for the raising up of modern day John the Baptists, saturated with the love and compassion of Christ.

An old Chinese proverb says, "If you want to know what water is, don't ask a fish." A fish only knows life in water. He is unable to perceive his own situation since he lives in it day in and day out. A voice must come to him from the outside to make known to him his true condition. This was the Baptist's ministry. He was separate from the people in their passions and pride, separate from them in their religion and government, separate morally and spiritually, separate from worldly ambitions—because he was separated exclusively unto God. As a result, John could see the reality of a sinful people who were at war with their Creator even though they believed they were "normal" and right with Him.

When there is no one to cry, "Prepare the way for the LORD," you may be certain there will be NO revival. Before revival can come, Christians must first be separated unto Christ, and then separated from sin and the world. It is vital that they live free from the passions of fame, wealth, and selfish ambitions while being rich in intimate fellowship with the Savior. Their lives must be fully yielded to Jesus, which means they will follow Him no matter the cost. Then they will begin to know the heart of God and the things that break His heart. Then they will weep over the nation like the prophet Jeremiah. "Since my people are crushed, I am crushed; I mourn, and horror grips me. Is there no balm in Gilead? Is there no physician there? Why then is there no healing for the wound of my people? Oh, that my head were a spring of water and my eyes a fountain of tears! I would weep day and night for the slain of my people" (Jer. 8:21-9:1).

Jeremiah was broken over the spiritual condition of his people. When he touched the heart of God he was transformed into a man of compassion. This drove him to his knees in desperate cries for the people to come to repentance. It also compelled him to warn them about their true spiritual condition. This was the love of God operating through the man. Such lives are instruments for revival. Saints who possess the heart of God will proclaim with courage, love and deep humility, "Prepare the way for the LORD!"

PREPARE THE WAY

Before a person, or a people, will prepare the way of the LORD they must yearn for Him and His appearing. Although God desires every believer to prepare for His coming, He will respond to the efforts of a few. This is not a justification for the indifference that plagues the majority of Christians in this nation. It does offer a tremendous hope to those faithful few aching for the LORD to rend the heavens. The character of the bold, yet humble John the Baptist is an encouraging example of a man who prepared the way for the Messiah. His purpose was clear, his message distinct, his sacrifice complete, his faith unwavering, his passion ablaze, his obedience to the death. These same qualities are necessary to accomplish an equivalent work today.

To understand Isaiah 40:3-5, and John's ministry, we must visualize what the prophesy portrayed from the cultural point of view of that era. In many ancient civilizations, a king would visit the villages of his realm to discern the condition of his kingdom and institute justice according to his own will. With undisputable power he would dispense mercy or wrath, blessings or curses, life or death. Emissaries would go before the king to prepare for his coming. A wise community, privileged to be visited by their king, would diligently prepare the way. They would clean the streets, paint their houses, and plan for the festivities. Every obstacle that would displease their king and incur his wrath would be removed.

Multitudes came to hear the Baptist preach and repent of their sins. John did everything within his power to ready the people for their King. He pointed to Jesus, proclaiming Him the Christ, the "Lamb of God, who takes away the sin of the world!" (Jn. 1:29). John prepared the way for Jesus with the message of repentance. Jesus took the message farther by saying He was the Way. Filled with compassion He touched multitudes of hurting people. Yet when the end came, those same crowds who were fed and healed by Him cried, "Crucify Him."

Everyone will not embrace the move of God when it comes. Revival means mercy for some and judgment for others. The annals of history record that the majority of Israel refused to accept the revival God offered them. Those that rebelled against their Messiah brought upon themselves the wrath of the Almighty.

Jesus prophesied the destruction of the Temple and Jerusalem because they did not recognize who He was (Lk. 19:41-44). When Christ stood before the Roman governor and the Jewish people, Pilate strove to release Him, but the masses cried out, "Let his blood be on us and on our children!" (Mt. 27:25). And so it was.

In 70 A.D. Jerusalem and the Temple were utterly destroyed by the Roman armies under Titus, son of Emperor Vespasian. The blood of the parents and their children came upon them for not accepting their rightful King. "Though God is longsuffering in the face of backsliding, there comes a time when His patience is exhausted. Ultimately it is either revival or catastrophe" (Coleman, *Dry Bones*, 47-48). Revival is the mercy of God freely offered to sinful humanity. Judgment is the unfortunate result of men and women rejecting His love.

Those who God uses to prepare the way for revival have the joy of witnessing vast numbers of people saved and delivered from lives of sin and rebellion. They will also see a greater portion of the people reject Jesus as Israel did two thousand years ago. The responsibility of those who prepare the way is only to be a voice crying in the wilderness. What people do when God rends the heavens is their own responsibility. The preparers of the way are called to be faithful to the LORD, His message and the calling no matter the response of the populous.

RESULTS OF NOT PREPARING

There are at least two forms of judgment that take place when the church does not prepare for revival. The first happens when God turns both the church and the world over to their own sinful desires (Rom. 1:28). Our indifference in seeing a move of the Spirit is proof of our lukewarmness. As Christians compromise their faith and morals they become more worldly and self-absorbed. Sin and compromise silences the church's voice, strips her of her authority and destroys her testimony. The unsaved are then left without the restraining influence of the Holy Spirit working through a holy church. Without this restraining influence secular society grows in wickedness. When God removes His protective hand from His people, the human race degenerates to baser lifestyles.

An honest assessment of the spiritual and moral condition of the American church exposes the raw truth that this judgment has overtaken us. Lack of the Spirit in the church has produced a lack of conviction over sin. Lack of conviction becomes a type of silent approval of unholy practices. Fornication is largely ignored in the church. Homosexuals can sit comfortably week after week in supposed evangelical churches without the slightest bit of concern for their ungodly behaviors. Pornography sweeps through the ranks of professed disciples from pastors to parishioners. The explosive divorce rate among acclaimed Christians is devastating subsequent generations. Because this sin is rarely addressed from a Scriptural perspective, divorce is now commonly accepted and even endorsed by the church and clergy. A plague of contention and strife runs rampant through congregations rather than being habitations of healing and peace. Nearly one third of churches seeking a pastor are doing so because they drove out the former pastor through acts of rebellion. This is just the tip of the iceberg.

There is another judgment that is far more severe than being turned over to our own sin; it is God withdrawing His Spirit from His people. Tragically, the majority of churches and Christians in western civilization suffer under this most disastrous of judgments and do not even comprehend that it has swallowed them up. Spiritually speaking, "Ichabod" has been stamped over their doorposts, which means the glory of God has departed from them (1 Sam. 4:21). For Christians to live contentedly without revival means they are either satisfied to live without God's manifest presence, have never known there is more to be received, or do not want God upsetting their lifestyles. One way or another, they are not seriously disturbed that God is not vitally present among them.

The deep moral decay of our nation is further proof of a prodigal church. She has ceased to be salt and light in this world. As salt, the church is to preserve society from moral and spiritual decay. This she has failed to do. Compromise has been her downfall. A syncretism (the blending of two beliefs to create a distinct third belief) has occurred between humanism and Christianity resulting in the formation of a third religion: the religion of American Cultural Christianity. This new religion, which is actually not new, is far removed from the Biblical version. It is a hedonistic, pleasure-driven religion that is self-reliant and self-centered. It makes man the center of all things, happiness and prosperity the prize, and God the subservient slave to their desires.

The moral and spiritual decline stated above can be turned around if we will see our sin and repent. Only the power of God can transform the church and secular society. We are in enormous need of voices crying in the spiritual wastelands of our nation. Those who prepare the way for divine visitation are average people who thirst for the Living God. They will do whatever it takes to see His glory revealed. The dead are hard to motivate, but desperate people live desperate lives that can shake their world. The LORD does not need our talent, intelligence, wealth or position. He is looking for radically-surrendered people who will passionately pursue Him no matter the cost.

MAKE STRAIGHT PATHS FOR HIM

Driving west on highway 10 across Texas is a long, arduous journey of more than eight hundred and fifty miles. It is a dry and rugged landscape. Imagine how difficult it was for the first pioneers to travel that territory and build a simple dirt road by sheer manpower. Think of the perseverance and determination it took to accomplish the task. Those who originally built the road were not the only ones who profited from it. Everyone who followed thereafter would benefit whether they understood the original cost or not.

Building a spiritual highway so God will reveal His glory is the responsibility of every Christian. Yet this duty offers a tremendous blessing. Making "straight paths for Him" requires us to diligently seek the LORD. The prize of Christianity is Jesus Himself. Intimate fellowship with the Savior is the greatest privilege offered to the human race. This truth moved the psalmist to proclaim, "O God, You are my God, earnestly I seek You; my soul thirsts for You, my body longs for You, in a dry and weary land where there is no water. I have seen You in the sanctuary and beheld Your power and Your glory. Because Your love is better than life, my lips will glorify You" (Ps. 63:1-3). David knew sweet fellowship with his Creator and passionately ran after Him, "As the deer pants for streams of water, so my soul pants for You, O God. My soul thirsts for God, for the living God. When can I go and meet with God?" (Ps. 42:1-2).

Rees Howells, a man in hot pursuit of God, daily enjoyed the gift of intimate fellowship with the Master. His entire Christian life was defined by one concept—making a straight path for Him.

He did everything within his ability to live a surrendered life so the power of the Holy Spirit could flow through him. After the birth of the Howells' first son, Rees felt an overwhelming burden for the people of Africa. He prayed that the LORD would send someone to reach them with the Gospel. The Howells told the LORD they would be willing to raise a missionary's child if it would allow that couple to freely minister in Africa since the health conditions were dangerous for young children. Instead, the LORD asked Rees and his wife if they would give their only son to relatives and go to Africa themselves. The LORD promised that in exchange for their sacrifice and obedience He would give them 10,000 souls. Mr. and Mrs. Howells lovingly obeyed the exceedingly difficult call and prepared the way for the LORD to visit South Africa. As a result, the fires of revival burned through them.

Mr. Howells visited Bethany, where the Queen of Swaziland lived. The first service lasted for thirteen hours. All the time he was dealing with the unsaved. The presence of the Holy Spirit increased as time went on. Rees stated, "On the third day, the power was there! It wasn't the preaching, it was the power."

"The Queen of Swaziland sent for me. She asked why her people were going after my God. I told her it was because they had met the living God, and had forgiveness of sins and the gift of eternal life. I told her that God had one Son, and He gave Him to die for us; and we had one son, and had left him to tell the people of Africa about God. She was much affected by hearing that my wife and I loved her people more than we loved our own son. She allowed me to have a private meeting with her chief men, but said I must not look at her, but speak as if I were talking to them! Later, in the chapel, the power of God was on the meeting, and when I tested it, fifty stood up, including the young queen, the daughter-in-law of the reigning queen.

"When we came back some time later the old queen asked to see us privately. She told us that she had just lost her daughter, who had become a Christian, and she had died in perfect peace, trusting Jesus. She seemed very much affected, and added that she too, in her heart, had accepted the Saviour" (Grubb, 174-175). Those who enter into a deep abiding relationship not only enjoy intimate fellowship with the Father, but will also be people who "make straight paths for Him" to visit as evidenced by this account.

The LORD used Rees Howells in Africa because he first prepared the way in his own life for God to come to him by removing anything that hindered His appearing. An intense love for the Savior compelled him to walk in obedience and holiness, which resulted in the Spirit coming to the people in an extraordinary manner. "The Sunday was October 10—my birthday—and as I preached in the morning you could feel the Spirit coming on the congregation. In the evening down He came. I shall never forget it. He came upon a young girl, Kufase by name, who had fasted for three days under conviction that she was not ready for the LORD's coming. As she prayed she broke down crying, and within five minutes the whole congregation were on their faces crying to God. Like lightning and thunder the power came down. I had never seen this even in the Welsh Revival. I had only heard about it with Finney and others. Heaven had opened, and there was no room to contain the blessing. I lost myself in the Spirit and prayed as much as they did. All I could say was, 'He has come.' We went on until late in the night; we couldn't stop the meeting. What He told me before I went to Africa was actually taking place, and that within six weeks" (Grubb, 167). God gave Rees and his wife well over the 10,000 souls He promised. What more profitable endeavor could Christians pursue than to pave the way for the Spirit to visit frail humanity?

This principle of preparing the way for us to go to Him and for the LORD to come to us is similar to what James taught when he wrote, "draw near to God and He will draw near to you" (Jam. 4:8; NKJV). In essence, the LORD is telling us that if we will take a step towards Him He will take a million mile leap towards us. Those believers who have abandoned their lives in a radical pursuit to gain intimacy with Christ will be used by the Spirit to prepare the way for His glory to fall upon the church and a dying culture. Jesus is waiting, even longing, for us to come near to Him so He can draw near to us. Yes, preparation precedes revival! This is an unalterable fact.

CHAPTER FIVE

The Work of Preparing

As is written in the book of the words of Isaiah the prophet: "A voice of one calling in the desert, 'Prepare the way for the LORD, make straight paths for Him. Every valley shall be filled in, every mountain and hill made low. The crooked roads shall become straight, the rough ways smooth. And all mankind will see God's salvation'" (Lk. 3:4-6).

Revival is obtainable! It is not like the proverbial carrot dangling before the helpless horse that never gains the prize. The preparation for revival consists of practical Biblical truths that are spiritually profitable for all who follow that way. In this chapter we will continue our examination of Luke 3:4-6 (Isa. 40:3-5) and see how this prophesy further relates to revival.

FILL EVERY VALLEY

In Biblical times, valleys were sites of great wars. Allegorically, they represent the difficult and painful seasons of life where we battle the enemies that come from outside us and within us. In preparing for the King of kings to visit His people, we must fill in the valleys of our lives. This means we must face the difficulties of life and overcome them through His grace.

The prophet Jeremiah had grown weary over the prosperity of the wicked. After he vocalized his complaint to God, the LORD responded with a challenge, "If you have raced with men on foot and they have worn you out, how can you compete with horses? If you stumble in safe country, how will you manage in the thickets by the Jordan?" (Jer. 12:5). The LORD was challenging the prophet to stand up and act like a man in the midst of strenuous times. If we cannot overcome sin, depression and fear in times of ease and prosperity, how will we ever stand in the heated battles over the souls of perishing humanity where the conflicts are fiercest?

THE VALLEY OF INDIVIDUALISM

Extreme individualism is one metaphorical valley of American life that causes us much sorrow. This philosophical belief is as old as the fall of mankind. It became the driving force of the 14th century Italian Renaissance and now has its expression in modern day humanism. The Greek philosopher Protagoras of the 5th century B.C. gave us the definition of humanism, "Man is the measure of all things." Extreme individualism is the philosophical underpinning of our entire American culture. It is a thread sewn throughout the fabric of our society. Individualism is a major breeding ground for depression, fear and a host of other sins.

Extreme individualism places man at the center of life rather than God. This is self-idolatry. Self-idolatry is the spiritual condition where the desires and ambitions of the individual become all-important and all-consuming. This hedonistic philosophy makes the pursuit of pleasure the primary purpose of man. The individualist proclaims, "I want what I desire no matter what it costs because it's my right to have whatever makes me happy." The goal of human existence then revolves around the fulfillment of one's own happiness at any cost. Extreme individualism produces self-indulgent individuals who, in turn, create a self-indulgent society.

The most powerful propaganda machines for advancing individualism and a self-indulgent society come out of our public schools and the television, movie and music industries. Millions of people are manipulated through these avenues by redefining what is spiritual, moral and immoral. They define for the American public what constitutes god, faith, success, love, family and personal worth. These propaganda machines are more involved in raising children than parents are. Strangers who define God, morality and purpose from a secular worldview shape a child's mind and conscience. The majority of Christians unknowingly incorporate this philosophy into their homes and then wonder why their children turn from Christ when they reach their teens.

Personal happiness becomes the all-consuming goal of self-indulgent people. Driven by their lusts they seek whatever they dream will make them happy or dispose of whatever does not. They search for that elusive possession, position, or person to satisfy their unfulfilled desires. Advertisers study the cravings of people and then manipulate them through their own obsessions. They announce, "You deserve a new Ford today" because they know you already believe it. The lust for more "stuff" (from our "Stuff Marts") has produced an economic system based on credit that has run amuck. Americans are no longer masters of their own desires but slaves to their evil passions—and this includes most Christians.

The offspring of extreme individualism and self-indulgence is a victim mentality. If the purpose of life is nothing more than personal happiness, then whatever robs us of our happiness we judge as bad. People consider themselves victims when they believe they have been robbed of their happiness. The vicious cycle begins of blaming others for our own sins and character flaws. Children blame their parents for their mistakes, alcoholics their family and homosexuals their genes. Where else but in America can a woman spill a cup of coffee in her lap while driving a car and sue McDonald's for six million dollars? We are a people who refuse to accept responsibility for our own actions and sins. When selfishness rules an individual's life, it does not matter how many people are hurt in his or her pursuit of happiness.

The futility of life apart from Christ will be a constant companion no matter how wealthy, famous or influential a person becomes. In our relentless search for significance, each of us craves a reason-for-being that gives value to life and death. After analyzing the American culture Ravi Zacharias stated, "I am absolutely convinced that meaninglessness does not come from being weary of pain. Meaninglessness comes from being weary of pleasure. And that's why we are bankrupt of meaning in a land of so much" (Zacharias). When the gods we serve are nothing more than the lusts of our own flesh, we are bound to come to a crisis of existence. The very things that defined our highly praised "freedom" have actually become the "tyranny of our own desires" (Hauerwas, 33).

JESUS IS ALL WE NEED

The same humanistic philosophy that manipulates the world has possessed the church. Why should pagans come to Christ when they see little difference between themselves and so called believers? It could even be argued that a very large number of Christians have become as pleasure driven as any proclaimed hedonist. This very issue provoked the infamous French atheist Voltaire to pronounce, "When it comes to money, all men are of the same religion" (MacDonald, 89).

To fill up the valleys of our lives we must first recognize the thoughts and passions that rob us of God's glory. We must then strategically dismantle them according to the Scriptures and through the power of the Holy Spirit. The very fact that Christians suffer under depression, fear and anxiety is proof that they do not believe Jesus is all they need. In essence, they are saying that Jesus is not enough, that He cannot satisfy their deepest needs, and that He is not able to give joy through all of life's challenges. We must reclaim the truth that people, possessions and wealth cannot gratify our profoundest needs. All the philosophies of men are only as strong as the frail, finite minds that created them. There must be a radical change in our lifestyles or we will continue along the same paths we have traveled for years, even decades.

It is time we fill in the valleys of our lives with something that truly satisfies. Only Jesus can satisfy the deepest longing of our souls, heal the rawest wounds of our heart and calm the raging storms of our minds. He will not force Himself into our lives. We must make our lives living temples where the Holy Spirit will freely dwell.

BRING DOWN EVERY MOUNTAIN

The Word of God refers to mountains in both positive and negative terms. Isaiah's prophecy portrays them negatively as mountains of pride and places where men worship false gods. These mountains must be torn down before revival can come.

Pride hinders revival just as it stops an individual from surrendering to Christ. Arrogance impedes holiness and is a barrier to intimate prayer. Conceit breeds contention. Our over-inflated egos reap havoc on families and churches (Pr. 13:10). The fear of man is another name for pride: fear of what others think, fear of not measuring up to expectations, and fear of sharing the faith.

Jehoshaphat was one of the few godly kings Judah had. One day the armies of Moab and Ammon gathered their forces to fight against Judah. The king resolved "to inquire of the LORD, and he proclaimed a fast for all Judah" (2 Chr. 20:3). He humbly prayed before a great audience, "O our God, will You not judge them? For we have no power to face this vast army that is attacking us. We do not know what to do, but our eyes are upon You" (2 Chr. 20:2). God gave the king a miraculous victory, not because he had a mighty army, but because he recognized his human weakness and the LORD's awesome power.

Pride compels people to trust in their own ability, strength and wisdom rather than the LORD. It keeps pastors from the place of prayer as they run after the latest church growth guru. Self-important leaders focus on natural abilities rather than a miracle-working God. The mountains of pride need to be pulled down in all of their various forms before revival can come! We overcome the sin of pride by humbling ourselves before the Savior. This process begins by comprehending our pride then repenting of it. This sin is so deeply interwoven into our character that apart from the Spirit's illuminating influence it is exceedingly difficult to perceive. As with Jehoshaphat, the LORD will pour out His power through those whose eyes are fixed on Him, not through the self-reliant.

MOUNTAINS OF UNBELIEF AND IRRESPONSIBILITY

Patrick Fairbairn believed that there are two major hindrances to revival that we need to confront. He said that most Christians have a difficulty with "faith in the possibility of the work, and a sense of personal responsibility in regard to its production" (Roberts, *Revival*, 126). These hindrances reside in our misconceptions about God and the purpose of man. The sin of unbelief is a byproduct of our distorted views about the Creator and His redemptive work in history. We would not be a doubting people if we truly knew Him and recognized what He is able and willing to do. We will never spiritually rise higher than our understanding of the LORD and the faith we place in Him. Great faith in a great God is able to accomplish great things, not because the people who believe are special, but because the almighty God they trust in is all-powerful and good.

Unbelief hinders revival because we doubt the Savior's desire and ability to transform our churches and nation. Unbelief can even dominate our prayers for revival. Nevertheless, spiritual awakenings come through faith. Jesus said, "I tell you the truth, if anyone says to this mountain, 'Go, throw yourself into the sea,' and does not doubt in his heart but believes that what he says will happen, it will be done for him" (Mk. 11:23). The prayer of faith can tear down the natural and supernatural strongholds that keep revival at bay.

The second hindrance Fairbairn pointed out related to our unwillingness to accept personal responsibility for revival coming to the local church, and in a broader sense, to the nation. James told us "faith without deeds is useless" (Jam. 2:20). This means that a desire for revival without action is worthless. We need to accept personal responsibility for the fulfillment of revival through prayer and evangelism. To tear down the mountain of irresponsibility each believer must accept personal responsibility in preparing for the LORD of Glory to visit His people.

Seeking God to send revival is the duty of every Christian. Yet there is a special obligation laid upon pastors and spiritual leaders to prepare for its coming. There is a profound truth that we cannot escape—as goes the leaders, so goes the church. Dead churches are the result of dead preachers, dead deacons and dead teachers. Thomas Trask stated, "Passionless pastors make for passionless pulpits that result in passionless people and empty altars" (Trask, 1).

Pastor, if your church is spiritually dead, then you must begin by looking at yourself. Stop blaming the congregation. If they do not have the fire of God, maybe it is because you do not have the fire to impart to them. They do not need another program or some tame Sunday morning service; they need an encounter with the Living God. "The preacher, by direct, divine appointment, is God's chosen servant to promote revival in his own church and community ... In a word, revival is the minister's main work. The church has never risen spiritually above the ministry" (Wadsworth, 81-82).

MAKE THE CROOKED WAYS STRAIGHT

To aid us in understanding what the Scriptures mean by "crooked ways" we should examine the English root word for "crooked," which is "crook." What is a crook? A crook is a person who lives by dishonest methods. "Crooked ways" are the unlawful, perverse and fraudulent ways we live (Strong's #4646). Our compromise with the world and "little" sins are crooked ways. They are the unlawful areas of our lives that we do not think are big issues, but God does. Our fraudulent conduct may seem innocent by the world's standards, yet it robs us of relationship with Jesus.

These crooked ways that abound in church folk hinder revival. Sin takes root in our lives when we neglect or reject the teachings of the Scriptures. Every dimension of our lives is to conform to the Word. We must never manipulate the Bible to fit our crooked lifestyles. The Word effectively communicates to us what is pleasing and displeasing to God, so we are left without excuse.

Charles Sheldon's challenging phrase, "What would Jesus do?" is still pertinent today. Would Jesus spend money the way you do on what you do? Would He watch TV shows and movies saturated with sexual innuendos, violence, vulgarities and anti-Christian philosophies? Would He listen to secular music filled with sex, drugs, and worldly values? The crooked ways destroys marriages and ruins children. By the Spirit of God King David commanded, "You who love the LORD, hate evil!" (Ps. 97:10a, NKJV). How can Christians embrace entertainment and lifestyle choices that are the very things that crucified Jesus? Consider Paul's uncompromised teaching:

"Be imitators of God, therefore, as dearly loved children and live a life of love, just as Christ loved us and gave Himself up for us as a fragrant offering and sacrifice to God. But among you there must not be even a hint of sexual immorality, or of any kind of impurity, or of greed, because these are improper for God's holy people. Nor should there be obscenity, foolish talk or coarse joking, which are out of place, but rather thanksgiving. For of this you can be sure: No immoral, impure or greedy person—such a man is an idolater—has any inheritance in the Kingdom of Christ and of God" (Eph. 5:1-5).

The key to getting the crooked ways out of our lives, families and churches comes from a hungry heart after God. Jesus told us, "If you love Me, you will obey what I command" (Jn. 14:15). Moreover, to those who love Him, "His commandments are not burdensome" (1 Jn. 5:3).

MAKE THE ROUGH WAYS SMOOTH

Have you ever driven over a highway that felt like a washboard? Your car goes bumpity-bumpity mile after mile. Now imagine someone driving a horse and buggy down that road. He would think it was fairly smooth. Get that buggy going 70 miles per hour and he would have a different opinion. Christians who are not pressing into God will never notice the roughness of the road since they are not spiritually going anywhere. For instance, people consumed with the accumulation of wealth or the pursuit of pleasure may never know how much they grieve God's heart or sense the warning signs of a troubled marriage.

Those who are aggressively pursuing the LORD will feel the roughness of the road the faster they go. Christians striving to walk near to Christ will even want the questionable things out of their lives. They become sensitive to the Holy Spirit and know whenever the slightest thing comes between them and God. Charles Finney was such a man. He stated, "I found I could not live without enjoying the presence of God, and if at any time a cloud came over me, I could not rest, I could not study, I could not attend to anything with the least satisfaction or benefit until the way was again cleared between my soul and God" (Finney, *Autobiography*, 38-39).

The man, woman, church or denomination that is hungry after God will remove anything and everything that may separate them from the Lover of their souls. Finney revealed passion for Jesus when he declared, "I had no desire to make money. I had no hungering and thirsting after worldly pleasures and amusements in any direction. My whole mind was taken up with Jesus and His salvation, and the world seemed to me of very little consequences. Nothing, it seemed to me, could compete with the worth of souls, and no labor, I thought, could be so sweet and no employment so exalted as that of holding up Christ to a dying world" (Finney, *Autobiography*, 28). As Jesus said, such wisdom is "proved right by all her children" (Lk. 7:35).

SO THE LORD WILL BE REVEALED

The ultimate reason for revival is so the "glory of the LORD will be revealed, and all mankind together will see it" (Isa. 40:5). All of our experiences, traditions, doctrines and methods must bow to the lordship of Jesus. Anything that robs Christ of His glory we are obligated to tear down and cast aside. Everything that advances His glory and Kingdom is our responsibility to press forward. Whatever is contrary to His will hinders revival, while everything that comes out of His good and perfect will advances His Kingdom and the cause of spiritual awakenings. Let us not rob God of His glory by hindering or resisting the outpouring of the Spirit.

In 1965, the Indonesian island of Timor experienced revival.

Unfortunately, they also experienced strong resistance from within the church. "The movement could have morally and spiritually transformed all of Timor, had all of the churches responded to the opportunities and the challenge of the moment ... However, most of the churches, enslaved by an ecclesiastical system failed. The churches thus lost an opportunity that may turn into a judgment upon it" (Peters, 34). Two hundred thousand were added to the church because of this revival. Imagine the millions that could have been saved if the entire church had embraced this move of the Spirit.

Many have shut down a genuine revival because it upset their lives or did not fit into their theological framework. Frank Bartleman gave an account of some deacons who kicked God out of their church in Los Angeles during the Azusa Street Revival of 1906: "I went to Smale's church one night, and he had resigned. The meetings had run daily in the First Baptist Church for fifteen weeks ... The officials of the church were tired of the innovation and wanted to return to the old order. He was told to either stop the revival or get out. He wisely chose the latter. But what an awful position for the church to take—to throw God out. In this same way they drove the Spirit of God out of the churches in Wales. They tired of His presence, desiring to return to the old, cold, ecclesiastical order ... Selfish spirits can never understand sacrifice" (Bartleman, 35, 37). What a terrifying situation the church leaders placed themselves in—to fight against the LORD of Hosts.

Revival is withheld from the land when Christians exalt experience, personalities, fame, wealth, denominationalism, or doctrine above the glorification of God. He will not share His glory with another! The great I Am will rend the heavens so mere mortals may gaze upon His magnificence and so salvation may flow like a river through our cities.

History reveals many men and women who learned to give the glory to God and became the benefactors of His presence as a result. One such man was David Morgan, who was involved in the 1859 Welsh Revival. After a powerful meeting on New Year's Day at Devil's Bridge, the minister and Mr. Morgan quietly walked to their lodging. Toward the end of their journey, the minister broke the holy silence saying, "Didn't we have a blessed meeting, Mr. Morgan?" Mr. Morgan replied, "Yes!" Then after a pause, added, "The LORD would give us great things, if He could only trust us."

The minister questioned, "What do you mean?" Morgan wisely answered, "If He could trust us not to steal the glory for ourselves." Then he proclaimed at the top of his voice, "Not unto us, O LORD, not unto us, but unto Thy name give glory" (Evans, 69-70).

Our land is in need of such men and women today. When God's people can be trusted with His glory, He will freely give it—but not before.

THE MOUTH OF THE LORD HAS SPOKEN

Isaiah's prophecy came from the mouth of the LORD and has a threefold fulfillment. First of all, John the Baptist was the direct fulfillment of this prophecy. He lived out the principles involved in Isaiah's oracle and saw the fruit of his labor when the Messiah was revealed. John literally prepared the way for Jesus to visit Israel.

Secondly, we can exercise this same principle of preparing the way of the LORD today. Whenever saints perform the words of this prophecy, the LORD will visit His people. Our present hope should be for a national awakening that sweeps America and even the entire world. The people of God must diligently prepare the way for His visitation. His Word is absolute truth and His promises never fail. The LORD is not the obstacle to revival—we are!

Finally, Jesus based His second coming upon the fact of His death, resurrection and ascension into Heaven. While many people saw Jesus ascend into Heaven, two angels spoke to the multitude and said, "Men of Galilee, why do you stand here looking into the sky? This same Jesus, who has been taken from you into Heaven, will come back in the same way you have seen Him go into Heaven" (Acts 1:11). We will see the culmination of history when the church throughout the world has prepared the way of the LORD. Jesus is coming back and we must prepare the way for His soon return.

John prepared the way for Christ and saw Him come. Church history contains wonderful accounts of the LORD revealing Himself in the beauty of holiness whenever the saints prepared the way. The Holy Spirit is the same today as He was when the church received her first Pentecostal outpouring and saw her first revival. He will do it again when Christians rightly prepare. When the fires of revival sweep our nation and world we are also preparing for Christ's second coming.

CHAPTER SIX

THE BEAUTY OF BROKENNESS

There are three facets of the Christian life that are essential to revival: surrender, brokenness and repentance. Surrender is relinquishing control of our lives to God. Brokenness is the state of being in which we yield that control. Repentance is brokenness and surrender in action. Surrender, brokenness and repentance are character traits of people desperately desiring the LORD. In this chapter we will look at how surrender and brokenness are integral elements to reviving the Christian life. In the next chapter we will examine the gift of repentance and its importance in the scheme of revival.

SURRENDER

Surrender is a fact of life. It may be voluntary or forced. In one way or another, every person yields control of their lives to someone else no matter their position in society. The question is not *if* we surrender, but *to whom* are we surrendering.

In view of God's mercy, humanity has but one acceptable response to the crucified and resurrected Christ—to surrender our lives to Him and live for His glory (Rom. 12:1-2). Anything else is rebellion! Repentance is an ongoing act of surrender, while holiness is the fruit of a surrendered life. Only yielded saints will live vibrant lives of prayer. Furthermore, surrender unlocks the door to the power of God and opens the windows of Heaven to flood a land with His holy presence.

To relinquish control of our lives to the One who both created and purchased us is foundational to the Christian faith. Jesus never *requested* our reckless abandonment, He demanded it. We cannot be loyal to two gods. When we refuse to surrender our lives, wills or wants to Jesus we walk in deliberate disobedience. By not submitting to the LORD people automatically submit to Satan and the principles that govern his kingdom. This may seem to be a hard statement. However, can any serious person believe that a compromise between serving God and serving Satan is possible?

Lack of surrender to God is a result of selfishness deep within our characters. Our selfish characters rob us of intimacy with Christ and the power to touch our family, friends and the lost with the power of the Holy Spirit. Liu Zhenying, known as Brother Yun, is one of the leading pastors in the Chinese house church movement. He recognized that "Multitudes of church members in the West are satisfied with giving their minimum to God, not their maximum. I've watched men and women during offering time ... open their fat wallets and search for the smallest amount they can give. This type of attitude will never do. Jesus gave His whole life for us, and we give as little of our lives, time and money as we can back to God. What a disgrace! Repent!" (Yun, 297).

There are three primary reasons why we have such a difficult time submitting to God. The first is our obsession with controlling our lives. In our effort to manage our own lives we attempt to manipulate the lives of others. Secondly, we struggle with submission because we love our sin and ourselves more than anything else. For some odd reason, we think that if we love God with all of our being we will be less a person or lose out on life.

Lastly, we resist surrendering to God because we have not been broken. We struggle to retain control of our lives whenever we do not comprehend our real spiritual condition and need. Many think submission to the Savior is weakness rather than a right response of fallen men to a holy God. So He must help us surrender to Him. This means that our pride and self-sufficiency must be broken, our love of sin and self must be broken, our love of pleasure and possessions must be broken. In truth, everything that is not of Christ must be broken. Here is the place where the Lord Jesus can freely live in and through us.

BROKENNESS

Brokenness is never weakness. It is coming to the end of one's self-life. Jesus said that the broken man is truly a blessed man (Mt. 5:3). Through brokenness we comprehend that we are finite people in tremendous need of a Savior. A person will throw himself at the Redeemer's feet only when he grasps the reality that he deserves divine judgment for his sin and that his sole hope is Christ's mercy. This is where a life of brokenness begins. "The broken man," observed William MacDonald "is quick to repent. He does not try to sweep sin under the carpet. He does not try to forget it with the excuse, 'Time heals all things.' He rushes into the presence of God and cries, 'I have sinned'" (MacDonald, 121).

Brokenness produces true humility. Until our pride is broken we will not humble ourselves before God or men. Brokenness and humility are the results of a deep consciousness of personal guilt before God over sin, seeing our overwhelming need of a Savior, and then clinging to Christ as a result. People who are in a right relationship with their Creator will grow in brokenness and humility until their dying day. "He has showed you, O man, what is good. And what does the LORD require of you? To act justly and to love mercy and to walk humbly with your God" (Mic. 6:8). Humility and brokenness are inseparably interwoven so as to bring a person to surrender, repentance and victory.

Revival is birthed through humble and broken saints who yearn to see the glory of God sweep the land. "In the local assembly, brokenness is the road to revival. It is a fixed law in the spiritual realm that the tears of brokenness are the prelude to shower of blessing. We generally try everything else first—new buildings, new campaigns, new methods, but God is waiting for repentance and humiliation. When we repent the blessings will flow" (MacDonald, 140).

The Christians in Uganda suffered tremendous persecution during Idi Amin's reign of terror (1971-1979). Revival is now sweeping that nation because the persecution helped bring believers to a point of brokenness. After the Christians lost virtually everything, they had no other hope than to desperately seek God's face. They longed for the LORD to rend the heavens and pour mercy upon a demonically battered nation. F. Kefa

Sempangi pastored in Kampala during this time. He wrote, "We must be 'broken,' even as Jesus was broken for the world. To be broken is to have no pride, for where there is pride there is no confession and no forgiveness. The broken one is he who is broken to heal a broken relationship. He is the one willing to 'give in,' who doesn't find his identity in always being right" (Sempangi, 39).

Idi Amin was the 1970s African equivalent of Hitler. The cruel bloodbath that he inaugurated was horrifying. The atrocities this Muslim leader inflicted upon his people, and uniquely upon Christians, created a true brokenness in the believers that allowed them to forgive the vilest of offenses. Brokenness heals relationships—pride and unforgiveness destroys them. The splintered American church with her astronomical divorce rate will find healing and anointing when brokenness defines her character. Until that time, our unbroken lives will rob us of revival and continue to destroy our marriages, children, churches and nation.

The LORD took the issue of brokenness very seriously with Pastor Sempangi (actually it is a very serious issue with every person, especially pastors). One day a brother from the Revival Fellowship gave Kefa the irreplaceable gift of a loving reproof. First the brother read Matthew 14:19. Jesus "directed the people to sit down on the grass. Taking the five loaves and the two fish and looking up to Heaven, He gave thanks and broke the loaves. Then He gave them to the disciples, and the disciples gave them to the people." Then he shared, "Until God breaks your will, He will never use you. You will remain only a nice loaf of bread."

Kefa said the brother explained that "unless I was broken I would be too proud to lose my life for sinners. I would be too proud to give my life away for people who were not perfect. I would wait for the perfect person and the perfect community, and I would never find them. I would end up like Judas, making only a partial commitment to the body of believers to whom I belonged and finding my identity in my rebellion from them" (Sempangi, 39). This is a lesson the entire church needs to learn. Hopefully, we will not have to pay such a high price in our country in order to learn true brokenness.

COMPREHENDING GOD'S MERCY

The strength of sin is greater than our natural self. A man who is broken before God will have a passion to walk free from the power of sin. The greater the yearning for the LORD, the quicker a man will seek forgiveness and grace to overcome sin and remain in fellowship with his Savior. King David repented of his adultery only when his pride and self-will was finally broken. He then mournfully declared, "For I know my transgressions, and my sin is always before me. Against You, You only, have I sinned and done what is evil in Your sight" (Ps. 51:3-4a). David finally laid aside his hurtful pride and rebellion when he was confronted with the ugliness of his sin in light of a holy God. Guilt was a gift from God to bring David back into right relationship with Him.

Guilt has little value if there is no hope for mercy. Only a cruel person or god would inflict guilt without hope. However, guilt that produces hopelessness in self is extremely profitable when there is hope in divine mercy. This mercy is most clearly seen in the face of Jesus Christ. The plan of salvation is based upon a God who desires to save the hopeless and helpless. The only remedy for mankind's hopeless state was for the Father to send the Son to die on the cross.

In 2 Corinthians 7:8-9 Paul said he did not regret hurting the church by preaching to them repentance, even though it broke his heart to do so. Though the message brought guilt, the church was broken and turned from their sin as they drew closer to the LORD. Paul stated, "For you became sorrowful as God intended." It was God's will for them to be broken through the knowledge of their sin. This healthy knowledge of sin produced godly sorrow that moved them to a deeper surrender to the Master.

GODLY SORROW

Godly sorrow is a fruit of God's mercy that is necessary to salvation and revival. This Spirit inspired emotion is exceedingly healthy. Godly sorrow can bring about a change of character that could never be produced through teaching, therapy or self-help principles. When the Spirit convicts a person of sin He always offers the remedy. As Paul wrote, "Godly sorrow brings repentance that leads to salvation and leaves no regret, but worldly sorrow brings death" (2 Cor. 7:10).

Worldly sorrow is a very cruel thing. It is guilt without hope. A man may possess a sincere remorse for hurting God, himself and others, but not to the point of changing his life. Quite often a person is only sorry that he got caught at his sin. Repentance is not taking place in any soul who is not actively turning from his sin. Prayer for forgiveness is worthless if the person does not want to be radically transformed by the Holy Spirit. It is impossible for worldly sorrow to produce genuine repentance that transforms the character because the person is not willing to surrender his entire being to Christ. Worldly sorrow produces death: eternal death, spiritual death, relational death and emotional death. It is hopeless because it is Christless.

For a person to know godly sorrow he must see himself entirely lost and undone without God. "A man must feel himself in misery, before he will go about to find a remedy; be sick before he will seek a physician; be in prison before he will seek a pardon. A sinner must be weary of his former wicked ways before he will have recourse to Jesus Christ for refreshing. He must be sensible of his spiritual poverty, beggary, and slavery under the devil, before he thirst kindly for heavenly righteousness, and willingly take up Christ's sweet and easy yoke. He must be cast down, confounded, condemned, a cast away, and lost in himself, before he will look about for a Saviour" (Iain Murray, 128). Godly sorrow goes to the root of the problem. It generates a righteous zeal to change the character of a person rather than just being sorrowful about the consequences of sin.

Godly sorrow produces action. After Paul rebuked the Corinthians for their sin he wrote on the holy aggression they had to get the sinful practices out of their lives. He penned, "For observe this very thing, that you sorrowed in a godly manner: What diligence it produced in you, what clearing of yourselves, what indignation, what fear, what vehement desire, what zeal, what vindication!" (2 Cor. 7:11; NKJV). The verbs (or verb phrases) of the above verse are: diligence; clearing of yourselves; indignation; fear; vehement desire; zeal and vindication. All of these passionate verbs relate to the actions of a person to right the wrongs he has done and to see his character transformed no matter the cost. Indignation and vindication are not acts of violence against a person, just against the sin and personal character traits that are the source of the sin. Indifference is crushed under the fervent desire to walk upright with God.

BROKENNESS BRINGS REVIVAL

John the Baptist was accredited as the greatest of all prophets even though he never raised the dead, made the blind to see or the lame to walk. He didn't part the Red Sea like Moses, or call down fire from Heaven like Elijah. Why did Jesus call John the greatest prophet? Because he prepared the way for the Messiah. What was the message that prepared the way? "Repent" (Mt. 3:2). John was a broken and surrendered man who knew he was not worthy to untie Christ's shoes (Lk. 3:16). Humbly and boldly he prepared for the coming of Messiah. The spiritual authority he possessed came through his brokenness and surrender to God.

John's message will accomplish the same thing today that it did in his day—the transformation of society through the salvation of men. The 1859 Ulster Revival, which swept Northern Ireland, is an example of conviction that brought the people to a place of brokenness and repentance. The strongest of men staggered and fell down "under the wounds of their conscience." They trembled and grew physically weak under the tremendous conviction of the Holy Spirit. The minister proclaimed, "Oh! It is a heartrending sight to witness. With wringing of hands, streams of tears, and a look of unutterable anguish, they confess their sins in tones of unmistakable sincerity, and appeal to the LORD for mercy with a cry of piercing earnestness. I have seen the strong frame convulsed; I have witnessed every joint trembling; I have heard the cry as I have never heard it before, 'Lord Jesus, have mercy upon my sinful soul; Lord Jesus, come to my burning heart; Lord, pardon my sins; oh, come and lift me from these flames of Hell!'" (Gibson, 25).

The conviction of sin produces brokenness when godly sorrow is present. Brokenness over sin brings repentance, which in turn yields the gift of salvation. These are some of the fruits of revival and how God heals individuals, families and nations.

THE COVENANT PROMISE

The covenant promise for revival found in 2 Chronicles 7:14 is based upon brokenness. It reads, "If My people, who are called by My name, will humble themselves and pray and seek My face and turn from their wicked ways, then will I hear from Heaven and will forgive their sin and will heal their land." This revival covenant contains four conditions for the people of God to fulfill and three responses from the LORD in answer to their obedience.

IF MY PEOPLE

The covenant begins with "If My people ..." Notice that revival is contingent upon the people of God, not the world. The church is either the obstacle to revival or the means by which it occurs. Billy Graham stated, "I believe that we can have revival anytime we meet God's conditions. I believe that God is true to His Word and that He will rain righteousness upon us if we meet His conditions" (Graham, 76-77).

Revival is the responsibility of every pastor and church leader. A primary part of the pastoral call entails leading the congregation and the community that God has entrusted to his care, towards a spiritual awakening. A revived pastor will produce a revived church, and a spiritually dead preacher can only build a spiritually dead congregation.

HUMILITY

The first condition for revival is humility. As stated earlier, brokenness and humility are inseparable. Without these two character traits none of the other conditions in 2 Chronicles 7:14 can be fulfilled. This is why brokenness is so vitally important in the scheme of revival.

James and Peter instructed Christians that, "God resists the proud, but gives grace to the humble" (Jam. 4:6b; 1 Pet. 5:5). The Greek word for resists presents the idea that God actively opposes the proud. Pride literally puts us at odds with Him so we are found fighting against the Almighty. William Gurnall revealed the destructiveness of pride when he wrote: "Pride was the sin that turned Satan, a blessed angel, into a cursed devil. Satan knows better than anyone the damning power of pride. Is it any wonder, then, that he so often uses it to poison the saints? His design is made easier in that man's heart shows a natural fondness for it. Pride, like liquor, is intoxicating. A swallow or two usually leaves a man worthless to God" (Gallagher, 47). Through brokenness and humility we find freedom from pride's destructiveness.

The LORD announced that He dwells with those who are lowly (humble) and contrite (broken). "For this is what the high and lofty One says–He who lives forever, whose name is Holy: 'I live in a high and holy place, but also with him who is contrite and lowly in spirit, to revive the spirit of the lowly and to revive the heart of the contrite'" (Isa. 57:15). Pride is thoroughly repulsive to a holy God who walked this earth as the meek and lowly Jesus. Pride stops men from repenting, surrendering their lives to Jesus and impedes Christians from compassionately touching a world in rebellion against their Creator.

Revival is kept from the land because pride is so thoroughly evil that it grieves the Holy Spirit. The Australian Renewal Fellowship in Brisbane organized a conference on revival during the 1992 Pentecost weekend. They decided to invite some of the aboriginal leaders of the Elcho Islands who were experiencing a powerful revival. The Aborigines ministered with the authority of the Holy Spirit and in the meekness characteristic of them. After the conference was over, the Aborigines were asked why the Spirit was sweeping through their people, but passing by the white churches. They humbly replied, "You are too proud" (Waugh, 88-89). Our self-exaltation is so ugly it literally keeps God from rending the heavens.

Pride is actually the belief in a lie! The lies of pride are exhibited in countless ways. From those who think they are better than others, to those who do not consider themselves sinners. The painful truth is that Jesus will not come in mercy to the arrogant. Pride and self-will are the fruits of rebellion that damns the unsaved to Hell and makes Christians ineffective in the purposes of God. Only the broken and humble will know the LORD's reviving power.

PRAYER

Prayer is the next condition for revival. Without impassioned prayer there can be no spiritual awakening. True prayer flows out of brokenness. This is not the recitation of cold, formal prayers, but those that come from hearts ablaze for the Savior. "We cannot live in the flesh and pray in the Spirit" (Maxwell, 119). Pride has no place in true prayer because God resists the prayers of the proud. Tozer declared, "Unless we intend to reform we may as well not pray. Unless praying men have the insight and the faith to amend their whole way of life to conform to the New Testament pattern there can be no true revival" (Tozer, *Keys*, 23).

When we understand the depth of our neediness, and of those around us, we will passionately petition God to pour out His mercy. Christians will move Heaven to shake earth when they comprehend the terrifying truth that the world is at war with their Creator and much of the church is estranged from God. Broken saints have come to understand their helplessness to change themselves or a perishing world. However, they are convinced that the Almighty super-abounds with the power and desire to transform lives and nations, so they live lives of prayer.

SEEK HIS FACE

The third condition of revival listed in our selected text is to seek the face of God. Prayer and seeking God's face are two distinctly different things. A Christian may pray and never know what it means to seek God's face. Seeking His face comes out of a burning desire to know the LORD in intimate fellowship. This is the result of an intense hungering after the LORD Himself, not after His blessings. As the psalmist wrote, "My soul yearns, even faints, for the courts of the LORD; my heart and my flesh cry out for the living God" (Ps. 84:2).

Prayer is necessary for a Christian's survival and maturity, but seeking God's face is the prize. Saints who have been broken of their self-centeredness become people who passionately pursue this greatest of treasures. They are driven to know their Savior. This is far more than seeking greater Bible knowledge; it is a quest for God Himself, for His heart.

People who seek God's face love Jesus more than they love themselves, family or friends. With reckless abandon they seek to know Christ in an ever-increasing manner. They have tasted of His glory and refuse to return to the mediocrity of nominal

Christianity or the vanity of worldly pursuits. Here is the place of holy desperation where one experiences an aching for God so deep and beautiful that they cry out as Moses did, "Show me Your glory" (Ex. 33:18). This is the heart and passion that births revival.

Repentance has no place in Heaven because wickedness is absent from its borders. Pride will never be found there since humility clothes its residents. There is no need of prayer as we understand it, for the redeemed speak face to face with Jesus, but to seek God's face is an eternal act, a privilege beyond comprehension that we can begin right now. This is what we were created for.

TURN

The final condition for revival as outlined in 2 Chronicles 7:14 is to turn from our wicked ways. To turn from our wicked ways is another term for repentance. A man will not turn from his sin until he has first humbled himself before God. And a man will not humble himself before God until he has been broken, until he has been brought to the end of his self-life.

The scribes and Pharisees attempted to turn from their wicked ways without first surrendering and humbling themselves before the LORD. They concentrated upon being morally correct with God rather than being relationally right with Him. They failed on both accounts.

The most powerful motivating force to turn from our wicked ways is a passionate love for Jesus. Prayer and seeking God's face is the means by which we receive all the power and desire needed to walk holy before the LORD. This is God's established plan for victory.

GOD'S RESPONSE

When the church has fulfilled her responsibility to this covenant promise God will freely carry out His part. First of all, He will hear our prayers when they are offered out of brokenness. He is moved when people wholeheartedly seek His face. Secondly, when we turn from our sin to draw near to God He will forgive our sins. Finally, the LORD promised that He would heal the land. God's plan for healing a land is through saving individuals. Revival accomplishes this in mass. Jesus heals the sin sick soul and sets the heart ablaze with a new love. Then He heals broken families which in turn transforms cities and then nations; all through the power of His presence.

God has not healed our land because we have broken covenant with Him. We have not changed the world, the world has changed us. All the while Jesus stands outside of the church, knocking at her door, calling her to wholeheartedly return to Him and fulfill her covenant vows (Rev. 3:20). The LORD will withhold His manifest presence until we meet the conditions of revival.

The prize to be won is Jesus Himself and the revelation of His glory among men. Nothing in all of creation compares to the boundless wealth of knowing how "wide and long and high and deep is the love of Christ" (Eph. 3:18). Jesus longs for us to know the gift of brokenness so that "times of refreshing may come from the LORD" (Acts 3:19). He "is attracted to weakness. He can't resist those who humbly and honestly admit how desperately they need Him" (Cymbala, 19).

Every issue that follows in this book begins and ends with surrendered wills that know the beauty of brokenness. Revival flows out of brokenness and surrendered lives. Repentance is an act of surrender, while salvation is the gift of God to those who have become living sacrifices. Holiness is the result of Christians yielding to the sanctifying work of the Holy Spirit. And only surrendered saints will rescue a perishing world.

CHAPTER SEVEN

REPENTANCE: THE GIFT OF GOD

Heartfelt repentance is a gift from God. It is a constant reality of every true revival. Sin is the great separator between God and man, repentance the great restorer. The Biblical message of repentance is the sword of the Spirit that brings salvation to the lost, maturity to the saints and hope for a Heaven-sent revival.

When revival falls from Heaven, the Spirit breaks into the lives of people in supernatural ways. He does this to accomplish the twofold work of repentance—turning men to God as they turn away from their sin. David Brainerd saw revival touch the Native Americans during the 1740s in the whole region of Susquehanna in Pennsylvania and in New Jersey. After one account Brainerd wrote, "The power of God seemed to descend upon the assembly 'like a rushing, mighty wind' and with astonishing energy bore down on all before it. I stood amazed at the influence that seized the audience almost universally and could compare it to nothing more aptly than the irresistible force of a mighty torrent ... Almost all persons of all ages were bowed down with concern together, and scarce one was able to withstand the shock of this surprising operation. Old men and women who had been drunken wretches for many years, and some little children not more than six or seven years of age, appeared in distress for their souls, as well as persons of middle age" (Brainerd, 379). During seasons of revival the Holy Spirit is manifested in remarkable ways to bring the gift of repentance to sleeping saints and to a perishing world.

DIGNITY AND DEPRAVITY

The Genesis account of Adam's creation and his willful sin reveals the dignity and depravity of mankind. In all of creation, only the human race was formed by the Creator's own hands in His own image. This bestows upon humanity an immense privilege, dignity and responsibility. God created mankind to walk with Him in intimate fellowship. Originally, Adam and Eve were predisposed to live holy. God's gift of a free will empowered them to choose either to keep His law or to break it.

The history of Adam and Eve's fall (Gen. 3:1-24) was meant to be literally interpreted as an authentic historical event. Their once perfect character, corrupted by sin, perverted their original dignity. Sin, guilt, shame and the desire to hide from God's presence are some of the repercussions of their purposeful act of rebellion. The unbelief and disobedience of our first parents brought misery and ruin upon themselves and on all their descendants. Now a universal depravity touches all of mankind. Both the Scriptures, and life itself, clearly reveals that every person sins. We become responsible to a holy God for our sins as soon as we are capable of moral actions (Rom. 1-3).

Adam's deliberate act of breaking God's law changed his original character of holiness to one of sin and rebellion. This produced a predisposition in him to sin that has been passed down to his entire progeny. Spiritual, physical and relational death is the wages sin pays. Jesus is the only remedy to Adam's fall. The Savior stated that a man must be born again to enter the Kingdom of God (Jn. 3:3). Through Christ alone can we be forgiven of our sins and find victory over the power of sin. The Author of Life imparts new life to the penitent sinner and begins restoring the dignity that was marred through the deceitfulness of sin by transforming the fallen character.

WHAT IS REPENTANCE?

By nature, by choice, and by character, every person is a sinner. Yes, even Christians. What is a sinner? A sinner is a person who sins. Sin is the transgression or breaking of God's law. "Everyone who sins breaks the law; in fact, sin is lawlessness" (1 Jn. 3:4). The unsaved practice their sin; true Christians strive to live free from it. God's call to turn from our sin is His goodness and love revealed.

The Bible is a book of repentance. Its primary focus is that the Father sent the Son to save sinners. The Old Testament looks forward to the coming Messiah while the New Testament is His self-disclosure. Together they comprise the history of redemption that teaches us how to walk in fellowship with a holy God through a lifestyle of repentance.

The Christian life both begins, and is sustained, through repentance. A lifestyle of repentance means a person immediately repents of sin the moment he comprehends its presence, and will even turn from the questionable things. This is a refusal to allow sin to "reign in your mortal body so that you obey its evil desires" (Rom. 6:12). A lifestyle of repentance allows men to walk with God in unbroken fellowship—a privilege beyond imagination. Unbroken fellowship with the LORD is the right motive to live such a lifestyle.

In ancient Hebraic thought repentance meant returning to God. The most commonly used Old Testament word for repentance is *shubh*. It fundamentally means, "To sigh, groan, lament, or grieve over one's doings ... [It is] such a sorrow for sin as leads one to turn away from sin" (Wright, 1). It is a radical change of one's attitude towards sin and God. *Shubh* incorporates the conscious moral decision to forsake sin in thought, word and deed and to enter into fellowship with the LORD.

There are three Greek words used in the New Testament that signifies repentance. The first is the verb, *metamelomai*, which indicates a change of mind, but not necessarily a change of heart. Judas, who betrayed Jesus "repented," or was remorseful, but did not change the direction of his life (Mt. 27:3). The verb *metanoeo*, along with the cognate noun *metanoia* are used of a true act of repentance that brings about a change of mind and purpose of life. "Repentance is a full-blooded, wholehearted, uncompromising renunciation of one's former attitude and outlook. It is a change of heart that always results in a change of course" (Wallis, 53).

God's call to repentance is a call to intimacy. "I love you child" is the Spirit's plea, "and I want to come close to you, but your sin is keeping Me from demonstrating My love to you. It is time to get the sin out." God's love is openly displayed through Calvary, which is nothing other than a call to repentance. Jesus did not come into the world to condemn it, but to save it through His tender mercies. "He is patient with you, not wanting anyone to perish, but everyone to come to repentance" (2 Pet. 3:9).

The convicting power of the Holy Ghost is NEVER, absolutely NEVER, a negative work. For the sinner to feel shame for his sin is a gift from God. Paul asked, "Or do you show contempt for the riches of His kindness, tolerance and patience, not realizing that God's kindness (goodness, KJV) leads you toward repentance?" (Rom. 2:4). To shun the Savior's call to repentance shows contempt for His kindness. To bring sinners to contrition is the kindness or goodness of God revealed. The message of repentance is the Biblical message of God's love to sinful humanity.

THE PREACHING OF THE CROSS

The preaching of the cross is the victorious message of repentance. Through the message of repentance people enter into relationship with the Living God, mature as disciples and by means of it revival can come. David Brainerd was a preacher of the cross. His first audience in Susquehanna was a few women and children. When the Spirit descended, men and women came from all over the region. With intense earnestness they pressed upon the missionary to hear the message of salvation.

Strong, brave men fell at Brainerd's "feet in anguish of soul." The Spirit pierced their hearts with His arrows of conviction. Their consuming cry became, "Lord, have mercy on me!" Brainerd was deeply moved by their passionate repentance. "The woods were filled with the sound of great mourning, and beneath the Cross every man fell as if he and the Saviour God alone were there. Gradually as the missionary spoke, there came to them, one by one, the peace and comfort of the Gospel" (Shearer, 37-38). The preaching of the cross can bring with it an overwhelming conviction of sin—this is the love of God revealed. Deep conviction that brings profound repentance yields the fruits of radical conversions.

When the preaching of the cross is neglected, or forsaken, men cannot be saved or delivered from sin. H. Richard Niebuhr lambasted liberal Christianity because they believed in "a God without wrath [who] brought men without sin into a kingdom without judgment through the ministrations of a Christ without a cross" (Dixon, 22). This old version of compromise has taken on a new face. Many churches desiring to present a "positive" message have removed anything that is offensive from their services. This crossless gospel of cheap grace has removed the Biblical Jesus, who is both a wonderful Savior and an "A stone of stumbling and a rock of offense" (1 Pet. 2:8; NKJV). Such marketing techniques may generate large gatherings on Sunday mornings but is powerless in building Christ's spiritual Kingdom.

It has become extremely popular in America to preach the positive messages of easy-believism that lulls people into a deathly spiritual sleep or that feeds the lusts of the flesh. Andrew Murray said, "It is comparatively easy to win people to a cross, but to a cross that leaves them uncrucified. Oh, beware of the cross that leaves you uncrucified" (Campbell, *Fire*). Duncan Campbell warned us in a sermon, "I dare not compromise in order to accommodate the world, the flesh or the devil. But see the tendency today is to do that. I want to say dear people; tolerance at the expense of conviction and righteousness is just playing into the hands of the enemy" (Campbell, *God's Answer*).

Churches that do not preach the cross are like fish deprived of water—death is guaranteed. They are nothing more than community centers filled with self-help programs. Paul stated, "The preaching of the cross is to them that perish foolishness; but unto us which are saved it is the power of God" (1 Cor. 1:18; KJV). There can be no revival apart from the preaching of the cross because the cross is the centerpiece of Christianity. Christ's death was God's redemptive mission to bring humanity to salvation and His resurrection the power that guaranteed our victory. The same cross that reveals our tremendous guilt offers our only hope.

THE PROBLEM OF UNREPENTANT HEARTS

To reject the preaching of repentance is to reject the Christ of the cross. The deceitfulness of sin, and the desire for a comfortable "Christianity," can make the preaching of the cross an unwelcome message. Yet, "No man can rightly value the redemption of Christ who has not seen himself lost and undone and absolutely without hope outside of the atonement" (Shaw, 7).

The Scriptures emphatically warn us not to harden our hearts, "as the Holy Spirit says: 'Today, if you hear His voice, do not harden your hearts as you did in the rebellion, during the time of testing in the desert'" (Heb. 3:7-8). Hard hearts are unrepentant hearts. The Hebrew writer forewarned the church that she could harden her heart just as Israel did and suffer similar consequences.

The Christians at Laodicea had hardened their hearts, so Jesus rebuked them saying, "You say, 'I am rich; I have acquired wealth and do not need a thing.' But you do not realize that you are wretched, pitiful, poor, blind and naked" (Rev. 3:17). Only a good God would warn a backslidden people of their dangerous situation. The LORD declared, "As many as I love, I rebuke and chasten. Therefore be zealous and repent" (Rev. 3:19; NKJV). This call to repentance was an act of divine compassion.

Hearts grow hard and reject the preaching of the cross when Christians think they have moved beyond the need of repentance. When some believers refused to repent during the 1950s Belgian Congo Revival they grieved the Holy Spirit. "One woman standing up with her arms upraised and her face radiant, talking about wheels within wheels and eyes within the wheels and patterns and above it all a great rainbow. It was straight out of Ezekiel. She spoke of the glory and began weeping when she said she saw the glory was in the midst of the Bible School and then it went out of the hall, across the courtyard and into the forest. She broke down, crying, 'It is because of our sin, our sin!'" (Roseveare, 2). The glory left when they ceased to respond to the call for repentance.

SELF-RIGHTEOUSNESS

One consequence of an unrepentant heart is self-righteousness. This is the spiritual condition in which people think they are right with God based on their moral goodness. You could think of it as salvation through moral living. Solomon forewarned us saying, "There is a generation that are pure in their own eyes, and yet is not washed from their filthiness" (Pr. 30:12; KJV). Whenever Christians forget they are sinners saved by grace they reject the preaching of the cross and ignore the guilt that accompanies the conviction of sin.

Multitudes of churchgoers think they are right with God because they have "accepted Christ" (but are they accepted by Him?), speak in tongues, or belong to a particular church. Trust, foolishly placed in moral goodness, water baptism, or a prayer once uttered but not lived out, puts people in a perilous position with eternal consequences.

Self-righteousness is the most hideous form of pride known to mankind. The LORD declared, "I have listened attentively, but they do not say what is right. No one repents of his wickedness, saying, 'What have I done?' Each pursues his own course like a horse charging into battle" (Jer. 8:6). The heart of self-righteousness is seen in the statement, "What have I done?" We are prone to view ourselves as innocent people. However, there is no such thing as an innocent sinner. Augustine stated that we must be so reduced in our own eyes "as to have nothing to present before God but 'our wretchedness and His mercy.' We are so wretched in our sinfulness that nothing else can ever save us except His mercy. But thank God, His mercy is all we need!" (Fenelon, 47).

Jesus dealt severely with the self-righteous. "For John came to you to show you the way of righteousness, and you did not believe him, but the tax collectors and the prostitutes did. And even after you saw this, you did not repent and believe him" (Mt. 21:32). Seven times in Matthew 23 Jesus pronounced, "Woe to you" against the self-righteous. This was a prophetic proclamation of doom from the lips of the Messiah. A stark contrast is seen between Christ's judgment of woe against the self-righteous and His compassion to rescue the worst of society. He said, "For I did not come to call the righteous, but sinners, to repentance" (Mt. 9:13; NKJV).

The religious Pharisees of Christ's day typifies the self-righteous in our own. This spiritual state blinds people to their true condition before God and causes them to reject the Biblical word that "all our righteous acts are like filthy rags" (Isa. 64:6). If our righteous acts are like filthy rags before a holy God then what is our wickedness like to Him? We need to see ourselves as sinners and take the way of repentance. Charles Spurgeon understood the place of victory over sin and self-righteousness when he admitted, "I find that my sweetest, happiest, safest state is that of a poor, guilty, helpless sinner calling upon the name of the LORD and taking mercy from His hands, although I deserve nothing but His wrath" (Spurgeon, *Praying* 75-76).

The lies that we are "good people" must be torn down before revival can come. Roy Hession stated, "The breaking in of the truth about ourselves and about God, and the shattering of the illusion in which we have been living, is the beginning of revival for the Christian as it is of salvation for the lost. We cannot begin to see the grace of God in the face of Jesus Christ until we have seen the truth about ourselves and given a full answer to all its challenge ... The result is that we have lost sight of things as they really are, and are now living in a realm of complete illusion about ourselves" (Hession, *We Would*, 31-32). Shattering the illusion is as simple as looking in a mirror and seeing the reality of our spiritual situation. Otherwise, we remain spiritually blind to our sin and will reap the sorrow sin produces.

REPENTANCE BRINGS REVIVAL

Repentance and revival are radical and inseparable. Revival is God breaking into human history, upsetting lives and earthly kingdoms by transforming all who will repent. James Burns illustrated this well, "To the church, a revival means humiliation, a bitter knowledge of unworthiness and an open humiliating confession of sin on the part of her ministers and people. It is not the easy and glorious thing many think it to be, who imagine it fills the pews and reinstates the church in power and authority. It comes to scorch before it heals; it comes to condemn ministers and people for their unfaithful witness, for their selfish living, for their neglect of the cross, and to call them to daily renunciation, to evangelical poverty and to a deep and daily consecration. That is why a revival has ever been unpopular with large numbers within the church. Because it says nothing to them of power such as they have learned to love, or of ease, or of success; it accuses them of sin; it tells them they are dead; it calls them to awake, to renounce the world and to follow Christ" (Pratney, 21). Revival brings with it the wondrous joy of forgiveness only after people have dealt with the heart wrenching reality of their sin.

During the Second Great Awakening, Charles Finney witnessed the overwhelming conviction that occurs when God rends the heavens. One account came out of a village near Antwerp, New York. "I had not spoken to them ... more than a quarter of an hour, when all at once an awful solemnity seemed to settle down upon them; the congregation began to fall from their seats in every direction, and cried for mercy. If I had had a sword in each hand, I could not have cut them off their seats as fast as they fell. Indeed nearly the whole congregation were either on their knees or prostrate, I should think, in less than two minutes from this first shock that fell upon them. Every one prayed for himself, who was able to speak at all. Of course I was obliged to stop preaching; for they no longer paid any attention" (Finney, *Autobiography*, 104). Spirit-empowered conviction compels sinners to flee into the loving arms of Jesus. This is the miracle of repentance—to take rebels at war with the LORD of Hosts and turn them into sons and daughters of the King.

A national awakening came in the days of Ezra when he led the people into brokenness, and repentance. Ezra prayed:

"O my God, I am too ashamed and disgraced to lift up my face to You, my God, because our sins are higher than our heads and our guilt has reached to the heavens. From the days of our forefathers until now, our guilt has been great. Because of our sins, we and our kings and our priests have been subjected to the sword and captivity, to pillage and humiliation at the hand of foreign kings, as it is today" (Ezra 9:6-7).

Such prayers of confession are an integral part of revival. Ezra had a healthy understanding of his sin, the spiritual condition of the people and of a God whose mercies are new every morning. As a result, he prayed according to the truth that would move Heaven to shake earth.

East Africa saw revival for approximately forty years. When it finally came to the Belgian Congo they were overwhelmed with its earth-shaking power. It began with Christians dealing with the reality of their sin before the revival burst forth among non-believers. At the Bible school in Ibambi the building actually shook. "It was seven o'clock on a Friday night. Jack Scholes, our field leader, had just come back from a trip in the south and he had seen revival down there. He stood up to speak about the revival and started to read from Scriptures. Suddenly we heard a hurricane storm. It was frightening!

"None of us stopped to think that this was strange because you don't get hurricane storms in July (we have them in February or March). We heard this hurricane coming and the elders began to take the shutters down ... We looked out and it was moonlight and the palm trees were standing absolutely still against the moonlit sky ... Then the building shook and the storm lanterns down the center of the building moved around. There was a terrific noise and a sense of external power around. We were all frightened—there must have been about five whites and 95 Africans present. You could sense fear all around.

"Jack stood at the front and said to us—'This is God, just pray—don't fear and don't interfere.' It was as if a force came in and we were shaking. There was no way you could control it and some were thrown to the ground off the benches as if someone had hurled them down! But no one was hurt. Everyone ceased to be conscious of anyone else.

"People began to confess publicly what you might call 'big sin' (and those were all Christians). They spoke of adultery, cheating, stealing, deceit... We didn't leave the hall that whole weekend! Most of the time God was dealing with our sins. Some needed help from the pastors who moved around with much wisdom and encouragement. Then joy struck the repentant sinners" (Roseveare, 1-2).

How could a people remain the same after encountering the Living God in such a manner? Saints who have experienced the manifest presence of God will ache to see His glory again and again until their dying day. With passion they will live a lifestyle of repentance so they may see Him rend the heavens once more.

CHAPTER EIGHT

PASSION FOR HOLINESS

When the LORD rends the heavens He unveils to mortal men the beauty of His holiness. That is why genuine revival always advances Biblical holiness. The holiness of God can be terrifying to sinful man. Yet for those who yearn to know the Holy One, it becomes beautifully attractive. A passion for holiness burns in those who long to be near the Lover of their souls.

Only the LORD Almighty is holy in and of Himself (Rev. 15:4). The Scriptures teach that people, objects, animals or certain days can be holy, but only in accordance to their relationship with God. Holiness, as it relates to mankind, is a twofold work. First of all, it is an act of the Savior whereby He makes a repentant sinner holy. Secondly, it is the pursuit of the believer to live holy through divine grace.

The second point consists of two parts as well. It begins with consecration unto God. Consecration is the devotion, or act of setting oneself apart, to the worship and service of the LORD. That is followed by the separation from what is sinful and common (worldly). The primary point of holiness is being separated unto God through intimate fellowship. This both allows us and empowers us to live separated from what is worldly and sinful.

Isaiah 35 prophetically revealed the splendor of Christianity more than 700 years before the church was born. It would be a time where the feeble find strength, the fearful are made strong, the sick are healed and judgment is executed. "And a highway will be there; it will be called the Way of Holiness. The unclean will not journey on it; it will be for those who walk in that Way; wicked fools will not go about on it" (Isa. 35:8).

To walk on the Highway of Holiness is a privilege. The impenitent will not be allowed to travel that road, for it is a royal road prepared for the King of kings and open only to His loyal subjects. This means that holiness is mandatory for every citizen of Christ's Kingdom. As the Hebrew writer taught, "Make every effort ... to be holy; without holiness no one will see the LORD" (Heb. 12:14). This is why the Scriptures command us to produce "fruit in keeping with repentance" (Mt. 3:8).

This highway is also the way for revival to come. Before we can examine holiness as it relates to revival we must first look at the holiness of God and the holiness required of every Christian.

THE HOLINESS OF GOD

The LORD God is infinitely holy! His character is holy, His actions are holy, His thoughts are holy, His words are holy, His justice is holy and He is the epitome of holiness. The holiness of God is so far beyond human comprehension that language miserably fails to adequately convey these truths. The infinite holiness of God may be the hardest thing for finite minds to grasp and explain. Nevertheless, we are called to know Him who "surpasses knowledge" (Eph. 3:19).

Two dimensions of God's holiness need to be mentioned: the LORD is absolutely pure and He is absolutely separate. God's absolute purity means that He is free from any form of corruption, fault or error; free from any outside influence that affects His nature and character; free from any need outside of Himself. The LORD remains perfectly consistent and uniform in being. "I the LORD do not change. So you, O descendants of Jacob, are not destroyed" (Mal. 3:6).

The LORD's purity also speaks of His ethical, or moral perfection. "Your eyes are too pure to look on evil; You cannot tolerate wrong" (Hab. 1:13). Whatever God does He remains true to His moral perfection. His justice is based upon His infinite ethical qualities and limitless knowledge. He makes no mistakes. His moral perfection is actually who He is, not something He does.

He never sinned, and even more than that, evil is totally absent from His being.

Secondly, the Almighty is absolutely separate and unique from His creation, including humanity (Isa. 37:16). There is no comparison between the Great I Am and man. The Creator is so far superior to His creation that our finite minds cannot fathom the distance. Not just that, He will always be totally other, separate and unique from His creation. Yet, He has made Himself touchable. Mankind will never become gods as Mormonism, New Age and Eastern religions assert. Besides such beliefs being thoroughly unbiblical, they are completely illogical.

The LORD created mankind in His own image. This means that God imparted to humanity only those attributes of His that are communicable (able to be transmitted or shared). We are privileged to share in His moral attributes such as love, kindness, and mercy. Mankind will never share in God's non-communicable attributes as omnipotence, omniscience, omnipresence, etc., which will always be unique to Him.

Those beautiful God-given attributes of love, kindness, mercy, etc. have been perverted through selfishness, lust and pride. Sin has distorted our ability to accurately perceive our spiritual condition and to correctly comprehend the character of the LORD. This is why we have such a difficult time grasping the perfection of His attributes. Nevertheless, God can open our eyes to His wonder and to our great need.

HOLINESS IN RELATION TO MAN

An unholy man is made holy only by a divine act. That person is then separated unto God for the purposes of God. When a person is truly separated unto the LORD, he will automatically be set apart from what is sinful and common. It is impossible for a person to be made holy by God and not be set apart from the sinful and worldly. Holiness and sin do not mix.

Scripture emphatically demands that His people reflect His ethical nature. The Pentateuch (first five books of the Bible) contains both ethical and ceremonial commands for holiness. The Psalms and the Prophets speak primarily of ethical holiness. The New Testament incorporates the ethical ideals of the Old Testament while adding the spiritual dimension of the heart. Holiness consists of moral purity and being separated from the love of this world unto the Savior. The LORD is calling His church (church means "called out ones") to be holy because He is holy. Through relationship with Him we begin to reflect His holy nature.

Holiness comes only through relationship with God. "Be imitators of God, therefore, as dearly loved children and live a life of love, just as Christ loved us and gave Himself up for us as a fragrant offering and sacrifice to God. But among you there must not be even a hint of sexual immorality, or of any kind of impurity, or of greed, because these are improper for God's holy people" (Eph. 5:1-3). To be holy we must fix our eyes on Jesus and draw near to the only One who is holy. As dearly loved children we must imitate Him as a child mimics every word and movement of his father.

SANCTIFICATION

The act of making a person holy is called sanctification and can be understood in two ways. First of all, a person is sanctified, or made holy by a judicial act of God alone. In other words, a man can receive a pardon for all the crimes he has committed because he begged for mercy. Salvation is solely the gift of God freely offered to undeserving sinners. The LORD imputes, or accredits His holiness to a person according to his faith. The moment a person surrenders his life to Christ he is made holy by God. The person then becomes the cherished possession of the LORD and is separated (sanctified) unto Him for His good pleasure. God responds to the repentant by cleansing him from sin through Christ's atoning sacrifice and then accredits him with the Savior's own righteousness. Paul said, "we have BEEN made holy" (Heb. 10:10).

Secondly, God commands those He has made holy to live in moral holiness. This speaks of a lifestyle that pursues holiness in an ever-increasing manner, also referred to as the progressive work of sanctification. True Christians have been separated unto God and must now live separated lives from what is sinful and worldly. "By one sacrifice He has made perfect forever those who are BEING made holy" (Heb. 10:14).

Day by day we should be developing in holiness by sinning less in thought, word and deed. There is no place for stagnation in Christ's Kingdom. If you are not more holy today than a year ago it is probably because you have grown lukewarm. Since God commanded us to be holy He is able and willing to empower us to live holy if we surrender all to Him. The LORD will never command us to do that which He will not empower us to fulfill.

Our natural propensity to sin keeps us in need of living a lifestyle of repentance and holiness until our dying day. We must never use our fallen nature as an excuse to sin since sin is always a willful act. There is power to overcome sin through the risen Savior.

NEED OF HOLINESS

Three ministers were among the crowd of people who responded to the evangelist's altar call. The first man held a Ph.D. in psychology and was the worship leader at a large Pentecostal church. He was an active homosexual. The second man was a youth pastor who was sleeping with his girlfriend. The last man was also a youth pastor who was living in sexual sin, but did not divulge his immoral practices. All these leaders were in brazen sin. The Apostle John plainly taught that if we practice sin we do not know Him (1 Jn. 3:4-10). Either these men were never truly converted or were blatantly backslid.

These three ministers claimed they were Christians even though they lived in outright rebellion against the Just Judge. They turned the precious grace of God into a cheap, vile thing by justifying their practice of sin while claiming to "live by grace." This cheap grace leaves the sinner in his sin because it is powerless to transform the person. People who live such lies have a perverted understanding of God's love, grace, holiness and justice. They think sin is not exceedingly wicked because they have not seen the LORD as absolutely holy.

The LORD's transforming power flows through repentance. Proof of salvation is manifested through a change in lifestyle and character. If there is not a transformed character then salvation has not come to the person! When personal growth in holiness cannot be found it is because the person is not in a right relationship with the Savior. Paul wrote, "I preached that they should repent and turn to God and prove their repentance by their deeds" (Acts 26:20). Genuine repentance will always produce a holy lifestyle. *Always!*

HOLINESS THROUGH INTIMACY

Holiness and revival are indivisible. Revival begins with the dreadful conviction of sin. At times the experience is overwhelming—men are convulsed under the weight of their wickedness, people weep uncontrollably, confession of sin and restitution become common. This is the goodness of God revealed. Men, women and children finally discern their true spiritual condition and mourn over their transgressions. Revival produces tears of conviction and the fruit of repentance yields holy lives. Anything else is not revival!

America's First Great Awakening changed the nation as the fires of revival burned the sin out and kindled the flames of holiness. After a sermon in Lyme, Connecticut, "many had their countenances changed; their thoughts seemed to trouble them, so that the joints of their loins were loosed, and their knees smote one against another. Great numbers cried out aloud in the anguish of their souls. Several stout men fell as though a cannon had been discharged, and the ball had made its way through their hearts" ... People had to be carried from the meeting house (America's *Great Revivals*, 19). Those terrified by their sin after encountering the Holy Spirit and repenting of their rebellion against a holy God will not quickly turn their backs on Him. Yet, the terror of sin is not enough to make a person want to live a holy life. The sinner must see his sin in light of a Savior who loved him and paid the penalty for his crimes so he might be forgiven.

The Scriptural concept of being born again implies new relationship. One cannot be born again and remain in the old lifestyle of the past just as a baby cannot be born and remain in the mother's womb. A new life is born and proved by the new relationship. Love for God is the most powerful remedy for sin. When sin enters the life love will drive it out with ferocious abandon. As Spurgeon emphatically stated, "I cannot trifle with the evil that killed my best friend [Jesus]. I must be holy for His sake. How can I live in sin when He has died to save me from it?" (Spurgeon, *My Conversion*, 15).

It is impossible for any human to overcome sin through his own ability. If we were able to conquer sin through our own strength then Christ died in vain. Jonathan Edwards struggled with this issue. He desired to be holy, but found he was unable to attain holiness through his own strength. Edwards said he pursued holiness, "with far greater diligence and earnestness than ever I pursued anything in my life, but yet with too great a dependence on my own strength, which afterwards proved a great damage to me. My experience had not taught me, as it has done since, my extreme feebleness and impotence, every manner of way; and the bottomless depths of secret corruption and deceit there was in my heart" (Edwards, *Memoirs*, 10). Such truths are painful, but life changing. When Edwards finally panted after the Savior, he abandoned himself to the LORD. He later wrote, "What a sweet calmness, what a calm ecstasy doth it [holiness] bring to my soul! ... there is no such near or intimate conversation between any other lovers as between Christ and the Christian" (Iain Murray, 46).

Edwards further revealed the joy of holiness that he found through intimate fellowship with Christ when he stated, "Heaven appeared exceedingly delightful, as a world of love; and that all happiness consisted in living in pure, humble, heavenly, divine love ... [Holiness] appeared to me to be of a sweet, pleasant, charming, serene, calm nature; which brought an inexpressible purity, brightness, peacefulness, and ravishment to the soul" (Edwards, *Memoirs*, 11). When a person desires Jesus more than his love of self and sin he will know the wonder of Christ's tender mercies and the power of holiness that flows with life-giving force.

ALIENS IN A STRANGE LAND

Holiness is a lifestyle! It is not subject to popular opinion, the dictates of government or enslaved to the whims of situational ethics. The Eternal Law Giver alone as revealed in the Scriptures defines the standards and authority for holiness. Love for God is the ultimate motivator for holiness. Compassion for the lost should further compel us to be holy so we can be living epistles that proclaim the life-changing power of a risen Savior.

As stated earlier, holiness is being separated unto God and separated from what is worldly and sinful. The LORD created mankind to be His precious possession, to be a holy community of faith so we could glorify and enjoy Him forevermore. Only as a separated community unto the LORD can we fulfill His purpose for our lives. Without a spiritually healthy body of believers, we follow the world and copy its ways.

The idea of being a separated community scares many people because of past abuses or misunderstanding. The accusations of being prejudiced, closed minded, and self-righteous have intimidated vast numbers of people. Nonetheless, the very nature of holiness demands that we live separated lives from the world no matter what the world, or other Christians, may think. The reason many do not live such lives is because they are more comfortable with compromise and worldliness than with holiness. The church has gone about "congratulating itself for transforming the world, not noticing, that in fact the world had tamed the church" (Hauerwas, 41).

The LORD commanded Israel to be a separated people so they could discern between the holy and unholy (Lev. 24:24-26). The same standard applies to the church. The church's "most credible form of witness (and most 'effective' thing it can do for the world) is the actual creation of a living, breathing, visible community of faith" (Hauerwas, 47). For there to be a vibrant community of faith there must first be a fully separated people unto God for the purposes of God. We are not called to be cloistered in a closed community, for what value is a community no one can see, be touched by, or become a part of? Those who hold to such a view, whether theologically or applicationally, have not truly separated themselves unto Christ.

Abraham was constantly pressing towards an eternal country since his citizenship was not of this world, but in Heaven (Heb. 11:8-16). He was on a lifelong pilgrimage to an eternal city and held everything in this life loosely because he lived unattached to this world. The psalmist tells us, "Blessed are those whose strength is in You, who have set their hearts on pilgrimage" (Ps. 84:5). This is the nature of Biblical Christianity. Since "our citizenship is in Heaven" (Phil. 3:20), we are on a pilgrimage, living as aliens in this "present evil age." Aliens think, talk, smell, eat, dress and live differently than do the nationals. They live in tight social groups because they are different from everyone around them. Their entire spiritual and social lives revolve around their community.

For the church to be a community of faith, she must live as aliens in this world. We should think differently, talk differently, act differently, dress differently and live differently. Our lives should revolve around our relationship with Jesus and the community of faith. Since our citizenship is in Heaven, the laws of Heaven should define our lifestyle. "Everyone who has this hope in Him purifies himself, just as He is pure" (1 Jn. 3:3; NKJV).

The Christian community should be open for the entire world to see as a city set on a hill. It should be open for non-believers to enter if they will flee from the wrath to come by living in intimate, holy, fellowship with the Lamb of God and the community of faith. A holy church should always be pleading with an unholy world to come up to the high standards of Christ's Kingdom. She must never condescend to the world's standards to gain a following.

We need to ask the question, "Are we changing the world or is the world changing us?" The very idea of compromise should be appalling to Christians. Compromise is rebellion against the King of kings. When our lives are driven with the pursuits of this world we stop straining towards Heaven and the standards that define Christ's Kingdom. We then cease striving for personal holiness and stop living a lifestyle of repentance. We become earth-bound people instead of Heaven-bound saints.

Those who are true residents of Heaven seek a spiritual revolution that will usher in Christ's Kingdom. We are called to be aliens on a mission to overthrow Satan's kingdom by building the Kingdom of God in its stead. This is what revival literally does. One eyewitness of the Rochester Revival in New York (1831) testified, "The whole community was stirred. Grog (liquor) shops were closed; the Sabbath was honored; the sanctuaries were thronged with happy worshipers ... Even the courts and the prisons bore witness to [the] blessed effects. There was a wonderful falling off in crime. The courts had little to do, and the jail was nearly empty for years afterwards" (Cymbala, 115). Within one year, more than 100,000 fled from the kingdom of Hell into the Kingdom of Heaven.

Revival is the amplification of the Spirit's call for Christians to live holy lives as aliens in this world. It is also the Spirit's plea to the unsaved to ascend the pilgrim's path of repentance to gain access to the Highway of Holiness.

HOLINESS AND REVIVAL

John Huss (1374-1415) lived in this world as an alien. His love for God was greater than his love of sin and self. Fearlessly he advanced Christ's Kingdom and the self-righteous were enraged. The Catholic Church was threatened by this humble man of God, so they seized him and put him on trial. The presiding bishops declared him guilty of heresy. They degraded him and stripped him of his priestly garments. The bishops placed upon his head a paper miter that had devils painted upon it with the inscription, "A ringleader of heretics." When he saw the miter he said, "My Lord Jesus Christ, for my sake, did wear a crown of thorns; why should not I then, for His sake, wear this light crown, be it ever so ignominious? Truly I will do it, and that willingly."

Huss was condemned to death. They took him out to be burned at the stake. When the iron chains were tied about him at the stake he said with a smiling countenance, "My Lord Jesus Christ was bound with a harder chain than this for my sake, and why then should I be ashamed of this rusty one?"

They piled bundles of branches and brush up to his neck. The duke of Bavaria demanded that he recant. Huss boldly retorted, "No, I never preached any doctrine of an evil tendency; and what I taught with my lips I now seal with my blood." The fire was then set. Yet as the flames arose around the body of the martyr a hymn burst from his lips in a loud and cheerful voice. He was heard above the roar of the flames and the noise of the spectators (Foxe, 192-93).

Huss lived and died with the integrity that holiness brings. Though wicked men raged, they could not silence his voice, for holiness speaks louder than evil. John set his eyes unswervingly on Jesus and remained faithful to the end. Huss lived a victorious life of holiness that did not supply his Romish accusers with a single reason to execute him. Like Stephen of old, they were enraged at a man full of faith and full of the Holy Ghost. Huss was a man aspiring to please His master in everything he did. He became an instrument for revival in his day and even for generations following his death. As Robert Murray McCheyne observed, "A holy minister is an awful weapon in the hands of God" (Spurgeon, *Self-watch*, 3).

Holiness is power with God and power with men. The LORD is attracted to holy people. He imparts to holy people an authority to speak to secular society and an anointing to set captives free. Furthermore, only holy saints can be instruments for revival. Sin and compromise robs the church of her anointing, steals her authority, and silences her voice to speak to a rebellious world. Revival renews the church's authority and restores her voice. Brian Edwards noted, "Revival is always a revival of holiness. And it begins with a terrible conviction of sin ... Sometimes the experience is crushing. People weep uncontrollably, and worse! But there is no such thing as a revival without tears of conviction and sorrow ... In 1921, in the revival that began in the East Anglican fishing ports of Lowestoft and Great Yarmouth, strong fishermen were literally thrown to the floor under conviction, until one eyewitness reported: 'The ground around me was like a battlefield with the souls crying to God for mercy'" (Brown, *The End*, 90).

When God rends the heavens He shakes men to the depths of their being. Holiness becomes normal as worldliness is swept away through the flood of the Spirit. Greed, drunkenness, homosexuality, fornication, pornography and the rest of humanity's lewd sins are forever forsaken. Even the questionable things are deserted as men behold the beauty of God's holiness. The worst of society can be found at altars of repentance next to lifelong church attendees. Marriages are restored, daddies come home, and wives get their husbands back. When the King of kings descends on the Highway of Holiness, men and nations tremble and are transformed.

CHAPTER NINE

HOLINESS TO SEE GOD

The Scriptures abound with awe-inspiring accounts of the Almighty revealing Himself to frail humanity. Church history is also rich with divine encounters where the LORD pulled back the veil so mere mortals could behold His splendor. To gaze upon the Great I Am will utterly change us. Isaiah saw the LORD and shared with us his astounding experience.

"In the year that King Uzziah died, I saw the LORD seated on a throne, high and exalted, and the train of His robe filled the temple. Above Him were seraphs, each with six wings: With two wings they covered their faces, with two they covered their feet, and with two they were flying. And they were calling to one another: 'Holy, holy, holy is the LORD Almighty; the whole earth is full of His glory.' At the sound of their voices the doorposts and thresholds shook and the temple was filled with smoke. 'Woe to me!' I cried. 'I am ruined! For I am a man of unclean lips, and I live among a people of unclean lips, and my eyes have seen the King, the LORD Almighty.' Then one of the seraphs flew to me with a live coal in his hand, which he had taken with tongs from the altar. With it he touched my mouth and said, 'See, this has touched your lips; your guilt is taken away and your sin atoned for.' Then I heard the voice of the LORD saying, 'Whom shall I send? And who will go for us?' And I said, 'Here am I. Send me!' He said, 'Go and tell this people'" (Isa. 6:1-9a).

There are nine points concerning this theophany (divine manifestation) that will shed some essential light upon the subject of revival.

THE YEAR THAT KING UZZIAH DIED

The reign of King Uzziah is recorded in 2 Kings 15:1-8 and 2 Chronicles 26. He was the eleventh king of Judah, came to power around 783 B.C. at age sixteen and reigned for fifty-two years. Uzziah's military success extended Israel's borders to the entrance of Egypt. His wise domestic policies built up their defenses and infrastructure.

Zechariah was the king's godly counselor who helped him walk upright before the LORD. When the king was about forty years old Zechariah died and his influence passed away with him. Uzziah began envying some of the pagan priest-kings that defined many eastern monarchies. One day he entered Solomon's temple to perform the duties that were only lawful for a priest. The Mosaic Law limited these responsibilities to the tribe of Levi and specifically to the lineage of Aaron. This unlawful and arrogant act was met by Azariah and eighty priests who undertook to stop the king. The egotistical monarch defied the priests but was unable to stand against God's holy wrath. Leprosy instantly broke out on his forehead and he was ushered out of the temple. Uzziah was forced to live the rest of his days in seclusion because of the contagious disease. Though he was still officially king, from that time on, his son managed the everyday affairs of the realm.

Pride was the downfall of Uzziah! Since God revealed Himself "in the year king Uzziah died" this statement could be allegorically understood as, "in the year that pride died." The pride of the king kept the glory of the LORD from the people. Only when pride died could the glory of God be made known. This sound, Scriptural principle still holds true today. When pride finally dies in the heart of Christians the Almighty will manifest His glory. We are the obstacles to revival, not the LORD. In whatever form our pride takes, it absolutely hinders the move of the Holy Spirit.

DWELLING IN THE PLACE OF BLESSING

Rabbinical tradition claims that Isaiah was a man of some rank, possibly a relative of King Uzziah. He would have been an educated man well acquainted with the Pentateuch and the account of Moses interceding for Israel after they sinned by worshipping the golden calf (Ex. 33). During this season of intercession Moses passionately pleaded with the LORD to see His glory. Isaiah must have had a similar passion. His spiritual hunger drove him to seek the presence of God no matter the cost. Isaiah longed to be near the LORD and was willing to have his entire life undone if only to gaze upon the beauty of His holiness. The prophet had become a desperate man, and desperate men live desperate lives and pray desperate prayers.

Revival is never a time and chance experience. It is always the result of diligent preparation. Isaiah "saw the LORD seated on a throne, high and exalted" because he deliberately prepared for God's visitation even though he did not know what that fully entailed. The Almighty is moved by His people when they passionately desire Him to rend the heavens and come down. The King of creation will reveal His majesty when His subjects have prepared themselves for His self-disclosure. He will not release His glory to unprepared vessels.

ISAIAH SAW THE LORD

The LORD's self-disclosure came to Isaiah in a way that the prophet could understand. Notice that Isaiah described God's throne (the seat of His authority) and the train of His robe (the symbol of His authority), not the One who sits upon the throne. In ancient Eastern and Middle Eastern times the length of the train on a ruler's robe signified his rank in the kingdom. An emperor would have a robe longer than those who ruled under him. God's train filled the temple. This was a visual statement to Isaiah that he was in the presence of the King of kings who had stepped down out of Heaven.

The LORD wanted to burn into Isaiah's heart and mind the reality of His authority and infinite holiness. Only through a confrontation with the holiness of God can we begin to understand that which intellect is unable to fathom. In other words, a man may theologically define God's holiness while never actually grasping it.

The seraphs that dwell in presence of the LORD understand His holiness far better than we do. By privilege, and by choice, they adore the beauty of His holiness. Exuberantly they cry, "Holy, holy, holy is the LORD Almighty; the whole earth is full of His glory." Their worship is not a burden to them. Quite the contrary, in the case of Isaiah's vision, their ecstatic praise shook the temple. This is true worship. We who know Christ should unashamedly extol Him in like manner and enthusiasm.

When the apostle John saw the glorified Savior he was overcome by His holiness and majesty. All he could do was fall as a dead man at the feet of his Redeemer (Rev. 1:17). In the fourth chapter of Revelation we are given a glimpse into Heaven. There we find angelic beings who cry day and night, "Holy, holy, holy is the LORD God Almighty, who was, and is, and is to come." Simultaneously, the twenty-four elders seated around the throne prostrate themselves before the Lamb. The residents of Heaven are constantly in awe of the LORD as they gaze upon Him with unveiled eyes. Unfortunately, we walk this planet virtually oblivious to His glory until the day He rends the heavens.

The holiness of God is terrifying and appealing, repulsive and magnetic (2 Cor. 2:15-16). There is a great mystery here—the same holiness that draws some repels others. People who do not want to serve God are repulsed by His presence because they are by nature God-haters even though they may speak of Him in sentimental terms. "Holiness provokes hatred," stated R. C. Sproul. "The greater the holiness, the greater the human hostility towards it. It seems insane. No man was ever more loving than Jesus Christ. Yet even His love made people angry. His love was perfect love, a transcendent and holy love, but His very love brought trauma to people. This kind of love is so majestic we can't stand it" (Sproul, 68).

Most of the religious people of Christ's day were repulsed by His holiness and wanted to kill Him. In contrast, the disinherited of society were drawn to the purity of the Savior's love and craved His transforming power. Those who find the presence of Jesus repulsive on earth will find the fullness of His presence in Heaven utterly repugnant. At their eternal judgment they will plead with Jesus to hurl them into Hell so they can hide themselves from the face of Him who sits on the throne.

Whenever Christians behold the glory of the LORD they will never be the same. Never again will they be able to live as they once did. Never again will they be content with a mediocre relationship with the Living God. In His presence they will find a love more powerful than sin, a passion more gripping than lust, a treasure worth more than the wealth of the world. Those who desire to be near Jesus may initially be terrified by His majesty as Isaiah was, and yet yearn for the wonder of His nearness all the more.

GOD WAS WORSHIPED

The prophet was given a glimpse of Heaven when he beheld the seraphs worshiping the LORD in humility and excitement. Their enthusiastic worship shook the temple. This was the spontaneous reaction of heavenly beings reveling in the presence of the Almighty.

Ignorance of God's awesomeness reduces worship to little more than sing-alongs or lifeless formalities. Tozer pointed out that, "Man's spiritual history will positively demonstrate that no religion has ever been greater than its idea of God. Worship is pure or base as the worshiper entertains high or low thoughts of God" (Tozer, *Knowledge*, 7). Only when we see the LORD high and exalted will we begin to comprehend the privilege and excitement of dwelling in His presence and worship Him as they do in Heaven.

Each of the heavenly beings that Isaiah saw had six wings. With two they flew, with two they covered their faces and with two they covered their feet. The covering of face and feet were acts of humility. They knew that it is only by the gift of God that they were allowed to adore the Sovereign Ruler of creation. The seraphs, or "burning ones," were ablaze with the glory of God, for the service of God, because they dwelt in the presence of God. The LORD is a consuming fire and only those who have been consumed by the fire of His presence will be able to spread His fire.

How could anyone dwell in the fire of God's presence and worship Him with indifference? Lifeless worship is a product of cheap Christianity and manmade religion. Such is the creation of people who have a perverted knowledge of the Holy One. By the very fact that they worship Jesus without a burning desire is testimony enough that He is absent from their midst. Isaiah saw the nature of true worship. It was alive and exciting, vibrant and free, filled with loud and joyful acclamations to the glorious eternal Creator. We disgrace Him when we worship Him with half-hearted devotion.

THE SIN OF THE PROPHET REVEALED

Terrified in the presence of pure holiness Isaiah screamed, "Woe to me!" The word "woe" is a lamentation of being "undone" or "destroyed." The prophet felt totally undone by the glory of the LORD. The awesome holiness of God revealed the depths of his own unholiness. The reality of his sin was laid bare to his conscience. Isaiah knew that if the Judge of all the earth administered justice at that moment he would be justly damned to an eternal Hell. His only hope was mercy.

Lack of conviction in the church is directly related to the absence of the Holy Spirit. Whenever God reveals His holiness everything that is unholy is exposed. "This is the verdict: Light has come into the world, but men loved darkness instead of light because their deeds were evil" (Jn. 3:19). Many people, including church folk, fight against revival because they do not want their sin revealed. But there is no other way for revival to come. For a holy God will only dwell with holy people.

Roy Hession writing on Isaiah 6 declared, "The lips are the tools of the heart, and if his lips (Isaiah's) were unclean it was because his heart was unclean. More than that, his lips represented his service: he was a preacher" (Hession, *When*, 22). The LORD justly accused the prophet/preacher of performing his ministry through unclean lips, which flowed from an impure heart. The glory of the LORD revealed the prophet's true spiritual condition. A man may think his life and ministry pristine until he sees Jesus in His infinite holiness. Oh, how ministers today need to be undone by His manifest presence. It will transform their lives and ministries.

When there is no revival in the local church the fault lies at the feet of the preachers and spiritual leaders. Very few pastors and spiritual leaders have the courage or desire to admit this truth and do something about it. Until the men and women in leadership are willing to let the Spirit expose the wickedness hidden deep in the recesses of their hearts their congregations will never experience genuine revival.

Our only hope is for God, who is infinitely good, to expose the corruption that lies deep within our souls so we may come to repentance. Tozer aptly told us, "Whenever God appeared to men in Bible times the results were the same—an overwhelming sense of terror and dismay, a wrenching sensation of sinfulness and guilt" (Tozer, *Knowledge*, 77). The power of Christ's blood can cleanse the worst of sinners and transform the worldliest of professed believers. The convicting power of the Holy Spirit is the love of God revealed. The Spirit does this to bring us into deep fellowship with Jesus.

THE SIN OF GOD'S PEOPLE REVEALED

After the Holy Spirit opened Isaiah's eyes to see his own sin, He then showed the prophet the sins of God's people. Those who have been confronted by the depth of their own sinfulness, and experienced the liberty that heartfelt repentance brings, can be effective in calling the church to repentance. Self-righteousness strips us of the Spirit's anointing to reach the heart of a people. Only through brokenness can a person rightly expose the sins of others. Before Isaiah could proclaim to Israel their sin he had to first see his own.

The Spirit revealed Himself in breathtaking power in Scottish Presbyterian communion services in Kentucky, beginning in 1800. At these two- or three-day outdoor services deep repentance took place as people examined their ways prior to partaking of the LORD's Supper. Repentance began with the churched and then flowed to the unsaved. These meetings were environments conducive to revival. In 1801 the revival exploded at a communion service held in Cane Ridge, Kentucky. This inaugurated the Camp Meeting era. Presbyterians and Methodists came from great distances. Some accounts say that nearly 25,000 gathered in this wilderness setting. Over half were unconverted when they came. Most were gloriously saved when they left.

James B. Finley, who was converted at Cane Ridge and later became a Methodist circuit rider, gave an account of the Cane Ridge Revival. "The noise was like the roar of Niagara. The vast sea of human beings seemed to be agitated as if by a storm. I counted seven ministers, all preaching at one time, some on stumps, others in wagons and one standing on a tree which had, in falling, lodged against another ... Some of the people were singing, others praying, some crying for mercy in the most piteous accents, while others were shouting most vociferously.

"While witnessing this scene, a peculiarly strange sensation such as I had never felt before came over me. My heart beat tumultuously, my knees trembled, my lips quivered and I felt as though I must fall to the ground. A strange supernatural power seemed to pervade the entire mass of mind there collected. . . I stepped up on a log where I could have a better view of the surging sea of humanity. The scene that then presented itself to my mind was indescribable. At one time I saw at least five hundred swept down in a moment as if a battery of a thousand guns had been opened upon them and then immediately followed shrieks and shouts that rent the very heavens" (Pratney, 125-126).

Only the Spirit of God can bring such deep remorse over sin. Neither the saved nor the unsaved escaped the convicting power of His presence. Such intense conviction is extremely difficult to understand unless you have experienced it for yourself.

THE SIN OF THE NATION REVEALED

The next fact that the prophet came to understand was the terrifying position secular society was in due to their obstinate rebellion against the Almighty. Isaiah saw that the sins of the nation would incur God's just and holy wrath if they did not turn from their wicked ways. The only hope for the nation was a divine encounter that would expose the sins of the people so they could receive the gift of repentance. When a nation comes face to face with the Living God the reality of their spiritual and moral poverty is exposed. Duncan Campbell relating to the Hebrides Awakening stated, "When God stepped down, suddenly men and women all over the parish were gripped with fear" (Campbell, *When God*). This is how the Spirit begins His transforming work of revival in a nation.

Similar to the days of Isaiah, America is suffering under obstinate rebellion against God. In this postmodern, post-Christian era secular society has replaced the Judeo-Christian morality with a relativistic philosophy void of God and void of absolutes. We have become a proud, self-indulgent nation in anarchy against the Creator. The non-Christian world does not comprehend this truth and many in the church are willfully ignorant of this nation's grave state of affairs.

The healing of nations comes through repentance. Before nations will change, people must change. Revival has produced some of the greatest social reforms known to man. For example, every social ill that produced the French Revolution was active in England in the early 1700s. God raised up John Wesley to hold back the flood of divine judgment looming over England by unleashing the transforming power of revival. Even secular historians give credit to the Methodist revivals for turning the reigns of a nation rushing towards catastrophe.

The poor English masses were gripped with a deep spirit of conviction as the Methodist Revival burst forth. "Wesley was a preacher of righteousness. He would exalt the holiness of God, the Law of God, the justice of God, the wisdom of His requirements, and the justice of His wrath. Then he would turn to sinners and tell them of the enormity of their crimes, their open rebellion, their treason, and their anarchy. The power of God would descend so mightily that it is reliably reported, on one occasion, when the people dispersed, there were eighteen hundred people lying on the ground, completely unconscious because they had a revelation of the holiness of God, and in the light of that, they had seen the enormity of their own sin" (Comfort, *Hell's*, 72).

As in the days of Wesley, judgment is hanging over America because of the enormity of our crimes against Heaven. If the mercy of God is not released through revival then we are faced with the grim reality that justice will be executed. Only the Holy Spirit can transform a nation for eternal good.

A BLOODY STONE

The Holy Spirit thoroughly convinced Isaiah of his sin and the sins of his people. The prophet knew that his only hope was mercy. How was mercy revealed? Through a hot bloody stone. That bloody coal came off the altar where lambs were sacrificed to atone for the sins of the people. After the prophet repented a seraph was sent to cleanse the preacher by touching his lips with a bloody stone. That stone represented Christ's sacrificial death on the cross as the Lamb of God. The only way for Isaiah to be made holy and useable was for the blood of Christ to cleanse him from all unrighteousness. That hot bloody stone burnt out the wickedness and set the prophet's heart on fire.

The glory of God always reveals the cross of Christ. The cross exposes the wickedness of our sin by manifesting the price for our redemption—a crucified Savior. Christ's death and resurrection offers sinners forgiveness from sin and victory over the bondage and love of sin. The LORD super-abounds with power to make His people holy if they want to be holy. "The cross of Christ, by the same mighty and decisive stroke with which it took the curse of sin away from us, also surely takes away the power and the love of sin" (Hannah Whitall Smith, 16).

Holiness flows out of a cleansed heart that is surrendered to Christ. A passion for Jesus will always produce a passion for holiness. It is impossible for it to be otherwise. As Evan Roberts preached, "You would not be cold if you had come here by Calvary" (Duncan, 41).

ISAIAH WAS CALLED AND SENT

After Isaiah was cleansed from his sin he heard the voice of the LORD saying, "Whom shall I send? And who will go for us?" The prophet quickly responded, "Here am I. Send me!" Then the LORD sent him saying, "Go and tell this people..." (Isa. 6:8-9a).

Whoever the LORD cleanses He sends! Those who are passionate for God will be passionate to obey Him. The sad reality is that most western Christians lack a passion for Christ, which results in a lack of fervor for holiness, obedience and evangelism. One reason revival passes by most churches is because they do not want to be sent by God. Whenever we grow satisfied with our self-centered lives we will not want the LORD to upset our comfortable little world.

One of the primary purposes of revival is to awaken the church to reach the lost. The power of God is for the purposes of God. Christians that refuse to accept the call to rescue the unsaved are living in disobedience. Those who sit at the feet of Jesus will know His heart and abandon themselves to His cause. As William MacDonald told us, "Those who are constrained by the love of Christ will count no sacrifice too great to make for Him. They will do because of love to Him what they would never do for worldly gain. They will not count their lives dear unto themselves. They will spend and be spent if only men might not perish for want of the gospel" (MacDonald, 58-59).

SPIRITUAL REVOLUTIONARIES

When God steps down out of Heaven, men and nations tremble. The LORD sent His Son to shake the kingdoms of men so He could raise a heavenly Kingdom in their place. That's radical! Biblical Christianity is revolutionary because Jesus came into this world as a spiritual revolutionist. He taught His disciples the principles of overthrowing Satan's kingdom. On the day of Pentecost the Holy Spirit was poured out and three thousand were saved. That's radical!

The church's first revival set in motion the revolutionary posture that was to define her spiritual life. The 1859 Irish Revival paints a wonderful picture of this point. "A poor man was converted at the beginning of the revival. Immediately, he became anxious for the conversion of the family with whom he resided, and his fellow-workmen at the mill. But they were an ungodly people. When they saw the change in the man they mocked, swore, sang impure songs, and did all they could to turn him from Christ. He saw that reproof was in vain, and resolved to pray for them. He prayed for a time until the answer came. Then suddenly one day the men in the mill were astonished at cries proceeding from their homes. The mill suspended business, and the men rushed to their houses to see what had caused the cries. They found their wives and daughters prostrated under strong conviction, crying to the LORD for mercy. The once despised convert was instantly appealed to for help, and led all the women to Christ.

"But the man's prayers were only partially answered. Some days later the mill had to again be stopped, but this time because of the men. While engaged in work the men were smitten down by the Spirit of God as they worked at their machines. Some of the strongest men and greatest scoffers fell powerless in a moment under the mighty and mysterious influence of the work.

"Strong men were prostrated and crying for mercy. Converted wives and daughters bent over them with tears of joy, giving thanks to God for awakening their husbands and brothers. The poor man's prayers were answered. The seven souls in the house where he resided were all saved, and about nine-tenths of the workers at the mill have been converted" (Davis, 58-60, edited).

The revolutionary nature of revival is seen in how it seizes the hearts of the lost and radically reforms all who would come to Christ. Then radical converts go forth as radical agents of change.

There is no such thing as revolutionary Christians who have not first revolutionized their moral and spiritual life. Only holy men and women can become spiritual revolutionists. When we harbor sin in our lives we destroy the very things that make us godly revolutionaries: the holiness and presence of God.

This revolution, which Christ began, was one of holiness through intimate relationship with Him. It will never be a revolution through violence, hate and the works of the flesh because that would make Christ's Kingdom no different than the world's rebellion. Our weapons do not consist of human might, nor natural wisdom and strength, but the Spirit of Almighty God.

The church militant is a holy church ablaze with the glory of God. Of such a church the world takes notice. A revived and holy church may be hated, as was the LORD; she may be reviled, rejected, beaten, killed or embraced; but she can never be ignored. It is time we accept the truth that if our Christianity is not revolutionary then it is not Biblical.

Jesus is building an army of saints that have been transformed by His holiness. They have stood in His presence, seen His glory, dealt with their sin and been cleansed by His blood. His holiness has permeated every fiber of their being so they strive with all their heart to fulfill the LORD's command to be holy because He is holy. Now the zeal of God consumes them. Then the call comes, "Whom shall I send? And who will go for us?" What will we do with His call?

CHAPTER TEN

REVIVAL PRAYING

Revival is a spiritual work obtained and advanced through spiritual means. That is why we cannot have a genuine spiritual awakening without Spirit-inspired prayer. Church history clearly validates this truth—that praying saints are the instruments the LORD has chosen to birth revival. "All true revivals have been born in prayer," penned E. M. Bounds. "When God's people become so concerned about the state of religion that they lie on their faces day and night in earnest supplication, the blessing will be sure to fall" (Bounds, *On Prayer*, 98).

Praying for revival should be a part of every believer's devotional life. Intercession remains the responsibility of every Christian without exception. Unfortunately, most Christians are unskilled in prayer, including the majority of those who call themselves intercessors. The purpose of this chapter is to highlight various dimensions of revival praying with the hope that many will eagerly enlist in Christ's school of prayer and subsequently storm Hell's strongholds.

A WAY OF LIFE

Prayer for the Christian is not an option; it is a way of life. God designed prayer to be the primary method of receiving His help and advancing His Kingdom. James taught that we do not have, because we do not ask (Jam. 4:2). There is virtually nothing the LORD will do for His people apart from prayer (this is an extremely important point). Not just that, a true man or woman of God will never live or act apart from that means of grace.

In this hectic American culture, we have become too busy for prayer, and our lives are spiritually bankrupt to prove it.

A Christian will never rise above his prayer life. Robert Murray McCheyne noted, "What a man is on his knees before God is all that he is, this and nothing more" (Campbell, *Heart*). The quantity and quality of prayer directly relates to the spiritual depth of a believer. The average Christian seldom, if ever, taps into the power of prayer. Through prayer, there is power for holiness, power to love God, power to serve, power to set captives free, power for signs and wonders, power to build Christ's Kingdom, and power for revival. Prevailing prayer opens the door to Holy Ghost power and without prayer that door remains securely closed.

The LORD designed prayer to be the lifeblood of a believer, an act of intimacy lived out between God and man. Oh! The joy of prayer! Few, however, avail themselves of the privilege. Most Christians know little or nothing of the joy that flows out of abiding in the secret place of the Most High (Ps. 91:1). We can be so concerned about what we get from the Savior that we seldom know the enjoyment of just loving Him and being loved by Him.

Jesus viewed prayer as an accepted fact of relationship with the Father. Prayer was His lifestyle, not a religious duty as the Pharisees reduced it to. The Messiah desired to build a community of faith based upon a lifestyle of intimate fellowship with the Father. To accomplish this, He developed a people who made prayer a way of life. Jesus demonstrated the effectiveness of such a lifestyle through the power He manifested in word and deed. He walked in perfect communion with the Father, which sustained Him each day, all the way to the cross.

How Christians understand prayer will determine how the local church functions and whether or not that church will ever experience genuine revival. We must define prayer according to Christ's definition, not our own. Consequently, to comprehend how Jesus characterized prayer we need to examine how He viewed the house of God.

A HOUSE OF PRAYER

Jesus was not like the religious leaders of His day. He lived in unbroken fellowship with His Father, walked in perfect holiness, preached with authority and shook the status quo. He directly opposed the dead religious traditions of the elders and denounced the popularized religion of the day by preaching the truth in simplicity and power. His righteous soul was filled with wrath against those who desecrated His temple through their religious pride and spiritual barrenness. He could not remain silent.

One day Jesus entered the temple courts and committed an act of holy violence. The radical Messiah was on the loose. He made a scourge of rope and drove out those who defiled His House. Jesus was declaring to Israel her sin. His voice echoed throughout the temple courts, "It is written, 'My house shall be called a house of prayer,' but you have made it a 'den of thieves'" (Mt. 21:13; NKJV).

Jesus was proclaiming that the temple was HIS house and He was defining the purpose of HIS house. This was Jesus, the radical, God incarnate in flesh and blood. He was teaching that His house was primarily to be a house of prayer, not a house of preaching, fellowship, social service or ministry—but a house of prayer. All those other dimensions of church life are necessary for her vitality, but should flow out of her prayer life.

When Jesus drove out the people that defiled His temple He was emphatically stating that prayerlessness is sin. Anything that keeps us from the place of prayer grieves His heart. Overturning the moneychanger's tables had less to do with their greed than with prayerlessness. Actually, their prayerlessness allowed their greed to flourish.

God created His house to be a house of prayer. If the church is not primarily a house of prayer then she is not a house of God. Whenever the church fails to be a house of prayer, she has failed her calling and become little more than a social institution. Restoring the place of prayer to God's house was a deliberate mission of the Savior. He purposely instilled in the minds of his followers that prayer must be the priority of their lives and that everything they did was to flow out of prayer. This was so important that Jesus went right into the proverbial lion's den and drove out those who dishonored His house. This event was engraved on the minds of His disciples and His words, "My House shall be called a house of prayer" burned inside of them.

Might not Jesus today accuse much of the western church of becoming a den of thieves because they have forsaken the place of prayer? Lack of Holy Spirit power is a direct result of prayerlessness. Jesus will never be glorified when there is an absence spiritual power in the local assembly. Instead of restoring the power through prayer, multitudes of churches have become nothing more than social clubs, self-help centers or pro-activist organizations. Prayerless churches are the result of prayerless pastors who reproduce after their own kind. Though filled with activity, such churches are devoid of supernatural power and worthless in the scheme of eternity. They may implement the most fashionable church growth teaching while never fulfilling the will of God.

Churches may be full of activity as the temple in Jerusalem was. They may supply services to help people as the merchants did, or even be busy with ministry as the priests were. Not realizing that Jesus is standing at the door, scourge in hand, ready to drive out the desecraters of His house. E. M. Bounds wisely instructed, "As God's house is a house of prayer, prayer should enter into and underlie everything that is done there. Prayer belongs to every sort of work relating to the church. As God's house is a house where the business of praying is carried on, so is it a place where the business of making praying people out of prayerless people is done. Any church that calls itself the house of God but fails to magnify and teach the great lesson of prayer, should change its teaching to conform to the divine prayer pattern; or, it should change the name of its building to something other than a church" (Bounds, *On Prayer*, 186). No matter how much activity a congregation produces, if the people are not a people of prayer then the church is not a house of prayer and they have failed their Christian calling.

The Kingdom of Heaven either progresses or regresses according to the prayers of the saints. Prayerlessness produces powerlessness, which in turn produces barrenness. A church can be spiritually barren whether it has a congregation of 50 or 5,000. Size does not constitute life or success according to the standards of Christ's Kingdom. Since prayer is a spiritual act, prayerless Christians and prayerless churches are helpless in advancing the Savior's spiritual Kingdom. They may even be detrimental to the cause of Christ and a hindrance to revival.

When true revival is withheld from the land, the fault lies at the feet of every pastor and believer who has ceased to be a person of prayer. Revival is the LORD's visitation, or habitation, among men. Without soul stirring prayer there can be no revival! The very idea that God's house should be a house of prayer implies that His people should be a people of prayer.

PEOPLE OF PRAYER

Prayer is so vitally important that a person cannot become a Christian, or remain one, without it. This means that prayerless people cannot be true Christians. Since the relationship between God and man begins with the prayer of repentance, it can only continue and grow through that same means. It is thoroughly unbiblical and illogical to believe that there can be a relationship with Jesus without deep personal communication on a constant basis.

Prayer is not something you do, it is who you are. A person of prayer is a person in continual fellowship with the Master. No greater privilege has ever been granted to man than to walk with God in unbroken fellowship. Paul called this walking in the Spirit. A husband and wife can talk while doing errands, but nothing takes the place of intimate communication without outside distractions. True intimacy is the place where dreams are revealed, and the joys and tears of life are shared. Few Christians experience the wonder of such a relationship with Jesus because they have not chosen to develop a lifestyle of prayer. "Our spiritual immaturity never shows up more than in our lack of praying, be it alone or in a church meeting" (Ravenhill, *Revival*, 29).

One day Jesus was invited to dine at the home of Mary and Martha. While Jesus was waiting for dinner to be served, a problem arose between the sisters, which was ultimately a question of priorities and lifestyle. Luke 10 gives the account. "Martha was distracted by all the preparations that had to be made." In contrast, Mary "sat at the LORD's feet listening to what He said." Martha began to complain, asserting that Mary should be helping her with the dinner preparations. Jesus intervened with a strong, but tender rebuke, "Martha, Martha, you are worried and upset about many things, but only one thing is needed. Mary has chosen what is better, and it will not be taken away from her."

Martha's fellowship with Jesus worked around her schedule; Mary's schedule revolved around Jesus. We could think of Martha as a person who prays and Mary as a person of prayer. Both made lifestyle choices; Martha kept herself at the center of her life while Mary centered hers around Jesus. The Martha type of person prays, but her prayers are selfishly motivated because self is still at the center of her life. A person of prayer sits at Jesus' feet and is consumed by the One who is a consuming fire. To know Christ's heart we must sit at His feet. Most Christians will never know His heart because their lifestyle choices will never allow for it.

Imagine Mary and Martha in their eighties. What memories would they have? Martha would be able to give tales of hot stoves, dirty dishes and fancy meals. Oh, but Mary gazed into those holy eyes that burn with fire and heard words from the lips of the Master that we have not been allowed to hear. What might our memories be when we are in our 80s? Of children or wealth, grown-up toys, or pain and suffering? Maybe they will be memories filled with dread as eternity looms near. What memories will endure into eternity? Would any of your life's labors be worth inscribing on the halls of Heaven as a testimonial to your love of Christ while on earth? Would you be ashamed to mention your earthly pursuits in those sacred chambers because they proved worthless in the scheme of eternity?

The diary of David Brainerd has changed countless individuals because his life had eternal value. He did not squander his life on meaningless pursuits but spent it on the eternal things of God. Above all else, Brainerd knew his Saviour on his knees. This is where his passion for the LORD and compassion for souls grew to be white hot. Day by day, he grew more powerful in the Spirit even though he was slowly dying of tuberculosis. "But as his strength ebbed his compassion grew, grew till it became a great hunger that would not be denied. Whole nights were spent in agonizing prayer in the dark woods, his clothes drenched with the sweat of his travail" (Shearer, 37).

In time, Brainerd's prayers brought revival to the Native Americans. His influence went further than he ever imagined, for his life aroused such men as Carey, Payson, and McCheyne.

Bounds stated, "All I want is simply to enforce this thought, that the hidden life, a life whose days are spent in communion with God, in trying to reach the source of power, is the life that moves the world. Those living such lives may be soon forgotten. There may be no one to speak a eulogy over them. But by and by, the great moving current of their lives will begin to tell, as in the case of this young man (David Brainerd), who died at about thirty years of age. The missionary spirit of this nineteenth century is more due to the prayers and consecration of this one man than to any other one" (Bounds, *Weapon*, 161).

The world today desperately needs men and women of prayer who know how to prevail with God as David Brainerd did. When he prayed, Heaven moved, Hell trembled, the earth shook and captives were set free. He accomplished great victories because he was a person of prayer.

PRAYING THAT CHANGES THE WORLD

The LORD has chosen to operate His Kingdom in this world through prayer. According to His infinite wisdom and goodness, the LORD will move, or remain silent, according to the prayers of His saints. That places a tremendous responsibility upon Christians to be people of prayer, yielded and obedient to the Savior. "In dealing with mankind," wrote Bounds, "nothing is more important to God than prayer. Prayer is likewise of great importance to people. Failure to pray is failure in all of life. It is failure of duty, service, and spiritual progress. It is only by prayer that God can help people. He who does not pray, therefore, robs himself of God's help and places God where He cannot help people" (Bounds, *Weapon*, 8).

We often rationalize our prayerlessness by convincing ourselves that no one gets hurt if we do not pray. Nevertheless, prayerlessness is sin! It is rooted in pride, selfishness, self-sufficiency and lack of surrender. By not being a person of prayer, we harm family, friends, neighbors, co-workers and the church. Lack of prayer causes sin and selfishness to run amuck in our lives. It produces lifestyles of compromise and hypocrisy that drives our children and friends away from Christ. Prayerlessness stops revival from coming so multitudes die without ever receiving salvation.

One of the first things prayer accomplishes is the transformation of the person who prays. He who does not pray stops the Spirit's revolutionizing power in his life. The Christian either rises or falls according to his prayer life. The Holy Spirit will not force His way through the barrier of prayerlessness. We must willfully open our hearts. True prayer is an act of surrender to God. Through it we place our lives in His service so we may advance His mission of building a community of faith by rescuing lost humanity. Only from the prayer closet are men and women empowered to take a city, state or nation for the glory of God.

For the lost to be saved in great numbers the Holy Spirit must be powerfully present to convict of sin. He can awaken the consciences of the hardest sinners or coldest church folk. An eloquent preacher might stimulate the minds and emotions of people, but only the Spirit can pierce the heart and conscience. Until the church becomes a praying church, it will lack Holy Ghost power to convict sinners and transform society. "The history of revival proves that conviction comes as a result of the prayers of God's people. Where there is fervent prayer there is deep conviction. Where there is no conviction there is lack of earnest prayer" (Paul Smith, 33).

One divine moment of the presence of God can do more for the evangelization of the world than all the combined efforts of our programs, crusades, and church growth seminars. The Great Korean Revival of 1907 is a wonderful example of the fruit and power of prayer. Earnest preparations began as early as 1903 and grew in intensity. In 1906, Dr. Howard A. Johnston brought news to the missionaries that revival broke out in Wales and in Kassia Hills, India. The missionaries began praying at noon every day for revival. After a short period, they started to grow weary and some even wanted to discontinue the prayer meeting. Discouragement had almost stopped the revival from coming. Missionary Jonathan Goforth related, "Instead of discontinuing the prayer meeting we would give more time to prayer, not less ... We kept to it, until at last, after months of waiting, the answer came" (Jonathan Goforth, *By My Spirit*, 23).

The LORD visited Pyengyang on the last day of a series of meetings where missionaries and national leaders had gathered to seek God's face for revival. It was Monday night, January 17, 1907. Graham Lee was leading the service. After a short sermon he called for prayers. The entire assembly began to pray out loud with such force that it became a roar, "like the falling of many waters," captivating the whole congregation. The sound of weeping was heard as a spirit of heaviness and sorrow for sin broke out among the whole audience. "They began to repent of their sins publicly one by one" (Lee, 76-77).

Missionary William Blair described the scene, "Man after man would rise, confess his sins, break down and weep, and then throw himself to the floor and beat the floor with his fists in perfect agony of conviction ... Sometimes after a confession the whole audience would break out in audible prayer, and the effect of that audience of men praying together in audible prayer was something indescribable. Again, after another confession, they would break out in uncontrollable weeping, and we would all weep, we couldn't help it. And so the meeting went on until two o'clock a.m. We had prayed to God for an outpouring of His Holy Spirit upon the people and it had come" (Lee, 77).

The next evening the outpouring of the Holy Spirit was even more intense. "Then began a meeting the like of which I had never seen before, nor wish to see again unless in God's sight it is absolutely necessary. Every sin a human being can commit was publicly confessed that night. Pale and trembling with emotion, in agony of mind and body, guilty souls, standing in the white light of their judgment, saw themselves as God saw them. Their sins rose up in all their vileness, until shame and grief and self-loathing took complete possession; pride was driven out, the face of man forgotten. Looking up to Heaven, to Jesus whom they had betrayed, they smote themselves and cried out with bitter wailing: 'Lord, Lord, cast us not away forever!' Everything else was forgotten, nothing else mattered. The scorn of men, the penalty of the law, even death itself seemed of small consequences if only God forgave" (Lee, 77-78).

Such accounts of revival are the direct results of saints who passionately grab hold of the Savior in prayer. No human effort will ever compare to the power of the Spirit released upon men, women and children. Spiritual outpourings like the one in Korea are what revival praying is all about. It is worth a lifetime of effort to see God rend the heavens and come down with such holy power. Jesus continues to hold before us the wonderful hope of His awesome presence revealed in our day.

Jonathan Goforth was an eyewitness of the initial outpouring of the Great Korean Revival. After he returned to his mission field in China, he saw revival sweep the land. While on furlough, he preached in his native country of Canada and also in the United States. He believed that the LORD could pour out His glory in North America as He did in Korea and China. However, revival did not come to these two nations. Goforth stated the reason; the LORD "does not get the yielded channels" (Jonathan Goforth, *When*, 25). What an indictment against the church.

Prayer is the primary means for the church to experience a fresh anointing from God. The Holy Spirit super-abounds with all the power necessary to awaken the church and save the lost. The Great I Am uses simple, hungry souls to pray in revival and advanced it with such force that vast numbers of people are thrust into the irresistible influence of the Spirit. What program or pop-church growth teaching ever accomplished such a feat? How we settle for refuse when the LORD wants us to feast at His table! Nothing else on earth can do the work of the Kingdom like the Spirit loosed upon men, women and children. Absolutely nothing!

CHAPTER ELEVEN

SPIRITUAL WARFARE

At this very moment a war is raging across the planet. Its battles are ferocious. Lives are lost, prisoners are taken, defections occur, atrocities abound and strategies are executed. The hostilities rage endlessly—it is a war to the bitter end. There is no demilitarized zone and there can be no compromise. This is the most important conflict the world has ever known—a war over the souls of men, women and children. Eternity hangs in the balance for billions of people. Satan has raised a *coup d'etat* against the Almighty. The devil must be put down!

Whether or not we believe this war is real does not alter its existence. Every human being is an active participant of this conflict by the simple fact that we are alive. We are either in God's camp or in Satan's. This is a conflict between two kingdoms where there can be no truce. Those who have not surrendered their lives to Christ are by sheer default soldiers in Satan's army. The unsaved are blind to this war and their part in it. This is true with most Christians as well, the majority of which choose to ignore the spiritual conflict that rages around them because they are consumed with their self-centered lifestyles.

Men will fight and die in war when they deem the cause worthy. Is there a more worthy cause than to rescue those rushing to damnation? Our active participation in this war is the most important thing we can do with our lives. This conflict is of such importance that the Father sent His Son to die on the cross so men could be delivered from their bondage under Satan's tyrannical rule. Yet Christians will not join the fight until they are liberated from their selfish living.

The advancement of Christ's Kingdom is the responsibility of every believer. Our weapons are not worldly in origin or design, nor are they used for the destruction of life. They are supernatural gifts to transform individuals and secular society (2 Cor. 10:4). They are deployed through prayer and can only be controlled through that same discipline. Every saint is obligated to learn and practice spiritual warfare. This begins with their reckless abandonment to God and is furthered through prayer, intercession and evangelism.

The majority of our conferences, programs and church activities leave the world untouched. Millions rush to Hell while we hide in our sanctuaries, rejoicing over our prosperity. Those that strive to reach the lost often do so with meager results. From businessmen to gang-bangers, the majority of the unsaved does not know, nor care, that the church exists. The raw truth is that, in recent years, Western Christianity has done little damage to Satan's kingdom. Our catchy slogans, conferences and campaigns will never transform cities and nations. Nevertheless, average people who are full of faith and the Holy Ghost can turn their world upside down (Acts 6 & 7). Let a few men or women like Stephen, Paul, Wesley or Finney loose on our modern cities and they will never be the same.

This chapter is not about methods to spiritual warfare, but about the condition of our hearts. Intercession is a heart issue. Set the heart on fire for the souls of perishing immortal souls, and intercession will take place. Genuine spiritual warfare begins by sitting at the feet of Him who vanquishes every foe and then rushing into the city with a baptism of Holy Ghost fire.

WAR FOR SOULS

It is time we take this war out of the church and into the enemy's camp. "Our biblical story demands an offensive rather than defensive posture of the church" (Hauerwas, 51). Where does the church's offensive strategy begin? On her knees! How is the church to advance? On her knees! How are the battles fought? On her knees! "Prayer is part of the primary business of life, and God has called His people to it first of all" (Bounds, *Weapon*, 64).

The war for souls is waged, advanced and ultimately triumphant through prayer. All that Christians do, corporately or individually, must flow out of vibrant prayer. Whether it is evangelism, discipleship or business, our lives should be saturated with prayer.

Ezekiel 37 is a vision of a valley full of very dry bones. The bones are the remains of a conquered army. After their defeat they were left to be devoured by scavenging animals and to decompose through the natural forces of the world. The unburied bones are a testimonial to their total demise. This vision graphically illustrates the spiritual death of Israel due to idolatry. It also prophetically speaks of those seasons when the church is defeated through compromise with the world. For the Spirit of the LORD to breathe new life into these bones presents a profound hope that God can resurrect the spiritually dead.

What defeats a spiritual army? Sin! What opens the door for idolatry? Compromise! How does this spiritual death begin? Prayerlessness! Whenever prayer ceases to be the church's primary function, she becomes nothing more than a defeated army in the valley of dry bones. Churches then become mausoleums—monuments to the spiritually dead.

The LORD designed prayer to be our most formidable weapon to transform society. It is an offensive weapon for taking the kingdom of darkness by force. Through prayer we can move Heaven to shake earth. John the revelator was given a wonderful vision of the power of prayer:

"Another angel, who had a golden censer, came and stood at the altar. He was given much incense to offer, with the prayers of all the saints, on the golden altar before the throne. The smoke of the incense, together with the prayers of the saints, went up before God from the angel's hand. Then the angel took the censer, filled it with fire from the altar, and hurled it on the earth; and there came peals of thunder, rumblings, flashes of lightning and an earthquake" (Rev. 8:3-5).

This vision vividly reveals that our prayers can move the heart of God. After the prayers of the saints are mingled with holy fire from Heaven's altar, they are hurled back to earth with such force that men and kingdoms are shaken. This is the result of Spirit filled believers who come before Christ's throne of grace with passion, purpose and faith. The picture of Almighty God shaking earth is an awesome representation of what revival actually accomplishes.

The time will come when the LORD will rend the heavens, not only in revival, but also in judgment. "I will take vengeance in anger and wrath upon the nations that have not obeyed Me" (Mic. 5:15). The prophet Haggai declared, "This is what the LORD Almighty says: 'In a little while I will once more shake the heavens and the earth, the sea and the dry land. I will shake all nations, and the desired of all nations will come, and I will fill this house with glory'" (Hag. 2:6-7). The LORD will shake earthly kingdoms so the "desired of nations" will turn from their rebellion against the Most High and know His tender mercies.

What solution does the church offer to America so that her judgment may be averted? We need to answer this question. It is not too late for us to arise from our valley of dry bones to become a living army. Joel cried out, let those "who minister before the LORD, weep between the temple porch and the altar. Let them say, 'Spare Your people, O LORD. Do not make Your inheritance an object of scorn, a byword among the nations. Why should they say among the peoples, 'Where is their God?' Then the LORD will be jealous for His land and take pity on His people" (Joel 2:17).

Revival can come either through times of peace or judgment. Both are expressions of God's love and mercy that brings to people the life changing power of repentance. The idea of revival in times of peace is far more attractive than as a byproduct of national calamity. If the saints will not arise to the occasion in times of peace then the LORD will allow disaster to overtake a nation so that revival may fall. In the end, revival will come either through peace or through judgment.

INTERCESSION

The revelation of God's glory is released through prayer. When the church fails to pray, His glory is withheld from the land. Divine glory falls on the church only in proportion to her hunger for His presence. True intercession flows through people of prayer who share in the passion that drove Christ to the cross. As Oswald Chambers penned, "The great difficulty in intercession is myself, nothing less or more." (Chambers, 74).

PEACE OR WAR

Paul admonished every believer to pray, "... that we may live peaceful and quiet lives in all godliness and holiness" (I Tim. 2:1-8). Unique to civilization during Paul's epoch in history was *Pax Roma*, or the "Peace of Rome." Because this peace predominately covered the known world, the Roman armies were free to build roads and police them. These roads allowed the quick deployment of Roman armies to areas of conflict. This in turn advanced international commerce by securing relatively safe and easy travel for merchants.

This peace was essential for the rapid expansion of the early church. Without it the Gospel would have never spread with the ease and speed by which it did. In spite of localized outbreaks of persecution, Christians had relative liberty to travel for commerce and for preaching the Good News. Free trade allowed the message to reach Rome before any apostle even visited the city.

The days of Elijah stand in stark contrast to the *Pax Roma* of Paul's era. During this epoch in Israeli history peace was not the avenue to revival. Israel needed divine discipline so she might repent. Peace in this situation would have been spiritually catastrophic. Therefore the Spirit instructed the prophet to pray according to their genuine need.

The LORD had respect unto Elijah's prayer because he was a man who deeply knew his Lord. "Elijah was a man just like us. He prayed earnestly that it would not rain, and it did not rain on the land for three and a half years" (Jam. 5:17). The man of God prayed a dangerous, yet merciful prayer of judgment so the descendants of Abraham could receive another opportunity to turn from her wicked ways.

The LORD was good to judge Israel. The judgment came according to the entreaties of an intercessor. Such prayers bring men and nations to their knees. C. E. Autrey expounded on the use of such drastic petitions, "The prophet had to pray such a prayer. It is always better that a famine stalk the land, that people thirst, that the nation be torn limb from limb, than that the people decay spiritually; better that a depression come and twenty million people walk the streets jobless than that the people, choked on prosperity, forget God and worship at the altar of crass materialism, drinking rivers of beer and champagne rather than the wine of holy communion. Physical destruction is a smaller calamity than moral delinquency. The love of God does not shrink from inflicting such suffering if by such judgment the plague of sin may be wiped out. It was a terrible prayer to pray, but it was necessary" (Autrey, 71).

Intercession that comes from hearts ablaze will be bold and radical. Prayers that cost us nothing are worth nothing. Prayer that costs us our blood, sweat and tears will change the world. Elijah was a courageous man of faith who unselfishly prayed that God would judge the rebellious nation he loved. The prophet knew he would suffer along with his people, but he loved them more than his own comfort.

In our day and age we are more concerned about our happiness, prosperity and ease of life than with the horrifying reality that Hell grows larger by the second. It takes men and women of courage, fortitude and compassion to pray that the LORD would judge a godless nation. True intercessors learn how to pray prayers that change men and nations, whether the need of the hour is for peace or judgment. Today, America is spiritually bankrupt under her peace and opulence. Now may be a season for the LORD's disciplining love. True peace can fill a nation or city after they have humbled themselves before God through repentance and loving obedience, but not before.

INTERCESSION AND COMPASSION

The All-Merciful One longs to demonstrate mercy in spite of the fact that we deserve judgment. Israel grievously sinned against The LORD by worshipping a golden calf after they were miraculously delivered from their slavery in Egypt. The Spirit moved Moses to intercede on their behalf (Ex. 32). This man of God learned the power of intercession. "Persevering prayer always wins; God yields to persistence and fidelity. He has no heart to say no to praying such as Moses did. God's purpose to destroy Israel was actually changed by the praying of this man of God. This illustrates how much just one praying person is worth in this world, and how much depends on him" (Bounds, *Weapon*, 19).

Moses prostrated himself before the LORD for "forty days and forty nights because the LORD had said He would destroy you" (Deu. 9:25). How many of us would pray like that for an obstinate rebellious people? His intercession was so passionate that he was even willing to suffer eternal judgment if only the LORD would spare the people. The justice of God decreed both mercy and judgment. Those who refused to repent would pay for their crimes; mercy would only be extended to the contrite. Paul prayed in like spirit, "For I could wish that myself were accursed from Christ for my brethren, my kinsmen according to the flesh" (Rom. 9:3; KJV).

People who think that the Judge of all the earth is harsh in His dealings do not understand His goodness and holiness. The LORD as chosen to work in the world through broken people who learn the discipline of prayer. He seeks for those who will intercede for a disobedient people so He can hold back His wrath to demonstrate mercy. In our day, the Savior is looking for a people of prayer who will intercede on behalf of a backslidden church, a sinful nation and a perishing world. He is calling the saints to do whatever it takes to bring salvation to the land, even if the intercessors themselves must suffer.

Two of Charles Finney's intercessors were Father Nash and Able Clary. Both were ministers who received a powerful anointing for intercession. Neither of them normally attended Finney's services because the spirit of prayer was so heavy upon them that they would break down with loud weeping for the unconverted. At times they would seek the face of God for twelve hours a day. One Sunday Able Clary happened to be in a service with his brother Dr. Clary. Afterwards, Finney was invited to Dr. Clary's home for a noontime meal.

"After arriving at his house we were soon summoned to the dinner table. We gathered about the table, and Dr. Clary turned to his brother and said 'Brother Able, will you ask the blessing?' Brother Able bowed his head and began audibly to ask a blessing. He had uttered but a sentence or two when he broke instantly down, moved suddenly back from the table, and fled to his chamber. The doctor supposed he had been taken suddenly ill, and rose up and followed him. In a few moments he came down and said, 'Mr. Finney, brother Able wants to see you.' Said I, 'What ails him?' Said he, 'I do not know, but he says; you know. He appears in great distress, but I think it is the state of his mind.' He lay groaning upon his bed, the Spirit making intercession for him, and in him, with groanings that could not be uttered. I had barely entered the room, when he made out to say, 'Pray, Brother Finney.' I knelt down and helped him in prayer, by leading his soul out for the conversion of sinners. I continued to pray until his distress passed away, and then I returned to the dinner table.

"I understood that this was the voice of God. I saw the spirit of prayer was upon him, and I felt his influence upon myself, and took it for granted that the work would move on powerfully. It did so. The pastor told me afterward that he found that in the six weeks that I was there five hundred souls had been converted" (Torrey, 22-23). Finney accredited the success of the revivals he experienced to praying saints such as Able Clary.

Those who follow in the spirit of Moses will endeavor to hold back the hordes of people rushing headlong into judgment. Those who walk in the spirit of Elijah will cry for the Great I Am to judge a people so mercy may be revealed when they repent. Compassion must be the underlying motive of true intercession. Unsaved multitudes desperately need those who will prostrate themselves before God's throne of grace until the fires of revival burn throughout the land no matter what their personal cost may be.

INTERCESSION AND PERSEVERANCE

Revival came to the Scottish Hebrides because many saints began interceding for an awakening. As stated in chapter four, after the elderly Smith sisters began praying for revival they compelled their pastor to gather some men to intercede until God would rend the heavens. The pastor secured seven men to pray in a barn while the elderly women interceded in their home. They prayed two nights a week from ten o'clock in the evening until four or five in the morning. They persevered until the LORD poured "water upon him that is thirsty, and floods upon the dry ground" (Isa. 44:3).

D. L. Moody received his baptism in the Holy Spirit because two elderly women refused to stop praying that he would receive the power of God. The results were tremendous. Nearly one million souls were saved through Moody's ministry in America and

England. Revival after revival has been birthed because saints became burdened enough to persevere in prayer until the LORD parted the heavens and came down.

Jesus taught about the necessity of persevering prayer through the parable of the unjust judge (Lk. 18:1-8). In the account, a widow kept pleading with an unjust judge to avenge her of her adversaries. Her persistence finally won the justice she sought. The Savior then made this startling statement, "When the Son of Man comes, will He find faith on the earth?" Christ was establishing that persevering prayer is an expression of authentic faith. If we desire to see revival sweep our land then it is extremely important that we express our faith through persevering prayer. We must give the LORD no rest until He rains His presence down upon us. Persevering faith is the true spirit of intercession that refuses to quit until the answer comes. There is no other way for revival to come. Jesus is asking us today if we will have persevering faith when He returns.

JESUS AND INTERCESSION

Christ's love and intercession was wonderfully portrayed while He hung upon the cross. In agony He cried, "Father, forgive them, for they do not know what they are doing." What was taking place in the heavenlies that compelled the suffering Savior to so pray? It may be suggested that the Father was ready to destroy the entire human race for the atrocities committed against His Son. This would have been a fitting act of justice for the wickedest crime ever committed. It was the Son's intercession that held back the Father's just wrath. This was the truest act of mercy ever performed. Directly, the Jews and Romans were guilty of crucifying the Messiah. In reality, all of humanity is guilty because it was each of our sins that nailed Him to the cross.

In Jesus the power of intercession was manifested in its purest form. He was the embodiment of absolute authority as God incarnate in flesh and blood. He retained that authority through His unbroken fellowship with the Father. Because of that relationship, Jesus received whatever He asked of the Father.

The same is true with us. The LORD responds to our intercession according to the quality of our relationship with Jesus.

Our fellowship with the Redeemer determines the authority He grants us. Through intimate fellowship with the Savior we can know His will and pray according to His good pleasure. Then miracles happen. Perseverance in prayer is faith in action. If we desire to be imitators of Christ, then cold-blooded prayers have no place in our lives.

PASSION IN PRAYER

Prayer must come from wholehearted devotion to the LORD. "He who prays without fervency," stated Spurgeon "does not pray at all. We cannot commune with God, who is a consuming fire, if there is no fire in our prayers" (Spurgeon, *Praying*, 36). Our prayers should never be lifeless and formal, but animated and alive. Yet, the only place to get a passion in prayer is to sit at the Savior's feet. At His feet intercessors are born and the prayers of saints become the birth pangs for revival. "For as soon as Zion travailed, she brought forth her children" (Isa. 66:8). We have not brought forth children at altars of repentance because we have not wept at His feet over our spiritual barrenness and the lostness of the world.

Our tame services and lifeless prayer meetings have accomplished little or nothing. There is a reason for our spiritual poverty and a remedy. Leonard Ravenhill offers a powerful answer, "Revival tarries because we lack urgency in prayer ... The biggest single factor contributing to delayed Holy Ghost revival is this omission of soul travail ... We will display our gifts, natural or spiritual; we will air our views, political or spiritual; we will preach a sermon or write a book to correct a brother in doctrine. But who will storm Hell's stronghold? Who will say the devil nay? Who will deny himself good food or good company or good rest that Hell may gaze upon him wrestling, embarrassing demons, liberating captives, depopulating Hell, and leaving, in answer to his travail, a stream of blood-washed souls?" (Ravenhill, *Why*, 59-60).

Passionate, persevering prayers can break open the heavens so the fires of revival burst forth. Such prayers come from people who know how to sit at the Savior's feet and are consumed by His holy fire. During the Hebrides Awakening the Holy Spirit was phenomenally present to convict men, women and children.

People could be found walking the streets weeping over their sins. In deep anguish of soul some even cried out, "O God, Hell is too good for me! Hell is too good for me" (Woosley, 130).

The revival had not reached one particular island where the minister, church and community were unconverted. As Campbell was driving a motorcycle to the church he found a teenage girl weeping along the side of the road. The evangelist stopped to minister to her and see what the Spirit was doing. He found that she was a Christian who had been praying with another teenage girl that revival would come to their godless island. Campbell knelt with the girl on the side of the road and began to pray. By the time they finished, three hours later, revival had swept the island. Young and old were driven to their knees with sobs of repentance. Not a home was left untouched and even the minister was soundly born again.

Those young girls heard the Savior's voice because they sat at His feet. While they were in prayer, God gave one of them a vision. She saw Mr. Campbell driving by that afternoon and the Spirit let her know that revival was finally coming, so she waited for the evangelist by the side of the road with tears coursing down her cheeks. The island was transformed through the persistent and impassioned prayers of two teenage girls.

PURPOSE IN PRAYER

Passion in prayer is the direct result of purpose in prayer. Christians without purpose offer passionless prayers that are always powerless. At times, the fervor in our prayer comes from the trials of life. However, as soon as the pain passes so does the enthusiasm. God desires to fill people with divine purpose so they will possess Spirit-inspired passion.

For the most part, born again believers have no idea what their purpose is on earth. They wander aimlessly about driven by little more than their selfish pursuits of life. Few Christians know their calling and even fewer have a passion to see the LORD powerfully fulfill His will in their lives. If we do not know our God-given purpose then we will never have passion in prayer or service. Every follower of Christ is called to minister the Gospel in one manner or another. There are no exceptions! Any saint that is not active in Christian service is in rebellion against the very One they claim to serve.

Scripture commands us to present our bodies as living sacrifices to God. This means that we can no longer live according to the standards of secular society but must be transformed by the power of the Holy Spirit (Rom. 12:1-2). When a person becomes a living sacrifice he will know "what God's will is–His good, pleasing and perfect will." We can deduce from Paul's statement that the reason we do not know God's good and perfect will is because we have not surrendered our all to Him. Our lack of surrender may be the result of hurt, fear, worldly ambitions, indifference, a busy life or just plain rebellion. Nonetheless, whatever keeps us from fully surrendering to the LORD, and knowing His will, is sin.

Knowing God's purpose for our lives and abandoning ourselves to His will produces passionate prayer. For example, many people teach Sunday school only because the church needs teachers rather than to fulfill a calling. This produces boring little lessons that are incapable of changing anyone. When a believer knows he is called to teach, and properly accepts that calling, he becomes passionate in prayer for those divinely entrusted to his care. Only through prayer will a teacher, preacher, parent or witness have anything of eternal worth to offer others. Purpose in life produces purpose in prayer, purpose in prayer produces passion in prayer, and passionate prayer can set our world on fire.

BROKENNESS IN PRAYER

Brokenness and prayer are irreplaceable ingredients to revival and spiritual warfare. George Otis Jr., commenting on James 4:6 stated, "'God opposes [or resists] the proud but gives grace to the humble.' This proverb, quoted twice in the New Testament, is linked contextually in both instances to spiritual warfare. And for good reason! If we want to resist the devil, we had better make sure God is not resisting us" (Otis, 244). This presents the potent truth that we cannot advance the Kingdom of Heaven if we are at odds with the Savior because of an unconquered character filled with pride and self-will.

Smith Wigglesworth taught, "To be poor in the spirit is when the human has been brought into helplessness. You are never rich to distribute until you are brought to poverty in yourselves" (Hacking, 62). The LORD wants us to see the depths of our spiritual neediness so we cling to Him with all that is within us. Because "God opposes the proud" the proud cannot bring revival. "The usual thing with pride [is] you are quite unaware of it until the Holy Spirit shows you; then you see you are full of it ... Pride, always an unpleasant thing, becomes particularly odious when it expresses itself in the realm of morals and religion" (Hession, *When*, 36 & 40).

In contrast to the ugliness of pride is the beauty of brokenness. Brokenness makes a people beautifully attractive to Almighty God. "The LORD is near to those who have a broken heart, And saves such as have a contrite spirit" (Ps. 34:18; NKJV). To become broken before the LORD we must see the truth about ourselves through the eyes of Jesus and His Holy Word. We are frail, needy people who can no more save or change ourselves than a leopard can change his spots. However, there is power with God.

From the altar of brokenness we obtain answers to our petitions and pleas for revival. Brokenness in prayer is as the incense that billows from the altar before God's throne and fills His senses with holy delight. The LORD loves the prayers of those who comprehend their neediness and cry to a merciful Creator to demonstrate His power on their behalf. "Prayer that does not stem from a life of humility before God is powerless, and is little more than a waste of valuable time. It is only as the Christian goes down in humility before God that his prayers will rise and be effective" (Paul Smith, 32).

The LORD demonstrates unique favor to those who live a life of brokenness. "The sacrifices of God are a broken spirit; a broken and contrite heart, O God, You will not despise" (Ps. 51:17). Again the LORD establishes, "This is the one I esteem: he who is humble and contrite in spirit, and trembles at My Word" (Isa. 66:2b). It is from the place of brokenness that true intercessors are born. Their small embers of passion for the Savior and a perishing world can burst into the consuming flames of revival.

CHAPTER TWELVE

DESTINY OF THE DAMNED

There is only one sure proof of revival—the visible transformation of secular society through vast numbers of radical conversions. Anything less is not authentic revival. Christians that have been genuinely awakened will never remain passionless about those who will spend an eternity in Hell. Awakened saints will have a fire burning in their bones to win a dying culture to Christ. That is why a revived church will always be a soul-winning church. H. Elvet Lewis, speaking on the 1904 Welsh Revival, gave the reason why the Gospel spread with such force, "Men who were before professing Christians were now evangelists, and men who had notorious fame hitherto as the curse of their homes, returned as missionaries" (Roberts, *Glory*, 79).

An immense number of Christians are not reaching the lost because they have forgotten what it was like to live without Christ. We have forgotten the hurt and sorrow our self-destructive lifestyles heaped upon us. We have failed to remember the loneliness and torment that accompanied our search for significance. We have forced out of our minds the painful rejections we endured in our quest for love. We no longer recall the emptiness that drove our selfish pursuits for pleasure. Yes, we can even forget the grief we inflicted upon our friends and loved ones through our self-absorbed lives. Tragically, we have forgotten the misery and sorrow that presently consumes every person that does not know Jesus as Savior.

Oh, how we need to sit at the feet of the Master until we remember what we were saved from and what we are saved to accomplish. Paul told us to "remember that at that time you were separate from Christ ... without hope and without God in the world" (Eph. 2:12). Hurting people are waiting for us to remember. Until that time, they suffer under their cruel bondage to sin. The Spirit is longing to make His appeal through us to those who do not know the bountiful love of Christ. The purpose of this chapter is to make plain to our hearts and minds the actual destiny of those rushing to damnation. May God "enlighten the eyes of our hearts" so that we would always live in the light of such truth. It is time to remember!

LAW AND CONSCIENCE

The Sovereign LORD gave humanity the gift of a free will and an active conscience. With these gifts comes the responsibility of their proper use. Free will grants individuals the right to choose between right and wrong. The conscience is the faculty for recognizing right and wrong. The problem with our free will and conscience lies in the fact that every human being possesses a sinful nature that is predisposed to rebellion against the Creator. This predisposition towards sin causes us to abuse these precious gifts of a free will and conscience.

To aid us in responsibly using these gifts, God gave us the Ten Commandments and the other moral laws expressed in both the Old and New Testaments. These commandments were given to be the moral and spiritual standards by which all of humanity is called to live. They are rules for right living in the sight of God and with one another. What individuals do with their free will, conscience and the divine moral law will either accuse or defend them before the Righteous Judge (Rom. 2:15).

Rejection of God's laws changes right and wrong into a subjective, relativistic morality. Morality is then socially engineered, reducing right and wrong to the whims of an individual or society. This gives way to a pragmatic, humanistic approach to ethics that is based upon cause and effect, or whatever works at any given time. To reject God's decrees is deliberate rebellion against the Eternal Lawgiver. It is an act of self-exaltation against the Creator that makes the individual god. This self-idolatry breaks the first of the Ten Commandments—"You shall have no other gods before Me" (Ex. 20:3).

The heart of an individual or society grows hard when they reject their Creator and His commandments. This deadens the conscience to right and wrong. What was once morally intolerable becomes acceptable, even to the point of propagating moral deviance. However, the truth is never arbitrary, changeable or pragmatic. So what happens when we break these God-given commands and violate the gifts of a free will and conscience? We become guilty before the Lawgiver as lawbreakers. Elevate God's righteous law and you restore divine power to expose sin and convict the sinner. This is the non-Christian's only hope to escape God's righteous wrath.

The law and the Holy Spirit work hand in hand in saving sinners. The law reveals the LORD's holy standards that have been broken, and the Spirit drives the truth home to the conscience. The law is good and it is the goodness of God that exposes our sin. Jonathan Edwards wrote that men have to be so dealt with that "...their conscience stares them in the face and they begin to see their need" (Iain Murray, 129). Finney asserted, "The law does its work—annihilates the sinner's self-righteousness and shows him that mercy is his only hope. Then, he should be made to understand that it is morally impossible for a just God not to execute a penalty when the law has been broken" (Finney, *Power*, 69).

THEY ARE LOST

The life of Christ was divine love in action. "When He saw the crowds, He had compassion on them, because they were harassed and helpless, like sheep without a shepherd" (Mt. 9:36). The Good Shepherd came to rescue the lost sheep wandering aimlessly through life in spiritual blindness, even though many thought they could see. He will leave the ninety-nine obedient sheep to pursue a wandering lamb that strayed through willful rebellion (Mt. 18:12-14). Great joy fills the Good Shepherd's heart as each wandering soul is rescued from their self-destructive estrangement from the Savior.

In the parable of the Prodigal Son (Lk. 15:11-32) a young man lived a life of self-determined rebellion against his father. The father knew that the rebellion in the young man's heart would only grow if he stayed at home. Though it broke his heart, the father allowed his son to leave home though it was contrary to his will. He knew that the wages of sin would eventually catch up to the young man and hoped that they would drive his boy home before they destroyed him. This parable differs from the lost sheep in that the father did not pursue the son as the shepherd did the sheep. The prodigal knew the way home. The lost sheep did not. Great joy erupts when the prodigal returns home.

These parables reveal two different kinds of unsaved people: those who have never served the LORD and those who have willfully turned their backs on Him. Regardless of the circumstances, anyone who does not know Jesus as Lord and Savior is at war with Him.

REALITIES OF THE UNSAVED

The Scriptures paint a terrifying picture of the eternal state of unrepentant sinners—they are destined for damnation. Below are six Biblical realities regarding their spiritual condition.

EVERY PERSON IS A SINNER

The Bible clearly teaches that sin is universal. It touches every individual whether he is a believer or not. The apostle John, writing to Christians, told us that those who contend that they do not sin are in essence accusing God of being a liar (1 Jn. 1:10). After King David repented of his adulterous affair with Bathsheba he confessed, "Surely I was sinful at birth, sinful from the time my mother conceived me" (Ps. 51:5). King Solomon, David's son, wrote, "There is not a just man upon the face of the earth that does good and never sins" (Ecc. 7:20). Non-Christians are willful sinners who obstinately continue their practice of sin. Though Christians sin, they have stopped its practice.

Sin is both destructive and deceptive. It literally puts the sinner at war with God. Sin in its very nature blinds the sinner to the depths of his rebellion so he thinks himself exempt from any danger before his Maker. Some think that their sin is not a real issue with the LORD, that He does not see, or does not care. Many even erroneously believe that there is no such thing as sin. Such attitudes flow out of rebellious hearts that say, "The LORD does not see; the God of Jacob pays no heed" (Ps. 94:7). Nonetheless, sin is direct, purposeful rebellion against Christ and the laws that govern His Kingdom. Since God's laws are founded upon His holy character, sin becomes an offense against His person, an enormous crime far beyond what we can fathom.

The sin of idolatry is a crime that every non-Christian commits. Because they refuse to worship the true and living God, they create through their own imaginations a god that thinks and acts just like them. Their manmade god condones their lifestyles and is undisturbed by their immoral acts. In spite of their beliefs, the LORD remains the same; He is not like sinful man. "These things you have done and I kept silent; you thought I was altogether like you. But I will rebuke you and accuse you to your face" (Ps. 50:21).

SIN IS A DISEASE

All of humanity suffers under the curse of sin and the resulting judgment. In Jewish thought, the disease of leprosy was far more than just a physical affliction; it was a judgment against a rebellious sinner. Leprosy symbolized the destructive force of sin and the consequences that follow (Lev. 13:45-46).

Lepers were expelled from the community to live in garments of mourning until they were healed. Because certain types of diseases classified as leprosy were contagious, lepers were cast out of the populace for the protection of the community. This signified that they were lost, outside of the commonwealth of faith, damned. They had to cry, "unclean, unclean" to warn others of their devastating disease so the plague would not spread. It was a miserable existence of weeping, gnashing of teeth and the utter darkness of despair. Such is the reality of sin. It always produces sorrow and will do so throughout eternity.

We read in Matthew's Gospel of a leper who cried out to Jesus, "Lord, if You are willing, You can make me clean. Jesus reached out His hand and touched the man. 'I am willing,' He said. 'Be clean!' Immediately he was cured of his leprosy" (Mt. 8:2-4). Jesus accomplished more than just healing the leper's body; He restored the man's relationship with God and with the community of faith. The Savior is always willing to heal those who suffer spiritual leprosy when they acknowledge their sin and cry, "Lord, make me clean."

Scripture employs the analogy of sin as a disease to illustrate its destructiveness in this life. However, the eternal ramifications of sin make it far more devastating than any physical disease. If sin was merely a hereditary disease then humanity would not be judged for it. However, sin is a willful choice, not a genetic disorder. "Before any sin can be enacted, it must be willed by some free personal agent, for that which is not willed is not sin" (Oden, 90).

SIN IS REBELLION AGAINST GOD

During the years of Isaiah the prophet, Israel and Judah rebelled against the LORD. Throughout his lifetime, the only ruler who walked with the LORD was Hezekiah. Listen to the prophet's opening oracle:

"Hear, O heavens! Listen, O earth! For the LORD has spoken: 'I reared children and brought them up, but they have rebelled against Me. The ox knows his master, the donkey his owner's manger, but Israel does not know, My people do not understand.' Ah, sinful nation, a people loaded with guilt, a brood of evildoers, children given to corruption! They have forsaken the LORD; they have spurned the Holy One of Israel and turned their backs on Him. Why should you be beaten anymore? Why do you persist in rebellion? Your whole head is injured, your whole heart afflicted. From the sole of your foot to the top of your head there is no soundness—only wounds and welts and open sores, not cleansed or bandaged or soothed with oil. Your country is desolate, your cities burned with fire; your fields are being stripped by foreigners right before you, laid waste as when overthrown by strangers ... Unless the LORD Almighty had left us some survivors, we would have become like Sodom, we would have been like Gomorrah" (Isa. 1:2-8).

This prophecy illustrates that a dumb ox can have greater awareness of who its master is than a man. Israel's rebellion was manifested through their lifestyles. "But these people have stubborn and rebellious hearts; they have turned aside and gone away" (Jer. 5:23). Their sin multiplied in the breeding ground of unrepentant hearts.

In addition, they refused to accept responsibility for their sinful lifestyles. The prophet described their self-destructive rebellion in light of a flesh-consuming disease, "only wounds and welts and open sores." Their sin placed them outside of God's salvation. Sin had become so ingrained into the lifestyles of the people that if justice was executed they would have been utterly destroyed as was Sodom and Gomorrah.

The sinner's revolt against the Creator is unmistakably portrayed in his refusal to surrender his life to the Savior. Such an act is nothing less than insurrection against the Almighty and is the work of a God-hater. (Isa. 63:10). All who refuse to bow to the lordship of Christ will in turn rebel against the laws of His Kingdom. Thus it follows that such persons after refusing to submit to the Sovereign LORD on earth would never want to go to Heaven where His Lordship is fully revealed.

SIN IS WICKED BEFORE GOD

Many believe the lie that a holy God will not demand and enforce His righteous laws. Such a belief degrades His holy nature by making Him a lawbreaker like us. The LORD of Righteousness punishes wickedness because it is unequivocally antagonistic to His character and the laws of His Kingdom. The prophet Samuel rebuked King Saul proclaiming: "For rebellion is as the sin of witchcraft, And stubbornness is as iniquity and idolatry" (1 Sam. 15:23a; NKJV). Sin, in all of its various forms, is rebellion against the Almighty!

Multitudes consider themselves to be morally good people. They say, "We're not that bad," or "not as bad as others." Such statements reveal a personal knowledge of sin but a refusal to accept responsibility for it. Sin remains exceedingly wicked regardless of our opinions. Our guilt is blatantly obvious if we have the courage to open our eyes and see the reality that our transgressions lie deeply imbedded within our bosoms.

Humanity is predisposed to do evil, not inherently good, as some have claimed. Jesus stated the reality when He said, "... how can you who are evil say anything good?" (Mt. 12:34a). No matter how many good deeds a person has done, sin always defiles the person and makes him guilty as a lawbreaker. "Who can say, 'I have kept my heart pure; I am clean and without sin?'" (Pr. 20:9). Truly, no deed can be acceptable to God if the person is not first accepted by Him. This means that there is nothing an unsaved person can do that is good or pleasing to God. No matter how good a person may think himself to be, sin still defiles him and places him at war with the LORD of Hosts. This war continues until the rebellious sinner repents and surrenders his or her life to the King of kings.

Our transgressions are rooted deep within the heart. "The LORD saw how great man's wickedness on the earth had become, and that every inclination of the thoughts of his heart was only evil all the time" (Gen. 6:5). All sin comes from the heart, "For out of the heart come evil thoughts, murder, adultery, sexual immorality, theft, false testimony, slander ... For out of the overflow of the heart the mouth speaks" (Mt. 15:19; 12:34). Jeremiah stated, "The heart is deceitful above all things and beyond cure. Who can understand it?" (Jer. 17:9).

UNREPENTANT SINNERS HATE GOD

All sin is anarchy against Christ's Kingdom. Sins are selfish acts of lawlessness. Selfishness is what defines the lifestyle of every unbeliever. Even when they perform benevolent acts, selfishness remains thoroughly entrenched in their hearts. Selfishness is rooted in their voluntary rejection of God and His laws. The Righteous Judge accuses the sinner, not for his nature, but for his willful acts that are contrary to God's moral standards.

Worse than the fact that impenitent sinners are lawless, they are by nature God-haters. "Here I would like to establish that unrepentant sinners positively hate God ... Sinners manifest great pleasure in sin: it is the element in which they live and move" (Finney, *Principles*, 137). Jesus said, "If anyone loves Me, he will obey My teaching ... He who does not love Me will not obey My teaching" (Jn. 14:23-24). Love for the Savior is proved through surrender and obedience to Him, while hatred for Him is demonstrated through rebellion. The very fact that unbelievers refuse to obey the commandments of Christ and yield their lives to Him in unswerving devotion confirms the truth that they are God-haters. This hatred for God is manifested in one's love of self and sin. Actually, the unsaved love their sin more than anything else, including God, spouse, children and friends.

Sentimental feelings or faithful church attendance does not mean a person loves the LORD. Willful rebellion is hatred toward God whether or not the person goes to church or has been baptized. James plainly expounded on this truth when he told us that the love of this world is "hatred toward God" (Jam. 4:4). The sinner's refusal to yield to Christ's lordship and Kingdom is no different than a terrorist's rebellion against a country. Both are in anarchy against a particular government. To the one it is the government of God; to the other the government of men.

THE SINNER'S SPIRITUAL FATHER

John made the terrifying statement, "He who does what is sinful is of the devil, because the devil has been sinning from the beginning. The reason the Son of God appeared was to destroy the devil's work. No one who is born of God will continue (practice) to sin" (1 Jn. 3:8-9a). If a person practices sin he is NOT a child of God, but a child of the devil, whether or not he claims to be a Christian. Jesus rebuked the religious people of His day saying, "You belong to your father, the devil, and you want to carry out your father's desire. He was a murderer from the beginning, not holding to the truth, for there is no truth in him. When he lies, he speaks his native language, for he is a liar and the father of lies" (Jn. 8:44). Examine the fruit and you will know the tree. Live in sin and your spiritual father is the devil.

GOD AS JUDGE

We champion the cause of justice, believing it to be a good thing in business, government and personal life. It angers us when politicians exempt themselves from the very laws they pass, or when businessmen use unjust means to increase their wealth. We believe in a judicial system that strives to execute justice, dispensing equitable penalties to the guilty while exonerating the innocent. Why then do we think God unjust when He executes justice in damning a soul to Hell?

We want God to be just, but we want Him to judge according to our standards. However, only God judges perfectly. He alone is infinite in wisdom, perfect in justice and absolute in holiness. His judgments are not corrupted by political bias, news polls, circumstantial evidence or the decision of a jury. Absolute truth is the basis of His judgments. He makes no mistakes!

The righteous judgments of the LORD go beyond our actions to the intents of the heart. Since He possesses perfect knowledge of every person, He is able to judge according to truth and is fully justified when He judges (Ps. 51:4). Many have attempted to vindicate their actions by saying, "God understands." You bet He does! No excuses on judgment day—only truth. The hearts of men will be laid bare before the living God. There will be no place to run, no place to hide and no attorneys to consult. "It is a dreadful thing to fall into the hands of the living God" (Heb. 10:31).

Everyone who does not know Jesus will be judged for his or her crimes against the Almighty. "Man is destined to die once, and after that to face judgment" (Heb. 9:27). This is not a game; eternity is at stake! "Do you not know that the wicked will not inherit the Kingdom of God? Do not be deceived: Neither the sexually immoral nor idolaters nor adulterers nor male prostitutes nor homosexual offenders, nor thieves nor the greedy nor drunkards nor slanderers nor swindlers will inherit the Kingdom of God" (1 Cor. 6:9-10). The LORD of Hosts does not make idle threats.

We have no concept of what it means to stand before God's infinite righteous wrath. It will be a time of terror beyond comprehension. His holy presence will fill the ungodly with dread, "Then the kings of the earth, the princes, the generals, the rich, the mighty, and every slave and every free man hid in caves and among the rocks of the mountains. They called to the mountains and the rocks, 'Fall on us and hide us from the face of Him who sits on the throne and from the wrath of the Lamb! For the great day of their wrath has come, and who can stand?'" (Rev. 6:15-17).

Eternal horror awaits those who have not known Christ. In anxious fright, they will stand before their Maker as the Book of Life is opened. "And I saw the dead, great and small, standing before the throne, and books were opened. Another book was opened, which is the book of life. The dead were judged according to what they had done as recorded in the books" (Rev. 20:12). Those whose names are not written in the Book of Life will be thrown into the eternal lake of fire.

When a person repents of his sin and surrenders his life to Jesus, his name is written in the Book of Life. The only way to guarantee his name will never be blotted out of the Book is to faithfully serve the Savior until his dying day (Ps. 69:28; Rev. 3:5). The wisest thing a man can do is to make sure his name is in that book. The most agonizing words anyone could ever hear would be, "Depart from Me, you who are cursed, into the eternal fire prepared for the devil and his angels" (Mt. 25:41).

HELL

Life beyond the grave is no less real than the one in which we now live. The LORD has "set eternity in the hearts of men; yet they cannot fathom what God has done from beginning to end" (Ecc. 3:11). All of mankind longs for eternal life even though we struggle with its Biblical concept because human experience suggests that everything has a beginning and an end. This means we lack any point of reference to eternity, which in turn presents us with the tremendous difficulty of grasping its mysteries. The only sure revelation concerning eternity must then come from beyond ourselves. Thankfully, God has not left us alone. He has revealed to us the realities of life after death through His Word. Even so, the Bible only allows us to see these realities from a distance.

Everything Jesus taught came from an eternal perspective. He possessed the authority to speak about eternal realities because He created them. As the author of truth, everything He taught about Heaven and Hell was based upon absolute truth. When we examine His teaching we find that He spoke more about Hell than about Heaven. In fact, Jesus went to great lengths to warn humanity of the realities of Hell. Love was the compelling force that moved Him to forewarn us about an everlasting judgment. It is interesting to note that our positive thinking, non-confrontational, cultural Christianity would label Jesus as a pessimist and a hindrance to church growth.

Jesus made every effort to change the destiny of the damned. What then remains for those who choose to rebel against the Savior? Death! Both physical and eternal. The Scriptures teach, "For the wages of sin is death" (Rom. 6:23a). The ungodly will not only experience physical death, but eternal death as well. "But the cowardly, the unbelieving, the vile, the murderers, the sexually immoral, those who practice magic arts, the idolaters and all liars—their place will be in the fiery lake of burning sulfur. This is the second death" (Rev. 21:8). All who die without Christ will taste the never-ending agonies of the second death.

The crime of murder is particularly hideous, especially since mankind was created in God's image (Gen. 9:6). Ponder for a moment the feelings of a man who saw his son brutally murdered. Would the death penalty for the perpetrator and ten million dollars compensate him for the loss of his son? Of course not! Now consider the murder of God's own Son. What punishment would be fitting for those who crucified the Redeemer? Not even an eternity in Hell would be a just recompense for the most heinous crime ever committed. In fact, all of humanity throughout time stands personally guilty for murdering the Lamb of God.

Throughout the ages, men have attempted to discharge themselves of this damnable crime of crucifying the Messiah. The truth will be revealed when we stand before the Father. On that day, what excuse will we offer, how will we absolve ourselves? Will any defense be sufficient to justify our sin and grant us a right to Heaven? Could baptism, church attendance or supposed good deeds cleanse such a wicked transgression? Absolutely NOT! Mankind has no remedy in himself for a sin so thoroughly horrendous. This is why Jesus died on the cross, to take upon Himself the punishment for our crimes against Heaven so we could obtain mercy and forgiveness.

Now what if God turned a "blind eye" in some special cases and let a few of the "good" sinners into Heaven? He would be neither just, nor good. The non-Biblical doctrines of purgatory and universalism (everybody goes to Heaven) may seem nice after living a rebellious life, but they are damnable lies. Life in this world is the only preparation time we are given for eternity. When we pass through death's door it is too late to pray, too late to repent and too late to change the way we live. Furthermore, it is thoroughly illogical to think that people who rejected the LORD in this life would want to spend an eternity with Him. All who refuse to love and serve Him while on earth will never want to love and serve Him in Heaven. Those who do not want to worship Him in this life will never want to sing His praises in those celestial halls, and everyone who does not want to live holy in this life will never want to do so in the next.

Hell was prepared for Satan and his fallen angels, not for humanity. Through mankind's willful rebellion against their Creator Hell became the eternal habitation of all who reject Him. "The wicked shall be turned into Hell, and all the nations that forget God" (Ps. 9:17; KJV). Human imagination cannot fathom the pain and suffering of Hell. John the Baptist called it a place of unquenchable fire. Jesus described it as "a furnace of fire: there shall be wailing and gnashing of teeth" (Mt.13:42). The wailing and gnashing of teeth refer to both their hatred of God and their eternal torments. Every resident of Hell will only know despair and absolute loneliness. There will be none to comfort.

Jesus counseled us to, "fear not them which kill the body, but are not able to kill the soul: but rather fear him which is able to destroy both soul and body in Hell" (Mk. 9:45-48; Mt. 10:28). There are no parties in Hell or moments of joy; only weeping, gnashing of teeth, hopelessness and haunting memories. They will spend eternity remembering their willful rebellion. Forever they will REMEMBER.

CHAPTER THIRTEEN

RESCUE THE PERISHING

Fanny Crosby, the blind hymn writer of the late nineteenth century, had a driving passion to win the lost to Christ. This burden compelled her to tell the salvation story to all who would listen, whether it was a homeless man at the Bowery Mission in New York City or a stranger on the streets. Once while addressing a group of workmen in Cincinnati, Ohio she had an overwhelming sensation that "some mother's boy must be rescued that night or not at all" (Ruffin, 104). She then pleaded with the audience for that young man to come forward, which he did. That night, alone in her darkened room, Fanny recorded on paper the pleadings of her LORD's heart:

> Rescue the perishing, care for the dying,
>   Snatch them in pity from sin and the grave.
> Weep o'er the erring one, lift up the fallen,
>   Tell them of Jesus the mighty to save.
> Rescue the perishing, care for the dying;
>   Jesus is merciful, Jesus will save.

The Father of mercies sent the Son to rescue a perishing world. This is what Calvary is all about and this is the Savior's ordained mission for every true believer, without exception. In the last chapter we examined the destiny of the damned—the reality that every unsaved person is going to a literal Hell. Now we must analyze how revival works into the divine scheme of reaching a fallen world.

The King of Creation designed the church to be a community of faith that is an instrument of the Holy Spirit to rescue the perishing. Whenever Christians possess God's heart they aggressively reach the unsaved. When we fall into lukewarmness our hearts are hardened to the temporal and eternal agonies of those without Christ. Ezekiel prophesied, "My sheep wandered over all the mountains and on every high hill. They were scattered over the whole earth, and no one searched or looked for them" (Ezk. 34:6). Tragically, most American Christians are not searching for the lost sheep Jesus died to save either. We have more than enough Bible knowledge to accomplish the task. In the end, failing to reach the lost is a heart problem, not a knowledge issue. Our self-absorbing love of pleasure and sin drains us of our compassion for the lost.

The LORD desires His church to resemble those who came out of the upper room on the day of Pentecost—filled with the Spirit's power to turn the world upside down. The lost desperately need us to be full of faith and full of the Holy Ghost or we will not have the power and authority to set them free. They need us to be Christ's hands to touch them, His feet to run after them, and His voice to call them home. George Macleod pleaded that "... the cross be raised again at the center of the marketplace as well as on the steeple of the church. I am recovering the claim that Jesus was not crucified in a cathedral between two candles, but on a cross between two thieves; on the town garbage heap; at the crossroad so cosmopolitan that they had to write his title in Hebrew and in Latin and in Greek ... at the kind of place where cynics talk smut, and thieves curse, and soldiers gamble. Because that is where He died. And that is what He died about. And that is where churchmen ought to be, and what churchmen should be about" (Dixon, 168).

It is time we become modern day John the Baptists crying in the wildernesses of our neighborhoods, schools and cities. To compassionately warn the ungodly, "Repent, for the Kingdom of Heaven is near" (Mt. 3:2) and plead with the careless, "Prepare to meet thy God" (Amos 4:12). Before we will allow our lives to be disturbed with the suffering and sin of others, it is essential that we know God's heart for humanity and allow it to change our lives.

THE HEART OF GOD

God's heart for the human race is perfectly seen in the face of Jesus Christ. The fifty-third chapter of Isaiah is a prophetic picture of the purpose of Christ's sacrificial death. This oracle was announced seven hundred and fifty years before the actual event took place. The fifth verse unmistakably reveals the crucified Savior's mission. "But He was pierced for our transgressions, He was crushed for our iniquities; the punishment that brought us peace was upon Him, and by His wounds we are healed" (Isa. 53:5). This section of Scripture explains why the Father sent His Son. A brief study of this verse will assist us in beginning to understand His heart.

Jesus was "pierced for our transgressions." The Hebrew word for transgression is *pesha*, which can also be translated as rebellion. Every sin constitutes a deliberate act of rebellion against God because all sin is the breaking of His laws. Our rebellion is so deeply rooted in our character that it is impossible to free ourselves from its evil control. The Messiah was pierced with nails, thorns and spear so we could be forgiven and find victory over our rebellious nature.

Jesus was "crushed for our iniquities." We are easily overwhelmed with the guilty burden of our transgressions and crumble under the regrets that weigh down our hearts. Jesus did not abandon humanity. The Lamb of God took upon Himself the crushing weight of our crimes against Heaven so we could be emancipated from the slavery of sin. Rebels will never experience freedom from sin until they know the joy of godly repentance.

Jesus bore the "punishment that brought us peace." Humanity is a rebel race convinced that their rebellion is normal. Unrepentant sinners are waging a real war against Almighty God. They fight against His Kingdom and willfully break His laws. Every non-Christian defiantly refuses to bow his knee to the King of kings in spite of the consequences of such an act of high treason. The Scriptures teach that "the wages of sin is death" (Rom. 6:23). There is no such thing as balancing the scales of life by doing more good deeds than bad. Nor is there a possibility of compromise between God and rebels. Jesus took upon Himself the punishment we justly deserve so peace could be made between God and man. The war ends when rebels fall at the feet of the Savior and plead for mercy.

By Christ's "wounds we are healed." Though sin may produce fleeting moments of pleasure, in the end it ALWAYS inflicts sorrow; sorrow in this life and sorrow in the next. Sin inflicts sorrow on us, our loved ones and even upon strangers. Earth is a planet of pain, a weeping world full of sorrow, suffering under the wages of our sinful labors. The Father saw the sorrow sin heaped upon fallen man and was filled with perfect pity. So He sent His Son to rescue all who would turn from their self-destructive ways by abandoning themselves to Him. He who knew no sin was beaten, bruised and crucified so we could find spiritual, emotional, physical and relational healing through Him.

The Father sent the Son to "seek and to save what was lost" (Lk. 19:10). Though He hates our sin, He loves us. The prize Jesus sought while hanging on Golgotha's tree was the heart of man. His love for us was so great that it drove Him to the cross. He purchased our deliverance with His own blood. What greater expression of love could be portrayed than the Redeemer laying down His life for a rebel race: the perfect for the imperfect, the righteous for the wicked, and the innocent for the guilty? The Lover of our soul aggressively pursued us, even when we did not want Him. This is the heart of God!

GOD'S HEART REVEALED

As the Father sent the Son into the world to save sinners, Jesus sent His disciples. How can we claim to be disciples of Christ when we do not live out the same mission that compelled Him to the cross? The apostle John taught, "Whoever claims to live in Him must walk as Jesus did" (1 Jn. 2:6). This command is not an option. We must love as He loved, forgive as He forgave, seek the lost as He sought them and sacrifice our lives in like manner. Paul presented this same teaching when he commanded all believers to be imitators of Jesus (Eph.5:1). We become imitators of the Master when we know His heartbeat and touch a suffering world with His tender mercy.

Missionary Jim Elliot was martyred in Ecuador when he brought the Saviour's love to a feared tribe of cruel Indians. His life was not his own as evidenced by a prayer he composed in his diary, "God deliver me from the dread asbestos of other things. Saturate me with the oil of the Spirit that I may be aflame ... Father, take my life, yea, my blood if Thou wilt, and consume it with Thine enveloping fire. I would not save it, for it is not mine to save. Have it, Lord, have it all ... Pour out my life as an oblation for the world ... Make me Thy fuel, Flame of God!" (Elliot, 58-59, 240). His blood, along with four other missionaries, baptized that stony spot where they were slain. The Conquering King then claimed that land as His own.

Elisabeth Elliot continued the work her husband Jim began. She took the saving message of Jesus to the very tribe that murdered her husband. In time, even those who slaughtered the missionaries were wonderfully converted. One person ablaze with the heart of God can do more than a hundred thousand lukewarm Christians.

Revival is one of the most beautiful expressions of God's heart. The outpouring of the Holy Spirit awakens the church and reaps a tremendous harvest of souls for the Kingdom. "The Christian man who studies the streets," taught William Riley, "will rightly interpret the spirit of Jesus, who, when He looked upon the multitude, was filled with compassion for them. With his Savior he will see that the poor are there, the maimed, the halt, the blind; yea, there are the wounded, the bleeding, the dying!" (Riley, 200). When we see the destiny of the damned through the eyes of Christ, we will weep as He wept and be filled with His compassion that transforms men and nations.

Jesus compelled the saints of all ages to, "open your eyes and look at the fields! They are ripe for harvest" (Jn. 4:35). The critical need in this hour is for laborers or the plentiful crop of souls will forever be lost. All we have to do is open our eyes and see that our family, friends, and co-workers are damning themselves to Hell through their rebellion. It would forever change our lives if we could gaze into the depths of Hell for a minute. We would hear the cries of the damned, smell the flesh that is ever burning but never consumed, feel the unending despair of utter hopelessness and hear the hatred for God that spews from their lips. Oh, how it would utterly change us.

One day while traveling on a train, Jesus revealed His heart to General William Booth, founder of the Salvation Army. In a vision he saw a raging sea. Above it loomed blackened storm clouds that sent forth lightning and peals of thunder. A massive rock arose out of the sea, breaking through the stormy sky, piercing the heavens. Around the base of the great rock a platform was built where people walked around enjoying themselves.

As Booth peered deeper into the sea, he saw the faces of men and women screaming in hopeless agony as they were drowning with no one to rescue them. One after another would sink down, never to rise again. The raging ocean was the sea of humanity in rebellion against God. The lightning and thunder were divine warnings of the eternal judgment awaiting those who reject their Maker. Christ was the rock that came out of the sea of humanity, spanning Heaven and earth. The platform built upon the rock was the church. The majority of those on the platform carelessly strolled about in their selfish pursuits, unconcerned that multitudes of immortal souls were drowning in their sin. They were far too busy with the cares of this life to be concerned about the perishing. Only a few saints selflessly surrendered themselves to the Savior's service to reach the lost. This was a picture of the church in Booth's day and now in our own.

The LORD shared with Booth His heart and thoughts (Pr. 1:23). He became a man consumed with reaching people who were dying in their sin. During the early days of the Salvation Army, his converts aggressively sought to bring non-Christians to the foot of the cross. They saw men, women and children radically saved, and in this way the Army flourished. Many of these radicals founded outposts around the world because they were thoroughly devoted to the Savior's mission. What a phenomenal privilege is offered to Christians that they could live and die in the service of their Redeemer. This kind of dedication is not extreme. It is the expected lifestyle of every true disciple.

REVIVAL AND REFORMATION

Genuine revival always incorporates reformation. Reformation is the restoration of Biblical truths and practices that were forsaken through neglect or false teaching. "I believe that the imperative need of the day is not simply revival," touted Tozer, "but the radical reformation that will go to the root of our moral and spiritual maladies and deal with the causes rather than with consequences, with the disease rather than with symptoms" (Tozer, *Keys*, 12). Such is the case with the doctrine of Heaven and Hell and the command to reach the unsaved.

The evangelical church in the west, including Pentecostals and Charismatics, may doctrinally believe in a literal Heaven and Hell, but applicationally live as though these doctrines were fairy tales. In practice, most Christians prove by their lifestyles that they do not care about those who are dying without Christ. Their assertions about wanting to see the lost saved are only worthless boasts to ease their consciences because their lifestyles do not line up with their claims.

Leonard Ravenhill related a story that revealed the conflict between our lifestyles and doctrine. "Charlie Peace was a criminal. Laws of God or man curbed him not. Finally the law caught up with him, and he was condemned to death. On the fatal morning in Armley Jail, Leeds, England, he was taken on the death-walk. Before him went the prison chaplain, routinely and sleepily reading some Bible verses. The criminal touched the preacher and asked what he was reading. 'The Consolations of Religion,' was the reply. Charlie Peace was shocked at the way he professionally read about Hell. Could a man be so unmoved under the very shadow of the scaffold as to lead a fellow-human there and yet, dry-eyed, read of a pit that has no bottom into which this fellow must fall? Could this preacher believe the words that there is an eternal fire that never consumes its victims, and yet slide over the phrase without a tremor? Is a man human at all who can say with no tears, 'You will be eternally dying and yet never know the relief that death brings'? All this was too much for Charlie—so he preached.

"'Sir' addressing the preacher, 'if I believed what you and the church of God say that you believe, even if England were covered with broken glass from coast to coast, I would walk over it, if need be, on hands and knees and think it worthwhile living, just to save one soul from an eternal Hell like that'" (Ravenhill, *Why*, 34). An applicational belief in Hell would compel Christians to change their lifestyles in whatever manner necessary to fulfill the privileged responsibility of being Christ's ambassadors to the world.

The church is shrinking in America and Western Europe. She has lost her voice to speak to secular society. Our compromise has caused the unsaved to think that the church is irrelevant in our post-modern world. If we do not wake up to this terrifying situation, we may soon be like many Western European nations where less than one percent of the population is born again. A modern dark age has fallen over much of Europe as the people reject Biblical Christianity for the pantheon of secular and sensual gods, and we are quickly becoming like them. We need a modern reformation to bring us back to New Testament Christianity in word, practice and power.

Many churches that have claimed to be in revival never obtained the genuine because they did not experience a reformation. Since their theology and lifestyles were not greatly altered from what it was before the alleged event took place, they never bore the proof of legitimate revival i.e., the transformation of society. Their Christianity did not line up with the Scriptural and historical model of a revived church that turns the world upside down. A move of God may have begun in the church but never became an authentic revival because reformation never took place. Tozer had something to add to this point. "It is my considered opinion that under the present circumstances we do not want revival at all. A widespread revival of the kind of Christianity we know today in America might prove to be a moral tragedy from which we would not recover in a hundred years" (Tozer, *Keys*, 12). What a terrifying indictment.

Revival and reformation changes the very belief, character and heart of people, who in turn become agents of change in their church, community and nation. We must be careful not to propagate as revival that which is nothing more than another version of self-centered religion or maybe something worse. The Prince of Peace wants us to know His heart and be renewed by the power of His Word. Then a revived church can take the reformation into the highways and hedges of our fallen world.

EVERY SAINT'S RESPONSIBILITY

Jesus commanded every Christian to "go and make disciples" (Mt. 28:19). We are called to reach the unsaved and instruct new converts in how to live as aliens and radicals in this world. Before we can repent of not rescuing the perishing we must first come to grips with the reality that it is sin. Our pride and fear of man has kept us from witnessing about the Lover of our souls. Our love of pleasure has driven us to avoid the inconveniences of touching the eternal and temporal needs of a hurting world. J. H. Jowett challenged the church, "Does the cry of the world's need pierce the heart and ring even through the fabric of our dreams? I can take my newspaper, which is oftentimes a veritable cupful of horrors, and I can pursue it at the breakfast table, and it does not add a single tang to my feast. I wonder if one who is as unmoved can ever be a servant of the suffering LORD!" (Jowett, 35). True compassion and obedience is far more than talk.

Every believer is called to be "Christ's ambassadors, as though God were making His appeal through us" (2 Cor. 5:20). What an astounding privilege that the Almighty would make His appeal to the lost through us. There is more to this than quoting Bible verses to unsaved people. It is presenting to them through the power of the Holy Ghost the very heart of God—that the Father sent the Son to save sinners. When we are moved by the heart of the Good Shepherd we will joyfully become His ambassadors— His hands, feet and voice to bring men, women and children into His eternal fold.

Some may honestly confess, "We know we should be touching the lost but the will and desire are not there." Obedience is not contingent upon emotion. Nonetheless, through a believer's honest confession God begins His reconstructing work. Whenever we comprehend the deficiencies in our characters and spiritual life we can begin to cry out for the Spirit's transforming power. We cannot change ourselves and the LORD never asked us to. The Spirit has promised to be our Helper and Sanctifier if we wholeheartedly plead for His help and cooperate in the process. "When Christian people are wholly yielded to God the result inevitably seems to be that God gives them a passion to win lost men and women to Christ" (Paul Smith, 51).

The LORD offers soul winners a joy unknown to anyone else. It is the joy of redeeming a soul from the eternal torments of Hell, of changing eternity, of seeing families restored, and of depopulating the kingdom of Hell. What a joy it will be to lay at Jesus' feet the souls of the men, women and children we won to Him while on earth. During the 1904 Welsh Revival, "A man made his way slowly along the densely filled aisle, towards the pulpit pew. When he was recognized there was a thrill of joy not quite free from fear. They knew him as one of the notorious characters of the whole district, a pugilist (fighter) of no light form, and leader of a gang of thirteen.

"They saw his face, stained with perspiration and tears, and, at first glance, more terrifying than usual; but there was a gleam of new life upon it. 'None of you will ever know,' he began, in a voice part shout, part sob, 'what I have passed through tonight.

I have wept a pool of tears where I have been sitting and they were the gladdest tears I ever knew. The agony before that! My head seemed to swell and swell, as if it would at last burst. But it grew easier when the tears came. You all know me: you know for whom I have fought; but I am changing sides tonight, to fight on the side of Jesus'" (Roberts, *Glory*, 74). He did indeed change sides. His evangelistic work began with his old gang of thirteen! He won them all to Christ.

This is the goal of our labors, the radical conversion of vast numbers of rebels and the total reconstruction of their lives and families. This is where men change sides, forsaking the kingdom of Hell to swear loyalty to Christ, to surrender themselves to the LORD with greater abandon than they did to the devil and the lusts of the flesh. This is the fruit of revival. This is New Testament Christianity!

FROM THE TOP DOWN

The prophet Amos rebuked the people of God because they strove to fill themselves with the comforts of life while never grieving "over the ruin of Joseph" (Amos 6:6). The unrestrained rebellion of our people is destroying the very fabric of our nation. Most Christians are not greatly disturbed by this until it affects their pocketbooks. The pestilence of sexual sins sweeps our nation and church as well. The media in all of its various forms are teaching both children and adults a relativistic morality. Our schools are breeding grounds for liberal agendas that are devastating our children and our children's children. Higher education has rejected the Judeo/Christian worldview and freely propagates their anti-Christian philosophies to young influential minds. All the while the church does not grieve over the ruin of our land.

Church leaders lead by example. When the shepherds do not grieve over the ruin of their cities then their congregations will not either. If the pastors fail to be soul winners, then their parishioners follow suit. Whether it is fruitfulness or barrenness, the church will reflect the spiritual condition of the pastor and leadership. This is the Biblical model, that spiritual life or death comes from the top down. Jesus demonstrated this throughout His ministry. For the Gospel to spread around the world the Savior would have to reproduce His heart and zeal in the disciples or the church would flounder and cease to exist.

Whatever Jesus wanted His disciples to do, He first lived by example. The Messiah sent the disciples out to preach the Good News, pray for the sick and cast out devils only after He showed them how. The Master did not expect His followers to live a crucified life until He first demonstrated it. Jesus was a living example, not a teacher without action. Here is an area in which we need a radical reformation. In our day, we are more prone to find a pastor hiding in his office behind a computer or out on the golf course than reaching his community. A lie has been propagated that the people win the lost while the preacher cheers them on. This is totally contrary to the discipleship method of Jesus. Not just that, a host of earthshaking saints throughout the Bible and history have proved that Christian leaders MUST lead by example. Then, both pastors and parishioners will see their spiritual barrenness healed as they together reach their unsaved neighbors and communities.

Jesus wanted the zeal that consumed Him to consume the disciples, so He lived as a radical with a fire burning in His bones. "I have come to bring fire on the earth, and how I wish it were already kindled!" (Lk. 12:49). The fire that burned in Jesus was contagious and the disciples caught it. A lack of spiritual fire in the congregation is directly linked to the absence of fire in the preacher. If the pastor does not have the fire of God how will the congregation ever know what it looks like? Before revival can come, preachers and churches must have a passion for the lost, for that is what revival is all about. How will congregations sacrifice their lives, time and money to reach a hurting world if the leadership does not first demonstrate it? Revival predominately begins with the pastors.

Pastor, it is not enough to teach the flock how to witness if you are not a living example. Do not make the excuse that your community has greater spiritual strongholds than other ones. There is not a demonic force on earth that can stand against the power of the Holy Spirit. And, dear pastor, don't claim that evangelism is not your calling because that is precisely what the pastoral ministry is all about—seeking the lost and discipling the saved. Remember, Jesus is the Good Shepard who exemplified the pastoral ministry.

The shepherds of this nation need to know God's heart and become living epistles of His heart to their congregations and communities. Then both pastors and parishioners will share the joy the Savior uniquely gives to soul-winners. Emma Booth-Tucker understood this when she penned, "The portions of my life which have given me the most satisfaction are the seasons when I carried the cross for Jesus, and the one regret which fastens down upon my spirit at the thought of turning from earth and entering Heaven is the realization that I shall never again be able to companion Jesus by bearing the cross, by suffering with Him for the salvation of sinners, and by ministering to Him by ministering to the sorrowing, suffering multitudes for whom His blood was given" (McPherson, 73). What a profound blessing it is to share in the fellowship of Christ's sufferings over those rushing to damnation (Phil. 3:10).

Every Christian, but especially the spiritual leaders of this nation, desperately needs their hearts filled with compassion for non-believers. Richard Baxter pleaded with the saints, "Go to poor sinners with tears in your eyes, that they may see you believe them to be miserable, and that you unfeignedly pity their case. Deal with them with earnest, humble entreaties. Let them perceive it is the desire of your heart to do them good; that you have no other end but their everlasting happiness; and that it is your sense of their danger, and your love to their souls, that forces you to speak; even because you 'know the terrors of the LORD,' and for fear you should see them in eternal torments" (Baxter, 121-122).

When the eyes of the pastors are dry, their congregation's will be likewise. Since pastors and parishioners are not soaking their altars with tears for the lost they do not see them saved. If Christians do not care about the destiny of the damned, who will? To our eternal shame we no longer grieve over the ruin of our people. The watchmen on the walls have fallen asleep, the enemy has broken down the defenses of our cities, schools and homes—he has taken the nation captive. What are we going to do about it?

CHAPTER FOURTEEN

THE WORD AND FAITH

The devil is more knowledgeable of the Word of God than Christians are. Yet this knowledge will never save him. Knowing the Scriptures and even holding a correct belief in them will never redeem a person, make one holy or bring revival. Brother Yun took this thought further when he said, "You can never really know the Scriptures until you're willing to be changed by them" (Yun, 297). John Warwick Montgomery, in taking up this issue wrote, "Salvation comes when, by way of personal contact with the Scriptures, we personally meet the Christ of Scriptures, who loved us and gave Himself for us" (Montgomery, 69).

Faith in the Living Word—Jesus and belief in the truths set forth in the written Word are intricately interwoven so that men can be saved. They are also essential elements in the scheme of revival. In this chapter, we will discuss how the Scriptures are a vital part of a spiritual outpouring. Then we will examine how faith in the Living Word and trust in the foundational truths of Scripture are indispensable to the commencement and advancement of a local or national awakening.

THE WORD

Revival is an explosion of divine truth upon the minds and consciences of men. When God rends the heavens, the pure truth of His presence exposes the lies and sins of men. The LORD is always true to His character and Word, for He does not change. The Author of Truth demands that His people walk in truth (1 Jn. 2:4). He gave us the written Word so we could know His commands and live His "good, pleasing and perfect will" (Rom. 12:2).

The written Word is the only sure revelation of divine truth and the only standard to define Christian faith and practice. Through the Scriptures, we come to know the character of God, the spiritual condition of mankind and the simple plan of salvation. The Holy Writ teaches us that the LORD desires to make His glory known to our fallen world. Great and precious promises have been lavished upon the Church so she can be empowered to move Heaven to shake earth.

There are no shortcuts that can manifest the glory of the Sovereign LORD. Those who yearn for revival must be determined to walk according to His Word while avoiding the host of strange and obscure teachings that continually pop up out of a fad-crazed Western Christianity. God will not rend the heavens because a preacher advances a "new" teaching or technique. The Almighty seeks to make His presence known to a people who will lovingly obey the timeless truths of His Word and faithfully fulfill His perfect will.

Repeatedly revival has died or been kept from the land because erroneous teaching crept into the church. The Great Reformation of the 1500s is a case in point. The Roman church, steeped in heresy and scandal, produced a spiritual wasteland throughout Europe and the known world. The Romish hierarchy kept the people in spiritual darkness by withholding the Scriptures from them. Men and women put themselves at enmity with the ecclesiastical giant so the life-changing truths of the Word could be read and plainly understood by the common people. As a result, the revival called the Great Reformation exploded throughout Europe. The moment people could read the Bible in their mother tongue the lies of the institutionalized church were exposed and they could be saved.

Doctrinal integrity is not a small issue with God. He gave us His Word for a reason and instructed us again and again to "FULLY obey the LORD your God and CAREFULLY follow ALL His commands" (Deu. 28:1). Many people, especially within the Charismatic/Pentecostal movement, have advanced "new" prophetic teachings, acts or rituals believing that they will produce a spiritual rain from Heaven. They often advance some very bizarre teachings and perform many outlandish ceremonies that they call prophetic. Yet the world remains unchanged by all their "words," strange beliefs and behaviors. The LORD of miracles will pour out His wondrous power when we carefully obey His written Word, not if we advance strange teachings and practices.

It is imperative that the Scriptures be restored to its rightful place in the Body of Christ. Brother Yun declared, "The first thing needed for revival to return to your [Western] churches is the Word of the LORD. God's Word is missing. Sure, there are many preachers and thousands of tapes and videos, but so little contains the sharp truth of God's Word ... Not only is knowledge of God's Word missing, but obedience to that Word" (Yun, 296). Jesus does not need our innovative thinking or church growth principles to turn the world upside down. He is seeking those who will place a childlike faith in Him and lovingly obey His every Word. "One of these days," proclaimed Leonard Ravenhill, "some simple soul will pick up the Book of God, read it, and believe it. Then the rest of us will be embarrassed" (Ravenhill, *Why*, 70).

JOSIAH'S REFORM

King Josiah came to the throne of Judah at the age of eight and reigned for thirty-one years. When he turned sixteen years old, he began to seek the LORD. Four years later he set in motion numerous religious reforms. In the 18th year of his reign, he ordered the rebuilding of the temple in Jerusalem. He followed the LORD to the best of his knowledge. During this period of Judah's history the Scriptures were not in common use. Though Josiah instituted many religious and social reforms after he turned to the LORD it was not until the Word of God was restored to its rightful place that the king and nation were radically transformed.

Before Josiah came to the throne, Judah suffered under many wicked kings who refused to worship the LORD and obey His Word. Possibly, under the evil reign of Manasseh, the Scriptures were hid so the wicked king could not destroy them. Since the people no longer had free access to the Word of God they fell even further into moral and spiritual decay.

After Josiah began rebuilding Solomon's temple, some workmen found a hidden copy of the Scriptures. When the king's secretary read the Book of the Law in the presence of the king he was greatly distressed. The Law revealed the horrifying truth that divine wrath was kindled against Judah because of her idolatry and the multitude of her sins. Through humility and the fear of God, the king tore his robes in a desperate act of repentance and the LORD responded with mercy (2 Kings 22-23; 2 Chr. 34).

A radical reformation came to Josiah and the children of Israel when the Word of the LORD was restored to the people. The king aggressively went throughout Jerusalem and Judah cleansing the land of its idols. He removed every vestige of idolatry from the temple and tore down the area that housed homosexual prostitutes. "Neither before nor after Josiah was there a king like him who turned to the LORD as he did—with all his heart and with all his soul and with all his strength, in accordance with all the Law of Moses" (2 Kings 22:25).

Though Josiah began many political and religious reforms before the Law was recovered, reformation and revival could not take place until the Word of God found its rightful place in the life of the king and the nation. For all of Josiah's sincere efforts to serve God, it was not until the Scriptures were planted in his heart that he knew how to recklessly abandon himself to the LORD. Only through the knowledge of God's will as revealed in His Word could the king walk in loving obedience and turn a nation back to their Redeemer.

In part, revival is kept from North America because we are ignorant of the Scriptures. This seems like a ridiculous statement in light of the phenomenal privilege we have, nonetheless, a spiritual famine has gripped the nation. The prophet Amos declared, "'The days are coming,' declares the Sovereign LORD, 'when I will send a famine through the land—not a famine of food or a thirst for water, but a famine of hearing the words of the LORD'" (Amos 8:11). We have a multitude of Bible translations, commentaries, dictionaries and study aids. The nation is flooded with Bible schools, conferences and seminars. The Christian book industry has skyrocketed which allows easy access to ancient, classic and pop authors. There are teaching tapes and videos, Christian TV and music, and tons of Jesus paraphernalia. In spite of all this, many are strangers to the Word. This is evidenced through the worldly lifestyles of the vast majority of acclaimed "Christians."

REFORMATION

The issue of reformation and revival needs to be addressed a little further. As stated in the last chapter, reformation is the restoring of truths that have been lost or neglected. Whole generations have lived and died ignorant of God's Word. In our time, the message of easy-believism has engulfed large portions of the church. Others are obsessed with teachings that feed the lusts of their flesh. All too often, we selectively apply the Word to our lives while diluting its radical demands so as to fit our self-centered lives. In the end, we want a gospel that makes us happy and does not upset our lifestyles or confront us with our sin.

In the days of Manasseh the Word was hidden from the people, however in our time, the people have willingly hidden Biblical truths from their own eyes. Our love of half-truths has hardened our hearts, so the LORD has given us over to teachers that feed the lusts of our flesh. "For the time will come when they will not endure sound doctrine; but after their own lusts shall they heap to themselves teachers, having itching ears" (2 Tim. 4:3). We surround ourselves with pastors and teachers who tell us what we want to hear, not what we need to hear. "When God speaks, we must listen," stressed Robert Coleman. "It is not our place to change or minimize the message. Nor are we called to defend what God says. The Bible is not on trial; we are. Our place is only to trust and obey" (Coleman, *Coming*, 42).

How strange it is when believers maintain that the Scriptures are divinely inspired and with the next breath claim that Jesus did not mean what He said. To illustrate this point let's examine Luke 14:33, "Any of you who does not give up everything he has CANNOT be My disciple." This is perhaps the most disliked verse in the Bible and possibly the most detested term of Christian discipleship. Many pastors, theologians and average church folk maintain, for a variety of reasons that Jesus did not literally mean what He said. Yet, throughout the ages, simple disciples have fully given themselves over to Christ's commands because they believed His words were true and that He knew exactly what He was saying. The fruit of these lives has repeatedly proved that the Master expected this verse to be literally interpreted and lived to the fullest.

Before we will radically live these Scriptural truths we must be willing for the Word to undo our entire existence—even our pet doctrines. Here is one reason why revival has not come to Western Christianity and why we are not seeing our cities won for Christ—we do not want the truths of Scripture upsetting our selfish way of living. There is a reason why we do not want to forsake all and follow Him.

The Word of God had to be restored and practiced before revival could come to Judah in the days of Josiah. This truth holds good today. We can move Heaven to shake earth when we are fully convinced that "the words of the LORD are flawless" (Ps. 12:6) and are willing to live those truths no matter the cost. Harold Spann noted, "There is little point talking about revival unless we believe what God says. If there is some doubt about the integrity of His Word, there is likely to be little concern for people to measure their lives by it ... Theological positions which discredit the Holy Scriptures never produce revival" (Coleman, Coming, 100-101).

Restoring God's Word to its rightful place will expose our worldly lifestyles and the sin that is deeply rooted in our nature. The "Sword of the Spirit, which is the Word of God" must be laid successively upon the root of our spiritual maladies (Eph. 6:17). Great pain accompanies the knives of a skilled surgeon. However, when his work is accomplished, there is hope for the dying patient. This is the hope the Great Physician offers a dying church. His healing hands will first inflict a holy pain that goes to the root of our spiritual afflictions. Then health can come to our sin sick souls and our sin sick churches.

WORD OF POWER

The power of the Holy Writ will only be realized when we abandon ourselves to it. "It is one thing to know the truth," charged Ernest Wadsworth, "another thing to understand it, but still another thing to feel its power ... Truth must be felt as well as believed" (Wadsworth, 60). When the Word and the Spirit are present there is power. Not some subjective concept of power that is unverifiable, but that which makes men tremble under the soul shaking conviction of sin.

The LORD has not called us to dead and powerless doctrines. He has called us to a living theology whose "promises have been thoroughly tested," therefore "your servant loves them" (Ps. 119:140). If the Word is living, then it should be obviously manifested through His people. "Many churches and ministries start out as places of power, then evolve into museums and end up as prison houses. Altars of fire become artifacts, miracles become methods, and people end up powerless" (Murillo, 65). All because the Living Word is replaced with lifeless doctrines and programs void of the Spirit. The Scriptures define this as "having a form of godliness but denying its power" (2 Tim. 3:5). Paul commanded, "from such turn away."

Jeremiah wrote, "When Your words came, I ate them; they were my joy and my heart's delight" (Jer. 15:16). We must consume God's Word so it becomes our very life, and we need to be consumed by it as well. To be consumed by the Word means that our selfish way of living ceases as the life of Christ pulsates through our entire being. The world has not turned to Jesus because we have not demonstrated that the Scriptures are true, powerful and worth the abandonment of our lives. Instead, "We inoculate the world with a mild form of Christianity so that it will be immune to the real thing" (Hauerwas, 91).

King Josiah saw the power of the Word when he fully yielded himself to God's simple truths. A revival followed that changed a nation. Jesus Christ is the same yesterday, today and forever (Heb. 13:2). What He has done in the past He can do today, for God does not show favoritism (Rom. 2:11).

FAITH

Biblical faith can only be founded upon Biblical truth. What value is it to believe in the existence of God if we will not believe that He is who He said He is and will do everything He said He would do? (Heb. 11:6). Genuine faith will cause us to abandon ourselves to Him through loving obedience whether His commands are convenient or not.

Faith, as it relates to revival, means that we believe the Spirit will bring a spiritual awakening to our churches and communities because we have fulfilled the covenant conditions of the Word. "Desire for revival is one thing," stated Duncan Campbell, "confident anticipation that our desire will be fulfilled is another" (Woosley, 112). Authentic faith is proved by the fruit it produces.

IDOLATRY

Lack of faith and surrender to the LORD is a form of self-idolatry. Tozer taught: "Among all created beings, not one dare trust in itself. God alone trusts in Himself; all other beings must trust in Him. Unbelief is actually perverted faith, for it puts its trust not in the living God but in dying men. The unbeliever denies the self-sufficiency of God and usurps attributes that are not his" (Tozer, *Knowledge*, 41).

Idolatry is placing one's faith in anything other than Christ, or endeavoring to share that place with another god. This means we cannot serve God and money, God and people, God and self or God and religion. Either Jesus will be our only Savior or not our Savior at all. Our faith must rest in Christ alone and the Word clearly expresses the fullness of His redeeming power. When Jesus is actually LORD of our lives there will be all the power necessary to correctly love people and rightly use the things of this world such as money, possessions and governments.

Idolatry, in all of its various forms, is breaking the first of the Ten Commandments, "You shall have no other gods before Me" (Ex. 20:3). It is also breaking Christ's greatest commandment to, "Love the LORD your God with all your heart and with all your soul and with all your mind and with all your strength" (Mk. 12:30). To not love and trust the LORD with all that is within us means we are placing our faith in something other than God. Our claims of faith in Christ are very shallow if we are not willing to trust Him with our entire existence and wellbeing. True faith trusts that Jesus will fulfill everything He has promised and that every command He has given is true and worthy of our complete and loving obedience.

As we tear down the idols in our lives we must replace them with a childlike faith in Christ alone. Before we can believe God for revival, we need to begin with the foundational principle of trusting Him to care for our lives and families. This was a message Jesus taught the disciples (Lk. 12:22-40). For faith to grow we must use the faith we have.

Smith Wigglesworth was a man of faith who proved his faith by the signs and wonders that followed him. Once while in Ireland he saw a powerful move of the Holy Ghost, "There were many sick carried to that meeting. Many people were seeking the baptism in the Holy Spirit. There were sinners there who were under mighty conviction. A moment came when the breath of God swept through the meeting. In about ten minutes every sinner in the place was saved. Everyone who had been seeking the Holy Spirit was baptized, and every sick one was healed. God is a reality, and His power can never fail. As our faith reaches out, God will meet us, and the same rain will fall. It is the same blood that cleanses, the same power, the same Holy Spirit, and the same Jesus made real through the power of the Holy Spirit! What would happen if we would believe God?" (Wigglesworth, edited, 194).

RADICAL FAITH

What moved the early church to follow Jesus and His teaching even at the expense of their wealth, reputations and comforts? What made them victorious in the face of trouble and persecution? And what compelled them to preach the Gospel at the cost of life and limb? They had a radical faith in Jesus and His Word. They possessed a faith based upon the evidence that Jesus rose from the dead and they believed ALL of the promises He gave them. Their lives produced the fruit of living faith. As Wigglesworth preached, "You must have the Word of God abiding in you if you want faith to be in evidence" (Hacking, 69).

The Word of God is "living and powerful" (Heb. 4:12; KJV). When average people believe and live its promises, they will see a miracle working God in action. Wigglesworth used to say, "God says it, I believe it, and that settles it" (Madden, 78). The LORD used this lowly plumber to see the lost saved, the lame walk, the blind to see and the dead raised to life. Wigglesworth gave this account of the outpouring of the Spirit on a train, "I stepped out of a railway coach to wash my hands. I had a season of prayer, and the LORD just filled me to overflowing with His love. I was going to a convention in Ireland, and I could not get there fast enough. As I returned to my seat, I believe that the Spirit of the LORD was so heavy upon me that my face must have shone. There were two clerical men sitting together, and as I got into the coach again, one of them cried out, 'You convict me of sin.' Within three minutes everyone in the coach was crying to God for salvation. This has happened many times in my life" (Wigglesworth, 83).

When we believe the Word, proof always follows. The cost of such faith is the surrender of our entire being to Jesus. Gary Harbaugh wrote, "Christ calls me to the righteousness of faith, which is a call for me to choose the death of my self-sufficiency" (Harbaugh, 127). There is no other path to revival and the power of the Holy Ghost.

One of the reasons we do not have revival is because we do not truly believe that God will bring it to our churches. The lack of faith in Christians is evidenced by their fear and hesitation to completely yield themselves to Christ and His Word. Before Charles Finney was converted he attended a prayer meeting in his hometown of Adams, New York. On one occasion they asked the young lawyer if they could pray for him. He emphatically said "no!" because he did not see that God answered their prayers.

Finney further told them, "I suppose I need to be prayed for, for I am conscious that I am a sinner, but I do not see that it will do any good for you to pray for me, for you are continually asking, but you do not receive. You have been praying for a revival ever since I have been in Adams, and yet you do not have it. You have been praying for the Holy Spirit to descend upon you, and yet complaining of your leanness. You have prayed enough since I have attended these meetings to have prayed the devil out of Adams if there is any virtue in your prayers. But here you are praying on and complaining still" (Finney, *Autobiography*, 11). Thank God Finney was radically converted in spite of those faithless church attendees and that he did not become like them.

Genuine faith produces verifiable results. There are times when Christians, to save face when their petitions are not granted, claim that their prayers have been answered in the spiritual realm even though there is no certifiable proof. Such claims are fraudulent. If the confident belief in a God who answers prayer has any legitimate value, then demonstrable proof will follow. Elijah prayed for it to stop raining and it did not rain for three and a half years. When he prayed for it to rain the showers came. This does not mean that we will always instantly see the answers to our prayers. However, the answers will come. People of faith will leave a trail of the fruits of their faith wherever they go. Hudson Taylor taught, "All God's giants have been weak men who did great things for God because they reckoned on God being with them" (MacDonald, 36).

TRUSTING GOD

The LORD commanded Moses to send one leader from each of the twelve tribes to explore the Canaan land. They returned with news that the land indeed flowed with milk and honey. Ten of the twelve leaders spread fear and doubt through the camp saying, "We can't attack those people; they are stronger than we are" (Num. 13:31). They told the people, "The land we explored devours those living in it" (Num. 13:32). These unbelieving leaders started a rebellion against Moses that spread through the camp. Unbelief is an extremely contagious sin that destroys individuals, families, churches and even nations.

Joshua and Caleb stood against the flood of unbelief. "Caleb silenced the people and said, 'We should go up and take possession of the land, for we can certainly do it'" (Num. 13:30). Joshua and Caleb chose to believe the promises of God while the other leaders gave themselves over to unbelief because they were convinced that the wisest thing to do was to not trust God. How often are we guilty of this same sin? We say to ourselves, "we can't go to the mission field because our children may not be safe;" or "we can't take a pay cut so we can work more for the LORD;" or "I can't preach the truth in my church because the biggest givers will leave." If we truly trusted in the Sovereign LORD we would surrender ourselves to His promises, knowing that, "Heaven and earth will pass away, but My words will never pass away" (Mt. 24:35).

As the Israelites continued to grumble and complain, Moses and Aaron fell before the Great I Am in intercession. Joshua and Caleb pleaded with the people not to rebel against the LORD. In spite of this, the whole assembly thought of stoning these four men of faith. Therefore, the wrath of God was kindled against the people. The LORD told Moses He would destroy all the Israelites. Even though the people had plotted to kill Moses, he prayed that the LORD would be merciful and not execute justice. The LORD responded to his plea by not destroying the people, but by sentencing the Israelites to wander in the wilderness until that unbelieving generation died.

The LORD said to Moses, "But because My servant Caleb has a different spirit and follows Me wholeheartedly, I will bring him into the land he went to, and his descendants will inherit it" (Num. 14:24). Caleb had a different spirit than all of the Israelites because he followed the LORD wholeheartedly. This wholehearted devotion was rooted in his simple faith and loving obedience. He believed in the Word of the LORD and lived according to those great and precious promises. Wholehearted devotion always produces a powerful faith.

As with Israel, unbelief resides in the hearts of most American Christians. The absence of revival in the land is proof enough of our unbelief. Not just that, we confirm our unbelief when we do not wholeheartedly yield ourselves to God, when we question His ways, doubt His Word and disbelieve His promises. How few truly have a different spirit as Caleb did.

The LORD is the great Transformer of men and nations. He works from the inside out. We must first lay aside our unbelief that compels us to grumble, complain, doubt and fear. Then we must wholeheartedly abandon ourselves to Christ and His Word. This will bring to an end our aimless wandering through the spiritual desert our churches have been living in. We do not have to die in the wilderness of unbelief. Through unreserved devotion to the Savior, we can build His Kingdom and see the fires of revival sweep the land. Revival can come. His Word has emphatically declared it. It's time we believe it.

CHAPTER FIFTEEN

UNITY

Unity among the saints makes them delightfully attractive to the LORD. This is one reason why unity is so vital for the promotion of revival. Whenever Christians conduct themselves in a manner worthy of the Lord Jesus they "stand firm in one spirit, contending as one man for the faith of the gospel" (Phil. 1:27). The opposite also holds true—division and strife are repulsive to God, grieves the Holy Spirit and thwarts the cause of revival.

UNITY AND DIVISION

There is an inherent tension between unity and division within the subject of revival. Unity is necessary for revival to come and be sustained, and yet when it comes there will be division. Every revival of which we have substantial information demonstrates that the fiercest opposition arose from within the church and religious community. When God steps down in response to the wholehearted prayers of a few saints some church folk will criticize the move of the Holy Spirit and at times even strive to shut it down. This happened to Huss, Savonarola, Luther, Edwards, Wesley, Whitefield, Finney, and countless others. Arthur Wallis commented, "If we find a revival that is not spoken against, we had better look again to ensure that it is a revival" (Wallis, 26).

A consensus in favor of revival will never happen in a local congregation or community. That is not the type of unity necessary for the LORD to rend the heavens. A spiritual awakening will come when He finds a core of unified believers who are earnestly seeking His face for the Spirit to flood the land. Opposition against such saints will arise out of the ranks of those who appear outwardly pious. "Very likely the leading men in the Church will oppose you," declared Finney. "There has always been opposition in the Church. It was this way when Christ was on earth" (Finney, *How To*, 135). Dr. Brown adds to this thought by insisting, "It is tragic but true, revival's greatest opposers will be the 'religious' people who refuse to repent" (Brown, *The End*, 9).

Critics often claim that revival is actually a work of the devil and that is why division arises. Logic not only dispels this argument, but the very fruit produced by an awakening should be proof enough to silence the most avid critic. The devil will never shut down bars, casinos and houses of prostitution through the conversion of sinners. He will never lead men, women and children to Christ, nor will he heal marriages and restore broken homes. It is ludicrous to think that the demonic hordes of Hell would awaken lukewarm Christians and turn them into pastors, evangelists and missionaries. Satan will never heal the sin sick soul nor cast himself out of an individual he has possessed for years. How ridiculous to think that the Evil One would voluntarily give glory to Almighty God in any way, shape or form. It would be foolish to reject a genuine move of the Spirit because divisions arise (remember what happened with Jesus). Not just that, much of the division found in revival may actually be motivated by satanic influences.

As noted in the last chapter, revival must be established and maintained upon the Word of God. Christians in the midst of a divine visitation need be conscious of how they direct the revival. Scriptural integrity and obedience to the Spirit's leading are of the utmost importance. There is much that can take place in revival that the Scriptures neither support nor speak against. This means that vigilance, self-control and sensitivity to the Holy Ghost are indispensable in pastoring the people in a move of God.

Even though God desires every Christian to embrace His visitation He knows that will not be the case. The LORD will pour out His glory through those who walk in loving obedience and passionately desire His fame to be known throughout the land. During the summer of 1828 a revival began in a rural community in Oswego County, New York. One hundred and fifty souls were irrefutably converted to Christ in a short period of time. "People were at a loss to account for it. But wonder was at an end with the godly when it was learned that two old men, living a mile apart, had selected a point midway, in a cluster of trees, and there at the down-going of the sun had met for months to pray for the out-pouring of the Spirit of God" (Riley, 23). In this case there were only two men who prayed in unity for the cause of revival. These two men prevailed with God and reaped a glorious harvest for the Savior.

RELATIONSHIP WITH JESUS

Jesus taught that a kingdom or house "divided against itself will be ruined" (Lk. 11:17). He further stated, "He who is not with Me is against Me, and he who does not gather with Me, scatters" (Lk. 11:23). The only way Christ's disciples can live in unity with each other is for them to be first and foremost in unity with their LORD. Everything that divides a person from the Savior will cause division with others and that which is detrimental to our relationships with people is damaging to our relationship with the Son. When people cause division, whether in their church, business or family, they do so because they have not fully surrendered to Jesus. As a result, they perpetuate the acts of the sinful nature which are always destructive to relationships (Gal. 5:19-21). When saints live in a right relationship with the LORD there will be power to restore and build right relationships with others.

Martin Luther made a powerful observation, "If the greatest commandment is to love God with heart, mind, soul, and strength ... then the greatest sin is the failure to do so" (Comfort, *Friends*, 122). When we fail to love the LORD with everything that is within us we will never be able to love others correctly. If we have not humbled ourselves before our Maker, we will surely be proud, prejudiced and critical towards others. Lack of right submission towards family, bosses and spiritual leaders is a sure sign of lack of surrender to Jesus. Our deficiency in compassion for a dying culture means that we do not know God's heart and are not willing to walk as He walked in this world. In short, what we are in relationship with God is all that we will be in relationship with others.

Unity with our Redeemer is directly dependant upon faith and holiness. The ancient word for faith, "feyth," is rooted in the idea, "to unite," and "to bind." This speaks "of the spiritual work of faith, as that which, on man's side, unites him to God for salvation" (James Orr, *ISBE*, vol. 4, pg. 12). Genuine faith incorporates the surrender of our entire being to the LORD, which in turn unites us with Him. Faith begins with believing that God "exists and that He rewards those who earnestly seek Him" (Heb. 11:6). As we live a life of faith we "are being transformed into His likeness with ever-increasing glory" (2 Cor. 3:18).

Holiness and unity work hand in hand. The Scriptures command us to, "Make every effort to live in peace with all men and to be holy; without holiness no one will see the LORD" (Heb. 12:14). Here we find that unity with others is interrelated to personal holiness. Everything that causes division among people is the result of unholiness in the lives of individuals. God, who is the absolute perfection of holiness, will not dwell with those who are unholy. Sin in all of its various forms makes us unholy and separates us from His presence. The sin that separates us from God is the same sin that separates us from each other. Lack of personal and corporate holiness grieves the Holy Spirit, which prevents His glory from being revealed in the home or local assembly.

The focal point of unity among Christians begins with their unity with the Savior. Paul instructed us to, "Make every effort to keep the UNITY OF THE SPIRIT through the bond of peace" (Eph. 4:3). Unity of the Spirit is unity by the Spirit. Harmony among the saints is contingent upon their walking in the Spirit so they do not fulfill the lusts of the flesh (Gal. 5:16). To walk in the Spirit we must "live in the Spirit." To live in the Spirit means we are to live in unbroken fellowship with God (Gal. 5:25). Through Colossians 1:8 we learn that brotherly love is a work of the Holy Spirit in our lives. According to our loving obedience to the Holy Spirit will be the depth of our love for others.

THE CITY-WIDE CHURCH

For revival to come to a church, city or nation, it is essential that a high priority be placed on unity within Christian homes, the local church and the citywide church. There has never been a genuine revival where there was not unity among a core of God's people. Just a brief look at present day revivals that are transforming cities and nations around the world reaffirms this truth. We are either agents for unity or agents for division. Unity is our personal and corporate responsibility and must be actively pursued. The unity may be limited to those desperate saints who aggressively pursue God; nonetheless, unity remains a criterion for revival.

As stated earlier, revival will always have its critics from within and without. Dr. Brown maintained, "You can have controversy without revival, but you cannot have revival without controversy" (Brown, *Answer Book*, 7). Jonathan Edwards said it a little differently, "If [we] wait to see a work of God without difficulties and stumbling blocks, it will be like a fool's waiting at the river side to have the water all run by. A work of God without stumbling blocks is never to be expected. 'It must needs be that offences come'" (Edwards, *Revival*, 133).

In considering the citywide church, most of the blame for division falls upon the shoulders of pastors. One example consists of pastors who become territorial, protecting their own turf. This happens both within denominational affiliations and in community settings. Our unwillingness to help other local Christian churches grow is a sure sign that this spiritual malady is present. Division and uncooperativeness among Bible-believing congregations prevents revival from coming to a community or from having far-reaching affects.

Another form of division that pastors often propagate can be seen in their lack of involvement in the citywide church. This could even be construed as a sin of omission, not doing what they are called to do (Eph. 4:3-6). Pastors can become so busy in tending to their own flock that they make no time to build relationships with pastors who commonly long for revival. This can be just as divisive as fighting over church hoppers, doctrine or polity. When pastors rarely go outside of their congregational or denominational boundaries to evangelize their city and support other churches they neglect Christ's citywide church and a perishing world. God has called His shepherds to look beyond their own congregations and become pastors to their city. Unity for revival needs to begin with the leaders. "Give us a revived ministry," challenged D. L. Moody, "and we shall soon see a revived church" (Moody, 216).

Part of the source of division among the citywide church is found in local congregations. Any assembly that is suffering under the satanic attacks of division will be worthless in advancing Christ's Kingdom on a citywide basis. Division in the local assembly destroys their spiritual vision, strips them of Holy Ghost power and incapacitates an entire congregation. Some churches have been plagued for years with the curse of a contentious, critical spirit. Paul warned, "If you keep on biting and devouring each other, watch out or you will be destroyed by each other" (Gal. 5:15). When pastors and parishioners grow weary from the strife they no longer see the pain of the unsaved living under the tyranny of the devil. They have fallen into a spiritual stupor where they have become self-absorbed with their pain, problems and divisions.

Division is always the by-product of the lusts of the flesh, whether it's in the home, local church or citywide church. To put it plainly, division is sin. Sin separates a man from God and a man from his family and friends. It divides husband and wife, parents and children, churches and Christian communities. The ugliest form of division is that which is supposedly perpetuated in the name of God. Possibly the greatest and most damaging form of spiritual blindness can be found in the man who thinks his divisive acts are divinely ordained. Jesus alerted us to this damnable problem when He said, "If then the light within you is darkness, how great is that darkness!" (Mt. 6:23).

Divisive people become tools of Satan to either stop a revival or never allow one to come. They are responsible for attacking and destroying God's anointed leaders and of harming Christ's little lambs. This sin is so hideously evil that it damns souls to Hell while those who commit such crimes against Almighty God think they are doing His service. King Solomon told us a terrifying truth, "There are six things the LORD hates, seven that are detestable to him ... a man who stirs up dissension among brothers" (Pr. 6:16, 19). God holds some very strong and passionate views about people who cause dissension in the local assembly and in the family.

James asked believers an important question, "What causes fights and quarrels among you? Don't they come from your desires that battle within you?" (Jam. 4:1). Many pastors and churches are held hostage by power-mongering deacons, ruling families, large donors or long time members. Bernard Jordan commented on this issue, "A person with a rebellious spirit exalts the importance of his own ideas above his leader's ideas ... A person with a disloyal or rebellious spirit develops a critical attitude towards his spiritual leaders ... [which] always manifests itself in murmuring and contentious words ... [He] distorts the views of his spiritual leaders ... gives recognition to others who are dissatisfied and justifies his opposition to his spiritual leaders" (Jordan, 71-73).

People responsible for causing division should tremble at the LORD of Host's intense wrath at that sin and thoroughly repent so they can be restored in right relationship with Him. Otherwise they may hear from Christ's lips, "I never knew you: depart from Me, ye that work iniquity" (Mt. 7:23; KJV). Thankfully, Jesus freely offers mercy to all who repent and prove that repentance with a changed life.

PASTORAL SUPPORT

One of the hardest ministries in the world is pastoring. A man or woman can start a new pastorate with joy and vigor and in no time at all be battling depression. Criticisms and personal attacks can be crushing to a leader and his family. Our spiritual leaders not only have to battle all that comes at them from the world, they must stand against contentious people who claim to be Christian. It's time we restore the truth that church members who fight against the pastor, his family and the pastoral leadership are actually raising a *coup d'etat* against the LORD of Hosts. To rebel against the LORD's appointed leader is to rebel against the LORD Himself. Virtually all church divisions are nothing other than people's sinful nature acting under the influence of demonic forces. Such actions are destructive, damnable and stop revival. This problem is a spiritual epidemic in the American church today.

How rare it is for rebellious and contentious church folk to repent of their divisiveness and make restitution (Ex. 22:1-15; Lev. 6:1-6, 24:21; Lk. 19:8). Revivalist Charles Finney emphatically insisted that those who surrender their lives to Christ must make restitution whenever possible. He asserted that when people do not right the wrongs within their power to do so that they have not truly repented and thus remain in their sin. Self-righteous pride blinds the eyes of contentious people to the great evil they have perpetuated and prevents them from receiving forgiveness, perhaps even salvation itself.

The success of a community of faith directly depends upon the pastor touching the LORD and then touching the people. When churches abuse or drive out their pastors rather than love and support them they are sure to be defeated congregations. Pastors are not disposable commodities; they are gifts to the Body of Christ. Those who fight against the man of God fight against

God Himself and those who try to control their shepherd strive to manipulate the Kingdom of Christ for their own selfish and evil desires. Such people do great damage to the Savior's Kingdom.

Contentious churches have disgraced the cause of Christ and their reputations are repulsive to the unsaved. Non-Christians will not want to be a part of a church full of ravenous sheep that bite and devour one another. Dr. Mark Rutland told the truth when he said, "... sheep can bite. In fact, they can knock a pastor down, stomp on him, and drag him into the bushes for dead" (Teykl, 38). If, perchance, an outsider became part of such a church the hypocrites would "make him twice as much a son of Hell" as they are (Mt. 23:15). God is good to keep the unsaved from becoming a part of a contentious church.

Without question, every pastor is looking for his Aaron and Hur, his Joshua and Caleb, his Timothy and Barnabas. The pastoral ministry is a great responsibility that weighs heavily upon a person. The load becomes easier when the saints support the man of God. Unity does not mean that we always agree with everything the leader does, just that we will stand by his side in loving support. "Obey your leaders and submit to their authority. They keep watch over you as men who must give an account. Obey them so that their work will be a joy, not a burden, for that would be of no advantage to you" (Heb. 13:17).

Unity brings victory while division offers sure defeat. Average leaders can accomplish tremendous things for the Savior when faithful men and women support them through the successes and battles of ministry. Revival is obtainable when the saints support the man of God and in unison cry out for the LORD of Heaven to send a Holy Ghost revival.

AUTHORITY THROUGH UNITY

Loving the brethren and unity are synonymous. Jesus thought that brotherly love was so important that He said, "By this all men will know that you are My disciples" (Jn. 13:35). The Savior gave the world the authority to judge whether we are Christians according to the love we show one to another. One reason He may have granted the unsaved this authority is because they can often discern our spiritual condition better than we can. Francis Schaeffer commented on this verse. "The church is to be a loving church in a dying culture. How, then, is the dying culture going to consider us? Jesus says, 'By this shall all men know that you are My disciples, if ye have love one to another.' In the midst of the world, in the midst of our present dying culture, Jesus is giving a right to the world. Upon His authority He gives the world the right to judge whether you and I are born-again Christians on the basis of our observable love toward all Christians" (Schaeffer, 12-13).

According to Jesus, the love we manifest to the brethren and a perishing world is the proof of our Christianity. He was not referring to a sentimental love that stays at a protective distance from others, but a holy love that moves men and women to turn the world upside down by laying their lives down for others. Through such sacrificial love, which is representative of Christ's love, we obtain the authority to speak to a spiritually dying world. Apart from such charity we are "only a resounding gong or a clanging cymbal," powerless to change the church or the world for their eternal good (1 Cor. 13:1).

King David presented two wonderful illustrations on the subject of unity in Psalms 133. First of all, David likened the unity of the saints to the anointing Aaron received as Israel's first high priest. The anointing oil used on Aaron contained a combination of principle spices, thereafter used to anoint every high priest, and in time, the kings of Israel. Without the anointing Aaron was not fit to serve the LORD and the people; without the anointing we are not fit to serve Christ, one another, or those who do not know the Savior. Notice that the anointing was given for the benefit of serving others, not for selfish ends.

The second illustration David portrayed was of the heavy morning dew that falls on Mt. Hermon. This regular Heaven-sent dew brings refreshing to a dry and weary land. Without this dew everything would die. So it is with Christians. Take away the unity of the saints and everything in the local church and community spiritually dies because the dew of Heaven is withheld. A spiritual dearth then sweeps the land killing all who would look for the church to be a place of refuge but find it a battle zone. But oh, when the saints dwell together in unity, it is a taste of Heaven on earth; it replaces death with life, refreshes the soul, makes beautiful the Body of Christ and anoints her to build His Kingdom.

In Christ's high priestly prayer of John 17 the Son interceded to the Father for our unity. He prayed, "I have given them the glory that You gave Me, that they may be one as we are one: I in them and You in Me. May they be brought to complete unity to let the world know that You sent me and have loved them even as you have loved Me" (Jn. 17:22-23). Jesus is offering to give the church the glory He shared with the Father so that the world may know that He is LORD and Savior. Contention, insubordination and unforgiveness destroys that unity and forfeits the wonder of His glory in the church. This quenches the work of the Holy Spirit to save and transform lives, which leaves the church spiritually barren and bankrupt.

Jesus prayed that we would be brought into "complete unity" so that the world may know that the Father sent the Son. Actions speak louder than words. Our division and rebellion declares to secular society that we do not really believe that Jesus is who He claimed to be (Jn. 17:22-23). Divisive churches actually advance a lie that God is not a God of love and that He is powerless to help the people love each other. Lack of unity between Bible-believing churches sends a false message to the unsaved that Jesus cannot unite His own people. The breakdown of Christian marriages proclaims an ugly falsehood that Jesus cannot change lives, heal marriages or impart love and forgiveness to Christian homes. This is no small issue. Our divisiveness has stripped us of spiritual authority to speak to unbelievers.

When the day of Pentecost came, the LORD found the believers in unity with Himself first and then with each other. This unity opened the door for Holy Spirit power that can transform the world. "In the last days, God says, I will pour out My Spirit on all people" (Acts 2:17). Here lies the answer we need for the church—the power of God's manifest presence—revival. We need a new Pentecost that produces the fires of revival that can sweep the world. The unity of the Spirit produces the authority and power of the Spirit. Pentecost came because the saints yielded themselves to Christ by going into the upper room to seek His face in desperation and unity. It worked! It still does!

CONCLUSION

Those who investigate the revivals of the past and present find the undisputable fact that unity is not an option, but a necessity. According to the depth of unity among the saints will be the influence of the awakening. Unity brings with it a great sense of expectation and joy. Such were the fruits of the revival that broke out at Charlotte Chapel in Edinburgh. "The people were now on tiptoe with expectancy for a revival. A Conference on January 22, 1906, addressed by several workers who had visited Wales, lasted from 3:30 p.m. until midnight.

"It was, however, at a late prayer meeting, held in the evening at 9:30 that the fire of God fell. There was nothing, humanly speaking, to account for what happened. Quite suddenly, upon one and another came an overwhelming sense of the reality and awfulness of His presence and of eternal things. Life, death, and eternity seemed suddenly laid bare. Prayer and weeping began, and gained in intensity every moment.

"It is useless being a spectator looking on, or praying for it, in order to catch its spirit and breath. It is necessary to be in it, praying in it, part of it, caught by the same power, swept by the same wind" (Olford, 129-132). It is of the utmost importance that the saints tear down the walls of division within the local and citywide church or revival will never come.

Pastors and congregations must look beyond their own self-preservation and recklessly abandon themselves to the Savior. They must live God's Word no matter the personal cost by walking in a childlike faith that simply trusts in His great and precious promises. The tremendous need of the hour is to tear down every thought, word and deed that destroys the unity of the saints and hinders the outpouring of the Holy Spirit. It's time we thwart the devil's plans and reap havoc on his kingdom instead.

Only radically surrendered lives will passionately endeavor to build the Kingdom of our dear Lord and Savior whether they receive recognition or not. There is a cause greater than our own congregations, personal fame, ease of life or secure incomes—it is Christ and His glory revealed. We have the promise that when Jesus is lifted up, He will draw all men unto Himself (Jn. 12:32). He is waiting for us to lift Him up in our homes, churches and cities so He can draw men, women and children unto Himself through the awesome wonder of revival. He gave us this promise and will fulfill His part when we have fulfilled ours.

CHAPTER SIXTEEN

THE END OF THE MATTER

The Book of Ecclesiastes is a sketch of King Solomon's quest for wisdom and significance. His journey took him on the painful path of sin and rebellion. Tragically, it left him staggering from the emptiness of a life without God. After the king effectively set forth the arguments that all of life's pursuits are "meaningless" and a "chasing after the wind" he boldly confessed, "Now all has been heard; here is THE END OF THE MATTER: Fear God and keep His commandments, for this is the whole duty of man" (Ecc. 12:13). The experiences of life and the wisdom of the Holy Sprit brought Solomon to the prudent conclusion that there is only one meaningful purpose for mankind—the pursuit of God and His glory.

Like Solomon, most American Christians have aggressively pursued lifestyles that are meaningless in the scheme of eternity. When all is said and done, we may be as guilty as Solomon of chasing after the wind, so what is the end of the matter after all the arguments of this book have been presented? That revival is not an option, but an absolute necessity. There is no other hope for the six billion people on this planet. Life and death, Heaven and Hell are at stake—eternity hangs in the balance. "Without a revival," stated Finney, "sinners will grow harder and harder despite preaching. Your children and your friends will remain unsaved if there are no revivals to convert them. It would be better for them if there were no means of grace, no sanctuary, no Bible, and no preaching, than to live and die where there is no revival" (Finney, *How*, 11).

If we ignore the importance and potential of genuine revival how will the mass of humanity rushing toward eternal torments be brought to Christ? What remedy are we offering the hordes of people who are bound by sin and the devil? What hope are we presenting to those who suffer every day under the meaninglessness of life without Christ? Are we ready to pray without ceasing until revival comes? As Andrew Murray admonished, "What is to be done? There is only one thing: We must wait upon God. And what for? We must cry, with a cry that never rests, 'Oh that Thou wouldst rend the heavens ... [and] come down, that the mountains might flow down at Thy presence' (Isa. 64:1). We must desire and believe, we must ask and expect that God will do the [unexpected] ... Let us band ourselves together as His elect who cry day and night to Him for things men have not seen" (Andrew Murray, 289).

The 1857 Prayer Meeting Revival burst forth from New York City and spread across America like a wild fire. Almost to the day, a prayer meeting revival began in Northern Ireland. Before long, news of revival in America and Ireland had created an intense hunger for it among the Scots. Within two years the Aberdeenshire Revival broke out in Scotland. James Turner was the simple man God used to continue the work begun by Reginald Radcliffe.

James Turner "was devoid of learning, and had no gift of utterance. He was consumptive (which means he had tuberculosis) when his great task commenced, a dying consumptive whose days were nigh numbered. He was little in stature, his voice was feeble, his eye deformed by a squint, but this frail, broken, disfigured vessel was filled with a passionate love to Jesus Christ, an intense hungering compassion for souls, and an invincible faith in God. He could pray! Therefore God was able to lift him up, out of weakness made him strong, and in two crowded years of glorious life, He used the dying consumptive to win for Him eight thousand souls!

"On December 6th, in the little fishing village of St. Combs, he began his memorable mission. From village to village he went, and everywhere along the seacoast his course was marked by a trail of divine fire. As he went on the blessing increased, and his coming was awaited with intense eagerness, and then, as happens when Revival reaches flood tide, a wave of great joy passed over the people. They thronged around him and marched in a body from town to town, singing as only those can sing who have drunk 'the royal wine of Heaven,' the joy unspeakable and full of glory.

"In this way he at last reached Banff ... It was found impossible to dismiss the people, and through the whole night a great reaping went on. Many of the most notorious sinners in the town were saved, and many who first saw the LORD that night went forth to declare His Glory in all parts of the earth. Turner had much of the spirit of McCheyne, and his end was like his. The matchless love of Christ filled his vision, and his last words were, 'Christ is all'" (Shearer, 87-88).

The Savior used a dying man to win to Himself eight thousand souls because Turner lived a surrendered life. How many healthy men did the LORD pass by before He found one yielded vessel that He could pour His power through? Though James Turner would not have fulfilled our modern criteria of a successful evangelist, he did fulfill the LORD's criterion. God used this frail, sickly man in a way that few have ever been used, because he abandoned himself to the Lover of his soul.

Throughout human history the LORD has raised up average individuals to change the course of history. In the Scriptures it was saints like Joseph, David, Elijah, Josiah, Daniel, Esther, John the Baptist, Peter and Paul. In church history they were believers like Luther, Wycliffe, Huss, Wesley, Finney, Woodworth-Etter, Roberts, Seymour, Lake and Wigglesworth. These are only a fraction of the men and women who turned their world upside down through the power of the Holy Spirit for the glory of a risen Savior.

It takes only one person—just one person—who will stand in the gap to see the mercy of God poured out to a people deserving judgment. The LORD asked Jeremiah, "Go up and down the streets of Jerusalem, look around and consider, search through her squares. If you can find but one person who deals honestly and seeks the truth, I will forgive this city" (Jer. 5:1). However, the city was destroyed. The LORD said He would spare Sodom and Gomorrah if there were ten righteous people. Tragically, the cities were destroyed. Yet at other times the LORD found the righteous and so spared cities and nations. It took just one Luther to spark the fires of the Great Reformation, one Edwards to see the Great Awakening break forth, one Turner to help spread revival through Scotland, one Lamphier to put in motion the Prayer Meeting Revival, one Roberts to set Wales ablaze and one Seymour to open the floodgates of Heaven for the birthing of the Pentecostal movement.

Every person reading this book has the potential to be used by God like the precious saints mentioned above. The LORD is not holding back revival until the rich and famous get right with Him, nor is He waiting for those who have great talent or profound knowledge. No! He is looking for those believers who will humbly, and wholeheartedly, yield themselves to Christ and the building of His Kingdom. We were born to see His glory flood the land. Yes, for "such a time as this" (Est. 4:14).

EPILOGUE

My prayer is that this little book has begun the work the LORD intended—to awaken your soul to the wonder of our great God and Savior Jesus Christ, to the awesome power of the Spirit manifested through revival, to the necessity of reckless abandonment and to the desperate need to rescue the perishing. The only hope for your family, city and nation is for the Sovereign LORD to rend the heavens. Jesus desires to use average men and women to turn the world upside down. May we passionately cry out to the God of all mercies until His awesome deeds of old are renewed in our day. It is time we move Heaven to shake earth.

"LORD, I HAVE HEARD OF YOUR FAME;
I STAND IN AWE OF YOUR DEEDS, O LORD.
RENEW THEM IN OUR DAY,
IN OUR TIME MAKE THEM KNOWN;
IN WRATH REMEMBER MERCY" (Hab. 3:2).

BIBLIOGRAPHY

Autrey, C. E. *Revivals of the Old Testament.* Grand Rapids, MI, Zondervan Publishing House, 1960.
Bartleman, Frank. *Another Wave Rolls In!* Northridge, Voice Publications, 1962.
Baxter, Richard. *The Saint's Everlasting Rest.* Rio, WI, Ages Software, 2000.
Bounds, E. M. *E. M. Bounds on Prayer.* New Kensington, PA, Whitaker House, 1997.
Ibid. *The Weapon of Prayer.* New Kensington, PA, Whitaker House, 1996.
Brainerd, David. *Remarkable Work of Grace.* In The Works of Jonathan Edwards, vol. 5. Rio, WI, Ages Software, 2000.
Brown, Michael L. *Revolution.* Ventura, CA, Regal Books, 2000.
Ibid. *The End of the American Gospel Enterprise.* Shippensburg, PA, Destiny Image Publishers, revised 1993.
Ibid. *The Revival Answer Book.* Ventura, CA, Renew Books, 2001.
Cairns, Earle E. *An Endless Line of Splendor.* Wheaton, IL, Tyndale House, 1986.
Campbell, Duncan. *Fire of God.* Audio sermon tape. N.p., n.d.
Ibid. *God's Answer to the Cry of Unbelief.* Audio sermon tape. N.p., n.d.
Ibid. *Heart Preparation for a God Sent Revival.* Audio sermon tape. N.p., n.d.
Ibid. *When God Stepped Down.* Audio sermon tape. N.p., n.d.
Ibid. *When the Mountains Flowed Down.* Audio tape. Sermon preached at Faith Mission Bible School, Edinburgh, Scotland. N.p., n.d.
Chambers, Oswald. *If You Will Ask.* Grand Rapids, MI, Discovery House, 1958.
Coleman, Robert E. *Dry Bones Can Live Again.* Old Tappan, Fleming H. Revell, 1969.
Ibid. *The Coming World Revival.* Wheaton, IL, Crossway Books, 1989, 1995.
Comfort, Ray. *Hell's Best Kept Secret.* Springdale, Whitaker House, 1989.
Ibid. *My Friends Are Dying.* Springdale, Whitaker House, 1991.
Cymbala, Jim. *Fresh Wind, Fresh Fire.* Grand Rapids, MI, Zondervan Publishing House, 1997.
Davis, George T. B. *When the Fire Fell.* Philadelphia, PA, The Milton Testament Campaigns, 1945.
Dixon, Larry. *The Other Side of the Good News.* Bridgepoint, Wheaton Books, 1992.
Duewel, Wesley. *Revival Fire.* Grand Rapids, MI, Zondervan Publishing House, 1995.
Duncan, Homer, ed. *Revival Fires.* Lubbock, TX, Missionary Crusader, n.d.
Edwards, Jonathan. *Jonathan Edwards on Revival.* Edinburgh, Banner of Truth Trust, 1995.
Ibid. *Memoirs of Jonathan Edwards.* Rio, WI, Ages Software, 2000.
Elliot, Elisabeth. *Shadow of the Almighty.* New York, Harper, 1958.
Evans, Eifion. *When He is Come.* London, Evangelical Press, 1967.
Fenelon. *Let Go.* New Kensington, PA, Whitaker House, 1973.
Finney, Charles. *How to Experience Revival.* Springdale, Whitaker House, 1984.
Ibid. *Power From On High.* Springdale, Whitaker House, 1996.
Ibid. *Principles of Revival.* Minneapolis, MN, Bethany House, 1987.
Ibid. *The Autobiography of Charles Finney.* Minneapolis, MN, Bethany House, 1977.
Foxe, John. *Foxe's Book of Martyrs.* Rio, WI, Ages Software, 2000.
Gallagher, Steve. *At the Altar of Sexual Idolatry.* Dry Ridge, KY, Pure Life Ministries, 1986, 2000.
Gardiner, Gordon P. *Out of Zion into All the World.* Shippensburg, PA, Champion Press, 1990.
Gibson, William. *The Year of Grace.* Belfast, Ireland, Ambassador Productions Ltd., 1989.
Goforth, Jonathan. *By My Spirit.* Elkhart, IN, Bethel Publishing, 1983.
Ibid. *When the Spirit's Fire Swept Korea.* Elkhart, IN, Bethel Publishing, n.d.

Goforth, Rosalind. *Jonathan Goforth.* Minneapolis, MN, Bethany House, 1937, 1986.
Graham, Billy. *We Need Revival.* Wheaton, IL, Van Kampen Press, 1950.
Greenfield, John. *Power From On High.* Muskegon, MI, Dust to Ashes Publications, n.d.
Grubb, Norman P. *Rees Howells, Intercessor.* Fort Washington, PA, Christian Literature Crusade, 1966.
Hacking, W. *Smith Wigglesworth.* Tulsa, OK, Harrison House, 1972, 1981, 1995.
Harbaugh, Gary L. *Pastor As Person.* Minneapolis, MN, Augsburg Publishing House, 1984.
Hauerwas, Stanley and William H. Willimom. *Resident Aliens.* Nashville, TN, Abingdon Press, 1989.
Hession, Roy and Revel. *We Would See Jesus.* Fort Washington, PA, Christian Literature Crusade, 1958.
Hession, Roy. *When I Saw Him.* Fort Washington, PA, Christian Literature Crusade, 1975.
Jordan, Bernard. *Mentoring—The Missing Link.* Brooklyn, NY, Zoe Ministries, 1989.
Jowett, J. H. *The Passion for Souls.* New York, Fleming H. Revell, 1905.
King, Darrel D. *E. M. Bounds.* Minneapolis, MN, Bethany House Publishers, 1998.
KJV—*King James Version of the Bible.*
Lee, Young-Hoon. *Korean Pentecost: The Great Revival of 1907.* Asian Journal of Pentecostal Studies, March, 2001.
Lindsay. Gordon. *John G. Lake—Apostle to Africa.* Dallas, TX, Christ for the Nations, 1994.
Madden, P. J. *The Wigglesworth Standard.* New Kensington, PA, Whitaker House, 1993.
MacDonald, William. *True Discipleship.* Kansas City, MO, Walterick Publishers, 1975.
Maxwell, L. E. *Born Crucified.* Chicago, IL, Moody Press, 1945.
McPherson, Anna Talbott. *Forgotten Saints.* Grand Rapids, MI, Zondervan Publishing, 1961.
Meldrum, Jessica. *Floods on Dry Gound.* Self-published, 2004.
Montgomery, John Warwick. *Damned through the Church.* Minneapolis, MN, Bethany Fellowship, 1970.
Moody, William R. *The Life of Dwight L. Moody.* Murfreesboro, TN, Sword of the Lord Publishers, n.d.
Murillo, Mario. *Fresh Fire.* Stockton, CA, Anthony Douglas Publishing, 1991.
Murphy, Owen. *When God Stepped Out of Heaven.* N.p., n.d.
Murray, Andrew. *Andrew Murray on Prayer.* New Kensington, PA, Whitaker House, 1998.
Murray, Iain H. *Jonathan Edwards, a New Biography.* Carlisle, Banner of Truth Trust, 1988.
NKJV—*New King James Version of the Bible.* Nashville, TN, Holman Bible Publishers, 1979.
Oden, Thomas C. *Life in the Spirit.* New York, Harper Collins Publishers, 1992.
Olford, Stephen. *Lord, Open the Heavens!* Wheaton, IL, Howard Shaw Publishers, 1969.
Orr, James, ed. *International Standard Bible Encyclopedia.* Rio, WI, Ages Software, 2000, original printing in 1915.
Orr, J. Edwin. *Evangelical Awakenings in Southern Asia.* Minneapolis, MN, Bethany Fellowship, 1975.
Otis, George, Jr. *Transformations.* Video. The Sentinel Group, 1999.
Ibid. *The Twilight Labyrinth.* Grand Rapids, MI, Chosen Books, 1997.
Peckham, Colin and Mary. *Sounds from Heaven.* Ross-shire, Scotland, Christian Focus Publications, 2004.
Peters, George W. *Indonesia Revival.* Grand Rapids, MI, Zondervan Publishing House, 1973.
Pratney, Winkie. *Revival: Principles to Change the World.* Springdale, Whitaker House, 1984.

BIBLIOGRAPHY

Ravenhill, Leonard. *A Treasury of Prayer.* Zachary, LA, Fires of Revival Publishers, 1971.
Ibid. *Revival God's Way.* Minneapolis, MN, Bethany House Publishers, 1983.
Ibid. *Why Revival Tarries.* Minneapolis, MN, Bethany House Publishers, 1959.
Riley, William B. *The Perennial Revival.* Chicago, The Winona Publishing Company, 1904.
Roberts, Richard Owen, ed. *Glory Filled the Land.* Wheaton, IL, International Awakening Press, 1989.
Ibid. *Revival.* Wheaton, IL, Tyndale House Publishers, 1982.
Ibid. *Scotland Saw His Glory.* Wheaton, IL, International Awakening Press, 1995.
Roseveare, Helen. *Revival in the Congo.* Jesus Life. World Wide Web (3-99).
Ruffin, Bernard. *Fanny Crosby.* Westwood, NJ, Barbour and Company, 1976.
Schaeffer, Francis. *Mark of a Christian.* Downers Grove, InterVarsity Press, 1975.
Sempangi, F. Kefa. *A Distant Grief.* Glendale, CA, Regal Books, 1979.
Shaw, S. B. *Old Time Religion.* n.p., 1904.
Shearer, John. *Old Time Revivals.* Philadelphia, The Milton Testaments Campaign, 1932.
Smith, Hannah Whitall. *A Christian's Secret of a Happy Life.* New Kensington, PA, Whitaker House, 1983.
Smith, Paul B. *Church Aflame.* Toronto, The Peoples Press, 1949.
Sproul, R. C. *The Holiness of God.* Wheaton, IL, Tyndale House Publishing, 1985, 1998.
Spurgeon, Charles H. *My Conversion.* Springdale, Whitaker House, 1996.
Ibid. *Praying Successfully.* New Kensington, PA, Whitaker House, 1997.
Ibid. *The Minister's Self-Watch.* Pensacola, FL, Chapel Library, n.d.
Strong, James. *Strong's Exhaustive Concordance.* Power Bible. Bronson, MI, Online Publishing, 2002.
Teykl, Terry. *Preyed On Or Prayed For.* Muncie, IN, Prayer Point Press, 2000.
Torrey, R. A., ed. *How to Promote and Conduct a Successful Revival.* Chicago, IL, Fleming H. Revell Company, 1901.
Towns, Elmer and Douglas Porter. *The Ten Greatest Revivals Ever.* Ann Arbor, MI, Servant Publications, 2000.
Tozer, A. W. *Keys to the Deeper Life.* Grand Rapids, MI, Zondervan, 1957.
Ibid. *The Knowledge of the Holy.* New York, Harper and Row Publishers, 1961.
Trask, Thomas. *The Assemblies of God Minister.* Springfield, MO, General Council Executive Office of the Assemblies of God (Jan. 1999).
Unknown Author. *America's Great Revivals.* Minneapolis, MN, Dimension Books, n.d.
Wadsworth, Ernest M. *Will Revival Come?* Chicago, IL, Moody Press, 1936, 1945.
Wallis, Arthur. *The Radical Christian.* Columbia, MO, Cityhill Publishing, 1987.
Waugh, Geoff. *Flashpoints of Revival.* Shippensburg, PA, Destiny Image Publishers, 1998.
Whittaker, Colin C. *Great Revivals.* Springfield, MO, Radiant Books, 1994.
Wigglesworth, Smith. *Smith Wigglesworth on Healing.* New Kensington, PA, Whitaker House, 1999.
Woolesy, Andrew A. *Channel of Revival: A Biography of Duncan Campbell.* Edinburgh, Scotland, The Faith Mission, 1974).
Wright, Fred Hartley. *If My People.* Butler, IN, The Higley Press, 1959.
Yun (Liu Zhenying) and Paul Hattaway. *The Heavenly Man.* Grand Rapids, MI, Monarch Books, 2002.
Zacharias, Ravi. *Getting to Truth: Who is Jesus?* (And Why Does it Matter?) Audio tapes. Lectures delivered at Harvard University entitled, "The Harvard Veritas Forum." Ravi Zacharias International Ministries, 1992.

WEB PAGES
crosswalk.com; 10/2001
logosresourcepages.com; 10/2001

In His Presence
MINISTRIES

In His Presence Ministries is the evangelistic team of Glenn and Jessica Meldrum. Radically saved from lifestyles of rebellion and drugs, they now proclaim the saving power of Jesus.

Glenn and Jessica came to Christ through the Jesus Movement and believe God is ever desiring to reveal His glory. Genuine revival is an invasion from heaven which brings a conscious awareness of God. When revival comes:

Conviction is wrought...
Choices are made...
...Saints are awakened and society is transformed.

Nothing less than this is needed for our time. This is the Meldrum's impassioned prayer; this is the heart of their ministry.

Ministry of Service...

Glenn is ordained and holds an MA in theology and church history. His 15 years of pastoral experience has included an urban, multicultural church, a rural church and a Romanian congregation. Jessica's calling includes teaching women's groups and ministering to children through mime. The Meldrums are available for church services, evangelistic meetings and conferences providing a special emphasis on holiness, prayer, revival and reaching the lost. Glenn also ministers in prisons and rehab programs such as Teen Challenge. Through the Meldrum's challenging and compassionate preaching, saints and sinners alike are called to repentance, surrender and intimacy with God.

For Booking Information Contact:
Jessica Meldrum
Phone: (651) 247-3979
E-mail: ihpministry@juno.com
Website: www.ihpministry.com

A TRUE ACCOUNT OF
Spiritual Awakening!

By Jessica Meldrum

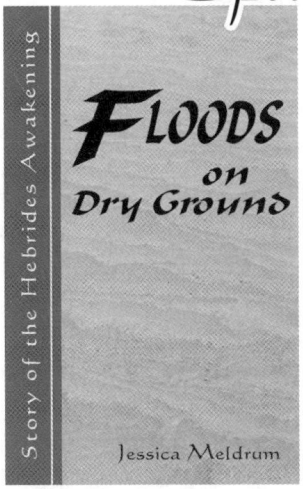

$8.00 postage paid

When God stepped down from heaven in 1949 the things of earth took second place. "An awareness of God was felt everywhere. You felt His presence and His power on meadow and moorland. You met Him in the homes of people. Indeed God was everywhere, you could not escape Him."

Conviction was so intense that people could not sleep, normal activities were halted and the lost cried out to God, terrified to face Him in their sins. Strong seamen could be found weeping behind their fishing boats crying out, "God, have mercy on me, a sinner!"

So many young people were converted that the places of entertainment were closed due to lack of interest. "There was no quenching of our desire for the Lord and for the things of God. There was no need to entertain us or put on any special program at the church. We were just hungry for the Word of God itself."

Floods on Dry Ground is the extraordinary account of the Hebrides Awakening. For a season, God pulled back the veil separating heaven and earth in response to the prayers of a few desperate saints. Their prayer? "Lord, forgive our waywardness and iniquities; 'pour water on the thirsty and floods on dry ground'" (Isa. 44:3). This book is a collection of the events leading up to the revival, accounts of the revival and Duncan Campbell's testimony, a minister greatly used in this historic visitation.

WISDOM'S GATE   P.O. Box 374, Covert, MI 49043
1-800-343-1943   •   www.WisdomsGate.com

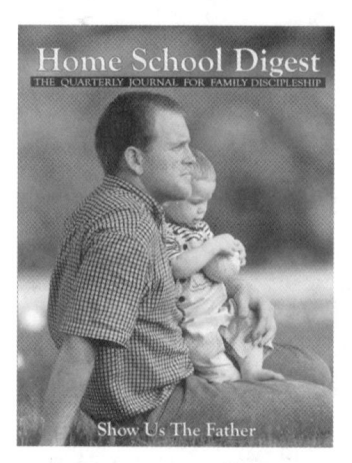

Home School Digest

A quarterly publication for families who are serious about raising Godly children in the midst of an unGodly society. Nearly 100 pages of articles and resources to help equip your entire family with a Biblical worldview. This trusted publication is known for its strong emphasis on character building and family discipleship. NOT just for homeschoolers!

Subscriptions: $18.00*

An Encouraging Word

A quarterly Christian women's magazine *"For women of all ages!"*

"Thank you for your uplifting, encouraging magazines. They never fail to help me in my walk with the Lord."
—A reader from Florida

Subscriptions: $16.00*

Order your subscription today and sign up a friend for a gift subscription ABSOLUTELY FREE!**

*Price for U.S. residents. **US residents only.
Canadian residents add $4. Other foreign add $8.

Wisdom's Gate   P.O. Box 374, Covert, MI 49043
1-800-343-1943   •   www.WisdomsGate.com